A Prayer for DEAD KINGS
— AND — OTHER TALES

AN ANTHOLOGY OF THE ENDLANDS
by
Scott Fitzgerald Gray

Cover, Design, and Typography
by (studio)Effigy

Cover Illustration by Alex Tooth
alextooth.com

Published by Insane Angel Studios
insaneangel.com

Monumental
WORKS GROUP

CONTENTS

To Colleen, Shvaugn, and Caitlin
For Infinite Patience

Wainamoinen, the magician,
Comes to view the blade of conquest,
Lifts admiringly the fire-sword,
Then these words the hero utters:

"Does the weapon match the soldier,
Does the handle suit the bearer?"

— *The Kalevala,*
Rune XXXIX

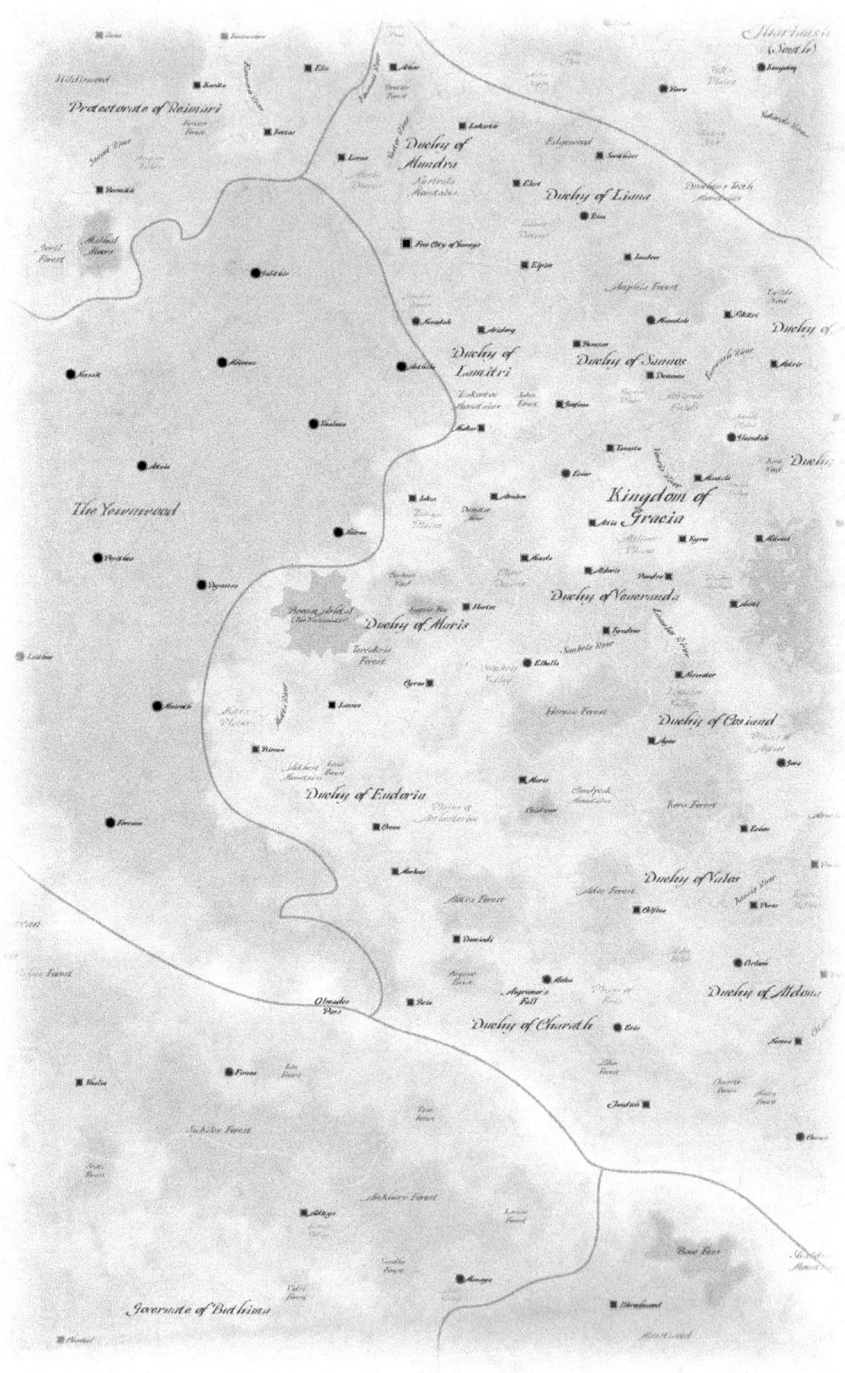

The Name of the Night

RAZEEN WAS STILL WARM when they found him, the rigor just beginning to set. Dead since dusk, no longer. From across the table, Scúrhand prodded the wizened figure with a scroll tube, the lifeless body rocking like a sapling in the wind.

The dark-haired mage spat. "Of course," he said, only to himself.

Across the tower chamber, Morghan circled warily, his gaze flitting across the destruction that had carried through the room. The subtle weight of the longsword shifted gently in his hands.

All is lost...

The voice was the whisper of a silk-lined sheath as it slipped within the tall warrior's mind. He spun fast like there might have been someone behind him, saw nothing but the walls of ransacked shelves and the dead sage they had come to see. Scúrhand inspected the bruising at the pale throat where Razeen had been strangled.

Where it gripped his sword, Morghan's hand was shaking. He squeezed his fingers shut, forced the tremor from them. Across from him, Scúrhand didn't see.

They had been three days on horse from the Highport before they reached the citadel, a narrow track breaking from the eastbound trade road to follow a rising line of scrub and sand along the ocean headland. The eastern sky was already dark when they arrived, the sun gone to a molten line beneath a black haze of storm cloud along the opposite horizon. The pounding of the surf was constant past tall columns of stone, the ruins of ancient battlements staggering their way across the rough beach and into black water beyond.

In the end, the shroud of darkness and sound had given Scúrhand and Morghan a chance to see the dozen or so figures hidden in ambush position along the road, long before they themselves could be sighted. The sentries wore dark leather and helms of blackened steel, scattered behind scrub trees as they watched for any sign of approach. This meant they left themselves open where Scúrhand and Morghan swung wide to the north and around, tethering the horses in a stand of salt pine and approaching unseen, away from the cliffs.

They moved to within sight of the sentry farthest from the gate-house, the others unseen but close enough to shout to. Atop a rise, behind a screen of wind-whipped sea grass, they watched for a long while.

"When I was last here, the sage was far more welcoming," Scúrhand whispered at last. "Perhaps he heard you were coming this time." The mage noted that Morghan didn't smile. "We should endeavor to find out who they are and why they're here."

"Agreed," Morghan said. "Take this one."

"An excellent suggestion. And one whose planning is worth long discussion, ideally back in the city."

"Take him." Morghan idly checked the longsword and dirk that were the only weapons he carried, his bow and quiver left behind him in the darkness, lashed to the saddle of his horse.

"Or perhaps another city entirely," the mage said hopefully.

"You take him or I will, and I'll be a lot less quiet about it."

Morghan shifted as if preparing to move, making an obvious threat of revealing his position where he stood a full head taller than Scúrhand and twice as broad. His mail was plate set within two layers of chain in an arrangement he had designed himself, apparently for the amount of noise it could make when he wanted it to.

The mage sighed as he felt for the power that threaded through him, summoning it with a whisper that knocked the sentry into the air and two strides back. He fell with a muffled thud, Morghan already moving. Too quickly, Scúrhand realized. Too ready for a fight that neither had known to expect. And even as the mage wondered what that might mean, the warrior dropped to kneel beside the motionless form.

Morghan had seen Scúrhand's magic drop enough sentries in the same way, and so should have known this one wasn't getting up anytime soon. But as the mage slowed, he saw that Morghan wasn't checking the pace of blood at the figure's neck as he assumed, instead fingering the insignia on the cloak. A boar's head sigil was embossed there, black on red, barely visible in the shadows.

"Who are they?" Scúrhand asked. The warrior only shook his head.

The citadel consisted of adjoining ramshackle towers leaning at dangerous angles into the ever-present wind. It was a military ruin, built and rebuilt by the succession of petty lords who had claimed this headland in the endless wars that were Gracia's greatest legacy. The space within it held two hundred warriors and their arms when it was new built. Before the long peace of Empire and the erosion of the sandy bluff turned its garrisons to fading memories and left it to be claimed by a lone Gnome who valued his privacy. Peace and the passage of time made for much irony in property values, Scúrhand had noted more than once.

One window lit in the cliffside wall made a gleaming gold beacon against the night. It was there that they had climbed, out of sight of the sentries below. To be accurate, Morghan climbed, clawing his way up along handholds found and carefully tested in the weathered stone. Scúrhand had an easier time of it, rising effortlessly through the air alongside him. The black cloak he wore over loose leggings and a high-collared jacket was of aristocratic cut, but in a style no self-respecting noble had worn in a dozen generations. Scúrhand knew the garment and the dweomer of flight woven into its threads to be older than that by far.

Though the mage was fairly certain he could have carried the warrior aloft as well as himself, he'd been reluctant to test the supposition with slightly more certain death promised on the rocks below if he failed. Morghan hadn't seemed to mind, not even breathing hard when they finally pulled themselves through the open shutters of some sort of study. It was there that Razeen had been found.

The body was draped across a high table, propped in a chair so ridiculously tall that the diminutive figure must have scaled it like a ladder. He had a selection of scrolls before him that Scúrhand took in at a glance, mundane alchemical texts.

Morghan was still pacing the room, listening carefully at each of three exits, stairs leading up and down. Velvet drapes in the same indescribable purple the sage wore were hung from tall pillars of yellowing marble. The air was heavy with the scent of old parchment and dust.

From below, loud enough for them both to hear, came the sound of smashing wood.

"We leave now?" Scúrhand said with little real hope. Again, Morghan didn't smile.

Vindicator...

Morghan took the stairs first. He didn't have to look back to know that Scúrhand was following.

Curving columns of black oak rose between levels of shadow above and below as they descended. A pool of light preceded them, cast from the pulse of lightning that traced the dagger Scúrhand had claimed from the ruins of Myrnan. The Sorcerers' Isle, legendary across Gracia and all five Elder Kingdoms and countless lands beyond. During a particularly violent squall that dogged them along the six-day voyage from Myrnan to the Gracian mainland, the mage christened the blade Storm's Light. Morghan had spent most of the remainder of the trip offering his opinion of those who named their weapons.

"A blade's a tool like any other. You don't name the plow any more than the oxen that pull it."

"I've never had an ox save my life," Scúrhand said. They were sailing through rain past sunset of the last day, the lights of the Highport visible ahead. "This might do that someday." The mage was doing handwork with the new blade at the rail. In the twilight, the pulse of its storm light shone.

Now, Scúrhand willed that light to darkness as Morghan waved him back. Where the stairs met an open balcony, they saw a faint light from ahead. Directly beneath them, the undying glow of magical evenlamps was filtered by some kind of latticed ceiling. Narrow beams crisscrossed below an empty space where the stairs turned and descended once more. There was room enough for Morghan to squeeze through, shifting slowly to spread his weight across the narrow beams. Scúrhand was close behind, perched at the balcony's edge.

Through narrow slats, the mage and the warrior watched the movement in the library below. A dozen figures in the same dark leather as the sentries outside worked with a silent efficiency as they tore through the shelves. Already, scrolls and bound volumes were strewn so thickly that they hid the floor. Scúrhand could only stare.

"That's a duke's ransom in lore they're stepping through," the mage hissed. "What in fate's name are they looking for that would make them discard that?"

Barrend's Bane...

Clear in Morghan's head again, an echoing voice, his own and not his somehow.

"What is Barrend's Bane?" Scúrhand whispered, and Morghan had to glance over to the mage's questioning look to realize that he'd murmured the name aloud.

A year before, in the midst of a long string of days spent trying to forget, Morghan had seen the boar's head along the Myrnan docks. A sigil on a cloak, black on red. It was an image he knew, locked into place in his mind. Scribed from the searing memory of a lash wielded by an arm that wore the same insignia. The memory of the pain was knife-sharp across his back, his chest.

The stone-faced warriors who wore the black boar on Myrnan had been led by a woman with hair the color of deep sunset. She and all the others were strangers to Morghan. But over the week that followed, he spent a modest percentage of the coin he brought out from the ruins to discover their names and mission. The secrecy that carried them to the Sorcerers' Isle was impressive even against the routine secrecy of most of those who sought Myrnan's hidden riches. In the end, though, all information had a price.

It was at a weaponsmith's stall along the muddy tracks of Claygate Keep's old Portown where Morghan found what he sought. The pale hair and sky-blue eyes marked the smith as Norgyr stock, his accent betraying him as not that long gone from the northlands. The flame-haired woman and her guard had visited him twice while Morghan tailed them. But when it came his own turn to step inside the stall, the smith met his inquiries with a sullen silence. Morghan noted the boar's head marked in ink at the smith's bare shoulder, a faded clan insignia beneath it.

In the dusky glow of the forge, the warrior pulled his sleeve down to reveal his own shoulder. Then he told a story. When he was done, the dark rage in the smith's eyes was one he recognized. He gave Morghan a name.

"What is Barrend's Bane?" Scúrhand asked again, but Morghan was moving. Shifting silently along the lattice of narrow beams, he strained to hear the voices filtering up from below.

"...the vault," a woman was saying. She was the leader of the searchers to judge by the manner in which she spoke. Her hair was flame-red in the pale light, as bright as it had been when Morghan first saw it in the dawn glow of the Myrnan docks. "Start again, top to bottom. Check every door, every passageway. Search for diaries, journals. What you can't read, bring to me."

The smith in his dockside shed had first seen the hidden mark on the shield at Morghan's back as he and the warrior drank at the hearth.

"You came out of Eltolitinus?" the smith asked gruffly when Morghan's story was done. "With this?" He touched the shield almost reverently. "I lost count of them that died trying to be you, lad."

The ruins beneath Myrnan were named for Eltolitinus, the greatest of the many mages who had tried to claim the Sorcerers' Isle as their own. A demigod of magic to the Aigorani who were the forebears of Gracia, his legend was built on the transformation of the entirety of Myrnan to a vast island-castle three thousand years before. It was the aftermath of the dungeons of Eltolitinus that had pushed Morghan to wander alone. Hoping to bury the memories of the dark month he and Scúrhand and all the others had spent beneath the earth.

In the end, the Norgyr smith told Morghan a story of his own. The legend of Barrend, who was weaponsmith to the magical court of the Sathnari, masters of the Sorcerers' Isle a thousand years before the island-castle was raised.

Avenge them...

As he watched the soldiers in black tear through the library, the voice in Morghan's mind was the voice of the smith suddenly. *Barrend's mark is what they seek. Weapons of the old age, secrets of craft long lost. Magics that can't be made by mortal hand no more.*

"Seek the signs of Barrend's Bane," the woman called from below.

Those who know it will kill for this mark.

"The lore we seek will be found or we do not return, by Arsanc's orders."

As the woman's voice echoed, Scúrhand saw a sudden darkness twist through Morghan where he watched.

Those who claim it lay claim to the power of kings.

Then the mage saw the warrior fall.

With a groaning crunch, the lattice of the ceiling gave way beneath Morghan's weight, the first arrows from below nocked and fired wild past him before he even hit the ground. Without a thought, Scúrhand launched himself into the air, cloak clutched tight and spread behind him as he soared silently to the apex of the arched ceiling. There was room in plenty to fly, the library huge, four passageways wending out of it where the great stairs ended their twisting path down.

The figures below didn't notice him, understandably distracted as Morghan landed with sword in hand and proceeded to carve his way through them. Scúrhand saw three down already, the rest pressing, but the warrior moved with a speed and grace that belied his size.

Then all at once, a pulse of white light wrapped Morghan like a shroud. The warrior's battle-scarred voice was choked off with a sudden finality. Rigid, he stood locked in a stillness that captured all the fury of his suddenly silenced attack. His eyes were dark between the line of his steel helm and the carefully trimmed beard. His blade was gripped tight, well-muscled arms locked in the midst of a backhand blow, held unwavering where he was frozen fast.

Scúrhand alighted on a section of shelf he hoped was sturdy enough to hold him. He saw the red-haired woman step up, hands still twisted in the complex gesture of the incantation that had taken Morghan out, another spell already on her lips that Scúrhand didn't want to wait to see the effect of.

"Stand down or die consumed by arcane fire!" he called with what he hoped was suitable bravado. He saw reflexive movement below, bows drawn and arrows nocked with a common bead on his heart, but he was already airborne again. He extended one fist, the plain copper ring there spouting flame to wrap his hand. He saw uncertainty in the eyes of those closest to him, fire flowing up his arm to the shoulder now. Where it billowed around him, the black cape gave him the imposing tone he hoped for, enough to hopefully hide the fact that the ring presented less threat to the foes scattering below him than if he'd simply fallen on them.

It was a relic claimed when he and Morghan first met, happenstance travelers who found themselves fighting at each other's backs when a cache of unguarded gold they had pursued independently on the frontier turned out to be less unguarded than was publicized. The ring's power was defensive, its dweomer swallowing the heat of mundane flame and eldritch fire alike, but its presentation proved almost as effective at keeping him out of the thick of combat as any blade might prove within it. Since that day he and Morghan met, the thick of combat was a place Scúrhand preferred to leave for the warrior whenever humanly possible.

On the floor below, the red-haired woman took a step toward him, and in her bright gaze, Scúrhand saw suddenly the youth she was trying hard to hide.

"If you wish to parley, say your piece," she said in the Imperial tongue. A tone of authority in the words but no strength in her voice to back it up, barely an apprentice's age by her look. Her accent marked her as Norgyr even if her ruddy features suggested Vanyr or the Kelist Isles. The guards with her all bore the pale hair and blue eyes of the north where they watched him coldly.

Scúrhand responded in the Norgyr tongue as a hopeful token of concord. "My partner and I mean no trouble nor harm. On the contrary, depending on your business here, we may find ourselves in a position of mutual benefit."

"Your partner has a unique way of introducing himself."

Scúrhand caught the dark looks of the three wounded men behind the girl, but the fact that they were merely limping was more than fortune. More times than the mage could count, Morghan had demonstrated a ruthless taste for the blood of those who deserved to shed it. However, Scúrhand had just as often witnessed the warrior's almost preternatural ability to leave less threatening foes standing, if a little shakily.

"My partner was set upon by your overzealous associates before being given any chance to explain his untimely entrance. Having watched him make it, I assure you that gravity was at sole fault. No one here intends murder. Least of all you."

The comment wasn't subtle, but the sudden darkness of the face beneath the rough-cut red hair told Scúrhand it worked. Not much of a gamble, given that of all the magic she could have cast, this one had chosen to simply freeze Morghan in his tracks rather than attempt to kill him outright. But before she could respond, from behind them both, a third voice barked out suddenly.

"Presume to know another man's intent often enough, and it'll eventually be the last mistake you make."

The tone was imperious, edged with a dark smile that Scúrhand could feel even before he saw it. He caught no sign of surprise from the soldiers, but the girl flinched. Scúrhand glanced back, careful not to move too suddenly.

A figure in silver mail strode up through the shadows at the back of the library, a squad of six archers arrayed to either side, shortbows drawn on the mage where he hovered. Scúrhand fought the urge to lift for the ceiling once more, dropping with a flourish instead, the cloak swirling in a calculated display. He managed not to stumble as he touched down.

"I am Naethdraca, called by some the Stormhand." It was the common translation of Scúrhand's patronymic that he never used himself, but which he had long practiced speaking with just a hint of menace. "That is Morghan. Our business here is research, nothing more."

He felt his dark features appraised as he let his long hair hang to cover them. The girl and the newcomer ignored the theatrics, but a look of sudden unease among the troops behind them told Scúrhand they had done the trick. He saw more than one figure glance to the dragon stitched in gold at the edge of his jacket collar, the mark of his given name. Naethdraca, the War Dragon who had been a grandfather he never met. They were old names, both promising power that the mage had yet to fully live up to.

"Ectauth," the mailed figure offered by way of a name, blue eyes ice-bright beneath a shock of pale hair. "My overly talkative servant is Thiri." Scúrhand nodded to the girl, her green eyes the color of wet leaves in the glow of the evenlamps. "Our business here is none of yours."

"Nor would I seek to know it," Scúrhand said evenly. "But if it please you, accept my services. I could not help but overhear that you search for some key within the lore here. Lore in which I am well versed. If my skills and knowledge can in some way smooth over the potential for conflict, they are yours."

Ectauth made to speak, but the girl Thiri cut him off. "Take the mage up on his offer, my lord. The sage's death has cost us time." She appraised him carefully, Scúrhand patient, ignoring the silver warrior's dark look. There was an odd dynamic here, one he wasn't quite certain of. The girl's skill with the spellcraft that held Morghan fast was good enough, but her demeanor marked her as a scholar, not a warrior.

Ectauth was another matter, though. The careful set of the armor, no weapon at his waist. Mail sleeves cut back of the wrist so that the movement of his hands would be unobstructed. He was a combat mage. A battle-caster of the Norgyr, his magical craft was focused and honed as a weapon. Whatever information might be hidden here, whatever this group had come in search of, it would be beyond Ectauth, leader though he was. He was thus obliged to depend on the girl's scholarly arts, Scúrhand decided. An obligation bound to rankle a combat mage.

"I expect you intended only to threaten the sage," Scúrhand said carefully. Another speculation, but a correct one from the reaction in the pale blue eyes. "Let us take the arrival of my companion and I as fortune, then. Or at the very least, let us get on with our research and leave you to yours."

Where he stood, Morghan watched and heard it all, motionless within the grip of Thiri's spell. His intact senses focused past the paralysis that the warrior suspected felt far too much like death would someday, and which was fading with each slow step Ectauth took around him. For all Scúrhand's postured tact, Morghan knew that the mage's words were also designed to fill up as much time as possible, allowing him to fight the effect of the spell that bound him.

From the start, the warrior had still been able to feel the sword against his fingers, the faint warmth of life pushing through his arms even as he forced himself to keep the blade steady in its interrupted stroke. As Ectauth considered Scúrhand's words, Morghan could feel sensation return to his legs as well, fought to stay steady. Thiri was watching him, though, where she paced around him. Cautious of any first sign that her binding was close to the breaking point.

The shield was slung to Morghan's arm, and he could see the faintest sign of the green eyes straying down to the mark there as the Myrnan smith's had. A thing that only one who knew of it would notice, the dark rune all but invisible.

Those who know it will kill for this mark.

Morghan couldn't shift his eyes without giving away that the spell's effect had passed, but at the edge of his vision, he saw the look of shock on the girl's face.

Ectauth saw that look, too. He saw the black rune that inspired it. With a shout, he twisted his fingers in a silent summoning of spell-power, a blade of white light suddenly erupting in his hand to stab for Morghan's heart. The warrior was already moving, though, finishing the stroke he had held motionless, driving the battle-caster's eldritch blade wide and catching him hard on the backswing as he wheeled away.

Morghan managed to fall back toward tall shelves at the closest corridor, protecting him from the first volley of arrows. Scúrhand took to the air to twist away from the knot of blades that erupted around him. As he sailed toward Morghan, he heard Ectauth's voice.

"Kill them both!"

"Call it," Scúrhand shouted.

Morghan appraised the mass of figures circling, another volley of arrows hissing past as he pressed back.

"Run," he said.

They ran. Out and down the narrow course of a winding stair, then into the shadow of uncounted corridors beyond. By an instinct Scúrhand couldn't name but was grateful for, Morghan lost their pursuit faster than he had any right to hope for. From shadow to darkness to shadow again, they ran blind through a maze of stairs and corridors where Ectauth's forces were already exploring ahead of them.

More than once, they tripped across patrols with no warning, the soldiers of the black boar left incapacitated by Scúrhand's spellcraft. The guards came by pairs, mostly. A squad of six once, but where the mage came up short against them, Morghan's sword was a blur of red and grey that made up the difference. No quarter given, the warrior slipping into the well-honed reactions of a lifetime at the blade.

Scúrhand was slower than the warrior, but Morghan kept himself and his armor between the mage and pursuit. He lost track of the turns they had taken, empty and crumbling chambers flashing past to both sides, when he had to signal Morghan to stop. In a five-way staggered intersection, he fought to slow his breathing. Morghan stepped far enough away to listen for any sign of pursuit, but there was only silence above and behind them.

"Do you have any idea where we are?" the mage whispered. Morghan shook his head. "Just checking."

"Traffic through here, though," the warrior said. He bent low to the floor, traced the dust with one hand, Scúrhand trying in vain to read the faint tracks there. All around them, pale light glowed from the frames of arched doorways, intact here. Marking off the deadly traps of Razeen's workrooms and archives, which Scúrhand would have struck any bargain to peer into under other circumstances.

"Where do you think…" the mage began, but then Morghan was on him, one hand pushing him to the wall while the longsword came up in the other. Scúrhand registered the footsteps racing toward them only an instant before he saw motion in the dark intersection, five figures on top of them. Morghan's blade slashed out even as Scúrhand stumbled back.

He felt the moment stretch, blind in the near-darkness that crippled his ability to target his magic with any accuracy. However, he knew better than to raise a light. Morghan was at his best in the shadows, able to pick out his targets with an uncanny ease. Scúrhand heard strangled cries, caught the movement of blood-dark steel in the half-light as five bodies fell.

"Light," the warrior hissed. Scúrhand set his dagger's lightning to life as he pressed back, the storm glow illuminating the landing and the stairs around them. Four Norgyr guards were beyond any aid he could give them, Morghan taking no chances in close quarters. The fifth figure was still moving, however, trying to crawl back into the retreating shadows. Morghan was there first, lifting the body as if it weighed nothing, slamming it back to the wall with a force that stunned it, head lolling forward as the figure went limp in his grasp.

"Blood and moons…"

It was the girl. Thiri. Scúrhand saw the gash where Morghan's blade had cut her leg almost to the bone. He noted the pool of blood spreading, the pallor of her face where the red hair framed it. Then he glanced to Morghan, following his gaze to the girl's shoulder. He realized that it wasn't the recognition of the young mage that had inspired the warrior's look of absolute shock.

Even before they stumbled out through Eltolitinus's ruined gates and gave thanks to sky above and ground below for their lives, Scúrhand had recognized a darkness lurking in Morghan that hadn't been there when they parted a year before on the Norgyr frontier. He had gone east then, Morghan catching up to him as promised by the time winter turned. But in that lost year, something had happened to the warrior.

When they met up in Yewnyr, the great Free City, Morghan had carried only the clothes he wore and an ivory-hafted shortsword Scúrhand didn't recognize. The wealth and the weapons the warrior spent the previous year amassing were gone, and there was an anger in him, threading through spirit and body alike, that the mage had never seen before. On the road to Myrnan, he loaned Morghan what he could for longsword and mail without complaint. When the warrior paid him back tenfold after the dungeons of Eltolitinus, he no longer needed the money but he knew better than to argue.

Only once, in the month of recovery from what Eltolitinus had done to them, did he ask what happened to Morghan in that year. The warrior's stony silence convinced him of the wisdom of not asking again.

There had been a moment within the ruins. Morghan was dressing a neck wound after a particularly brutal skirmish with Eltolitinus's undead hordes. Scúrhand saw the mark. A narrow sequence of three interlocking loops, barbed like links of spiked chain. It was set in black ink at the warrior's shoulder, tattooed with a precision that suggested whoever had done it meant it to last. Now, where Thiri's shoulder had been bared by her torn tunic bunched in Morghan's fist, Scúrhand saw the same tight knot of jagged line on her pale skin.

In the ruins of Myrnan, close to the breaking point already, Morghan had drawn steel against the mage when he caught Scúrhand's gaze on the black mark, seemingly ready to kill. He spoke of it much later, only to apologize. Never an explanation.

From behind and far off came faint footfalls. Scúrhand willed the dagger's illumination away, startled suddenly to find Morghan's bloody hand at his wrist, squeezing with a strength that the mage had seen break bones.

"Light…"

In the warrior's voice, Scúrhand heard a need he didn't recognize. In the pulsing gleam that the dagger's lightning conjured again, Morghan was on his knees. His sword was cast to the side as he pulled out his own dagger, laying the girl gently to the floor. He checked her breathing as he cut the legging away to fully expose the wound beneath. A deep gash, dangerously close to the fast blood.

Morghan motioned to Scúrhand for his waterskin. He flushed the wound, hacking an edge from Thiri's cloak to bind it. He motioned again, Scúrhand digging within his cloak, pulling free a carefully packed glass vial. A healing draught within it, gleaming pale blue with its own light. The mage thought to remind Morghan that the two of them might have better need for it later, but he said nothing as the warrior slipped the vial to the girl's lips, checked her suddenly even breathing, her eyes still closed, face ashen.

Scúrhand wasn't watching, focused only on the footsteps getting closer. "She'll have aid soon enough," he whispered. "Or we could take her. They might ransom…"

"No." Morghan's voice held a dangerously dark edge as he grabbed up his sword and stood, appraising the girl's unconscious form. He pointed down the passageway in the direction that Thiri been running. "Move," he said.

As they pounded along endless corridors of black stone and dark stairs, Scúrhand lost track of time, lost track of where the noise of pursuit was coming from. He was already gasping air, Morghan barely breathing hard. They hit more patrols twice, Scúrhand taking them out with routine spellcraft, leaving the Norgyr warriors to slumber or to wander befuddled, stripping their armor and weapons off as they went.

Against a foe set for the fight, the subtler spellcraft was often the best offense, Scúrhand had discovered long ago. As he always did when the stakes were high, he felt the call of the eldritch power in him. The darker energy of his blood, the birthright of the names he bore. Waiting always for its chance to be unleashed, but he was content to hold it back for now. It was more than a hunch that told him he would be needing it later.

Ahead, there was sudden darkness. They skidded to a stop where the corridor seemed to disappear into empty space.

"Light," Morghan whispered. Scúrhand obliged.

At the end of the finished passageways they passed through, a space of raw stone opened up. A blister of shadow, a rough-edged rock dome rising where the floor suddenly fell away. It was cold there, Scúrhand feeling it in the air, in the stone at his feet. Across a space of perhaps a dozen strides, a narrow stone bridge arced into shadow, open space to both sides.

Far below them, a pool of black water faintly caught the light of Scúrhand's blade and the gleam of lamps where Ectauth's force was spreading on the opposite side, shifting into defensive positions along a wide terrace.

Footsteps grew louder behind them. Scúrhand glanced ahead and back as Morghan stepped up. "Call it," the mage said.

"We fight here, we're closed in. We break for the bridge fast enough, we have a chance."

"Of course."

With a snarling cry that he could only hope sounded like battle-ready rage, Scúrhand soared out across the stone arch, Morghan one stride behind him. The first hail of arrows hit like black rain, Scúrhand summoning up the dweomer that sent each dark-barbed shaft splintering off into empty space. Morghan ran the rough stone of the arch at a speed that made the mage's stomach turn, the warrior already shouting tactical directives for when they hit the other side. Scúrhand only dimly registered them, all his focus directed to protecting them and hoping that Morghan could avoid looking down to the dark water below.

Ectauth hit them just past the halfway point, as Scúrhand knew he would. He sought out the silver-armored battle-caster in the ranks, but there was no sign of him where he must have been holding back behind the protective cordon of archers and shield fighters. The flare of spell-force exploded in the darkness of the chasm nonetheless, smashing into him and Morghan both like a hammer blow.

He heard the rending of steel, saw the warrior's longsword sundered. It was a dweomered blade with the strength of ancient magic, Ectauth's spellcraft as strong as Scúrhand had feared. The warrior's armor and shield, the mage's black cloak all flared as they were scoured with eldritch energy, but they were spared. Morghan cursed as he hurled the broken hilt-end of his blade toward a well-armored axe-fighter leaping to the attack, its jagged edge punching through the figure's neck to unleash a fountain of blood.

Scúrhand touched down along the rough stone ledge that fronted the terrace, breaking hard right behind Morghan exactly as the warrior had called it, heading straight for the thickest bulwark of defenders where they massed behind pillars some dozen strides away. Ectauth missed them completely with his second attack, sending the full fury of his arcane blood slamming down into the ledge behind them. Scúrhand felt a moment's elation that they were clear, the battle-caster caught off guard by their suicidal charge. No chance to hit them again as they closed with the dark-cloaked Norgyr forces.

Then he heard the grinding of stone twist through the echo of the eldritch blast, and the rough ledge beneath his feet gave way. Ectauth had hit behind them on purpose, judging the relative weakness of the ledge where it was carved from the rough face of the chamber. The bridge cracked and split behind it, cutting off escape. Nowhere to run.

Scúrhand found himself admiring the battle-caster's tactic as the floor ahead of them cracked cleanly and detached. He hoped he might stay alive to use it himself some day.

Morghan stumbled as the floor disappeared, his feet churning empty air as he fell. Then he felt hands on his shoulders, Scúrhand swooping in beneath him, cape spread like black wings in the shadow. There was a lurch as the mage fought to hold him against the pull of gravity. Then they were rising clumsily, the collapsing bridge shunted off into endless shadow below them.

Ectauth hit them dead center with a pulse of spell-fire as they climbed. The shattered landing was almost within reach, Morghan feeling a blast of heat and light swallow them both, Scúrhand taking the brunt of it as he screamed. A razor-point of pain erupted where the mage's hands gripped beneath Morghan's shoulders, the copper ring burning as it swallowed eldritch flame.

Then those hands slipped. The warrior twisted in midair, grabbed at Scúrhand's smoldering form as they both fell. All around was motion and shadow, the black pool circling far below at the edge of vision, no time to react, no time to think.

Morghan felt for a moment's desperate instinct, obeyed it without question even as the thought flitted through his mind that Scúrhand would have pointed out the futility of his actions if he had been conscious. Through an endless moment of falling, he pulled the cloak from the mage's shoulder, managed to force most of one arm into the sleeve as he willed the dweomer there to fly with all his will.

It didn't work. Not enough to send them skyward again at any rate, though Morghan somehow managed to slow their frenzied flight. He felt a lurch as they twisted and shot sideways, felt them slowing even as the water rushed up at them.

There was a moment of crushing impact, then a moment of numbing cold. There was a darkness that Morghan fought hard, but it took him anyway in the end.

When he awoke, he was sprawled on cold stone, no light to betray any detail of place or position. The fact that he was soaked to the skin was the only reason he didn't wonder idly if he was dead, the ice water of the black pool still clinging to him. He felt the pain in his side that told him he'd broken ribs, senses reeling as he fought to stay awake. He gave vague thanks to fate that his limbs were whole as he rolled to sitting, then began the slow shifting through the blackness to find Scúrhand's motionless body where it lay three strides away.

He checked the mage's blood, found a reassuring tremor of life at his neck. Another moment's grasping and he had the dagger free from its scabbard, awkwardly willing its storm-light to life. A quick turn to all sides, making sure they were alone. The vaulted space around them ran to dark walls on all sides, empty save for the rubble of the collapsed bridge where it spread in chalk-white drifts.

In Scúrhand's wet cloak, Morghan found a second and last draught of healing. He forced it between the mage's lips and saw his breathing grow less erratic. He remained unconscious, though. Some injury beyond the physical, or the taint of death magic in Ectauth's spellcraft. Nothing to do but wait.

In the dagger's bleaching light, Morghan reached for his longsword before he remembered it was gone. Taken from the ruins of Eltolitinus, the ancient blade had seemed destined for Morghan's hand when he claimed it. A sign of a new beginning after all that had come in the long year before. Broken now, just as every blade broke in the end.

Around him, Morghan recognized the lines of a tomb with uneasy familiarity, but where six stone vaults stood spaced between the buttresses, their tiers were empty. An equal number of columns circled the center of the chamber, but there was no sign of stairs. No ladders, no handholds, no door or other egress above. No means of exit apparent, no sign of the emptiness ever having been disturbed.

Then above, he saw the buttressed ceiling, and a dark plane of rippling shadow that he realized with a shock was the bottom of the ice water pool they had plunged through. Morghan stared in disbelief for longer than he liked, the water held there somehow by strength of sorcery. Deep enough to cushion the fall from above, then to slow them for the second leg of the fall to the floor below.

He had to assume that up through the pool offered an escape as straightforward as their entrance had been. He tried not to think about what happened if the unseen spellpower that held the water up also prevented them from passing through it again.

Even sharper than the ache in his side, he felt the pain at his shoulder where the black tattoo still burned even after a year. He felt the dark memories that dogged his sleep and that he had spoken of to no one, conscious of the questions always lingering. That spring, when he followed Scúrhand to Myrnan at last, he had tried to turn his back on the dreams that pursued him out of the frontier.

People who had followed him, dead now. Their faces still with him.

Too many times, he had dreamed of the Sorcerers' Isle. Too much, he dreamed of the darkness of Eltolitinus.

The ruins of Myrnan were a knacker's bone mill through which would-be heroes were ground. Too many lives spent dreaming of places like it. Too much wealth to be had in the catacombs and tombs that underlay the lost Empire and the empires that fell before it. But even after the thirty centuries since the island-castle was lost, no place in the Elder Kingdoms, perhaps in all the world, held as much lore and wealth of the ages as Myrnan. Rumors spoke of the farmers of the Sorcerers' Isle too frequently tilling some relic, some blade or other item of arcane power, up from the dead past with the passage of a plow.

Their group had gone in as twenty-one. Only eleven came out again. Morghan had learned the names of most of those who were lost only the night before they took the Black Stair down beneath the earth. All the dreams that had carried them to the Sorcerers' Isle, all their ambition lingered now only as dust and the memories of those who survived.

Too many dead in the name of unearthing the past and the secrets it held.

Avenge them...

In his head, the unknown voice resonated with a sudden familiarity that made Morghan realize he had all but forgotten it in the chaos of the levels above.

He had too much left to do.

That was the thought that tore at him now. Out from the dark dreams came the memories of the slave caravan that had set out from the foot of the Ceilamist Mountains and wound its way through frost and forest to the barbarian kingdoms of the untamed Jharlaash.

Now, as then, he hadn't been afraid to die. Not exactly.

Among the Vanyr, it was said that all life, all the world was the balance between dark and light, between good and malice. That great western realm of the Elder Kingdoms was a land whose folk had clashed with the brutality of Norgyr northward and the cunning of Ajaeltha to the blistering south for four millennia, and which had never been conquered.

At nine years old, Morghan had been taken in by a mercenary band in the southlands, his parents barely a memory even then. He held a dagger for the first time. He'd been shown how to kill with it, quick and dirty. Over a fire the night before the young Morghan fought his first sortie, a one-eyed veteran watched for a long while. And seeing the fear in him, the warrior quietly told the boy to not be afraid.

We hide from the darkness all our lives, though darkness takes us all in the end. But those who embrace the dark, those who meet death and are not afraid, can face that end with power, for we know the voice of death when we hear the shadow speak.

The memories he carried now were all that remained of those who had followed him.

We face the dark without fear, the old warrior said. *We who know the name of the night.*

He had too much left to do.

Vindicator...

He saw the blade then.

Beyond one pillar indistinguishable from all the others, unseen until he circled slowly around it, a figure sat. The mummified warrior was in chain shirt and helm, dead for longer than Morghan cared to guess. The clothes and the leather of belt and scabbard were shredded and split with dry rot and age. The figure sat upright, back to the pillar, legs crossed and head bowed as if deep in the throes of some endless contemplation. The sword in its hands flared in the dagger's pale light.

It was a hand-and-a-half blade, tapered wide to the base, and hilt-wrapped with pale leather showing no sign of age. The guard was black steel in the shape of what looked like the teeth of some creature Morghan was glad he'd never met. It curved opposite directions at either end, no sign of where it ended and the steel of the blade began. Down the center of that blade, a damask pattern caught the light in blue-white lines. The dust that clung to it was spread evenly, but even as Morghan touched the blade, he watched it slough off like gently falling snow.

In the center of the pommel, he saw the mark of Barrend. The same sigil that his shield bore where the Portown weaponsmith had shown it to him. A black rune that seemed to swallow the light.

Avenge them...

The voice had been calling to him since he set foot within the citadel, but there was a clarity to it now that left no doubt where it was coming from. And where it almost seemed his own voice at the outset, his own thoughts tripping him up as they sometimes did, Morghan felt the words of the blade now as a metallic echo in his mind.

He crouched low, appraising the body carefully for a long while. "Barrend's Bane," he whispered, and as he spoke, he felt a faint twist of power thread through him. He ran a callused thumb along the blade, felt its razor edge draw blood. The dead figure's hands had kept their grip, fingers locked tight to hilt and guard where Morghan was forced to snap them off, one by one.

When he finally seized the sword, Morghan felt the power again, spiking in a sensation like the emptiness of unspoken words. A bloodless rage twisted through him just as the voice had twisted through him before, and in that instant, in a heartbeat, in the rawness of memory where it clawed at him from the dark dreams that the day tried to push away, he knew that anything was possible.

Too many things still to be done.

So many debts to repay.

Avenge them...

"The black mark, on the girl's arm. What is it?"

Morghan started, spinning back to where Scúrhand was rising shakily. "Not important," the warrior said as he handed the dagger back, tried to mask the tremor in his hand. He didn't ask after Scúrhand's return to consciousness. No other pleasantries between them. Not necessary anymore.

Morghan raised the new blade carefully, felt its balance send the subtle signals of control through his arm. "What is this place?" he asked as he began to swing the sword in long arcs, working to assess its subtleties, adjusting to them. Working on a level below thought, below consciousness. The sword seemed almost weightless in his hands, shifting like something alive.

"Old," was all Scúrhand said. He was pacing slowly, still finding his strength as he circled along the walls. "Older even than the citadel, judging by the stonework here. The one built first, then the other raised above it."

"What was that one's story, do you think?" Morghan gestured to the figure, slumped in shadow now.

"In a tomb, one shouldn't be surprised to find the dead," Scúrhand said. The dagger was still the only light, shadow lurching around them each time he swung it to scan to either side.

"No dead here except him, though. And usually you arrange to be laid down, not sit."

Morghan saw the mark then. At the figure's shoulder, a faint red glow flared through a dark shroud of rusted chainmail links. He stepped back instinctively, the bastard sword up before him as if he expected the figure to suddenly rise.

Scúrhand saw. He followed Morghan's gaze to the corpse, staring for a moment before he stepped up to kneel at its side. He felt the warrior's blade follow his movement, ready.

"Unless the one you have to arrange to bury is yourself," the mage said thoughtfully. He carefully pulled away the screen of mail to reveal a mark still etched in the leathery flesh beneath.

It was a shape Morghan had never seen before. Three part-circles turning around each other, interlocked like a harrier's claws. At their ends, three scalloped blades were nocked, their edges locked into a triad. The symbol pulsed with a blood-red gleam, rising and fading in a steady pattern like the beating of a dying heart.

Vindicator...

The warrior felt the voice as much as he heard it now. A presence pressing in on him, threading through his hands where they wrapped the haft of the bastard sword tightly. He felt that red glow burn his eyes suddenly, felt the pain of the slave brand at his neck. Three loops, interlocked. Their shapes were wholly different, but he felt the two sigils reflected in each other in a way he didn't understand.

"What is it?" he hissed.

"Was, not is," Scúrhand said. "Lotherasien. But he's as dead as he looks, I assure you."

Morghan's eyes narrowed. "The Imperial Guard?" He had little interest in history, but it was a name he knew.

Morghan's eyes narrowed. "The Imperial Guard?" He had little interest in history, but it was a name that even he had heard. For the fifteen hundred years that the Empire of the Lothelecan held sway across the continent, the Lotherasien were the force by which they ruled. Elite troops, legendary in their dedication, falling to shadow just as inevitably as the Empire had in the end. Fallen to the unnamed cataclysm that turned the distant capital of Ulannor Mor to a sheet of black glass. "Why is he here?"

Scúrhand said nothing in answer, but he glanced back to the sword in Morghan's hand. "Is that the blade they seek?"

Morghan only shrugged. Scúrhand was thoughtful a long while. "So long as we hold it, negotiations might go in our favor..."

"They won't have it," the warrior said.

Scúrhand laughed. "This is hardly the time for trophy hunting..."

"Arsanc will not hold this blade while I live!" Morghan's cry cut the silence, cut the cold.

The smile died on Scúrhand's lips, no sound now except the warri-or's breath, visible in the chill air. Morghan looked up to see the mage's gaze fixed on the guard of the blade, the black mark there.

"This Arsanc," Scúrhand said carefully. "The one the girl spoke of. This one you seem to know, who is he?"

"Just a name."

"Indeed. The Freelord of Thorfin in Norgyr goes by that name."

Morghan wouldn't meet his friend's gaze. "And when did the poli-tics of the northlands become one of your endless fascinations?"

"When politics crosses over into history, I pay attention. Arsanc of Thorfin was poised to become High King of Gracia, five years past. The height and end of the Wars of Succession that restored Gracia to monarchy and sanity. A long fall from grace for him since then, or so they say."

"Do they." Not a question. A spark of anger in the warrior now as Scúrhand pulled history from memory.

"He was killed even as he tried to claim the throne," the mage said thoughtfully. Remembering. "Gone for a time, then brought back to the light. Or so they say."

Morghan said nothing, but Scúrhand saw the uncertainty in the flicker of the warrior's eyes as he looked away. "He controlled all the northlands once. Threw it away for the sake of wanting more. Re-claimed Thorfin after a time, or most of it. You fought in Reimari, you said. The battles for the borderlands. Those were Arsanc's lands you were warring for, after he'd lost them."

Morghan glanced back quickly. The look in his eyes told Scúrhand he hadn't known any of it, and that he was angrier now that he did. He shrugged coldly. "My interest is more recent."

"Recent enough to have brought us here," Scúrhand said, under-standing suddenly. "You knowing that this force of Arsanc's would be here to meet us. Yet you asked me of Razeen, said you sought the lore and history of the shield. That maker's mark. But that quest meant nothing, didn't it? A ruse to keep my company."

Morghan stood in dark silence a moment. "Can you fly us out?"

"I can fly myself out," Scúrhand said. He pulled the black cloak tight around him as he paced away.

Twelve days into the nightmare of Eltolitinus, Morghan had done his closest dance with death. Twelve days in, fate only knows how many levels deep into the ancient dungeons of Myrnan that were once the foundations raising up the entire Sorcerers' Isle in towers of white stone. In a dead garden of onyx trees, he was scouting with three mercenaries of the Vanyr, battle-hardened and senses sharp as slivered glass. He was leading, not watching behind as they were cut down by living shadow that seeped from the stones.

Morghan had tried to fight his way through to them, only to fall beneath the paralyzing cold of living death, nearly consumed. Scúrhand saved him, pulled him up from a narrow well of black where the shapeless forms of the three who had already fallen tore at him with taloned fingers, their faces, their bodies shredded by a darkness with no end.

In their names… the sword whispered to him. Morghan started, stumbled back even before he realized he was moving. With effort, he loosened his grip on the pale leather of the haft, knuckles white where his fingers were locked tight.

"When I left you in Einthra a year past, I traveled north." Against the silence, Morghan heard his own voice, uncertain. Across the chamber, Scúrhand turned back, the warrior pale at the fading edge of the dagger's glow. "I took up a call to arms. Mountain giants of the Ceilamist raiding farmsteads, sweeping down as far as the Thorann wood."

"Thorann in Thorfin. Those are Arsanc's lands."

"Those were Arsanc's lands. He abandoned the frontier two days past High Winter. Didn't want to commit the resources necessary to defend it. Homesteaders, farmers. I told myself I could save them."

In the mountains of Jharlaash, in the blackness beneath Myrnan, Morghan had learned the name of the night. But rather than quelling the warrior's fear, that name had scarred him. Cut him through flesh, bone, and spirit. Filled his dreams with the faces of those who followed him and were gone now.

Scúrhand was silent a while. "The girl. Thiri."

"She bears the slave mark. One of those given up, cleared from the mountains. Marked for sale to Jharlaash along with me. Arsanc must have found some worth in her. Bought her back."

Scúrhand felt something change in the warrior's manner. He thought he saw the darkness shift just slightly.

"The slavers wore Arsanc's own black boar. He used the threat of raid to cut away his own lands. Sell the people that paid him fealty. Betray them all."

Through the darkness, within the pain that threaded the voice, Scúrhand heard the Morghan he knew. The answer unfolded in his mind, making sense of what he had seen even as it spawned more questions that he ignored for the moment.

Instead, he asked, "You've faced him? This Arsanc?"

"No."

"Stood against him? Incited uprising?" Scúrhand sighed as the warrior shook his head. "You know that vengeance really only works best when the other party has some inkling that they've wronged you."

"This isn't about vengeance."

In all their names...

Threading through the warrior suddenly, a shredding pain rose and faded in a heartbeat. Morghan felt something twist inside him, Scúrhand seeing it where he circled closer, wary suddenly.

"You see something," the mage said. Not a question. "You've seen it since we arrived here. What?"

Morghan shook his head slowly. "I hear it. The blade has a voice. For me, at least."

Where Morghan held the sword out, the mage appraised it, the blue-white damask seeming to shift and flow in the dagger's pale light. He glanced to the shield, saw a hint of the same pattern in the shimmering steel of its rim. "The arms of Barrend are too-long separated, perhaps. Anxious to know each other again."

Morghan only shrugged. "Arsanc had a people who looked to him for protection, and he sold them as chattel. I called for those who would follow me and found six strong enough, six brave enough. If you'd gone with me, you'd be dead along with them." The warrior's voice was even. "Arsanc will not hold this blade."

Scúrhand was silent again.

"Can you fly us out?" Morghan asked.

The mage glanced to the darkness above them. "They'll be waiting for us. We should regain strength, let them wonder if we're dead before we surprise them."

"They won't wait. What's here is too important to them." Morghan raised the blade. "They'll kill for this mark..."

As if in answer, there was a dull crash of thunder from above. Along the lines of the tall arches, dust shook and fell.

Morghan appraised the flat shadow of the pool bottom above him, faint light rippling beyond it now. "Ectauth expected to pick us up from the water, dead or alive," he said thoughtfully. "Claim the shield. He'll be panicking now. Vulnerable."

Another blast from above. Scúrhand shook his head. "Of course..."

As with every other time, it was more a moment of awareness than an actual decision. An acceptance that the fight closing in on them was the only path open. No other options, no alternatives to that final stand. Neither of them spoke as they checked weapons, Morghan unslinging the empty scabbard of his shattered longsword and casting it aside. He fit the new blade to belt and hand, swinging it carefully in ever-wider arcs.

It was a warrior's ritual, Scúrhand knowing it from observation. Morghan had been trained to the sword from those first mercenary days of his childhood, and it showed. Each morning, each evening, every moment of respite in campaign or exploration, the warrior checked each weapon he carried for heft and weakness, a blade or bow fought with a hundred times examined as if it might have been brand new.

Scúrhand's skill with a dagger had been mostly accidental when he and the warrior first met, and checking that his scabbards weren't about to fall off was the extent of his preparation for combat. So many showdowns in the three years since then. So many times like that first time, back to back against an ever-shifting sea of foes and running on the timeless instinct to just survive.

They were older now, stronger. Always in the end, though, there was someone a little stronger, a little better than you.

Always in the end, it came down to something deeper than strength.

They shot out through the pool faster than even Scúrhand thought himself capable of flying them both, a half-dozen passes made around the inside of the tomb to build up speed before they climbed. Morghan held tight to the mage, didn't blink against the shock of cold water that hit him like a body blow, then against the sudden riot of light and frantic bowshot that met them as they emerged into the chasm.

Morghan had already picked their spot, Scúrhand twisting as they soared. Arrows passed harmlessly by them as he dropped the warrior to the open terrace where the bridge had fallen, Ectauth standing at the fore this time where his force was circled to all sides. Scúrhand stayed aloft, the air a blur before him as the screen of arcane force he summoned up shattered a wall of bowshot that came his way. The silver battle-caster's voice rang out against the stones, frantically ordering the archers to stand down, but Scúrhand could see that their attention was already fixed firmly on the opposite side of the cavern.

There, Morghan stepped to the terrace edge, every eye in the Norgyr troop following the slow swinging of the blade in his hand where he held it out over dark water below. The damask pattern of its steel caught the bright light of evenlamps around the room, flaring like the sun on clear water. No one moved.

Ectauth's gaze looked to be as dispassionate as he could make it, but Scúrhand noted the anger in the battle-caster's eyes as he drifted slowly closer. There was no sign of Thiri with him, no time to look for her. "If you wish to parley, speak your piece," he called.

"That one drops the blade safe to the ground," Ectauth shouted. "Both of you submit. When we've crossed the frontier, you'll be released to your own fate."

Where Morghan shifted suddenly, a dagger that hadn't been in his hand a moment before flashed as it buried itself in the neck of a lone scout coming up almost unseen from the side. The would-be assassin fell noisily.

"Let's assume the surrender option is off the table," Scúrhand called.

"Here are our terms," Morghan shouted over him. "Your lord Arsanc needs a message sent. You can take it or I can, delivered along with your head."

There was a rustling of bows, Arsanc's archers eager to begin the bloodletting. Too eager, Scúrhand thought.

"Madmen, fools, and heroes all fit the same grave." The young voice caught him and Morghan by equal surprise, both wheeling to see Thiri standing alone where she had slipped through the ranks. She was limping, her leg still bleeding. When Scúrhand tried to meet her gaze, she looked away.

Beneath Ectauth's anger, there was no trace of the uncertainty that Scúrhand heard in Thiri's voice. This should have been a precision operation, a night of stealth and recovery. The sage's death was something the girl had already paid for in her conscience, but the battle-caster was thinking only about what he might pay if he failed to deliver the goods whose retrieval he was charged with. A tension between the two Norgyr spellcasters that Scúrhand hoped desperately he and Morghan could use.

"The message is this." Morghan called to Ectauth, but his eyes were on the girl. "The right to wield power is earned by deed. Not delivered by proxies, stolen and paid for by murder."

Ectauth only laughed, Morghan's glance shifting to where the Norgyr battle-caster stepped forward. "And what deeds have earned you the right to a king's blade?"

"Arsanc sold his people..."

"The Lord Arsanc made rightful disposition of those who rejected his flag and his will," Ectauth shouted. "The Lord Arsanc surrendered lands in the name of peace that could not be defended, except by those with a wish to die beneath your banner, mercenary."

Only because he was watching, Scúrhand saw Thiri's reaction to the Norgyr captain's words. Where he had shifted to keep his shield between the closest archers and himself, Morghan froze.

"I know you," Ectauth laughed. "All your pathetic pursuit on the Sorcerers' Isle, you thought you wouldn't be noticed? Watched in return as you watched us? Your name came easily enough. Then came the memory that one of that same name led a futile assault from the Lord Arsanc's lands to the mountain lord's own halls. A self-styled warlord and his mercenary band taking on a mountain giant garrison. How many made it out alive behind you?"

In Morghan's hands, the sword called Barrend's Bane flared blue-white. Then it began.

It should have been over quickly. They were outnumbered, outpowered, the odds too much like those of too many previous fights that Scúrhand had been sure would be his last. He counted eleven figures surging even as Morghan slammed into them, saw Ectauth curse as a bolt of spell-fire intended for the warrior struck one of his own lieutenants instead.

In each fight like it, there was always a moment when the tide turned. A point where odds first were evened, then the balance tipped in favor of improbable victory or timely escape. There was no tide this time, though. There was only Morghan, moving with a speed and a fury that drove him through the ranks of Arsanc's forces like a bloody storm.

He was gaining no ground, though, Scúrhand in the best position to see it from the air. Too many, more coming, a dozen pouring in from above. That was Morghan's plan, though, and Ectauth's dark expression showed that he knew it. The battle-caster's spellpower was focused for maximum destruction, and all but useless now where the warrior fought within the screen of bodies pressing against him.

Scúrhand stayed in motion as he watched, not bothering to waste his own spellpower against Ectauth and the wards of protection he could sense even at the distance between them. The girl Thiri was another issue. But though Scúrhand did his best to draw her fire along with the attention of the archers, in the ebb and flow of the power that passed between them, he noted the uncertainty in the young mage's tactics.

His own first salvo was ice and fire, but she countered it with an ease that astounded him. In response, she filled the air around

Scúrhand with darkness and mist that kept him moving, prevented him clear line of sight to the battle below. She was focusing on harrying him, he realized. Ignoring Ectauth's shouted orders to target Morghan, the battle-caster trying in vain to break through the press of bodies.

Shadow blurred Scúrhand's vision, Ectauth unleashing spell-fire in close quarters even as Morghan slipped back and three more of the battle-caster's own warriors were cut down. The pulse of light and flame suspended the melee into motionless moments, frozen images.

In one of those moments, Scúrhand saw the snarling Ectauth finally break through. He tried to shout where Morghan spun in the mortal dance his wrath made, but the mage had no voice to overcome the screams of the dying and the steady crash of steel that surrounded the warrior where he fought.

Spellpower pulsed in the battle-caster's hand, a twisted whip of smoke and shadow lashing out, coursing through Morghan as brands of piercing black flame. Scúrhand heard the warrior cry out. But then even in the moment that it should have taken for Ectauth to finish him, the battle-caster's sudden scream rose as a dark echo of Morghan's own. Tendrils of black fire wrapped tight in his fist flickered and flared out as twin bolts of white light tore through his armor and convulsed him as if he'd taken a blade in the back.

Morghan reacted without seeing, screaming with pain as he twisted back and around and drove the blue-white blade through the battle-caster's throat.

From the air, Scúrhand could only stare to where Thiri stood, eyes wide as if somehow only just realizing that her spellpower had put her captain down. Then she was moving even as cries of treachery arose from the warriors closest to her, a surge of shock and anger rising as she ran to Morghan's side.

The dagger the girl drew told Scúrhand that her spellpower was close to spent. She unleashed a last barrage of magical force against a howling axe-fighter who struck from the side, and who fell to Morghan's blade as the warrior spun past in a blur of blood and steel.

Then four more were on them, Thiri slashing awkwardly at the closest attackers as they pushed in. Scúrhand laid down three points of arcane shielding around them, but the fight was too fast. He could see Morghan shouting, could feel the words without hearing, telling the girl to run.

She didn't.

Where a pair of archers erupted from the shadows, she spun toward them. Four arrows that would have claimed Morghan unleashed a shroud of blood as they tore through her.

Afterward, when he looked back on it, when he tried to remember, Scúrhand couldn't summon up the images that should have recalled for him what happened next.

In his head, he thought he heard a scream. A voice that was Morghan's but not Morghan's somehow. He saw arrows fly, saw the shield the warrior had borne from the Myrnan ruins seem to pull them from the air as he fought with a ferocity Scúrhand had never seen before. And through the fury of the warrior's movements, the mage imagined for a moment that he could see a blue-white light in Morghan's eyes. A glow to match the steady pulse flaring now from the damasked heart of the blade as it bit deep again and again.

Scúrhand couldn't see the moment when Ectauth fell in the chaos, but he was dead with the rest of them when Morghan finally slowed. The warrior's armor was flecked red with gore, breath white on the air, the cold of the chasm chamber deeper now. He wiped his face and arms with Ectauth's black cloak. He didn't wipe the blade as he slipped it to his belt. Didn't need to, no blood clinging to the blue-white steel.

"What in fate's name was that?" Scúrhand was crouched in the shadow a short distance away, faint light showing above through narrow windows he hadn't noticed before. Dawn breaking outside. He briefly considered holding the question for a better time, realizing in the end that he had no idea what that time would look like.

"That was staying alive."

Where Thiri had fallen, Morghan knelt at her side. Her skin was white as ice and blood-streaked, the arrows fanning out across her chest. But even as Morghan fumbled bloody fingers at her neck, Scúrhand called out to see the faint movement of the black shafts.

"She's breathing..."

Morghan felt the blood weak at her neck, saw the steel-edged hunting heads where they punched out through her back. He had the skill to bind the wounds, but there was no point. The girl was at the edge of death, no way to pull the arrows without only hastening the end.

"Search Ectauth," he whispered to Scúrhand, fear in his voice. "He'll have healing..."

"I did. Nothing."

Save her... whispered the breathless voice of vengeance as it threaded through his mind, and Morghan's vision blurred suddenly, eyes burning.

— 28 —

He remembered Eltolitinus. He remembered the faces of the others and saw the dread in their eyes that was their last sight before the final darkness, as they were consumed body and soul. He remembered the mountain giant's halls, heard the howling of wolves and the screams of those who had followed him. All the ones he couldn't save.

"Save her," he whispered, and he felt the words twist in him like a thing closer to prayer than any oath the warrior had ever spoken.

He felt the metal of the bastard sword grow warm beneath his gore-streaked hand.

Without thinking, he grasped the girl's fingers, forced them closed around the haft. He felt her shudder, saw color twist through her cheeks as he quickly snapped the shafts that pinned her, grasped each in turn and pulled. In the dark sleep of pain, she screamed, but even as she did, Morghan saw the wounds close over as she consumed the healing power held in that blade of damasked steel, the blood-streaked skin smooth again as her eyes snapped open.

The sword slipped from her hand, clattering to the stones as she scrambled back. Scúrhand was close by now, catching the disorientation in her eyes that he knew would quickly pass. But it was the sword he stared at as Morghan picked it up.

The warrior turned away, looked to the light above and walked toward a distant flight of stairs twisting up from the shadows of the cavern.

"It's done," Scúrhand said to Thiri. He saw her staring to the carnage around her, wide-eyed as if waking from a half-remembered dream. "You're safe, with us at least. If you're still here when Arsanc sends another force to discover what happened to this one, I wouldn't like your chances."

She followed him shakily as he followed Morghan in turn. The stairs led on to a passage he recognized from his previous dealings with the dead Razeen. The main doors of the citadel were ahead, open now where the sentinels they first avoided had been called in by Ectauth. The scent of sea air and the rising sun were beyond.

Scúrhand fought the urge to break for the library, the incalculable worth of lore still scattered there. When he had searched the dismembered Ectauth, he found scroll tubes that he slipped to his pack by quick instinct. Another time for the rest, he thought. He had a more important mystery to assess at present.

Beyond the doorway, Morghan stood atop a rise of stone a dozen strides away. He had the sword in hand, was swinging it idly, a dark silhouette against the sky.

"Vindicator," the warrior called.

"You?" There was an edge in Scúrhand's voice. It took him a moment to hear it, then another moment for him to recognize the fear there. "Taking vengeance against whom? You blame Arsanc for what happened here? Ectauth?"

"I blame myself. For all of it."

There was a familiar weariness in the warrior's voice, but something else as well. A kind of peace Scúrhand hadn't heard in all the time since Morghan returned from the north, but it chilled him now, the mage not sure why. In any of the previous narrow escapes he had followed Morghan into, fear was never in short supply. But before he could think on it, Thiri's voice came from behind him, stronger than he would have expected.

"You seek vengeance against your own past, you fight a foe you'll never defeat."

Morghan turned to appraise her for a long moment, a darkness flashing momentarily in his gaze. And then he laughed out loud. From somewhere below the cliffs, the call of seabirds rang out as if in echo.

The warrior shook his head. " 'Vindicator' is the blade's name. He was right," he said, pointing to Scúrhand. Thiri's look told him she didn't understand, but Morghan only laughed again.

Scúrhand watched, smiling himself after a time. "Are you absolutely sure you're quite all here?" He caught Thiri's eye as he glanced back, but it was Morghan she moved toward.

"More sure today," the warrior said. He shrugged as he nodded to Thiri. "We'll see what tomorrow brings."

There was nothing more to say as they returned to the horses, just waking from a fitful sleep within the hissing curtain of the wind. They rested themselves only for a short while before they set off, Morghan with Thiri behind him, Scúrhand thoughtful as they rode out against the red flood of dawn.

The Wood

WITHIN THE WOOD, yellow-green tendrils of creeping snow-vine thread the eye sockets of a frost-splintered skull. *Old magic lingers in these secret places of the world,* the Quick Ones say. He hears their songs. Knows that this place that is his is one such place they sing of.

The skeleton spreads beneath the green shroud of endless branches. Its fingers of grey bone, still as death, clutch the ice that binds them. His fingers of black wood shift slowly with a silent wind, scratching distant sky. Great roots hunch and rise like talons dug deep into freezing earth, a wide swath that pushes up and out as thick ridges of buckled stone. Ice-choked rills mark the shattered lines of the land, root-web twisting down and out through a skin of earth and wood-bark, shrouding the living ground beneath.

He knows the ancient magic of this place, drinks it deep through the roots that are his feet. He spreads it to sky and air through the ancient bare fingers of his blackened arms. He feels the sun, cast along the edge-precipice of western horizon, jagged gash of crimson flaring beyond cloud and freezing haze. The dome of dark sky presses down, split by pale dusk like cracks in the acorn that let frost seep within. He feels white flowers thread their way between weathered teeth, triggered to life by winter's first breath.

He knows the reckoning of seasons since the body fell and turned to bone. Seasons come and pass endlessly for him, each stretched and twisted out to the next, glistening mirror-moments of time catching each other's reflections like raindrops striking still water. For an age, golden grass grows up and through the skeleton's weathered bones, fragile mineral of life fissured and broken, overgrown and swallowed in a heartbeat of passing days.

The bones are of a Quick One, whose kind pass only rarely through the wood, but who are not of the wood. Born of blood as are all the creatures of the world, the Quick Ones are set above the world by bright minds, by spirits that burn like no other creatures'. Quick Ones come in smooth and tall, scaled and short, the green and grey of forest shadow, the pale rose of first light at dawn. Sharing shapes and colors with other Beasts and Birds, but standing always tall where their kin of blood crouch low.

The Quick One fallen at his feet had been smooth-skinned, had borne a shell of steel long years before. That shell has long ago turned to rust in his slow senses, fused with bone and rock, flaked finally to nothing. Steel is a secret of the Quick Ones, who collect the soft stones of the open desert to burn and hammer to a cutting brightness.

From the day when the Quick One fell, only the sword is left behind.

He knows blades from the past. He feels axe and adze raised against the groves around him when he is young. Even in that ancient youth, though, his visage and power drove the Quick Ones from the wood. In later years, they did the task themselves with dark legends and warning tales, felt through the touch of those few who once walked within his shadow. Warriors, mostly, avoiding the wyrms that prowl the dry wastes and the mountains that are the lands within which the wood is set. The old magic that lingers here is thing that the Quick Ones do not understand, and so their fear builds on the dread rumors of this place that is his.

His perception is all the living things he touches through the roots that bind him to the land. His perception is all the living things that touch him in return. In the touch of those that once came with offerings of sacrifice and totem, blood and bone, he feels the world. Memory made and unmade. Taken in to become part of the time that is his.

Along the highest of the narrow ridges outthrust from the great roots that are his feet, the sword is a steel-grey spike buried in white stone. Its edges are straight like the line-paths of shooting stars, tall even with two-thirds of its length swallowed by the earth. Vine-twined and silver-bright in winter. Flanked by flowers in summer whose sun-white cups catch each day's dew, wind whistling razor-clear through crown of haft and hilt.

Few Quick Ones have come here since even long before the sword fell. The world outside the wood is changing. No shelter sought at his twisted feet, in cool shade where ever-stretching fingers spread their net of green. The grey blade stands unchanged beyond that green, untouched by winter and summer, never rusted, never weathered.

Midway along the ridge, shrouded and all but unseen within the green, a cloak of black leather survives the same long cycles of bitter cold, blinding heat. Lost now, covered with layer-years of leaf and mold, creeping tallgrass kept at bay in a twisted circle all around. None see it. None watch the blade mark out the passage of years by the shadow of the sun, moving from horizon to height to horizon again as it circles slowly around the sky.

With no warning, he feels the shadow cast by the blade flicker in the last light of a winter's day. A shift of time touches it, twists through him like bitter wind across the white-black etching of his skin.

The world changes.

Something catches his indistinct attention then.

Movement twists beyond the trees that grow to the line of his roots and stop there in a reverent grey-green wall. The howling of wolves, an echo of rasping breath tracing through snow-shrouded silence. An instant later, a Quick One bursts out from frosted shadow, skin limned with a bloody light within the haze of sunset as it runs. A dozen paces behind it, three wolves crash through the screen of trees, flanks winter-lean. Fierce voices lash the air, blood at their tongues.

The Quick One sees him there, twisted-trunk wall of shadow against the sky. And in the touch of its desperate life that unfolds through freezing air, he feels a recognition that he does not understand. The Quick One hungrily sucks air, struggles ahead on feet wrapped in leather and fur, red tracks staining the unbroken white of the ground.

He feels the Quick One's mind as a blur of fear and shadow. Feels thoughts and future trace out as rippled lines. One step ahead of death's pursuit across a bloodied crust of snow, it will leap to his lowest branches, his trailing fingers, thick around as the Quick One's legs. It will climb to safety, rest in resin-scented shadow, cling tight to his blistered skin. He feels that future, as he feels all futures. Feels wolves circle, howl to the black sky, eventually slink off to seek easier prey. Answering the hunger of empty stomachs, starving white eyes.

A dozen strides away, the Quick One sees the blade.

The world changes.

The figure lurches, slowing. Stares in wonder. Recognition. Fear. It looks back behind it, sees the wolves but its eyes are glazed, blue like summer sky beneath a dirty shroud of sun-red hair.

The ripples of the future twist through him, then are gone. Swallowed by shadow. In its moment's hesitation, the Quick One has turned from him, turned from the future in which it climbs to safety. He feels those almost-moments fade, shred like morning mist beneath bright sun.

The Quick One runs again, bolts for the narrow ridge of ice and stone, but the wolves are already there. It stumbles on the snow-shrouded skull of the one who is there before, falls to its knees and claws forward, thrusts gloved hands toward the blade even as the wolves hit.

Forgive me...

He feels words slip into chill air. Feels the screaming start and finish in an unmarked moment of time.

The wolves feed until long after the pale Clearmoon rises, sets again. More wolves come, following the faint scent of offal on the frozen wind. He feels their voices, feels them fight for the life they take from the dismembered body, but his thoughts are gone from the moment, gone from this place.

He is in the past. He remembers when the first Quick One falls.

It is warm. He remembers the moment of it. Feeling and fear as the Quick One crawls forward from the thick shadow of the closest trees. The sun is high, the red of the Quick One's life marking its path back across the green as that life drains away.

That first Quick One finds its way beneath him, lingers within his shadow for an unmarked moment of time. Its eyes are bright, taking in the wonder that is the wood. Cicada song is a silver haze, but against the chill of death, the Quick One wraps a cloak of black leather tight despite the heat of sun and air. The black leather is clasped at its neck, pinned with metal in the circle-shape of three twisted lines, linked and intertwined. Sharp-edged like the unsheathed blade in its gloved hands.

It crawls up and along the ridge, scrabbles across the mounded crowns of white stone thrust up through grass and vine. It weeps in the honey scent of flowers gold and white as it moves to the edge, to that highest point that marks the unseen vortex of the old magic that threads through this place.

That first Quick One lies there, weeping. It has no strength left. It rises all the same. He feels dying fingers drive the grey blade down,

down, striking the crown of white rock with a scream of dweomered steel. Sending it deep within a sheath of stone and black soil.

He feels the clasp that holds the cloak rend as the figure falls, dead weight tearing it free. Unhooked, the cloak touches the rising wind, pulled back to twist like broken wings along the ground.

On my life, the Quick One whispers. Then impression and memory and deed are done.

Cold metal cuts deep, slices through leather gauntlet, finger flesh and bone as the Quick One dies.

Its hands are tight around the blade of the sword. Clinging vines wrap its dark metal with a longer grip as the land brightens, darkens, fades.

A ripple in the long line of time twists through him. A moment whose power he feels but does not understand. But it passes, disappears in the name of new moments, new days, new seasons.

Time shifts. The world changes.

Winter again. Now. Bone and sinew spread in the flat-pounded circle of blood-streaked snow, all that remains as the last of the wolves slip away to the wood and he is alone once more.

Memory twists through the silence of his senses. Faint resonance. A shimmer though black air and white ground. In the lingering energy of the Quick One's death, he reads the impressions of a life, feels names and memories flit unfiltered through his mind.

Holy woman. Priestess of the Green Path.

The days slip past. Light to dark again a dozen times by the time he absorbs those names, makes them part of his understanding.

For the first time, he reckons the seasons back to that bright-sun day when the first Quick One falls. A different creature than this second Quick One, whose blue eyes are plucked out by the crows at dawn. The second Quick One is slight, fair of hair and flesh. The first is taller, thicker, eyes dark, skin dark beneath its metal shell.

The first Quick One has a mark at its shoulder, revealed when the carrion cats dig in through the seamed metal skin, burst it blood-bright from the inside. The same mark as the clasp that holds the cloak, and which breaks and fades away in time to rust. But this second mark is carved into blackening flash. Burning with a red glow that pulses and fades in slow rhythm.

The same circle-shape of bright-edged lines. Three crescents all interlocking, set at their edges with straighter shapes, sharp like the razor edge of the grey blade thrust deep into rocky ground as the first Quick

One dies. Only when all its flesh is gone, bones all that remains, does the magic of blood-red mark fade beyond the threshold of his senses.

The bright Clearmoon in the sky those nights is the crescent whose shape echoes the bright marks at the Quick One's shoulder. It swells to full as he thinks, then wanes again, days turning colder in a haze of hoarfrost and grey skies. Snow falls to shroud red ground with white. Then the bones of the flame-haired Green Priestess are gone to all senses but memory.

He remembers the future of the Quick One who is the first to die. That day, he feels the mind of the steel-shelled figure, a blur of fear and shadow. He feels future-lines twist out from the Quick One's staggering steps, spread like ripples in the unseen shroud of the old magic where it circles him like an endless storm.

He hears names then, as he hears names now. He casts himself back, digs deep as days lengthen one by one and snow melts to rivulets of blue water curling between the roots of his feet, eddying along the rills and away. The bones of the Green Priestess are kissed by the sun, last remnants of flesh scoured by the first flies and stripped clean by the warmer day when he finally recalls the name.

Lotherasien.

The Quick One who died and thrust the sword deep into stone and ground names itself thus. Names its place and purpose as a knight of the Blood of the Commonwealth, and in the last will and purpose of that dying mind, this name is all the Quick One is and was and will ever be.

He remembers now.

Twenty-one full cycles of the sun, carefully reckoned, reckoned again. Brief pulse of time and time passing, barely visible within the record of his endless memory. Back to times before time, seasons without end that flare, pass, fade before him.

The Blood Knight is running, but no wolves follow this day. Only staggering footfalls, tracing back beyond the edge of the grove and past him. His long fingers trace the air as gently hanging curtains of green leaves, drinking rain and sun as the figure falls.

He feels the Blood Knight's desire then. Its eyes are set on the edge of the ridge that crests beneath his outstretched arms. It feels the ancient life that steeps these stones, the power of this place that is the power of earth, of heat and deep magic pulsing within the earth.

The power of the sword fights against the old magic that is here. The power of the sword knows what is coming.

To hide the sword is the vow the Blood Knight has made, but the strength that is its will and purpose is nearly consumed by the sword. Nearly consumed by the ancient hunger that is the birthright of the great grey blade. A power that pulses like the red flow of life that marks Beast and Bird and Quick One alike. A power all but drained from the Blood Knight as it collapses at his feet.

Twenty-one years ago, the sword is the fulcrum around which the Blood Knight's life ends. The momentary distraction of life and death so quickly embraced by earth and time.

Twenty-one years later, the grey blade calls the Green Priestess through the gate of life to death, and he feels a darkness spreading out from the great sword, twisting through the wood around him.

He ruminates while the dull bruise-light of the Darkmoon trails behind its brighter brother, blooming to its fullness over long nights, fading again. He feels the blood-black shadow the blade casts upon the open space around it.

He tries to understand this thing, but he cannot.

Twenty-one years ago, the Blood Knight's goal is to bury the sword in the ridge of stone and earth that thrusts out at his gnarled feet. The old magic that is the magic of this place is a thing the Blood Knight feels, a thing it seeks over the endless leagues and hardships that bring it here. The desire to lose the grey blade in this place that is his. To see it hidden for all time.

He feels that desire reaching for him, feels it twist through his awareness with an acuity that slows all thought for two seasons. Then winter is done, and other things must be thought on, and only in the passage of time has that long-ago day now come back to him.

The Blood Knight dies in anguish as its goal is met. Embracing the death it sought. And as he feels that death resonate again, he casts back through time and memory to taste the sorrow that died with the Quick One that day.

Through the spring and into the close days of the long sun, he thinks. Then finally, he decides.

From one of the great roots that hold him fast to rock and soil and the vastness beneath, buds unfurl. Shoots twist forth at his thought, pale green. He flexes them, guides them, feels creeping movement over the slow passage of days. The season swings by. Wind blows, hissing through his upper branches. The heat of summer cracks the few bones the wolves left whole. Fat hornets feast at dried marrow scraps as they nest within the Green Priestess's splintered ribs, leave a screen of paper walls behind.

As autumn falls, wolves howl, reminding him what it is he waits for.

As the cold rains come and the screen of leaves begins to fall, he is ready to set his will within the twisting tendrils. A reach across long days, marching almost into winter, then he is there.

Tufts of grey grass rise through the eyes and mouth of the Green Priestess's skull where the wolves discarded it. The Blood Knight's empty eyes are half-shrouded by creeping violet. He sends shoots through and within both caverns of bone, splitting within the shadows. Cold tendrils spread, touch all the space within.

He feels day shift to night, reckons off a dozen sunrises before it is done.

The morning is cold, bright and cloudless and carrying the night-chill of empty sky and white stars. The vines reach the sword, surround it with all his senses.

He feels the freezing aura of arcane dweomer in that grey steel. The magic of the Quick Ones, drawn from the mana of the unliving world. The newer power whose strength twists counter to the life that is the old magic of him and his kind. He holds it at a distance, lets it twist and expand like the slow unfolding of leaf-showers on the rising wind.

The priests of the Green Path hold the old magic, or some small fragment of it. The Quick Ones who are so-named for the speed with which they pass through life tame the old magic to themselves, but only as a single stallion is tamed within the larger herd that darkens the grey plains. The old magic of life and green and living things, set against the new magic of stone and mana like oil and water. No convergence of forms. No underlying connection between both magics, but he remembers the Green Priestess falling before the blade in an act of final supplication. Remembers the longing to touch, to hold, to possess that weapon that is the Quick One's last thought.

Over the passage of days, he wraps his subtle perception tighter around the sword's grey blade, sends it up to touch the cold metal of the guard. A single slab of bright steel is forged as an unbreaking cross, wrapped with filament lines of dwyrsilver that gleam a pale grey.

He feels the life of the Blood Knight, its memory held sharp within that steel now.

Lotherasien.

The energies of life are ripples in the world. Points from which time and past and future split off, forged and broken and cast back to the unwrought realm of possibility once more. These are things he senses, feels as he touches a thousand centuries of history all at once. All the infinite futures, shed and split off as singular paths. Like the unseen magic of this place, twisting through him and spreading out to fill the wood as the unseen touch of a world lost to time.

I am the Imperial Guard, and in my blood runs the honor and duty of the Lothelecan...

He feels the names unfold again, faint play of words surrounding and supporting them with the history of the fabled and fallen Empire. With the words comes again the shape, the interlocking circles. The shadow of life and spirit that touches and imprints on grey steel.

It isn't enough. He feels for the fullness of what it means. The blade's power of new magic spikes, flares white-hot against his unfelt touch, but he ignores it. He thrusts deeper into the maelstrom of faint impressions, seeking the stronger truth beneath. All the scars of mind and memory set upon the sword by all the hands that ever wield it, by the hands that forge and fight for it. The Blood Knight, last to touch it. The Green Priestess, reaching for it with the last strength of life. Not knowing the dark power promised by that touch.

He feels the past split open, his faint caress of mind and under-standing tearing away the veil of lost impressions. He feels a spider's web hung with dewdrop spheres of crystal, feels it shredded by the chaos wind that is all those futures denied, splitting off from a single line of the past.

He feels the Green Priestess, feels the Blood Knight. Feels the cold spirit of the grey blade as sight and voice ringing separately, then as one.

Death...

Once, this is the sword of a warrior-folk on a green isle far to the east, and from the hands of those warriors, the Lotherasien steal it. He hears it named by long-dead voices. *Kelastaen.* The Kelist Razor, blade of the war-kings. He sends his touch to wrap haft and pommel, feels that impression break off from the faint trace of memory that the Blood Knight's hands have left imprinted on steel and tight-wrapped white leather that shows no sign of age. But when he tries to seek the reasons for that theft, he finds only shadows and secrecy locked deep beneath an oath whose name he cannot know.

Death...

On a day of first frost, brown-black leaves plucked from his sway-ing limbs by the icy wind, he feels the Empire fall. A moment of long years ago. A time well within his reckoning but beyond his ability to judge by its faint reflection in the Blood Knight's life as the unseen scars in blade and bone reveal it.

From the fall of Empire, a thousand years pass backward, and then twice that long again, and he senses a great plain of grassland and wandering watercourse. A pristine land whose air is clear morning mist, pushed by the soft-scented breeze of distant woods. A ring of high mountains, molten-gold sky of the rising sun. On those peaks gleam towers and bridges of ivory white, shapes reflecting the gently twisting lines of trees along the forest slopes beneath them.

Then something passes his perception and twists away the shroud of light to reveal the shadow beneath. He senses the plain boiling with the shapes of unnatural creatures of stone and metal, feels war unfold and spread and scour the living land like plague. Black fire sweeps across the endless grasslands, white towers shattered and fallen, built again to be torn down once more.

Death.

It is the memories of the Blood Knight that thread through him now. Memories of a dark age lost to time but never forgotten by those who sought to hold that darkness from rising again. Against the shadow of those memories, the blade is hidden, found, taken, hidden again. He reckons off this time over which the Lotherasien keep the sword safe. From the day it was claimed from the hands of the last Kelist war-king, he feels the passage of a thousand seasons flash four times past. Old impressions, locked in cold steel and the spirit-memories of all the Quick Ones who die in the sword's name.

He senses the sword lost in the aftermath of the Empire's last war. The great war-king betraying a nation's birthright and beholden to a darkness that has no name. He senses a shadow pass through the strength of steel, a thousand years turning for the blade with barely any touch of living hands.

Memories and legends. Over the fast-blurred space of a hundred winter days, the blade is forged within a fallen castle, a shadowed tower of a distant golden land. A force of spellcasters with power enough to lay waste to cities gathers to infuse that power into molten steel. New magic, fell and pure and black as midnight's storms. A strength in the dweomer of that steel that will keep the grey blade from ever being destroyed.

Memories and legends. He senses the hands of the king that wields the sword, feels the unreckoned hands of other sovereigns seize it from the dying grasp of the hands before. Fathers and daughters, mothers and sons in a long line, ruling by dint of history and the blood of kings in their veins.

Against the shadow of those memories, the Blood Knight takes an oath that the blade which cannot be destroyed will stay hidden, far from the hands of those that would wield it. Those that would succumb to its shadow. A pledge that the Quick One will die to uphold.

The Blood Knight runs with the blade, even as it feels a dark despair course through its mind for the oath that cannot he upheld anymore. The Empire is fallen, and the grey blade is found and stolen back again. But when he falls as he knows he will, there will be no one to hide it again. In the aftermath of the Lothelecan, the Blood Knights are cast to the winds. Spread as a memory already fading to legend.

Pledged unto death, the Blood Knight seizes the sword and carries it across dangerous realms to a place of faint legend. A forest where the old magic might be stronger than anywhere else across the world-land the Quick Ones call Isheridar. The shroud of magic that is the legacy of this place, that is his name and birthright. A veil within which the blade might be safe, might be lost for all time.

The ancient magic of this place will wrap and conceal the dark dweomer of the blade. Or so the Blood Knight hopes as it dies driving the sword into the living ground at his dark and twisted feet.

He feels darkness again, feels it chill him as the first vision wraps around him once more. War on the black plain, the sword in the hands of its first master, whose name is burned away even as the memory shapes it.

The wind drives leaves turned frost-white and black. He loses track of time passing, of memories playing out like the songs of wind and rain that make up each storm scouring the distant mountains.

He sees himself now, cast in the final memory of the Blood Knight's lost gaze as it looks up to the sky. The spread of his own great arms are a welcoming embrace through the Quick One's eyes, bright sun flaring to whiter light that occludes all else, then is gone.

On my life, the Blood Knight whispers, and its life is no more.

Spring blooms again.

Grey-brown fingers of vine flare green, drinking the life of sun and sky as they entwine the sword, the skeletal shadows still grasping for it. Summer comes, and the Green Priestess is all but gone now within the tall grass and the shroud of sun-touched flowers.

In his mind, he is moving. Running with blade in hands and across his shoulder, his body not yet stilled by death as it shadows him close, a predator's step running fast behind him.

Death.

This is the song sung by all the memories of the grey blade, and he is joined to them now. Feelings and impressions, a single mind within his. Broad web of past and futures threading through dull steel from molten birth to this space of shade and sheltered wind.

Within that mind, he feels the great distance between the two lives inextricably bound to this place. The Blood Knight, the Green Priestess. A clash of spirit and purpose.

He focuses. Reaches within himself for the selves he has become, splitting and shaping them. Seasons pass in a blur, the first taste of frost touching his fingers. The wind turns from the north once more.

It is the heart of winter, the wolves prowling the deep forest again, and he is the Blood Knight. He is the Lotherasien in whose doomed heart burns the fear of what the grey blade is, of what it becomes.

It is the heart of summer, the cicada song a silver haze, and he is the Green Priestess. He is the holy seeker of the Kingmakers, the name that is given to the Green Priestess's path. His is the longing to restore the greatness promised by the sword that is Kelastaen, the long history reflected in a razor edge of grey steel. A line of kings once straight as haft and blade, then broken. Waiting to be restored now with the hated Empire's fall.

He feels the enmity of these two spirits that die with no knowledge of each other. Feels a hatred twist out between them, entwined in his own experience. Caught within the warp and weft of the past unfolding as a thousand histories touching those minds.

He looks forward then.

Ripples spread out from the blade where the wind sends spiral clouds of autumn leaves around it. That shroud of red is the color of the Green Priestess's hair, falling and spreading like a stain of blood when the storms come. He feels the shadow spread in echo, senses the future open up within it.

For long years, the sword stays hidden within his shadow. But in every future, every line of time forced open before him, there comes a time when he senses a figure step up to the crown of the narrow ridge once more. When it leaves, it holds the grey blade in its hands.

On each path, the figure's shape is different, shifting between all the possible futures that the shadow holds. On each path, a thousand-thousand blades fit two thousand-thousand hands, all the unreckoned possibilities branching out from this place, this time. But as far as he follows, he feels each path lead to the same place of blood and shadow. Black and red occluding all futures into a dead haze.

From the depths of the spirit heart that has defined him since the beginning of time, he mourns.

A storm of seasons passes. He loses track of them, senses the stars sweep past as endless arcs of blue-white fire.

He slips back, senses the Blood Knight fall, claw its way forward, die, fall, fall and die in an endless cycle. But no matter how many times the Blood Knight dies, no matter how many ways the grey blade is hidden, no matter how strong the magic of this place that hides it, he feels the sword reclaimed.

He knows this. The future unfolding before his thought.

As the Green Priestess does, other Quick Ones seek and find the sword. They die in battalions to track it to this place, seizing it as they crush the bones of the Blood Knight, the Green Priestess beneath their feet. The grey blade is taken, its wielder slain, claimed, slain again over endless lifetimes of the Quick Ones in their endless search.

For untold thousands of undone years, he touches the Quick Ones, feels their movement along the fringes and boundaries of his realm. He hears their spirit songs carried on the summer wind, senses the impressions their lives and minds make on the other creatures of the wood. Ripples of shadow.

Within the spirit of the Green Priestess locked tight inside him now, a light burns like white fire. He feels it sear him, looks within the fate of the Green Priestess to feel it flare brighter, scouring the shadow of the Blood Knight's oath.

He feels it as the sword is born, senses liquid steel glow the white of first daylight, poured in a shroud of smoke and shrieking flame. The weapon's mold is a slab of perfect black marble broken off from the throne that once sits within a ruined hall, walls pulled down and overgrown five hundred years before. The history and power of that throne is drawn within the blade, and as its white metal cools first to blue, then grey, its heat splits that great slab asunder, leaves it rent upon this makeshift foundry floor.

A song threads within the lives of the Quick Ones that he hears for the first time. And over a year of days that are a moment for him and the earth from which he drinks and the sun that is his heart, he comes to understand that he is wrong in all that he knows. He is wrong in all he feels in the long years of observing the Quick Ones and the pattern their short lives make against the slow passage of seasons.

The Quick Ones move from life to death in a single heartbeat of the world, and they slay each other with a focus that he has always understood to mean they embrace death. It has been clear to his reckoning always that the Quick Ones welcome death's release, and the chance to become one with the world from which they arise and to which they return. Death the end and beginning of the cycle of all seasons.

He is wrong. He knows now. The Quick Ones do not embrace death.

They fear it.

For a season, he ponders.

In the time that another winter approaches, then passes, he decides.

All the possible futures he perceives. All the endless exchanges of madness and war that branch off as ripples from this spot.

All the death that surrounds each vision of the blade, each facet of the future and past splintering like ice. Steel and stone and blood lock together in a delicate and deadly embrace across the chasm of time. Within the spirit of the Blood Knight that lives now only within his memory, he senses shadow that threads through him, freezing all the innermost veins of the liquid of life.

His is the old magic. But in the space beyond all history, there lives a magic that is older still.

It is a thing that he and his kind do not dwell on, do not think about. A thing they turn their senses from, always unknowable. This is the sword's magic, he realizes. The deep magic that is older than he, older than any living thing.

It is the deep magic that forges the grey blade long ago, imbuing it with the shadow that will scour the world if that magic is ever unleashed. The deep magic has no equal anymore, no force of life or spellcraft in all Isheridar that might stand against it.

Except for one.

Old magic lingers in these secret places of the world, the Quick Ones say. He hears their songs. Knows that this place that is his is one such place they sing of.

For the first time, he thinks on how very old he is.

He thinks on the world that is older still, and on the Quick Ones who partake of so little of that world in the short time given to them. He thinks about the death they face, and the history that reaches beyond life.

He thinks on the endless death that twists out from this place, this time, because the presence of the grey blade here creates a single future that will not be denied. The quest of the Green Priestess, the sacrifice of the Blood Knight. No difference made. The Green Priestess falls, the Blood Knight falls, and the rift between these two is never breached. Cut by long years between them and the door of death that closes off their perceptions.

There stands a future beyond which he cannot feel. There stands a place that seethes with the noise of storm wind across the dry grasslands, that burns with the heat of the unseen earth that will consume all the wide world in the end.

This is the end of each future in which only death unfolds each time the grey blade is seized, claimed by another that will turn its power to destruction in the name of the hunger that the deep magic brings.

All futures save one. An impossible place where the Green Priestess and the Blood Knight are made to see the things each knew. Things the other should have known.

He reaches deep within himself.

He summons all the old magic that is in this place. He creates a moment beyond which he cannot stretch his endless thought. A moment beyond all the long centuries of his awareness and the farthest expanses of all the futures he can touch. A single future that he will shape. A possibility that is all he is. All he can be.

The Blood Knight's dedication burns bright in the dead heart of every oath ever uttered in the Empire's name, and in the knowledge of a darkness hidden from the world at the cost of blood and in the name of the common good. In the name of the commonwealth of the Lothelecan, gone now.

The Green Priestess's hope flares within a shroud of white-hot anger and defiance at the Empire that steals the Kelist Razor away, and the death that shreds the dream of reclaiming the sword becomes the sword, because death and the grey blade are one, the knotted cord of life tearing before its edge like rotted gauze.

He feels spring turn as he begins it, and by the time of deep summer, he feels nothing at all.

There stands a place that seethes with the noise of storm wind across the dry grasslands, that burns with the heat of the unseen earth. This is the future beyond which he cannot feel.

In the blindness of that last moment, he understands what it means.

* * *

She awoke in the spring, lurching to life in a wave of pain and bright blindness. She heard wind and water, twisting over her, flowing beneath her, impossibly loud. The sun was high above her, stabbing her eyes as she reflexively turned away. Rolling to her side on her bed of soft grass, she froze suddenly with a guttural fear, seeing the sloping edge of the broad and crumbling ridge she rested upon. She felt a pounding pain in her head, felt a spell of dizziness take her that caused her to seize the very ground beneath her, hold it tight.

She saw the sword then.

It stood where her memory placed it, buried to more than half the length of its broad blade in a crest of white stone, as if it had been plunged there to cool its final forging. A vision came back to her in a rush of cold. She remembered running, remembered wolves behind her. She lurched to her feet in sudden fear, half-fell, half-stumbled back and away from the edge of the ridge. She felt her heart race in the expectation of jaws clamping hard against her legs, tearing flesh and muscle, pulling her down. She screamed with the memory, and then it was gone. Just a dream.

She looked down to see herself, staring in shock. She stood naked as her birth, wrapped only by the crumbling tendrils of dead vines. She brushed them away in frantic fear, felt her pale skin drink the heat of the sun that slowly sent the chill away. Before her, in the space where she had lain, were spread fragments of leather that she knew with unknown certainty were all that was left of the armor she once wore. She picked up a section of breastplate and rusted buckle with shaking hands, felt it crumble with the rot of endless years.

She remembered running, remembered seeing the sword even as she sprinted for safety and felt herself stumble at that long-dreamed-of sight.

She remembered running, remembered the sword's great weight in her hands as she drove it down to shatter the rock and tear the soil that would sheathe the blade until the end of time.

She blinked, felt both sets of memories twist past each other in an impossible embrace. The sword was three strides away from where she fell. The sword was where she left it, thrust down as a vine-strewn offering into the earth itself.

Above and around her, a whisper traced the still air.

She wheeled, stumbling again as she looked up, but all she saw above and around her were the skeletal arms of an ancient oak. Its heavy branches were dead black, leaves hanging dark and slicked with grey mold. The size and spread of the tree spoke of incalculable age, its great base as wide across as a castle tower, countless trunks splitting off from it to spread like a vast wall. Around her, great roots furrowed the ground, touched by rot where winter had peeled their ancient bark away.

In a shudder of memory, she saw the great tree spreading above the snow, black branches limned with frost. She felt her heart twist with that memory, felt a sudden spike of pain and longing for the mission that set her against the will of a dead Empire. She felt her sight clouded by the dead eyes of the knight who was pledged to die in the defense of that Empire, and who had tried to stop her mission even before she was born.

Around her, inside her, she felt the old magic sing.

This was the magic from which life sprung, coursing now in every breath, in the space where that breath became the wind, in the wind's caress of golden leaves and the white bark of the lesser trees that spread out and around the open space of ridges and ravines above which the great oak had climbed. She felt it in the burning heart of the sun that was the source of all life, watching its twisting shadows across the grove around her.

She felt a fear she didn't understand.

Old magic lingers in these secret places of the world, the high priests said.

She found a black cloak with which she covered herself. It lay half-hidden beneath a layer of loam and dead leaves, but she knew it was there, had always known it. Two strides from where the cloak was fallen, she saw the same dead vines that had clutched at her twisting through an ancient skull.

She remembered everything. Remembered nothing. All the hope that brought her here, that had carried her across half a world. She was one of hundreds, scouring the farthest corners of a dozen kingdoms in search of a legacy stolen from her people twelve hundred years before.

She was one of hundreds taking the oath of blood to defend an Empire against the rise of ancient evil that spread like a dark stain from the deeps and legends of the past.

She was the last of the Lotherasien, following ancient portents and the shadowed signs of divination to the dark wood. Last of a fated handful who had sworn to die in order to bury the dread blade beyond all thought and memory. Out of the reach of any who might seek it.

She was the knight whose skull had lain here for uncounted years, twined now by dead vines and wind-touched grass. She was the acolyte that had died within sight of her peoples' dream, was the spirit of life reborn and hope rekindled, and of a future that dwelt in her as a dark memory she could not name.

She tried to tear the cloak but its strength was beyond her. She felt the strength of spellcraft in its weave, keeping it whole against the passage of time. In the end, it took the sword itself to cut it, the cloth snapped taut and drawn against the razor edge of grey steel standing immobile in its cradle of stone.

She wrapped the haft in the shorter piece of cloak, twisting it tight in three layers before she would draw it forth from the ground. Careful not to let any part of it touch her flesh, just as they had all been taught. As he had been taught, she realized. The other mind in hers, all the fear that had been someone else's once, guiding her now in a way she didn't understand but could not ignore.

It took the better part of the day for her to slowly wrench the grey blade free of the grasp of ancient stone. She stood it before her carefully when she was done, only half a head taller than the sword at its full height. She weighed in her mind the difficulty of carrying it, measured out the effort of finding shelter, finding clothing, finding sustenance as she dragged it in secret across the distance home. A journey she would make because there was no one else to make it.

With the larger piece of cloak, she wrapped herself against the chill that advanced with the setting sun. She would set out in search of a more sheltered space, the open ridges too exposed to spend the night before the first day of that long march.

She heard the whisper again. But when she turned, she saw only the stooped and twisted trunks, the time-bent limbs of the ageless oak above, its black leaves spreading to cover all the bluff like a shroud. She thought she felt eyes on her, felt a timeless touch thread through her like the incessant stitching of a silver needle. She heard the voice of the wind, heard the hiss that carried a black storm of dead leaves to the air as she turned away.

A Space Between

THEY WERE FOUND IN THE MIDST of their tryst by the Khanan Irnash'an himself, the steel-bound door of the abandoned White Tower gallery breaking beneath his shoulder like it might have been a courtesan's cork-paneled closet. The voice of the High Emperor of all Ajaeltha when he saw them was a scream of purest rage. He held the scepter of his reign in hand, hefted like a mace with all the strength and fury that had conquered the uprisings of three governors before the two of them were even born.

Jalina screamed, clutching the sweat-stained satin sheet to her as she scrambled back on the cushioned pallet, eyes downcast from instinctive deference as much as fear. Charan met the aging sovereign's gaze as the scepter swung high. He hit the floor rolling, naked flesh slamming against cold stone as the mass of gilt-edged steel and razor-sharp gems hissed past his head, a finger's breadth from killing him.

Across the ancient line of statues set in an uneven colonnade to both sides of the door, his clothing was scattered as an unseemly web. Cloak and leggings, shirt and linens. The stone faces were ancient courtiers and forgotten sovereigns, all of them staring blankly. Banished here to dust and silence, far from the white marble of the khanan's great halls.

Jalina would be safe enough, Charan knew as he scrambled to his feet, feeling the ancient warrior twisting behind him but not daring to look. He understood that the second blow would come for him, just as he knew that it would hit with certainty, no room to maneuver in the narrow confines of the cluttered chamber. Snatching at his leggings and belt, Charan grabbed up his knife, the scabbard left exposed as it always was. Force of habit. He spun as he hurled it with no thought, felt the momentum of his movement twist through his arm like the crack of a teamster's whip.

He was planning only to distract the khanan, hoping to divert that follow-up killing stroke to his shoulder or side rather than his skull. What he might do to prevent the next blow was a matter he was still frantically thinking on when the scepter lurched from callused hands.

The khanan clutched at the knife where a hand's-length of damask steel had buried itself hilt-deep in his chest. He hit the floor with a soft thud and the gasp of his last breath. All was silent after that.

Neither of them spoke for a long while. Charan fought to slow his breathing, realized numbly that the continued quiet meant the khanan had made his careful way up the tower stairs alone. He slipped to the buckled door, closed it carefully against its shattered frame.

"You killed him," Jalina whispered at last. The ash-brown eyes were wide, set within their frame of auburn hair. Her hands were shaking, fingers reflexively forming the death-sign before her.

"A knife in the heart will do that."

Charan stood over the corpse, turned from her so she wouldn't see the wonder as he stared. It wasn't the first body he had seen. Not even the first whose death was nominally his responsibility, but it was the first to have fallen by his own hand. He half-expected to feel something. Fear, perhaps. The weight of hubris, the dread of vague doom. Some guilt or misgiving.

Instead, his mind was empty. As he looked down absently, he saw his sex still standing rigid, unhooded where it reached for the empty air before him. He tasted metal in his mouth, dull copper like the stippled blood rising in the khanan's dead eyes.

"He is the khanan and your father," Jalina whispered, hoarse. "Is that all you have to say?"

Charan smiled bitterly. A hand absently ran through the black hair shrouding his face, pushed it back to hang to his shoulders. He turned to his sister with a flash of black eyes that were reflected in her own cold gaze.

"Gods save the empress," he said.

He saw Jalina flush, a rush of crimson rage that made her eyes flash brighter. It twisted from face to neck, pushed down to spread across her breasts as she stood regally, wrapping the sheet around herself. "We bring him back," she said.

"He's dead," Charan responded idly. "There's a degree of permanence involved."

"I mean bring him to the priests, fool. Impose the rites of return while the spirit still lingers…"

"When the spirit returns, the memory comes with it. Bring him back to recall how I put a blade in his heart? I think not." Charan stooped to lift the diadem from his father's brow, felt the flesh already cooling beneath it. He pulled his shirt from a statue of the great-grandfather who named the empire that his sister had just inherited, dropped it to shroud the face and its sightless eyes.

There was less blood around the knife than he imagined there would be. He absently tossed the crown over his shoulder, turned to see Jalina snatch it by instinct before it hit her. By a less well-practiced instinct, she recoiled from it like it might have been a serpent, sending it to the ground with the dull thud of its golden weight.

"I thought you might like to try it on," Charan said evenly.

"It fits your ambition best." His sister's voice was ice, the full mouth set in an imposing blank line.

He only shrugged. "Should have thought on that before you clawed your way from mother's womb ahead of me."

He saw her look away, close her eyes and mark the death-sign again in response to the mention of their mother. The maker's cross, both hands scribing the air before her. The circle of the sun above, the quick intersection of the sword below.

Charan scowled. "No matter how often you wave your hands to your gods, she stays just as dead."

Jalina dropped the sheet as she stood, slunk to the window ledge where she had carefully folded her own clothing. She stood in silence a while. "I want neither the crown nor the throne," she said at last. "I'll refuse both. Take them and be happy for the first time in your life."

Charan's dark eye followed the curve of her back as she fastened her underskirts, the faint gleam of lantern light showing the wetness at her thighs and in the dark tangle of her sex. He felt the ache in his loins thicken. "Our first purpose here will make us both happier by far," he said carefully. "For a time, at least."

He saw the shudder of revulsion slip through his sister. As from a sudden shock of cold water, his tumescence waned.

"You stopped needing to prove your depravity to me long ago." Jalina's hair showed whorls of sun-brightened copper in the light as she tied it back, tightened a belt of spun sheen-silver to fasten her shift.

This she adjusted to the courtly style, the globes of her breasts revealed from the wide-cut sleeves.

"My so-called depravity has had no shortness of call from you these past years." But his sister was silent as she slipped her knife in its scabbard to her thigh, adjusted a patterned skirt of blue and yellow silk over it.

Charan turned from her in anger, tripped over something. At his feet, their father's body. He stared at it like it a thing suddenly and somehow forgotten. "We need to think," he said.

"Match our stories up." Jalina's voice was a child's suddenly. Charan heard it as he dressed with his back to her, saw a vision of her in his mind suddenly at age twelve, their mother dead that summer. In her chamber in the White Tower of the Empress, in the scant time before the priests arrived and the body was whisked away, both he and his sister had seen the marks of his father's hands at her throat.

When the spirit returns, the memory comes with it.

Charan remembered the brown eyes wet with tears, his sister's hand in his as the sepulcher stones were sealed in a haze of blue-white fire. An eldritch consumption, the healers called it. Beyond their skill to pull her back from the darkness. The people had believed them, because it was easier that way.

"We can say we found him," Jalina whispered. "Throw a concubine or two to the councilors. A crime of passion."

"No."

"Assassination, then. Lure a guard here, make it look as though…"

"No," Charan said carefully. "No story. Anything we do, any involvement with the body, no matter how fleeting, makes us suspect."

"Then what…"

"We dispose of it."

In the sigh that followed a sullen silence, Charan knew that Jalina had already realized there was no other way forward. She needed Charan to be the first to voice it, though. As always, he thought.

"A place no one will ever go." He prodded the body with his foot, felt it unyielding but with no stiffness of the blood yet. The last of his own stiffness had finally faded.

"They won't believe we know nothing of this."

"They will when we show our surprise. Show our uncertainty along with everyone else at the khanan's disappearance…"

"You're as big a fool as he was. The councilors will look to us…"

"They won't dare. The hint of murder puts the empire in their hands, yes. But an unexplained disappearance creates a constitutional crisis that threatens the council's hold on power. Let them come up with the idea of covering for it. They'll invite the two of us to rule as regents in father's place. Tell the people he's gone in secret to the temples at Terhetu, or leading a warband to the Dragonspires."

He looked back quickly, saw her force the quiet smile from her lips. Her eyes were ice where she watched him. Dry, suddenly. He hadn't seen her wipe the tears away.

"What do we do?" she said.

The castle was dark, the corridor lanterns shrouded, but the light of the near-full Clearmoon at the windows was a bright guide as they made their way slowly from the White Tower, down to the distant kitchens far below. The first leg down the endless winding stairs was the hardest, both of them staggering. They had stripped the body, using the robes to staunch the slow flow of blood. Then they wrapped their father in the silk sheets, Charan taking him by the shoulders, descending backwards to watch Jalina struggle as she gripped his feet and followed. The scepter, Charan had lashed tight to his father's waist with the jeweled belt he wore, its bone-crushing weight a scarcely noticed addition to their father's well-muscled bulk.

They moved in a regular pattern, setting the corpse down so that Charan could scout ahead, listening with held breath and pulsing heart for the telltale sound of footsteps. It was late enough that there was little chance of them being seen in the side corridors and wall-passages they moved along, but he had no great desire to explain his presence. Or, more inevitably, to make more murder against whatever courier or wayward servant they happened across.

As disturbing as that thought was, he knew with unasked certainty that he would do the deed without hesitation if it came to it. One death on his hands and he was still shaking. He would have expected that to make the next harder.

Through the wide-open windows, the heat of day was finally past, broken by the dark breeze of the bay. Moon's-light gleamed silver on the water, gold on the towers and minarets of Sasaerin, jewel of Ajaeltha. The city's sloping peaks of clustered spires rose across from them as he and Jalina descended, working from the castle's upper tiers to the servants' levels below.

Luck or fate was on their side, it seemed. Charan could hear slaves in the kitchen along the final stretch of darkened corridor, but the cutting room adjacent was empty. He caught the familiar steel tang of sanguine air as he thrust open the damp-swollen door, saw a half-dozen yearling buffalo dressed and hanging in the darkness. He was much younger the last time he had any reason to pass this way, but a quick inspection showed that the wide black grate at the center of the stained stone floor still hadn't been repaired in all the time since.

When they had dragged their father's body inside, Charan pushed the door shut, kicked a wedge of splintered bone from the detritus of the floor into place along its foot to jam it. He leaned across a dark-stained table, needed to rest his aching back a moment. Across from him, Jalina limped as she paced, staring around her.

"You're a fool," she said at last, as he knew she would.

"I'll take that under advisement."

"You think they won't search for him here? Or were you planning to cut and dress him for feast and hope no one notices?"

Charan moved past her to drop to his knees. He gripped the stinking grate, ignored the heady slime of blood and offal that clung to its corroded bars as he shifted it from practiced memory. A particular twist, a specific positioning that would disengage it from the stones that surrounded them. He felt it come loose, lifted it carefully. Below, the mouth of a narrow well opened up to darkness.

The khanan's stiffening legs were forced into that darkness only with effort, but Charan needed to use the steel and gold scepter to shatter the bones of his father's splayed arms and wide-set shoulders. A half-dozen blows forced the torso into the space of the drain, the broken arms up in a dark gesture of surrender as Charan pushed down with his foot. He kicked a half-dozen times to force the mangled corpse through, watching as it slipped away finally with a sickening lurch.

He dropped the scepter after it, heard the faint echo a moment later as both it and the body hit water below.

"The sewers?" Jalina said from behind. "They'll search every sewer and tunnel within a league of the castle to find him."

"If you insist on telling me things I already know, put them to a tune at least." With a flourish, Charan stood back, beckoning her toward the open sluice drain. The day's wash water was still slick on the stones, dripping at the edges like a rank rain.

"You're mad," she said.

"And a fool, apparently, and proud of both. Get in."

"I will not…"

"You will," Charan said, "whether you climb or whether I drop you." Smiling, he advanced on his sister as one moved on a disobedient dog, saw her flinch despite her own best effort. "This isn't done yet, but when it is, you'll have an empire to rule. The scent of blood is the first thing you need to get used to."

He held her ashen gaze, felt the depth of the anger there. Anger and something else, but he had no time to try to read it.

Not fear, he knew. Of all his sister's moods, that alone was the one he would always recognize.

Jalina turned away. She stepped to the mouth of the black well.

"There's a ladder," Charan said, more softly. "The smell is worse above. Hold your breath to the bottom, you'll be fine."

The narrow chute was roughly chiseled, a wide drain descending what might have been the length of two dozen paces. As his sister lowered herself, Charan saw her find the ladder, its rungs inexplicably extending a hand's-breadth from ancient stone with no sign of support. Steel cylinders descended the length of the shaft, thin as a finger and impossibly strong, hung there and protected from corrosion by the unseen strength of spellcraft. He had stolen them from his father's arcane armories on a whim when he was a boy, even before he had any idea what use he might eventually put them to.

She needed both hands to cling carefully as she descended. Charan went one-handed, the other holding an evenlamp he had taken from the corridor along the way, its eternal cold flame casting the glow of an unnatural sunrise across the stones. He slid the grate back into place from below as he made his way down.

The air was cloyingly damp, Charan's light shimmering on water below them. He heard Jalina jump to wet stone as she reached the bottom, her footsteps loud but steady. He was behind her a moment later. Their father's shrouded body lay in a shallow puddle of black water. Charan stepped over it carefully.

The ceiling was barely tall enough for him to stand beneath, vaulted stone holding the weight of ground and castle above, slick with moisture and the sheen of black mold. True to his word, the air within the sewer passage was clean, scoured by the salt tang of the sea. The broad tunnel was of finished stone but had no entrance, no exit, no doors. The well they had just descended opened up as a rough chute in the arched ceiling. Midway along the walls, a dozen vents opened up to darkness, each as wide across as a child's shoulders.

On the wall beneath the ladderway, a larger grate opened up, as wide to the eye as the drain in the cutting room above. Charan stepped close to it, Jalina staring, her expression unreadable. "You've been here before?"

Charan ignored her. "Look here," he said instead.

The bars of the slime-slick grate were set at cross-angles a hand's-width apart. Beyond them, a shadowed tunnel of cracked and black-ened brick opened up, a grated aqueduct whose mouth dripped water in an intermittent rhythm. A distant pulsing roar echoed from the darkness.

"It connects to the harbor, beyond the deep docks," Charan said. "Seawater flows in at high tide to clean out this and all the other sewer traps beneath the castle. As the tide turns, it empties again. We remove the grate. We ensure the body can't be identified." He felt his hand ab-sently stray to his knife, forced it away. "Let the sea take what we leave of him. Consign him to the depths."

The grate was black sea-iron, strong as crucible steel but untouched by rust. The stones around it were weaker, however, their mortar eaten away by age and the salt-rot of the sea. Charan pulled a chunk free with little effort, tossed it to the black water where his father's body lay.

"Tear a stone wall down with our bare hands?" In Jalina's voice, he heard a familiar disdain that told him she had secretly appraised and approved of the plan. "We'll be here a week," she said. "They'll be looking for him and us before we're halfway finished."

Charan smiled as he suddenly grabbed for the wall, pulled himself up as the jet of water he had heard approaching broke through the bars. He watched it crash across their father, breaking along the stone floor to make Jalina scramble back. It pooled in a slick haze, ankle deep now. The inflow returned to a trickle, steady against the distant howl of the surf.

Charan set the evenlamp on an outcropping near the ceiling. "Then we'll need to work more quickly than that," he said.

They labored together wordlessly, side by side in the wet gloom, knives hacking at the crumbling mortar that held twisted bars to weathered stone. At intervals, Charan struck the grate hard with his father's scepter, gold plating and gems worth a rogue's fortune torn away with each echoing blow. Jalina glanced above her each time he hit, but he knew from experience that no sound would make its way up the dark well to the castle above.

His shoulders were already aching, but he wouldn't let Jalina see it. He watched her as he worked because she was refusing to meet his gaze, focused wholly on the digging. She paused only when one end of her knife's guard snapped off at her attempt to use it as a lever. The death-sign she made at regular intervals didn't slow her down. One hand working, the other with fingers twisting to ward off the fear that he knew her father's body was inspiring in her. She would whisper names each time, a faint trace of movement at her pale lips. Benedictions and the names of deities long dead.

"The gods have already had their say in the matter of the khanan's life," Charan said quietly. "What do you hope they add to it now?"

Jalina's eyes narrowed as she redoubled her attack against the ruined wall. "Mock my faith all you wish."

"I don't mock your faith. I'm thinking I should embrace it. Seek the guidance of sun and moons as did the khanans of old." He twisted his knife, feeling for and carefully avoiding its breaking point as he dug his way into crumbling stone.

The fear had been in Jalina when their mother died. Charan felt it that day when her hand found his at the edge of the funeral bier. He felt it that night when he drew her to him for the first time, yielding when he pressed his mouth to hers. He felt it as he led her through silence and shadow up to the White Tower that had been their mother's court, empty since the week of mourning, its servants feted and drugged and burned still living with their empress-consort on the pyre.

"The khanans of old Ajelast were masters of sun and moons." Jalina took the bait, as he knew she would. "The god-emperors captured the magics of the heavens, and with it built a world the likes of which will never be seen again."

Twenty centuries before, Ajelast had been built on the bones of the great empire of Nesana before it died out in fits of corruption and bloody magical war long ago in its homeland across the sea. In an age where the secrets of magic were long divided between the power of life and the power of mana, the animys and the arcane, it was the hierophants of Nesana who had married and perfected those disparate sorceries. Those same hierophants had later been the power behind the ancient empire of Eria that first bound the lands of the western Leagin as one.

"Your precious Empire cast down that faith and made all Ajaeltha slaves to others' ambition," Jalina said, defiant. "Even as they stole the power that was once ours. Those who revere the Lothelecan are the dogs never knowing any life but the search for scraps at their masters' feet."

With one final thrust, the last mortar holding in the left side of the grate fell away beneath Charan's knife. His father's blood still clung to the grooves of the blade, he saw. "The khanans of old Ajelast married blood to blood. Brother to sister."

A darkness fell across Jalina's face like a mask. She turned all her attention to the keystone at the upper corner of the grate that had loosened but would not yet move. He stepped in behind her, slipped his hand in to grasp it. She flinched as he pressed against her.

"It is not for anyone else to tell us what we can and cannot do. Not anymore." Charan's voice was a faint echo over the shadowed rasp of stone on stone. "I do not claim to know the will of heavens or earth or what gods live above or below our own lives. I only know what I believe in, and what I believe in is you."

"It's over, Charan."

There was a resounding crack as the crumbling keystone came loose, a shower of dust and mortar rubble following it. The slow flow of water was disrupted for a moment as the grate lurched. Charan was suddenly very cold.

Jalina threaded herself through his arms and away while he stood unmoving. He watched the stone fall absently from his hand to strike black water.

"We walk this path together," he said, but his voice trailed off against the dripping hiss of the shattered duct. He fought to speak, but his sister's words filled his mind and drove all else out.

He had expected those words, but not here. Had known from the first that this moment would come one day. Jalina pushed along the wall as splashing footsteps, turned back toward him. The brown eyes burned with contempt. The taste of metal came to his mouth again.

"We walk together," he said. "Now more than ever. We pledged oaths…"

"We were children then," Jalina said, and Charan once more heard the child she had been thread through the words. An echo in her voice that cut him. "Children's oaths mean nothing. Set the past behind you, brother."

"We are bound," he said. He sheathed his dulled knife to seize the bars, pulled with all the strength his rising anger gave him so that he wouldn't have to look at her. He heard stone and brick give way, felt the muscles knot across his back and shoulders as the bent and ruined grate shifted in his grasp. "Now more than ever. We…"

"There is no we. Not anymore."

With a rumbling echo of steel and stone, the grate came loose, and the response Charan would have made to his sister was choked off behind that sound and the certainty he heard in her. An argument, he would have expected, could have dealt with. A carefully crafted distraction, his sister jockeying as she so often did for any subtle advantage in the eternal tension that hung between them.

She had sensed the fear in him. Seeing deeper into him, perhaps, than even he was capable of. Using that fear just as he should have expected she would.

He dropped the grate to the pool of the floor, heard its drowned echo ring out. "Father only just cold, and already you speak with his voice," he said evenly. "He has no say in what we do anymore…"

"What we did," she said, all stress on the past. "What we did, what we were, is why he died."

He felt it then. Saw it like a mirror held up to his own uncertainty. She was testing him, he realized. The fear he had learned to recognize twisted through her words, hiding a truth he could almost see. A thing he could extract and claim if he was careful, as he had been so many times before.

The evenlamp on its shelf shed its light behind him. He moved slowly, Jalina wrapped within his shadow. A hand on her shoulder made her flinch. Then slipping across, rising to her cheek.

"If your gods do exist, it was their hand that guided my blade today. They have brought you here. Placed you at the apex of the power that was promised you the day you were born. They have made you their agent in Ajaeltha now, and placed me here at your side."

Charan didn't see the arch of the ceiling shudder and split above his head until he felt Jalina's hands on his arm.

With a strength he had never suspected in her, his sister pulled him off his feet, dragging him backward land atop her across the floor as the age-weakened vault collapsed on the spot where he had been standing. The noise was an echoing roar in the narrow confines of the sewer's stone walls, a blast of stale air slamming past to blind him with grit and black mold.

When he could open his eyes, the chamber was silent once more. The evenlamp had fallen when Jalina saved him, its light shimmering now where it was half-submerged in the ebb and flow of black water. The scepter and the grate were both gone, buried beneath a jumbled fall of shattered brick and rubble rising knee high. A pall of ash-grey dust hung over it, twisting like storm clouds in the uneven gloom.

"My thanks," Charan said awkwardly. He felt his sister push him away as he stood.

Jalina moved back to crouch against the wall, eyes closed and breathing hard. He stepped toward her, touched her shoulder. She didn't flinch this time, but when he put his hand to her waist, she shrugged him off, turned so she could slip past him.

Charan saw the ashen eyes widen, flicking past his gaze to something behind him. The fear he recognized again. He crouched low as he spun by instinct, knife in hand.

At the corner of the haphazard mound of rubble, half-buried and barely visible beneath the fall of stones and shattered brick, a body sprawled.

Charan scooped up the evenlamp, brought it to bear on the apex of the collapsed wall. Through a shattered fissure, he saw darkness opening up above the narrow confines of the sewer chamber. A rising passageway of worked stone, closed off from the trap at some point in the past. Or perhaps an ancient sublevel, beneath which the sewers had been extended when the foundations of the castle were first laid.

"Who is it?" Jalina was at his side, her fingers trembling as they made the death-sign. Despite himself, Charan fought the hope that those fingers would seek his when they were done, watching as his sister's hand went to her breast instead, clenched tightly there.

The mummified form was the black of weathered silver, wrapped in a torn shroud of rotted cloak and twisted ropes of cobweb. "Dead," Charan answered.

"I can see what it is. I asked who."

"Death makes all the answers the same."

It wasn't the sight of death that his sister feared, Charan knew. It was the spirits of the past. The superstitions of children and old men were the foundations on which the faith of her once-dead gods was built. Their church had been resurrected a generation before in the aftermath of the distant Empire's fall, and while he heard the liturgy as often and as endlessly as she, it had never amounted to any more than any other folk tale in his mind. He had thought his sister of the same mind, once.

When their mother died, Jalina had changed.

"Imperial Ajelasti," Charan said softly as he bent close to the body. Jalina gave him a quizzical look. "Judging by the age of him."

Ajelast, whose ancient empire was the foundation on which Ajaeltha was raised, had been the most bitterly contended of the lands destined to become the Elder Kingdoms. Long after Nesana was only a memory, Ajelast stayed strong. First of the Elder Kingdoms to fight the encroach of Empire. Last to fall to the Lothelecan's iron embrace, or so the official histories said. More accurate accounts told less flattering tales of the complicity of Ajelast's last free khanans in the Empire's final assault against the independence of the east.

However, all tales spoke consistently in describing how Ajelast rose in the aftermath of the fall of Empire as Ajaeltha. A new empire forged in blood and steel by their father's grandfather. A strength for rule in their line that Charan saw in his sister in each waking moment, but which for some reason he had never warmed to himself.

Even under the rule of the Lothelecan, the Ajelasti made sport of assassination like no people before or since. Military history had been Charan's single point of interest in his lessons as a child, forgoing languages, astronomy, natural history, literature and all else in favor of the endless recitation of organized bloodshed that his father's military advisors held in seemingly endless supply. Wars they themselves had seen, political uprisings before their time, endlessly talked of and analyzed. Tales of generals and the nobles who ruled them murdered in more glorious and disturbing ways than Charan would have thought possible.

His father had always spoken proudly of his son's predilection for the bloody politics of history. He found himself wondering now if the khanan's opinion had changed in the last few moments of his life.

Their father's spirit was still locked within his already rotting flesh. Or so it was reckoned by the beliefs of the temple, and by the magic of the priests that could have enervated that dead flesh to life with the ancient rites. For people such as his sister, those rites proved the renewed presence of the once-dead gods. Banished by Empire and lost to the faithless but never truly gone, the priests said. For Charan, however, the rites did the opposite, and he was always quick to point out that the priests' magic functioned just as well under the Empire's godless ochlocracy as it did now.

"Captain or castellan," Charan said idly. "Or a queen's consort, or a king's lover. Killed and sealed up behind stone. Or sealed alive, more likely. Open up the old tunnels beneath any castle, you'll find more like him."

Charan saw his sister make the death-sign again. He let her hear him laugh. "You spend your life afraid of shadows, you soon fear the sun and moons that shed them."

"I make the mortal warding for you," she said calmly. "Not for me."

Charan felt a flush of heat rise at his chest, twisting up to his cheeks. In his sister's voice, there was a sudden edge that he had heard before and learned to fear. Something had changed in the two dozen words that just passed between them, and he had no idea what it was.

"Do I look afraid, sister?"

"The dead cast their shadows even in the absence of light," Jalina said, not answering. Her face was pale in the glow of the evenlamp, not meeting Charan's dark gaze. The water at the ruined duct was a steady rain now, dripping in an uneven curtain against the stones. "He's been here all along, turning this place to a tomb. You let the dead witness your corruption, their spirit becomes a part of that corruption, tainting it further. Tainting you. You should be afraid."

He understood then. He cursed himself silently, even as he angrily conceded Jalina credit for this thing she had hidden, blindsiding him expertly. His focus on getting their father through the castle, down into his makeshift sewer tomb kept his thoughts scattered. He should have seen it. Would have seen it under any other circumstances.

He laughed in an attempt to cover for the slip, knew that it was already too late. "So my soul is tainted, is it?"

"Brother, your soul was tainted from the moment of your birth."

At the grate above, Jalina had told him she wouldn't descend, her revulsion all too real. But she hadn't bothered asking about their dark destination. Hadn't needed to, Charan realized now, because she already knew where they were going.

"Your darkness brought you to this place from the time you were nine years old," she said simply. "It made you bring a long line of serving girls with you, each discarded with silver in hand when you were done with them. When they had finished pretending they were me."

The words carried themselves with an ease that made Charan knew she had waited years to speak them. He only smiled in return, tried desperately to judge her true tone, her mood. Something was happening. A plan whose foundations had been laid long ago. Disrupted now by the death of their father, he guessed. Put into motion early. Or was the khanan's death merely the catalyst? A moment of disaster long waited for, in whose aftermath Jalina would act?

He went for the feint by instinct, summoned up a suitable degree of chagrin that he could pretend was a response to her discovering his secret.

"If only I had known all those years how much the pretending would pale against the reality of you." He stepped close, the sound of his breathing loud even over the hiss of water as Jalina watched. A shiver threaded through her. He moved his head down to kiss the nape of her neck beneath the tightly drawn auburn hair.

He felt her push back against him, too quickly. He lost track of what happened next.

Steel flashed as she spun away from him, his own knife in his hand somehow. They locked guards at the first strike, then Jalina was fading back, footsteps splashing clumsily as her blade slashed past Charan's neck. He slid to let it miss him, parried the next blow, returned with one of his own that she caught and twisted past, behind him suddenly.

Where Jalina crouched, her eyes were bright with the fear he recognized. "I knew it would end this way," she whispered.

Charan's hand was shaking, the battered blade of his knife weaving points of bright fire in the half-light. He tried to trace back the two dozen heartbeats just past, but his sight, his mind and memory were the same blur of red.

He had drawn on her, he thought. But he wouldn't have. Couldn't have. The evenlamp was in the water behind him. He had dropped it in expectation, needing to free his other hand for balance. Impossible. He shook his head, saw his sister flinch in expectation of another strike.

The feeling he was forever afraid to name rooted deep in his chest. He felt the scent and the sight of her overwhelm his memory.

He felt the pain that her words made, felt the fear in her that was the knowledge that her brother had tried to kill her rather than lose her. The knowledge that he would try again. He felt the weight of the knife in his hand.

At the conduit they had torn free of ceiling and wall, a surge of black water exploded as shadow and white foam. The sea-channel had tipped past the aqueduct's unseen halfway point and was flowing steady now, pressing in with a steady hiss of salt air and the distant moaning of the pounding surf beyond the harbor's breakwater stones.

Charan felt for the hot shard of anger at his breast, cooled it with slow breathing. He lowered his knife as much as he dared without compromising his ability to parry, wasn't sure the notched and blunted blade could even withstand the force of an attack.

"You are the one they will watch," he called, voice as clear as he could make it. "Jalina, whose beauty and grace will redefine an empire in mourning. While all the while, I will be your right hand, silent and invisible and devoted to your bidding. It was fate that brought you first from mother's womb, because you are the one who can lead. Some of us are fated to follow."

Jalina tried to laugh, voice ringing out like a cascade of silver over the dank echo of water on stone. With sudden dread, Charan realized why. He cursed himself for the slowness of his wit. His father's murder had rattled him. His father's death. He corrected himself absently, felt the weight of it press down on him all the same.

"You've spoken those words before," his sister said.

Charan felt the memory of the White Tower twist through him, hot wires beneath his skin. He shook his head but kept his silence.

"Do you think often on that night?" she whispered. "Does the memory come unbidden? And knowing now that it ends, do you feel sorry for yourself, brother?" Her voice was twisted through with a honeyed sweetness that brought the taste of bile to his throat. "Cut off from your carnal sanctuary? Denied this forbidden tryst?"

"It was more than that," Charan said, and he felt his tongue suddenly turn to lead even as the words were formed.

"Whatever you thought it was, Charan, you were wrong."

She struck with the speed of a brush-viper, too fast to see. Charan managed to twist away in the barest nick of time, felt her knife's broken guard tear his tunic and the flesh beneath. And in the sudden blossom of that pain, his only thought was that he would never know whether her renewed fury was a sign that she believed his words. Or the final proof that she didn't.

The flash of blades between them was a steel-grey rain as they fought across the shadows of the rapidly flooding chamber. All the effort and eager practice of two childhoods lost to the training floor of their father's war-masters showed now in the grim set of Charan's mouth, in the smoldering light of his sister's eyes. They hit fast, unforgiving, a succession of killing strokes turned wide by the narrowest of margins. Both their blades dulled by stone but hitting hard enough to punch through skin and bone if they hit, Charan knew. Brother and sister striking like the twin serpents they truly were.

Charan had no illusion about having the speed that would be necessary to disarm his sister, just as he was sure she harbored no vain hope that she might wear him down. A terrible passion twisted between them now that replaced the stolen emotion of the time just passed, of the months before, of the five breathless years since they had first taken each other in the silent aftermath of their mother's ash-rites.

All their lives, mother and father had been the twin poles around which so much turned. With their mother's death, they had found a measure of peace within each other.

With their father's death, they had found something else, it seemed.

But even as he thought it, Charan fought to recognize this rage, this sudden and inescapable fury that twisted between them now with each pass of the blade. A new emptiness, he thought. A space between them that he had never felt before. But in feeling it now, he wondered whether it was a thing that had always been there, hidden by choice and the sweet darkness that cloaked them both, night after long night.

He was breathing hard, heard the roaring in his ears that was more than just the pounding of his blood. His feet were numb, water calf-deep now where the inflow churned it to black foam.

For all the late-childhood trysts that brought him here, Charan had never lingered belowground to watch the high tide cleanse the trap and the sewer channels beyond. He had no idea how long it would take for the water to fill the chamber, but he could guess that the end was coming quickly.

Jalina glanced to one side, avoiding the worst of the spray. Time enough for Charan to move. He drove hard for her heart, couldn't risk pulling the punch of the killing stroke, but even still, he caught her knife instead as it flashed up to parry, impossibly fast. He screamed as he forced his hand around, felt hers twist against it, sliding to catch her knife with his guard and snap it. The shattered blade caught him above the eye as it flashed past, a spray of red blinding him. He lost his footing for the moment it took Jalina to spin in the haze of water, up to her knees now, one leg out and coming up to connect a kick that nearly broke his jaw.

He blacked out for a moment. Fought his way back to consciousness even as his own knife dropped from his hand to hit the water with a dead-black splash. Jalina was there, dropping to hands and knees with a shout of triumph, but the blade was already beyond her reach in the dark water. Charan stumbled through the fast-flowing surge of the sea, tried to grab his sister, but she was rolling away from him, wet silk like oil against her lean body as sharpened fingernails raked his face.

He swung at her, missed beneath her subtle movement as she spun again and drove her fist into his side, just missing the tight knot of nerves that would have dropped him. They shifted past each other, clumsy and freezing in the rising water as they attacked hand to hand, neither managing to land a blow, their moves too familiar. From the long years of training, from the shorter time of the dark trysts in the White Tower's empty halls, each of their bodies was a map that the other knew too well.

Their father's corpse was floating, a slick of blood spreading across the oily blackness of the thrashing tide. The evenlamp was underwater, its golden light cut to a rippling silver sheen across dark walls. Even in the grim shadows that the body threw to the ceiling, Charan could see that the ladderway was all but gone beneath the roar of dark water at the inflow, no way to even get close enough to climb it now. Before the inflow, the ancient corpse had been torn apart by pressure, blasted to a shadow-swirling storm of bone and rotting cloth.

And in that ancient figure's fractured hands, previously unseen where the shroud of dust and cobwebs had hidden them, a pair of bare-bladed daggers gleamed in the evenlamp's faint glow.

As one, they moved. Charan got there first, only to have Jalina drive the full force of her fist into the side of his neck as his focus drifted from her for just a moment. He saw a haze of red, felt the cold as he hit the water, but then something warm was in his hand and he was up, thrashing side to side to clear wet hair from his eyes.

His sister stood across from him, brown eyes unblinking, a dagger in her hand to match the one in his. Razor-edged stilettos, each set with a wickedly clawed blood-edge that looked as if it might saw through bone with enough force behind it. Their twisted guards were shaped to suggest the flow of water, each set with a diamond at its heart, but one gleaming black, the other brilliant white.

In Jalina's hand, the metal of the dagger was the blue-white of the hottest forge fire, glowing now as if it was fresh-struck in her living grasp. The blade that Charan held tight was black steel that seemed to mark the emptiness between them, unwavering in his hand despite the pain and the blood-dark haze still hanging at the edge of his sight.

The water was at his groin now, his legs numb as the two of them held there, an arm's breadth apart. Both ready to move with the final strike that would spell the end.

Charan felt a strength surge through him then. He felt all the rage, all the uncertainty that had been set in his heart, all of it focused and made sharper. He felt the weight of his father's death leave him, felt the pain of his sister's love torn away like a shroud of leaves on the wind. He felt nothing, felt everything. Felt alive. Jalina's eyes blazed, her teeth set in a hissing smile that told him she felt it, too.

Charan felt something touch him, felt a bond he couldn't explain stretch out across that empty space of longing and laughter and pain. Something stronger even than the forbidden thirst of the blood and the mind that had brought them to the tower earlier that night, then brought them to this black-water tomb.

When he was nine years old, he had slipped into the Red Tower of courtly magic by dark to steal two talismans from a young vizier just graduated from the apprentice's suites. Charan knew the relics would be missed, of course, but he had already planted rumors of a taste for gambling and the temple virgins in the vizier's name. After a well-placed bribe to the castellan's office saw the young mage arrested, Charan had made a point of not paying attention to his particularly unpleasant fate.

For almost a year, he waited for a night of full Darkmoon rising blood-red with no light of Clearmoon in the sky, as the crumbling scroll that accompanied the pieces in their leather case had bade him. When the time came, he drugged the servants outside his sister's rooms, stole into Jalina's bedchamber. He slipped one of the frail star-silver pieces beneath her pillow.

Then all that endless night, as he had longed to do since he was old enough to remember thought itself, Charan slipped inside his sister's dreams.

A sudden rush of understanding swept through his mind with the force of the sea, surging toward his waist.

In his hand, along his arm, in his ear and mind and only for him, the black blade sang.

Power threaded through him, touching and amplifying the power of the white blade as its own song rose. It was a thing beyond words, beyond thought. A power he and his sister shared suddenly, a nexus of energy that threaded through them. Their bodies turned to silk, scoured by the warm desert wind.

The haze that was all that remained of the broken body was a faint outline beneath the water, but even as his gaze flicked there, Charan was moving suddenly, faster than thought. He sensed a blur of blades, felt twin arcs of white and shadow slash between them as he and Jalina struck, parried, a fast strike caught and spun off a crossguard, the return seeking flesh and striking empty air, again and again.

His vision sharpened in the darkness, a warmth flooding through him. But even as it did, he heard his own voice harsh in his head. *Fool,* he called himself, and a chill twisted through him, helped him focus. Smarter men than he had felt their lives cut short by the dark dweomer of a cursed blade. Relics left for the finding by those their fell magic had already killed.

He felt the passage of time slow around him. Felt a wholeness that filled his mind and forced out all thought but the memory of that perfect connection he had once felt between his sister and himself.

He saw Jalina start as if she sensed his thought. He heard her voice, but in the haze of shadow that suddenly shrouded his sight, his mind, he couldn't be sure whether she spoke, or whether it was her very act of thought tracing through him, or whether he dreamed it in the end.

"Whatever you thought it was, you were wrong."

He parried, spun the black blade through a feint as a blur of shadow, struck hard as he slipped beneath Jalina's return strike. He felt the flesh and bone of her breast yield with the softness of sand. But even as it did, pain like white-hot fire flared at his own chest, and a blade that wasn't there shattered his collarbone and drenched his freezing-wet shirt with a gout of hot blood.

As he had tried and failed to do ever since that dark night, Charan remembered. As he tried to do each time he pulled the shadow over the two of them, slipping into the wordless space where they were one, he felt that wonder of touching his sister's mind.

Charan screamed, scrambling back as his blade pulled free from Jalina. His hand was locked to the haft by searing pain, teeth set against it. His sister's pale face was a mask of fear as she fought her way back through the flood, clutching at the jagged rent in her tunic to reveal no blood there, the pale skin unbroken.

Charan fought to stay on his feet, pressed his shaking knife hand hard to the gash at his chest. He had struck the fast blood, no way to staunch the wound that should have been his sister's, the black blade turning the blow back against himself with all the strength it had borne. The dark dweomer, he thought. But stronger even than the fear of that magic was the knowledge that the blow he had taken would have killed his sister had it struck.

He remembered his father's rage at the tower door. Remembered seeing that same rage too many times to count, a lifetime of anger that was his legacy. He remembered the reflection of that anger, bright in the last light of his father's eyes when the blade left his hand.

Jalina's eyes were wet, her voice all but lost against the roar of water, lapping at her breast now.

"Brother," she called. "Some of us are fated to follow."

She hesitated just long enough to let Charan understand that she knew what she was doing. His utter betrayal of her was the only thing that mattered to her now, as she lunged forward to plunge the length of the gleaming blade into his heart.

Charan felt something twist in his chest, felt his breath stolen away. He saw Jalina's shift suddenly turn black in the shadows, a blood-flower blossoming there in time with his own pulse as she fell.

The roar of water swallowed his scream as it swallowed her body, slipping like a stone beneath the foam. Charan felt the pain at his chest surge as he pushed forward, but then it was gone and replaced by a sharper agony that twisted from gut to heart to head, pounding now with the strength of his own blood and a fear he had never known before.

He was blind in the surge of water and shadow as he fought to dive. He felt her, lost her. Grasped her again by the edge of her shift and hung on to seize her fiercely, fighting the current.

He pulled his sister up from the darkness, screamed her name this time, but her empty eyes were blank. Desperate, he slung her to his shoulders, unaware of her weight as he looked to the ladderway but saw it already gone, the vents submerged where black water boiled.

Behind him, against the last grey flare before the light from below was swallowed, he saw the faintest flicker of firelight. There, beyond the shattered ceiling where the ancient body had once hidden.

Each slow step was agony as Charan fought his way through the freezing inflow, aware that the bitter cold staunching his bleeding was the only reason he was still on his feet. He tried to feel some sign of Jalina's breath where her face was slumped against his, but his vision was a pounding haze, red shadow roaring in his ears. At the ragged opening where the grate had been, he felt his way along the wall as water poured past and out through the ancient drain, threatening to sweep him off his feet.

All was darkness. Then from the passageway that had been sealed came the faint glimmer again. Charan pushed Jalina up, followed close behind her lifeless body into the narrow darkness. He didn't remember climbing, his sister slung across his back as he pushed himself up a narrow chimney of dusty stone and cobwebs. The gleam ahead grew steadily brighter, the red flicker of firelight calling him on even as his mind slipped closer to shadow. He felt the names of all Jalina's dead gods slip unbidden to his mind as he prayed.

His legs were numb, feet bleeding where they gripped rough stone when he arrived at the end of the chute. The glow he followed was blazing bright now, a perfect lozenge of firelight forced through a haze of dust that billowed with his frantic breathing. A keyhole, it looked like. The bottom side of a concealed trapdoor, unlatching easily with a shoulder's pressure from below.

Bright braziers hung by golden chains where Charan pushed himself through. The air was a shimmer of heat haze, darkness claiming him for a moment, but then he was back. Jalina's body sprawled alongside him where he collapsed silently to a floor of night-cold stone. He couldn't see, couldn't feel anything beyond where he groped with shaking fingers for the blood at his sister's throat, found only stilled silence.

He was in the sepulcher, he realized. His sight was shadow and the braziers' faint golden smoke, everburning with the spellcraft of the silent priests. The great tomb of khanans on the lowest level of the castle. Its vaulted columns of white marble held up a ceiling of shimmering black stone brought here a thousand years before from the Mountains of the Moons, far eastward and overlooking the end of the world at the edge of the Great Sea of Storms. His father's ashes would have been laid here, once. Now, they would burn an empty bier, scattered only with the signs and objects of his reign, ready to be reclaimed in the next life that all the dead gods promised.

Charan had been here last when his mother died. Though he told himself he should have known which space was hers among the lines of narrow upright ash-vaults lining the walls to both sides, he couldn't recall it anymore.

From that first night he and Jalina shared, that night of dreams that had inspired the hunger of all the nights that followed, Charan remembered his own face in his sister's mind. Remembered the longing for him that struck his heart like some god's ghostly fist, left him limp and sweat-soaked in the darkness when he awoke.

On that night when he walked in Jalina's dreams, the talisman had turned to ash on his pillow, as he had been warned it would. He had squeezed those burning embers in his hand as though he might will them to reshape themselves again, tears flowing and body aching. Suddenly crippled beneath a weight he had always carried but never felt before.

With shaking hands, he tore the blood-soaked shift from his sister's body. He pressed hard at the jagged wound the white blade's magic had torn at her breast, but her flesh was ice.

On the floor beside him, the black and white steel of the twin daggers caught the flickering light.

Charan felt his breath cut off suddenly. He stared.

He didn't remember slipping the weapons to his belt. Didn't remember even seeing the gleaming white steel of the blade with which Jalina had taken her life. He must have grabbed it even as she fell, he thought. But he couldn't have. Must have been holding it the entire time without realizing. Impossible.

Carefully, he reached for them. First one, then the other. He felt their warmth as they slipped into his shaking hands, left and right, white and black. And without thinking, without understanding, he shifted to press the pale blade into Jalina's unfeeling grasp.

As it did before, the silver-white dagger began to glow. A shimmering ghost light, the mottled ice-sheen of his sister's dead flesh.

Charan felt a trace of faint energy thread his trembling fingers, suddenly stilled as it flowed through them and up his arm. When it reached his chest, the pain there flared again to remind him how he had forgotten it. But then it slowed. Stopped.

Where his sister sprawled before him, he saw the jagged wound at her heart slowly close within its shroud of blood.

Charan had felt the power of the healing magic before, the animyst-priests of his father's court ministering to him when he shattered his leg in a childhood fall from the White Tower roof. He had seen the rites of returning only once. A captain of his father's had been brought back from beyond the veil of death, struck down in combat but deemed too valuable to be left to that darkness. He died again less than a year later. Took his own life, the stories said, driven mad by what he had seen in that shadow before the light returned.

Charan's eyes were wet, breath coming ragged as he saw his sister's fingers flinch against the cold haft of the white blade in her hand. Her skin was silk smooth, all the marks of their dark labor in the sewer washed away.

As he watched, Jalina shuddered, convulsed once as she vomited blood and black water and her eyes opened wide. The wound at her breast was closed, the pale perfect skin sealed over without so much as a mark. She stared up, meeting Charan's gaze where he loomed over her, trembling. He fumbled for her soaked tunic, found one corner cleaner than the rest and gently washed the slick of blood from her face and neck.

Shaking, she raised herself up to kiss him hard, wrap herself in his arms.

They stayed that way for a long while, and when their clothes had dried well enough in the braziers' golden heat, they slipped back through the deep-night castle, then to the secret ways only they knew that led past the servants and to their separate chambers. The same secret ways that had taken them to the White Tower, a lifetime ago now. The ghost blade was clutched tight to Jalina's breast, the dagger whose darkness was the endless night in Charan's hand when their other hands reluctantly parted at last. Fingers slipping from each other, they went their separate ways without a word.

Apart, Charan waited, watching and dozing at the high windows that opened up to the great green-garden courtyard across from his sister's suites. First dawn touched the gleaming towers of the city, twisted the shroud of shadow to a veil of gold across the sky and the star-shining black of the bay.

He remembered the night of shared dreams. From the dark shelter of his own slumber, he walked inside Jalina's mind, feeling the song her thought made, seeing the bright desert dawn that was the backdrop to all her fear and youthful longing.

He felt her dreams and the warmth of a kindling passion he had never felt before. He remembered his own face seen in her mind's eye. Remembered what it felt like to love and be loved that way.

He felt the hunger that had so long twisted through him finally settle and shape itself to something else. He was dreaming of Jalina, the day breaking blue and bright beneath a cloudless sky, when the frantic knock came at the door and the rest of their lives began.

Dark Road

SHE HAD BEEN NAMED Szirha'mun, which was the Darkmoon in his people's tongue. So it was that he dreamed her always watching him over nine days of blood-red shadow that were the nights of sacrifice and remembrance. Those nights when he could be himself once more.

The grey wind was cold along a heading from the distant sea, threatening a storm but seemingly unable to make up its ageless mind when it should arrive. He was naked now save for a necklace of yellowed bones around his neck, looking every bit the monster he was. It had been a decade of exile since he was forced to forget the flesh into which he was born. Long years as the Mockery that he was now, his features pale as cloud, no color or strength to his sickly-smooth flesh.

Ten years ago, he fled the Sorcerers' Isle and the wild marshland that had been his clan's home since the time before the first songs were made. Now, his mottled flesh was wracked with cold, the shivering hands stunted and deformed. Less strength in his spindled fingers than he had commanded as a child.

His senses, too, were dulled in the Mockery's form, but he had long grown used to that weakness. So it was that even against the hiss of wind, he heard the telltale rustle of movement in the tall grass behind him.

He was weak and he was bent, kneeling in muck and pain throughout the long day to await the red moonrise. But the instincts of the warrior he had always been still lingered at a level deeper than the prison of his flesh. From the ground where he set them, he pulled his knives, locked his hands in a defensive stance as he scrambled back, staying low to the ground. He felt the blood loud in his misshapen ears, felt the taste of metal in his mouth that was the Mockery-body's fear.

It was the ninth day of those nine days of the full Darkmoon, and he was waiting for the change that would let him die. Let him pass from this world as he once was, remembered by fate as more than the monster he had become. And staring, his weak eyes saw a girl with a sword standing on the far side of the mottled clearing, curtained by the regular rhythm of grass rippled to fast-whipped waves by the wind.

At the fore of his mind, held tight in the rage that broke and was lost within the weakness of his flesh, there was a name he had not spoken in ten long years. He had saved it for this moment of waiting, had waited to whisper it with his last breath, but the moment was ruined now. He silently cursed his weakness, cursed the child standing motionless in shimmering shadow.

She is named Szirha'mun, which was the Darkmoon in his people's tongue, and he watches her die.

He lowered his hands, felt a sudden shaking twist through them as he turned the knives clumsily down. He carried no sheathe to set them in where he stood naked as the day he was born, so he locked them to the soft skin of his arms, held them there. Conscious of the pain where their edge threatened to cut him. Not caring.

The girl was young, barely a child. The sword that she held point-down before her was the dull grey of brushed silver, its guard and grip of black leather. In his own hand, even with this stunted body, it would have been a short arming blade, suitable for close-quarter fighting and little else. Where the child clutched it, the pommel came almost to her chest, the leaf-shaped blade comically broad.

He didn't flinch as he stood, felt needle-points of pain shoot through bird-thin legs. Though he was naked, he felt no shame. The Mockery-body possessed no feature that would have startled a child, even one as young as this. The girl's golden eyes were wide, but not with the fear he expected.

"I saw you pass along the edge of the village," she called. She spoke the trade tongue that was the common speech of the uncivilized, like him. Like those who wore the form he wore. Her voice had a reedy quality that carried an echo of the wind around her, the words coming matter-of-fact. "It was nine days ago."

"So? And so?"

"I followed you."

"And found me. What of it?"

"You were sneaking, so I followed you."

"Those who have reason to sneak are often best left alone." He spat the metal taste from his mouth, felt a string of spittle bitterly catch the grizzled hair that clung to his misshapen chin. "Or did your parents not teach you this?"

"My parents taught me to look after myself," the girl said. Something changed in her voice. A faint echo of sadness shadowed the bright eyes, but still there was no fear in her. And even as he heard that sadness, he looked into those eyes and felt himself caught there. He felt the pain again, rooting deep and bitter in him as he turned away.

The clan lord, name ever-unspoken and burned ember-bright in his memory takes her innocence in the hot blood of the Darkmoon's night, and she is broken mind and spirit, flesh and bone.

Crumbling shadow blurred his vision as he squeezed his eyes shut, fought back against the memory. He opened them only to take a final glance behind as he pushed himself into the screen of tall grass. She was watching him as he turned from her, looked quickly away, as if she saw the weakness that was his legacy.

He was a sellsword now, and had been for a decade of days spent living hand to mouth. The southern deserts were his home most of that time, a place where the Mockery he was now would fit in. He knew of other lands he could have fled to, certainly. On the Sorcerers' Isle where he was born, there dwelled countless folk who lived with the weakness that was his curse, and monsters in plenty more frightful still. But that road was closed to him now, by the pain that pushed him over the narrow sea, down through Gracia and the mountains. Away from where the voices alone would have been enough to remind him who he had been.

He had needed new voices, new songs, new names when he took the first of the long caravan trains from the foot of the Shieldcrest, the great mountains snow-shrouded and silent as the secrets he left behind. So far north now. So far gone.

As the months wore on, he grew more and more accustomed to the crippling heat that rose from the slate-grey sands. Accustomed but never fully accepted, the harsh air of Ajaeltha's desert scrubland still tearing at his throat as he breathed it. But despite the hardship, he found himself in time counting the unintended blessings of this desolate land.

When they come for her to invoke the rites, she fights them. For her audacity, for her insolence, they beat her nearly to death, but in that cunning way of hard killers who fill the narrow window between near-death and life with the memory of all the pain a body might endure. Let her linger long in the knowledge of all they do to her, body broken and mind ravaged and no way to stop for her the sight those memories make.

No lakes spread here in the land of sunburned soil and scrubland. No great flow of waters tumbled, save for the trade rivers to the north, wending through their green fields. No seasonal ponds, no standing water to speak of, and all the wells of the thousand villages he passed through covered against the harsh and endless drift of sand. So it was that he could go for days, for weeks, for whole months without ever catching sight of his reflection. Whole months without being blind-sided by the self-made sight that was the Mockery he had become, staring up at him from pool or still stream bank, his narrow eyes set like pale coals in a malformed head.

He had walked a score of his weak strides into the shadows where his meager camp was set when he realized she was following. He glanced back again, saw her watching him as intently as before.

"Are you not afraid of me?" he called. From his gear, he sought for the cloak that would wrap his unnatural form. It covered him while he slept, the softness of the Mockery's flesh feeling the cutting edge of every chill night and storm wind. He had set it aside that morning, discarded the heap of his belongings in it. Making it easy for whoever found him to dispose of what was once his.

"I am afraid of your outside. But I know that what is inside is good. The sword tells me."

He set the cloak across his slack shoulders, watched the girl for a long while. She shifted where she stood, let the blade lean back against her. Where the Darkmoon's sanguine gleam caught it, even his weak eyes could see the razor sheen of its edge. "Be mindful of that."

"But it will not cut me." She shifted again, let the blade stand centered over its own weight. He fought the revulsion of imagined pain as she drew her palm along its edge, lifted it to show him. No mark. "It protects me," she said.

"Some sword," he said.

"I will sell it to you," she said, and there was an even tone to her voice that told him this is what she was wanting to say, what she had practiced, waiting for her chance to approach him. Beneath the words, he felt the unease. A sadness that told him the girl held other words still unspoken that were more important by far.

"They say that your kind carries gold and silver," she said. "They say you covet it above all else. I see your knives, but they are not strong. You could use a sword like this."

"Because I am weak? Misshapen?" He took three steps toward her, felt himself lurch as the sharpness of an unseen stone cut the cracked flesh of his foot. The golden eyes were impassive.

"You are ugly," she agreed in the matter-of-fact appraisal of the innocent. "But it is not your fault. The sword told me."

He felt a chill that was not the wind. He wrapped the cloak tighter around himself. "What is your name, child?"

"Hoi'ul," she replied. "It means green."

"It means more than that," he said. "Hoi'ul is the green of spring's first leaves, wet with sunlit dew." To her look of mild surprise, he said "I know your people's tongue, child."

"What is your name, then?"

He had practiced his answer to the question for all the long years of his new life, but he faltered now for the first time.

"I am called Lárow," he said.

The girl laughed, a musical sound. "I know your people's tongue," she said. "Lárow is not a name. It is what your kind call the leaders of the silver-slave gangs. 'The boss.' "

He was silent a while. The Darkmoon was cresting the trees now, fighting to stay afloat on a torrent of thin cloud boiling in from the distant sea. "That is what I am."

"But what is your name?"

He heard the wind, hissing in the ears set low on his head as lumps of gristle. "My name is gone. My story is gone. What I am now is what I do. I am Lárow."

"All folk have a story."

She is fighting to breathe when he finds her, fighting to shed the last tears that mask the sight of him as she dies in his arms. He sees only darkness, feels the dank must of water and rot that claims her body as she slips into the fen and away. And he rages then with the fury of all his ancestors. Pushes into the rope-vined trees with a strength that shatters branches, drives his footsteps at a silent run, clears the path between him and bloody destiny.

In his memory, he saw the eyes that had been the bright amber of the girl's own gaze cloud over. She looked down to the sword still leaning against her, appraised it as if she had forgotten it was there. He felt the pain of heart and memory, felt his vision blur. Grasping for words, for some distraction.

"What is your story, Hoi'ul?"

She looked up again, and the weight of that golden gaze drove into him like a mailed fist. The wind picked up, clawing the clouds as twisting shadow scoured the trees.

"The sword belonged to a lord named Voosal'hal. I killed him."

He is young then, and he bears both the name and form he was born with. She is named Szirha'mun, which was the Darkmoon in his people's tongue.

For the nine days that the Darkmoon blossomed full against the fading dusk, he had lived in this isolated arm of a larger spread of swampland, its scent and the low whistle of night wind in the reeds speaking to him of the home he made himself forget. He came here alone, moving always in the shadow of dusk and dawn to hide from those who might see him. Those who would react with fear and distrust to the Mockery-face he had learned to hate.

He had found the village after nightfall. At the edge of the larger watercourse that lost itself in the mire where he rested, then trickled to a muddy wash twisting south and east to meet the sea. He passed by once, was drawn back to gaze at the small cluster of huts and stockade pens rising from the wetlands. Shallow-bottomed swamp boats rocked gently at a dock of sweetly rotting redwood, bells glimmer-singing along their prows to ward off the spirits of the night. He smelled roast meat, saw the firelight at shuttered windows. He heard the music of laughter, sensed the warmth within as he passed by again, unseen.

The clan lord, name ever-unspoken and seething venomous in the pain of dreams, dies shrieking that night, as do all the rest who broke her. Dying slowly. All of them. The clan lord is last, throat torn out to mark her last breath, anointing the green-black of his regal robes with blossoms of blood that are the Darkmoon's glowering red. Limbs shattered in thirds to mark the breaking of her once-strong body. The flesh of his sex torn free and eaten blood-raw as he screams, for the sorrow visited on her, the final words she whispered to him. Faint through the haze of blood at her lips, all vigor drained from her as he cradles her tightly in the dizzying tremor of his fear.

"I killed him," the girl said again, and the sweet timbre of the voice was no less musical as it crafted the dark confession. Direct in the manner of one repeating something for the sake of its own acceptance. Even through the cloak, he felt another tremor of cold and fear thread his pale flesh.

The girl was younger than he first thought. Too long since he had walked among his own kind, so that their form and movement were grown foreign to him.

He had to turn away for a moment. He crouched and pretended to fumble with something within his meager belongings. His hands were shaking, fear snaking through him to thread his weakness, tie a knot in his throat that he could not swallow.

"He threatened my father," the girl called. "He lusted for my mother. It is the way among our tribe, and the sword gave him strength and put the fear into those he hurt."

"But not you."

A trembling glance back. The girl shrugged.

They come for him then. His people's nobility is a razor-sharp blade too easily rusted, too quick to corruption. Too eager to forget that rank is born of honor, instead giving honor to rank. Order is their way, and the way of clan lords to lay claim to unwed maids in the nine days of the full Darkmoon that are the nights of sacrifice and remembrance. And so they come for him, too late to stop his wrath and vengeance, but ready to invoke the law to send his spirit after hers.

Too slow to catch him, though. Never expecting the rage that fuels him that night, betrayed by fate and blood and clan. And so he betrays them all in turn, for the sake of the blood-black madness that consumes him.

"The sword was his," she said again, as if she was trying to focus the light of her memory on that one specific truth. "He slept with it in his hut, and no one would go there because they were afraid."

"When you hate," he whispered, "you forget how to be afraid."

The meager relics that were all he possessed were a handful of coins and polished stones. Totems he had collected on his recent journeys. Mud-streaked cloth with which he shrouded himself, hiding the vile sight of the Mockery body. Things temporary and fleeting and mundane, carried for their inability to trigger the dark memories that stretched behind him. Anything that threatened to become a memory was cast aside.

"There was blood," she whispered, the wind echoing the emptiness in the words. "He threatened my father and he lusted for my mother, and his sword called to me and I took it and I killed him."

As from a dream, he wakes once that fateful night. Sees his village burning, sees his people dead and dying.

Within the vision that the flames make, he sees her face. Eyes that are the gold of a summer sunrise, warm against the skin.

"Swords do not speak," he said evenly. He tried to focus, tried to force the memory away. "You hold a sword in your hand, you can't help but be aware that you hold the power of another's life and death. That by that power, others might trade life and death with you. But it is your own voice you hear. Warning you to watch for the simplest incaution, and of what you might become if you fail."

"The sword talked to me," she said again, as if he hadn't heard her properly. "The sword looks inside. In his hut, he had pillows and mats of silk and reed. The sword lay on its own pillow like a bed, next to his bed where he slept and where I killed him. I seized the sword and I killed him. There was so much blood..."

He felt the helplessness twisting in him. He fought it, stilled it with the careful training of thought and mind that had kept him alive this long. The calm in which he learned to drown himself as he tore himself from the past. He cleared his eyes of the wetness that came with the Mockery's weakness. The girl was watching.

"I touched it and it looked inside him. There was something black in him, and I knew what I had to do."

He was silent for a long while. He felt an ache in the weak shoulders, the frail body's signal that he had stood for too long. "And now?"

"Now I don't want to do it again," she whispered. "I saw you sneaking, because you are not of this place. You will not stay here. You could use a sword like this. You can take it far away where it will not call to me."

The wind was rising. He thought he caught the scent of the distant sea, another memory he tried to crush, felt it slip out of reach, hanging there. He shivered again, not from the cold.

"Show me this lord of yours."

On that first long trip south as a hired blade, he had watched over a caravan carrying a fortune in gold to be exchanged for illicit magics of Ajaeltha's self-styled southern empire. Through all those long months of the desert, he felt the memory of his birthplace. Felt the hunger for that lost land burn in him like the heat of the Ajaelthan sands.

Then on the night they were to return, he heard the night wind call her name. The Darkmoon was waxing, filling out within the reddening shadow of the sky.

That night long ago, he had turned his back on the way home and sought the dark road, slipping away from the caravan and the others who had come to trust him with their lives and who had never learned his real name.

She led him now on a roundabout route through the bog, racing easily through the tall grass even with the sword dragging behind her. He was winded keeping up to her, stumbling on legs not made for this soft ground. The body lay in a shallow pit roughly hacked out beneath a bank of black peat. He saw the rough edges, knew that the girl had dug it with her bare hands.

Whatever regal bearing this so-called lord managed in life, it was far beyond reach now. He gagged at the scent, needed to move upwind. Another of his weaknesses. The girl barely seemed to notice it. The body was face down, a bloated mass of green-black flesh stained red where the denizens of the swamp had been at it. Three days since the girl dumped it here, he reckoned. Three days it took her to work up the courage to talk to the monster he was now. A monster so weak, so base, that it would need this blade to match the strength of normal folk.

As from a dream, he wakes twice. Sees himself reflected in black water, falling. Cut down by the madness he unleashed.

These nine slow days, the red Darkmoon hung full in the sky as the bright Clearmoon pulled steadily away from it along the far horizon. On this ninth day, he awoke at dawn and prepared the rites that his people called Ma'atlese. The deepening. As he had every other morning of his watch, he sensed the long road home that he had turned his back on, felt it calling him with a voice of firelight and friend-song and laughter and fresh fish roasted on low coals.

Betrayer and betrayed.

Where he looked for the road that lay ahead now, all was darkness.

He is young then, and he bears both the name and form he was born with. She is named Szirha'mun, which was the Darkmoon in his people's tongue.

He blinked back the memory, locked the Mockery's soft teeth to stifle the sudden rush of breath.

She lives long enough to whisper words in his ear that he cannot hear for the coursing storm of rage. Ears only for the blood pounding in his chest, for the fury burning forge-hot in the tight-squeezed space of heart and mind.

As he appraised the body, he felt her eyes on him, knew she was wondering why he brought her to this place.

"Leave it here," was all he said.

His people's ways are the old ways. But in the golden mire of the fen that is his people's home, there lives a magic older still.

"That ends it," he said. "For both of you."

The girl shook her head, didn't understand.

He spoke evenly. He found the words in her own tongue, which had been his tongue once. The Mockery's voice was clumsy in all but its most common speech, but that speech had no words to fully capture what he must say.

"With his life, he has been made to pay. With the pain of your heart, you have paid, but your mind and conscience will try to make you pay again as long as this blade stays in your hands. Don't let them."

He reached within the cloak, felt for the pouch he knew was there. He drew it forth, slipped its weight to the girl's grasp. The golden eyes narrowed in suspicion, her hand flinching to feel the shift of coins within weathered canvas. It was copper and silver, the cold currency of the distant towns. He carried the gold of the cities as well, but the girl's family would have no more way to spend it than he would. These folk, a village this size, so far from the trade roads, meant that the girl's father had likely never worked for coin. This gift of his was more wealth than her family would earn in a lifetime.

"Never show it all at once. Spend it only among strangers, the traders along the river roads. Never among anyone who might question your getting of it."

"Why are you doing this?"

"Because when we sleep, we travel," he said. "When we dream, we come to the place where each new day's journey starts. At this place, there stands the light road. There stands the dark road."

Over years, over centuries, more creatures than could be counted are lost in the golden mire of the fen that is his home, his people's home. Over years, over centuries, lost and dead, pulled down and trapped in the place between, held in the muck and mire of the witching water lapping at the ruins of ancient castles that were the signpost-bones of long-forgotten history.

"I understand," the girl said softly. Her hands on the sword were trembling.

"No," he said. "Because folk think that the difference between the light road and the dark road is the destination. But all roads lead to the place that fate and choice take them. It makes no difference in the journey."

On the air, the storm that the day had promised was finally stirring. Even his weak senses caught its scent, and the faint aura of distant thunder that brightened the sky.

"Once you step down the dark road," he said, "you can no longer see the path back. On the light road, when you look back, you always see the way you came."

"What if you are afraid to look back?" she said quietly.

He dies in the witching water that night. Embraces the clutching-claw darkness that is the sweet shroud of forgetting that he craves above all else, with which he might burn away the final memory of her face as she touches her tongue to his tear-streaked lips and dies.

Black water. The red moon hanging heavy and full within a sea of cloud that twists on the wind like ripples of blood.

"Set the blade atop the body," he said, and she did.

Countless creatures were lost in the fen, but few of his kind. Tough, hardened by life along the black and gold of the witching water. The dead here are the Mockeries that rise to rule the isle from within the weakness of their soft, fat flesh. Drawn to the fen by the light of gold and silver, coveted above all else. Drawn to drown and die there by the score, by the hundreds as their softness is shredded by tooth and claw, choked to stillness by vine and black water, swallowed whole by magic dark and old.

"Go now," he said, and she did.

Dead and not dead, drawing life from the old magic that reshapes and reforms him. Like raw clay clumped to the base form of nature, slowly sculpted by fate's laughing hand to final shape. Body shattered. Soul suffusing into the witching water to be reborn.

He felt the first drops of rain strike from the hissing sky. Grey cloud overhead was a billowing shroud that swallowed the stars, but still the Darkmoon on the crest of the empty horizon blazed bright, filling his sight and his mind as if he might drown within it.

The curse was a thing he could not talk about. A thing not of his making, not of his control. The curse had saved him all those years ago. The curse had let him live past the point when he should have died, had brought him now to a place where he wanted to die, where that thought had gripped him time and time again. And each time, he heard her voice from that night long ago, when he clutched her dying form tight to his breast and wept for both their pain.

We are born of earth and fen, blood and water, fire and bone. We are the journey, not its end, and we will go together in memory where we cannot walk in body and mind.

From the black sky, the rain advanced as a chill curtain. He felt it hiss through the grass, racing toward him as a striking serpent. He closed his eyes, let it fall across him. He felt his soul drink the life-giving wetness that he needed, felt the pain and the strength tear through him as it always did.

Always look back, she told him, and he had turned her words to silence and let the madness take him that last night of both their lives.

Do not walk the dark road...

In a sudden and endless agony, the body of the Mockery that was his rebirth was shredded away by the storm of blood and bone that erupted inside him. He felt the soft flesh of weakness turn to scaled strength, felt the muscles of arm and back, leg and shoulder ripple and twist like knotted whipcord. He knew the exquisite ache as bones broke and reknit, as his joints twisted and thickened. He felt his face and maw reshaped as his swelling tongue laughingly flicked through a screen of razored teeth thrust from bleeding gums. He felt the weak fingers harden to talons, tearing out through the last vestiges of soft flesh with a strength that could lay open the deadly bog-drake from heart to head with a single strike.

The crest on his shoulders twisted and flared as it unfolded from the line of his spine, catching the rain that pounded down harder now even as its chill numbed the pain. He felt his sight sharpen, saw the faint haze of storm and red moon's-light flare like the bright of noon, and the song of wind and thunder was a symphony to all his senses of sight and scent and sound.

He was on his knees, fighting to breathe through the beautiful agony of the change to who he was. Who he had been. The life he lost that night. He looked up, shouted in triumph to the wet sky. He felt his tail thrash behind him in uncontrolled ecstasy, heard laughter that he realized suddenly was not his own.

The girl was jumping, dancing as she watched him. Where she had slipped back to the bog's edge, her amber eyes were bright with laughter, sealed against the rain that sluiced the dust from her skin and turned her scales to a sheen of green-gold in the faint light.

He expected her to be afraid, he realized. He had counted on that, the deep darkness of his spirit seeking that fear and the pain it carried with it. Affirming what it was he already knew.

"You are like me," the girl shouted. She flicked her tongue through her serrated grin, lashed her tail in the tall grass. Her claws, free finally of the sword, pawed the ground as she crouched.

Red shadow shimmers across the black-silver surface of the shallow bog where he claws his way screaming from the darkness of death, then drinks the foul air of the fen like sweetest nectar. For the nine days that the Darkmoon's crimson weight flares full, its light stains the mire around him, body held fast there, floating in thickening ooze like an errant leaf as the witching water bathes his wounds, stifles his frenzied screaming, fills his lungs. Weaves a song of pain and flesh and spirit knitted whole once more.

"I was like you," he called. The voice that sounded in his ears was his voice again, the deep-throated hiss within which was held all the music of the people he had left behind. "I am the Mockery now. Pale and weak. Helpless within soft flesh and dependent on steel."

On the ninth day, he rises. He feels the ancient strength of his people, feels life surge within muscle and bone and spirit. And as he claws his way from the mire to stand again for the first time, he weeps for what he has done.

He leaves the water behind. A dozen strides or less and he feels his flesh dry. Feels the old magic that hides his true form and leaves him the Mockery that night.

"Now you are both," the girl said. She hissed with laughter again, and he did not understand. "My father said that a secret is like the moni tree that sets only in the company of its own kind. On its own, it withers and dies, but as a pair, it issues all the best sweet fruits. And so secrets must come in twos to be properly kept."

She sprang toward him, slid to a halt in the soft loam. She motioned him down, and he crouched without thinking. She stretched to come close to the membrane of his ear.

"We know each other's secrets," she whispered. "They will shed sweet fruit now."

He was weeping as she scampered off, salt in his mouth as he properly swallowed his tears.

He understood then.

That morning, he awoke at dawn and prepared the rites that his people called Ma'atlese. The deepening. He sensed the long road ahead, felt it calling him with a voice that promised dreamless sleep. Ten years before, he had betrayed his people in the name of a memory that has burned in him through endless days of dryness, uncounted nights of pain.

That night, for the first time, he weeps for what he is. The Darkmoon passes full, leaves him the Mockery. Leaves him solitude-shrouded, choking on darkness and hatred coursing black in his blood like fever.

The girl made it as far as the edge of the clearing when he called.

"You know what I have done…"

Lightning flared in the darkness overhead. The girl turned back. She appraised him for a moment, watched him standing tall in the crash of stormlight, tail thrashing in the mist.

"You saw it," he called, and she nodded.

"The sword showed me," she called. "It sees inside people."

So many years since then, and this is his fate. To live as the Mockery until the slow progression of the Darkmoon turns his blood once more. Lets him transform at the touch of the life-giving water that is his people's home. Lets him remember who he was only long enough to feel the pain of losing that all over again.

"Do not walk the dark road, Lárow," the girl said, and she was gone.

He let the cool of the storm thread through him for a time. He found the cloak where he had discarded it, shuffling to the pit and spreading it beside the rotting remains of this lord who had lost his life to his own avarice and a child's pain. He rolled body and sword onto the cloak with ease, the eyeless skull grinning where scaled skin pulled away from jagged teeth. He gathered rocks from a dry rise nearby, lined the corpse with them as he wrapped it tight.

Then with all the strength of his new form, he hefted the body to his shoulders, the broken tail emerging from the shroud of the cloak to hang twisted down his back.

This or any pit dug in the soft loam of the swamp would leave the body too long to the beasts of land that would come back this night, and to those who would come after. For the girl's sake, it could not be found.

This lord had been an elder bull, the body twice his own weight, yet he carried it effortlessly. He imagined the girl dragging it here in the dead of night, a feat that he would have been hard-pressed to match at her age. This was the strength of his memory, of the dark dreams that called to him with the voice of the past. Dreams that took him in the deep night and told him his daylight life was the real dream. Dreams that snatched away that feeble hope and left him broken once more when morning came. Left him the Mockery. Left him the prisoner of his own weakness, and of the pale skin so soft that the dullest blade could cut it.

He took the body back to the swamp and set it adrift, then watched it sink in a stuttered haze of lightning, the weight of stone and sword dragging it down. The body would be consumed by morning, shroud and blade lost eventually in the depths, for a while at least. Someone would find the sword eventually, he knew, though it would not matter by then. Such things never stayed hidden for long.

He flipped one of the knives he had snatched up at the girl's first approach, felt the supple movements of his fingers shift it easily. As he had before her presence stopped him, he set the jagged blade to his neck. He knew how easily it would have bitten into the soft flesh of the Mockery just a short while before. Had thought of nothing else for nine days.

He held it there for a long while, felt it warm, harmless set against the strength of scaled skin.

He felt the rain stop. Felt his flesh dry and contract, weakening with each breath of cold wind that stole the life-giving moisture away. He felt the pain of the transformation, felt the pain of the blade where it pressed in, the leathery skin of his neck fading to the weakness of pale flesh once more.

He caught his reflection in the water as it stilled with the passing of the storm. He saw the face of the Mockery staring back at him.

She is named Szirha'mun, which was the Darkmoon in his people's tongue, and he watches her die. One last time.

He reached down, slipped his other hand into the embrace of its own reflection. Watched as his skin shivered and rippled and stretched green once more. One moment of memory.

Slowly, he pulled his hand back. Slowly, he lowered the blade to his side.

She had been named Szirha'mun, which is the Darkmoon in his people's tongue. So it was that he dreamed her always watching him over nine days of blood-red shadow that were the nights of sacrifice and remembrance. Those nights when he could be himself once more.

It didn't take him long to pack up. He had the gold that ten years on the desert caravans earned him. More than enough for the tall ships that set sail from Deema and Ebondar, but he would work again if he needed to.

He watched the sky change as the Darkmoon set, a trace of blood at the horizon fading with the dawn. Bright now where the long road home was waiting.

STORIES

IT WAS THE BLADE of Ngrehim, forged by Dugaam in the name of Jhanasaath, Bladelord of the Carbáin, slayer of Moiriar, destroyer of Sollyra, destined ruler of all the world. Or at least that's what it said to Hjorn when he brushed up against it in the back of Garna's wagon.

I can grant thee the power thou seekest... the axe whispered.

Hjorn blinked.

Garna was the best wagon trader between Jandich and Cunoch on the great river, and no matter how often you looked through his overflowing wares, you were bound to find something you'd never seen before. But even within the carefully racked stacks of Gorbeyna pottery, cast-off Ilvani leather, oil-polished armor shards, and bones of questionable vintage, a talking axe that promised you the power you seek was unusual.

Hjorn blinked his black eyes again, stroking the russet beard that ran nearly to his knees, hanging as long braids set with links of silver chain. "That's unusual," he said.

At the head of the wagon, Garna looked up from the ledger he was poring over. He furrowed his brow, pocked skin the grey-green of a dangerously overripe cheese. From his dismissive glare, it was clear that the trader hadn't heard the axe talking.

"That's quite unusual," Hjorn said. Garna's pair of withered mountain ponies glanced back where they cropped the short scrub grass that clung to the trail.

Hjorn had the wagon to himself. He was Garna's only regular client on this isolated stretch of switchback, but his coin was good and the Gorbeyna had made his two-season stop on this high pass between the mountain villages for years. Hjorn had the pass to himself, had the mountain to himself. He liked the solitude. He liked the peace that carried in the empty echo of his sky. Still, when that silence pressed down as it did sometimes in the night, Hjorn had more than once found himself thinking that it would be nice to have someone to talk to.

He talked to Garna twice a year when the cart came, but the wizened Gorbeyna met most attempts at conversation with only the sullen silence and the poison glare well known among his kind.

"How much?" Hjorn asked him now, because it was one of the few phrases the trader did respond to.

He hefted the axe, holding it high so that the sun gleamed along the bright steel filigree that traced its way along the leather of the haft. It was a weapon of war, double bladed and razor sharp, though the style of its casting was old. Hjorn swung it once, twice, the weapon's weight growing quickly familiar to his hands.

He felt a guilty thrill as a story slipped within his mind.

With the axe in hand, he was his grandfather suddenly, at the battle the clan-singers called Fignarmald. In the depths of the burning mountain Rodangrim, he stood alone against a horde of Darkfolk and dragons, his family's battle flag flying proudly above him. Then Hjorn felt a twinge in his shoulder where his gout was still acting up with the slow fading of winter.

The story went away with the sudden pain. The Gorbeyna appraised the axe where Hjorn set it back down, wincing.

"Could get a pretty price for it in Galindo. Ninety argryns."

"Galindo is dirt farmers and woodcutters that couldn't scrape up that much silver if the old gods came collecting."

"Jandich, then," Garna said dismissively. "The city."

"They'll string you up in Jandich to find out who you stole it from."

Garna scowled. "Found it on a dead guy in the Helexia hill woods. Nice and legal."

"Five chrysans." Hjorn's coin was the old gold favored by his people, and the offer was more than Garna would earn in any of the villages on either side of the pass.

"Six."

Thou wilt rule the world... the axe said.

Hjorn shrugged as he paid.

•

It was a long walk back to the small stone house that Hjorn had raised above the narrow cut of a river that had no name. As he made his way, he swung the axe jauntily over his shoulder, letting his hand rest casually on the haft as he had seen the warriors do when he was a boy. In the clanholds of the Duncamb, the young and the old, the crafters and miners and hearth keepers all turned out to line the wide, dark boulevard before the gates, watching the guards of the Rohizum heading off to their dangerous patrols of the darkness.

When he was young, Hjorn dreamed of making that march himself. However, hammer and handbow had never felt as right in his grasp as did pick and shovel. From the time he was apprenticed to the master diggers of the anthracite seams that rooted their way deep, deep into the mountains, he forgot about that dream. But today, with the axe in his hand, he felt it fresh in his mind as he hadn't for a long while.

He walked in silence, suddenly awkward as he thought about what a person should say to a talking axe. Living alone on his mountain, he was sadly out of practice.

"Do you like stories?" he asked finally.

I will tell thee stories of greatness, the axe replied, which wasn't really what Hjorn had asked. However, he said nothing as the weapon's voice in his head began to speak.

In the white fire of Andolin was I forged, the axe began. Then it went on for a long, long time. And though Hjorn was interested at first, and then just listened politely for a while, his attention began to flag after the first thousand years or so of the axe's long and bloody history. From the strength of its haft and the edge on its steel, he wouldn't have thought the blade to be that old, nor to have undertaken the number of battles it claimed.

For the first time ever, Hjorn found himself wishing that the long walk back to the small stone house was quicker.

At the midpoint of the climb, a rise of rock offered up a view of his distant front porch, from which he could look out upon the edge of the bluff where the nameless river tumbled out over rocks to drop to the foot of the narrow ravine below. In the spring and fall, the sun would set there, dropping down behind the cloud of spray and turning the sky the color of bright copper. Within the ravine, the river disappeared into a whirlpool that plunged down into the unseen depths of the mountains. He liked its howling sound, which reminded him of the wind in the high peaks but which wasn't as cold.

In his head, the axe had killed another in a long line of kings and been passed to yet another's hero's hand, but all the names began to sound the same to him. It was a complicated tale that the axe told him, and not for the first time, Hjorn wished that his own story was more interesting than it was.

Hjorn loved his ravine, his river, his sky because he was different than his kin. Since he was a boy, he had loved the scree slopes in a way that marked him as odd by most of his folk, their hearts held enraptured by the mountains' depths but not their heights. Even before he left his parents' house, Hjorn always used his leave time from the mines to follow the trade trails out toward the Duncamb Pass that bore his people's name, where he would sit to while the day away watching the sun and sky.

For all his young life, Hjorn had worked and saved away the coin he earned, and kept safe what his parents left him. And when he had enough, he bade his folk goodbye and left the caverns. He made his own walk down the dark boulevard before the gates, a well-stuffed pack and his tools strapped to his back. Only his close kin were there to see him off, but their shouts of well-wishing had a hollow quality as he passed through the darkness that last time.

Thou wilt name me, the axe said as Hjorn made the final turn that led to the great wooden staircase he had built along the side of the bluff. This was a great out-thrust horn of stone, studded with jack pine and juniper that clung tenaciously to the rock. When the wind blew, the trees whistled an off-key tune that Hjorn liked to hum along to.

"Excuse me?" he said.

Thou wilt name me, the axe said again. *When I was carried in the Duranholds of Dugaam, I was Rasilnar the Deathcleaver, but I have claimed and forgotten five score names besides. In Galgaila, I was Immaru, the Blade of Gods. In Liryan, I was the Shrike, the Butcher Blade, before I was lost to the ages and mortal sight and found again by thy hand.*

The axe didn't speak in words. Not really. Rather, it seemed to Hjorn that he heard the axe's feelings and such in his head, and that his head was turning those feelings into words. If other people heard the same feelings, no doubt their heads would speak them differently, he thought.

Hjorn stared, uncertain. He was anxious suddenly. He had never needed to name anything before. "Deathcleaver is nice," he said awkwardly.

Thou must name me...

Hjorn hadn't even named his house, though the way of his folk was to christen their great underground estates. He hadn't named the river that wasn't on any map that he had ever seen, nor had he named the bluff or the mountain or anything else.

Name me!

"Steelblade!"

The axe was silent a long moment. Where it rested on his shoulder, Hjorn thought he could feel its disappointment.

"Killer Steelblade," he added. "The Terrible. That's a good name."

He swung the axe off his shoulder, slashing it from side to side in what he thought was a threatening way. He felt the twinge of the gout again.

The axe said nothing more as Hjorn climbed the steep stairs, their log planks painstakingly cut and planed over the long months when he first found his bluff and its sunset sky. He was as skilled at rock climbing as all his kin, but he liked stairs. He liked their straight edges and their smooth lines, and the fact that they were a thing he had built with his own hands. He was proud of the things he could build. He was proud of his house and his view of the sunset through the mist of the river where it boiled away into the caves below.

On the stone porch, Hjorn sat beneath the twilight sky. These were frontier lands, the stony wilderness of the northern slopes of those mountains the Tallfolk called the Shieldcrest, but which were Tharseen, the Great Peaks, to Hjorn's folk. These territories showed up on the maps of the Tallfolk but were all but unclaimed by the distant dukes of Gracia, only a few tenacious villages marking the track that wound its way between the great mountain passes of Duncamb and Olmades. These were Dwarven lands and Gorbeyna, the frequently warring clans of both peoples living in their ancient warrens deep, deep in the darkness.

Hjorn's house was far from that darkness, set upon its isolated granite shelf and looking out over the steep slopes below. Far south and east were his own folk, who he turned away from in order to dwell beneath the sun. He loved the sun, though it burned his skin sometimes when the weather was hot. He wore a straw cap on such days to keep his eyes shaded, but the sun was cool today.

That long first summer when his wanderings had led him here, Hjorn built the house with his own hands, cutting and laying the stones in carefully squared lines. He built a guest room, because he always imagined that someone would visit him some day. But through all the long years that he had retired to this place and watched the sky from his porch each night, no one ever came.

Because the axe was still silent, Hjorn talked to it now. Tentatively, he told it some of his stories, the favorite tales of the clan-singers and the hearth-rites that were the memory of his mother's sweet voice in the darkness. Hjorn knew the old stories because he told them to himself in the quiet evenings as the fire burned low. He told the stories to himself because he had no one else to tell them to anymore.

While he lived in the mountain halls of his kin, he told stories to his grandfather and he listened to those his grandfather told. Those were real tales, he knew. Stories of far-off war with the Gorbeyna of Kiengiraka, and of legendary heroes delving deep beneath the mountains of the Shieldcrest, pursuing great wealth and even greater danger in the darkness.

The stories Hjorn told only to himself were often tales of history and lore and his people's long travails within the earth. However, more and more often since he had come to his bluff and built his house above the river that had no name, Hjorn's stories were those he made up himself. Tales and songs of the mountain slopes, and of the wide world under the sun that he had first heard of in his grandfather's songs but explored now each day in his imagination and his dreams.

He liked to remember the old days, before his grandfather died. He had so few reasons to remember now.

He told the axe the story of the sleeping curse that claimed the life of the Ilvani princess Lealyan, but it seemed unimpressed.

Hjorn spoke of pirates on the wide waters of the Leagin Sea that he had heard of but never seen, and he told of the twelve Kings of Death who challenged the great hero Hjorna for whom he was named. He told how they had been defeated one after the other by bravery and great cunning.

As he sat at the top of the stairs beneath the spray of stars that slowly revealed themselves to streak the cloudless sky, the axe spoke again to tell him another story of its own. This was the story of a great battle between the kings of three races and the dark sorcerer who stood against them. The dark sorcerer's warrior-slaves fought with great blades of power whose magic transcended the greatest powers of the gods and titans of old. The axe talked of the endless battle that had laid waste to whole nations, leaving them burned and blackened and leached of life.

"Do you know any happy stories?" Hjorn asked uneasily.

I will grant thee the power thou seekest, the axe whispered in a voice like winter wind. *I will grant thee all thy heart's desires...*

Hjorn was confused, and because he didn't know what to say, he stood. His back was stiff from sitting, so he stretched beneath the stars, scanning the sky above and the bluff below and his house with its shuttered windows and stone walls carefully scrubbed each spring, pale now in the starlight.

I will grant thee all thy heart's desires, the axe whispered again.

Hjorn shrugged. "I have all I need," he said. And then because he felt a sudden smoldering darkness in the axe's silence, he added, "We should go in now."

Inside the small house, the hearth fire he had left blazing that morning was down to coals and ready to be rekindled. Hjorn soon had the stone firepit burning cheerily with a carefully stacked pyramid of well-dried pine that he cut himself from the slopes of a close-growing grove a half-day's walk away. Hjorn liked the walk. He made the journey down every other day, cutting deadfall to fill the leather-and-wattle shoulder basket he made himself.

When he walked to the grove in spring and fall, Hjorn also set snares for grouse in the narrow vales of the wood. He ate them fresh-cooked when he could and salted through the winter. When the weather was nice, he caught fish in the small streams that cut their way through the rough scree slopes of the foothills. It was grouse he cooked tonight, along with sweet snowroot that grew wild in the soft loam of the lower slopes. He ate it with a goblet of last season's best wild honey wine, which he decanted himself into bottles bought from Garna, then stored in a hidden cellar tucked into the bluff on the far side of the porch.

It would be good, Hjorn thought as he ate, to have someone to talk to. But though the axe hadn't warmed to his stories, Hjorn was sure it was going to like the surprise he hadn't yet talked about. It was an idea that came to his mind at his first sight of the axe in the back of Garna's wagon.

Hjorn's house was three rooms set in a row. There was the main room that was kitchen and hearth and a place to sit, with Hjorn's room to one side and the guest room on the other. Opposite the hearth in the main room was a rough plaster wall. Set into it were hundreds of gleaming crystal agates, collected from the banks of Hjorn's fishing streams over the first year that he lived here. The wall had been the last part of the house to be completed.

The stones were water-green and sky-blue, red like glowing coals and gold like the winter sunrise, shining and polished smooth by the scouring water. He had prepared the wall carefully, plastering it over with white mud he made from river stone crushed in a rock mill he built himself. Into this, he set the brightly colored stones with a careful hand. At night, when the fire was burning bright, the stone wall would gleam and flicker like a rainbow sunset. He would sit and watch it. It made him smile.

At the head of the shining wall, Hjorn had built a mantle on which he set a constantly changing collection of interestingly shaped rocks, and abandoned birds' nests he found along the autumn woodland trails, and abstract wood sculptures that he carved himself on the porch on warm summer nights.

Carefully, he set aside the current collection, which included a blue-glass prism he bought from Garna the last time the trader passed by, and which Hjorn thought was the most beautiful thing he had ever seen. Until now, at least.

Carefully, he lifted the axe to the mantle and set it there. He used one of his wood carvings to raise the end of the haft so that it sat almost straight. He stepped back and smiled. The blade of the axe gleamed majestic in the firelight, throwing its shadow against the subtle shift of summer-flower colors across the wall behind it, and Hjorn thought of how impressive it would look if only someone came to visit.

"You look good up there," he said, and he was happy for the axe as he turned to take the kettle from the hearth.

A curse on all thy line, caitiff fool, and blessings of power on all those who will shed thy craven blood in the end...

Hjorn turned back. He stared for a moment.

"Did you say something?" he asked, but the axe was quiet.

It stayed quiet until morning, when Hjorn awoke and ate a small breakfast of dried sausage and pine nuts at his carefully polished stone table, sitting and looking at the axe all fine on the mantle where it belonged.

I can help thee, the axe said.

Hjorn considered this as he scrubbed dishes at his small stone sink. "I'm fine," he said.

I can grant thee all thy wants and needs, came the voice in his mind, but he thought he heard a subtle tone of anger this time.

"I have all I need," Hjorn said again, and he heard the axe laugh darkly.

Seize me, and I will show thee magic...

Hjorn had seen magic once or twice and found it not to his taste. He didn't really need to see it again, but he was worried that he had hurt the axe's feelings somehow when he turned down the offer of his desires and needs. When he finished the dishes, he walked over to the mantle. He carefully grasped the axe, its weight comfortable in both hands.

Now, the voice said. *Think of some other place, a place thou knowest. A place to which thou hast a yearning most zealous to go.*

Hjorn didn't know what a yearning most zealous was, so he felt awkward suddenly. As a result, the only place he could think of was his front porch, but even as he thought it, his vision blurred out to streaks of grey like rain against the rippled glass of the windows.

He felt the chill of the morning air and the damp against his bare feet. The wind was twisting the branches of the closest trees, its hiss drowned out by the steady roar of the dark whirlpool below.

"That's unusual," Hjorn said.

By thinking it, he jumped back to the main room, then jumped again twice more between the house and the porch. He sensed a subtle thrill of power flaring within the axe as he did.

Thou seest what I can do for thee? the voice said. Hjorn nodded, most thoughtful as he set the axe carefully back on the mantle.

What dost thou?

"Going out to the pine grove for firewood," Hjorn said. He laced up his boots, found his good walking jacket.

I can take thee there in the blink of an eye, the axe said. *I can take thee to the top of the highest peaks, and to both ends of the world!*

Hjorn was confused. "There's plenty of deadfall just down in the grove," he said.

I mean thou hast no need to walk, impudent fool!

"But I like to walk," Hjorn said.

The axe said nothing more, so he left. It was likewise silent when he returned that afternoon with his basket full of firewood. Hjorn thought he might have hurt its feelings, so he took the axe in hand and jaunted a half-dozen times from the house to the bottom of the stairs and back again.

"Oh, I hate taking these stairs," he said loudly, to make sure the axe was listening. "I am so happy to have this magic."

That night, as Hjorn baked biscuits he made with ground snowroot from an old recipe of his mother's, he told the axe the story of the Dancing Daughters of the Ilvanking, and of how they were stolen away deep into Khimerean realms and rescued by the Shieldsons of the first Dwarf Queen. The axe in turn told him the story of the fall of Sollyra. It talked of great mountain citadels rising as tiers of white walls, and of the unliving forces of the Bladelord crashing against them as a never-ending wave, breaking bone and stone alike and slaying all who fell before them until the mountain slopes ran red with blood.

"Do you know any stories that don't have so many people dying in them?" Hjorn asked when the axe was done.

There are no other stories, the axe said coldly.

It went on like that for a long week, Hjorn making his regular trip to the pine grove and the axe lying on the mantelpiece and filling the room with the unseen shroud of its disappointment. Hjorn could feel the blade's dark thoughts, and by the fire each night, he told his happiest stories in an attempt to cheer it up. Nothing seemed to work, however, and the stories the axe told him each night got darker as a matter of course.

At the same time, Hjorn couldn't help but notice that strange things were beginning to happen. Gorbeyna bandits attacked the house just before lunch on the third day, and while it wasn't the first time, these bandits were particularly tenacious. As he always did, Hjorn simply locked his doors and stone shutters and let them rail away on the porch for as long as it took to appreciate how well he built his house, and that he hadn't left anything on the outside of it worth stealing.

On the fifth day, he got back from his journey to the pine grove to find that his porch had become a nest for a giant bird. It saw him as he approached the bottom of the stairs, shrieking a warning as it rose up on great taloned feet and clacked a beak large enough to snap a spar in two. Hjorn spent the night outside, waiting for the bird to budge, then finally drove it off by lighting a green-branch smoke fire at the foot of the stairs.

The seventh day, a plague of bark beetles came down the chimney to swarm in his kitchen, and as he spent the rest of the day and night swatting and sweeping them out, Hjorn began to grow suspicious.

He spent the better part of the following day carving and staining a proper stand for the haft and blade, but even that didn't improve the axe's foul mood. Then as he was sitting and watching the firelight play across the shining wall and listening to the axe tell him the story of the month-long, limb-by-limb execution of the traitor Moiriar in excruciating detail, Hjorn had a wonderful idea.

"I have a wonderful idea," he said. "I know what will make you happy."

Thou wilt enter the nearest city and slay its champions like dogs! the axe called with dark enthusiasm. *Thou wilt exsanguinate their virgin women at the height of rapture, and all will bow down before us and despair!*

Hjorn was silent a moment. "I have a different wonderful idea," he said, and he tried to ignore the axe's bitter disappointment as he stoked the fire and went to bed.

The next morning, Hjorn ate quickly and left the dishes standing to dry. The axe was silent, but he felt its expectation, its dark will seeking out his thoughts. He did his best to hide those thoughts, wanting to keep his special plan a secret. He took the axe carefully from the mantle, swung it over his shoulder as he headed out.

The pine grove was still cool, faint trails of mist rising as the heat of the sun worked its slow way down through the trees. Hjorn could sense the anticipation in the axe, even as he felt it silently willing him to break from the trail and run screaming through the dark woods in hopeful search of something to kill.

He stopped instead at the black tangle of a deadfall snag he had been working around for the better part of the previous week. Its brittle branches were picked clean, cracked and snapped and carted back up to the house. However, the main bole of the ancient pine was thick and gnarled, and had resisted all Hjorn's attempts to break or cut it.

"Here we go," he said.

He swung fast. The blade was sharper than anything he had ever seen, chopping through the sun-kilned hardness of the snag like it might be a sheaf of dry grass. He felt a quick rush as he swung again and again, and he imagined himself suddenly as the wood-ranger Dyssa, who had been the protector of the Mosstwood and slayer of the dread war-trolls of the Bone Fens. Only he and his trusty axe would slay deadfall instead. No stand of firewood would be safe.

He stopped suddenly. Where his hands gripped the axe, he felt a kind of buzzing.

A silent horror twisted through the blade, the voice in Hjorn's mind speaking not in words suddenly but in raw emotion that made his head ache. His heart was pounding. His hands shook, and he had to squeeze them tight to keep the axe from slipping from his grasp.

"I thought you might like something to do," Hjorn stammered. "Always lots of firewood to chop." He suddenly had the feeling that this might not have been as wonderful an idea as he first thought.

Thou wilt die the death of body, spirit, and mind, the axe said on the walk back home, *and only the worms that feast on thee will remember thy passing in the end.* It said nothing else after that.

The axe drew the first foes to him the next day. These were real threats, not just the dark distractions of the previous week, which Hjorn belatedly realized must have been attracted by whatever dark magic had been kindled by the axe's even darker mood. These were warriors, Gorbeyna from the closest tribes to start. Hjorn recognized them by their livery, shields and faces war-painted with a dark red X. As he had with the bandits, Hjorn was content to let the first two waves batter themselves senseless against the great stone door, and finally to turn against each other as their level of frustration rose.

The axe still wasn't talking to him, but he could hear it darkly muttering that night from its place on the mantle. It was a language he didn't understand, but he sensed the rage that underlay the unknown words all the same.

Three more Gorbeyna warbands came the following day, but Hjorn was ready for them this time. Before dawn, he toted three barrels from the cellar and set them out and open on the front porch. The first group threw themselves at the wine with unbridled enthusiasm, drinking themselves into a stupor and collapsing in a snoring, sodden heap. The second group drank was what left. The third turned on the first two when they found the barrels dry.

They left six dead on the porch before they fled back to the forest, Hjorn sadly rolling the bodies over the edge of the cliff as a fourth group, newly arrived, burst from the tree line at a run. He waited until they were halfway up the steep stairs. Then he rolled the empty barrels down one after the other, the shrieking Gorbeyna bowled over to tumble back down in an undignified and badly bruised heap.

Hjorn watched them slink off, but he stayed out past the rise of the Clearmoon on the porch, watching carefully for any further movement along the narrow paths below. The night passed quietly, except that over the hiss of wind and the roar of the river below and even in the short stretches when he could sleep, Hjorn could hear the voice of the axe faint and dark in the back of his mind.

The Hogorba arrived shortly after dawn, great hairy brutes that were twice the size of their Gorbeyna kin and proportionally unpleasant. Torches and guttural war chants heralded their movement up the switchback paths. Hjorn watched them from the porch and lost count of their number. He saw the mark of a white dagger on their shields and breastplates, the sign of a tribe he didn't know. He also saw the steel-spiked battering ram they carried as they eyed his front door.

He went inside to retrieve the axe, its hilt strangely cold in his hands. The tight-wrapped black leather had taken on an oily texture that made his skin crawl, but he held it firmly as he strode to the edge of the porch, raised the blade above the horde advancing now with shields up. Then he carefully chopped away the supports that held the stairs in place, the closest Hogorba only halfway up as the long flight of steps collapsed beneath them and sent them screaming to the ground below.

There will be more, the axe whispered unhappily. Hjorn only shrugged. He dug out his knife and hatchet and filled a small pack with rope. Then he held the axe tight and thought about the edge of the ravine where the trail squeezed through a gloomy grove of close-growing willow, and suddenly he was there.

There was no one else around, but he thought he heard distant shouts from farther down the mountainside. He was wary as he worked, but no one showed up for the better part of the afternoon as he carefully laid a series of tripwire snares along the path. They were of a design he had shaped himself over long years of hunting, and of convincing the mountain cats to take their own hunting away from his house and his ravine. Each was anchored with a thick-twisted trunk, bent low to the ground and holding enough spring strength to stun a horse in its tracks. He hid each loop of rope with a mulch of mold and broad blue-weed leaves when he was done.

With the axe's magic, Hjorn jaunted back to the porch and waited the time it took for the first screams to be heard over the river's echoing roar. He saw the trees shake where whoever was coming for him was tossed left and right. Hjorn hoped it would make them think twice about another assault. They came again at dawn to tell him he was wrong.

For four days, he watched as the Gorbeyna and the Hogorba and their huge reeking Birgard barbarian-cousins of the western mountains threw themselves at the cliff face but were turned back. On the fifth day, he heard shrieks and the clash of swords before dawn, and the horde gave ground to mud-streaked Tallfolk of the hills, who howled and fired a hail of heavy stone-tipped arrows at the porch for the better part of the afternoon.

The next morning, individual warriors sent ropes and steel hooks up to the porch, which Hjorn dutifully cut free with the axe as he protected himself from arrows by sliding beneath his kitchen table like it was a turtle's shell. The day after that, the mountain tribes squabbled with a mercenary band of hulking Tallfolk and the more graceful Ilvani for the right to assault Hjorn's house. Two stealthy rogues clambered up the cliff face but were driven back with hails of arrowheads that Hjorn collected from the scores sent against him the days before. He had no way to shoot them, but carefully dropped from the top of the tall cliff in clusters, they picked up a healthy amount of momentum by the time they hit.

He was dozing the following dawn, when a two-score strong force of Tallfolk warriors in full armor and on horseback announced their presence with trumpets and sent the mercenaries scattering. How they made it up the switchback trail, Hjorn was afraid to even guess. They charged from the tree line with lances at the ready, but then circled around aimlessly when they saw the bluff rising before them.

Hjorn was getting angry now. It had been a long while since he slept more than a few fitful winks at a time, forced to stay on his guard through night and day. The faintly heard voice of the axe was a constant dark droning in his mind.

"Go home and leave me alone!" he yelled to the riders circling threateningly below him, but a hail of arrows and insults drove him off the porch and inside. He grabbed the axe from the mantle, ignoring its vicious curses as he jaunted into a poplar bluff a day's walk down the trail. He jaunted back a short while later with an enormous hornets' nest in hand that he pitched off the edge of the porch. The vicious insects had no time to notice that they had even been moved until they smashed into the riders and their mounts at high speed.

For another week, they came. For another week, Hjorn carried out hit and run attacks on the growing number of warriors and mercenaries amassing below his front door. Using the power of the axe, he shifted between his home and the wilderness around the bluff in search of increasingly ingenious ammunition.

When the Ilvani war-mages came, they blasted his porch and front door with fire and lightning, but the stones that Hjorn had laid using the ancient craft of his people held fast. In response, he collected boulders from the shattered rockslide wall that was as close as anyone could come to the dark chasm where the river disappeared. He dropped them from the edge of the porch, sending them down the bluff with a sound louder than the spells that had scorched his walls.

He jaunted into the camps of some sort of doglike creatures that walked on two legs, leaving with them a brace of skunks he plucked from their twilight dens in a distant meadow. Over long days and sleepless nights, he countered the fury of the horde below him with his best ideas, but Hjorn's ideas were beginning to run out. The axe's voice was growing more and more erratic in his mind. It had moved beyond threats aimed at him and was shrieking about how it wanted to kill everyone, everywhere, just because.

Or were those his own thoughts he was hearing? Hjorn wondered suddenly. It was getting hard to tell.

One morning, there was a great battle in the camps below, various factions laying into each other with fire and steel as if the horrific vengeance that the axe screamed for had overwhelmed them. When it was done, the day was passing and the woods were in flames. Bodies littered the foot of the bluff, the Tallfolk and the Gorbeyna and Hogorba and Ilvani and Doglings slinking away into the twilight shadows of the trees.

Two figures stood alone, both of the Tallfolk. One was an armored warrior, pale of face and dark of eye, his gore-flecked black mail glowering crimson in the light of the setting sun. The other was a mere boy, some sort of squire or page by Hjorn's view. He carried an oversized pack on his back. A battle standard showing a white horse rampant on a field of blue fluttered atop a long pole leaning on his shoulder.

With calm determination, the warrior walked to the foot of the bluff. Slowly, methodically, he began to ascend, the greatsword that was near as tall as he was slung to a back scabbard. Despite the weight of weapon and armor, he clambered up the cliff like a shadowed spider. His squire stayed below, watching with wide eyes and gamely waving the knight's banner aloft to catch the twisting breeze.

Over the previous weeks, Hjorn had learned a hundred different ways by which he might have dispatched this new threat. But as he heard the axe's voice murmuring dark benedictions in its unknown tongues, he understood something suddenly. A thing he silently cursed himself for not having realized before.

Though he still couldn't understand the axe's words, he knew their meaning now. The blade was calling for a new master. One worthy of its dark ambition. All the fighting, all the bloodshed, and he could have ended it at any time if he had only known it sooner.

Hjorn was no hero. He wasn't his grandfather, standing in the firestorm of Fignarmald like a resolute wall of sinew and steel.

He was tired. He stood and watched the warrior climb.

As the armored figure clambered over the ledge where the stairs were once attached, he drew the greatsword in a fluid motion. He swung it one-handed in a wide circle before he let it come to rest before him, tip down as he clutched grip and pommel to his armored chest. He pulled his helm off, tossing it aside as he shook his head, a thick mane of black hair rippling like dark cloud against the sunset. He appraised Hjorn with glaring eyes.

"You are an unclean scion of a darkling race," the knight said in a commanding voice, and Hjorn's eyes narrowed because he wasn't entirely sure what 'scion' meant. "You have sullied a great blade of power with your touch, and you will pay."

In the words, Hjorn heard a thread of nobility and grace, all but lost now within the dark voice that twisted through his mind and the warrior's alike.

Kill him, the axe whispered.

"Your life is forfeit," the warrior said.

Vengeance left sleeping cold for over five thousand years is thine, and in the name of Immaru and Rasilnar which is the Shrike which is the Butcher Blade, thou wilt rule the world!

"I will rule the world…"

"Great," Hjorn said. "Here."

He took a single step forward. He spun the axe so that the haft was held out toward the warrior. He sensed a moment's uncertainty in the knight and the axe alike.

"Take it," Hjorn growled. "I don't care anymore. Rule whatever you want."

Kill him! the axe screamed, and its voice was a dark pain rooting deep in Hjorn's skull. *Thou wilt kill him for ignorance and impudence and leave his bloated corpse for the crows!*

"Treachery!" the warrior screamed, but his hand shot out to grasp the black leather of the haft. Hjorn felt the strength in that grip as he was yanked forward, stumbling to one knee as the knight hefted the axe high with his free hand.

Thou art the chosen one! Thou art the master of blades and the heir to Jhanasaath, and the power of ages dwells in this steel!

"I am the chosen one!" the warrior screamed, and his voice was the axe's voice suddenly, twisted through with an evil whose darkness echoed down an endless well of years and longing.

"So just take it then. Go!"

But the knight only flung the greatsword aside as if it weighed nothing, letting it clang to the stones of the porch as he raised the axe above Hjorn's head in preparation for a killing stroke. Hjorn stared, wide-eyed. Where the blade caught the last light of the sun, its edge gleamed red like the madness in the dark knight's eyes.

"I am the master of blades and keeper of the Shrike, and its power is mine!"

"Suit yourself," Hjorn said.

Still on one knee, he shot up a heavy-fingered hand to slow the axe's descent. Not enough to stop it, but in his instant of contact with the haft where it joined the blade, Hjorn thought of a place he knew well. It was a place he saw each morning when he stepped onto his porch to breathe in the cool air of the early dawn, and that he saw each night as he watched the sun set through the haze of mist.

He concentrated on that place even as the descending axe twisted from his grip. With the blade a finger's breadth from his face, he felt the beginning of the quick lurch as the weapon jaunted. A sensation as familiar to Hjorn now as sight and touch after weeks of sending himself hither and yon across the mountains. At his direction, the axe carried the warrior out a hundred paces into empty air, high above the whirlpool where the river coursed away beneath the mountain and into shadow.

The dark knight screamed all the long way down, but his was the only voice Hjorn heard.

He stood in the familiar roar of the river for a long while. Along the edge of the woods below, he saw the last straggling camps of those who were defeated by the dark warrior pack up and leave. In the touch of the wind, where he had heard the axe's dark voice for long days now, there was only silence.

Carefully, Hjorn kicked the helmet, then the greatsword to the edge of the porch and over, watching as they tumbled noisily down the cliff and disappeared into the dark below. He hadn't heard the sword talk, but he wasn't taking any chances.

He turned back to the house, more tired and sad than he had ever been. Then he stopped.

Hjorn stepped to the edge of the porch again. Below him, alone in the twilight, the young squire stood at what would have been the perfect location to watch the dark knight drop to his death. The standard had fallen at his side.

Hjorn made his way carefully down the cliff with a lantern, dropping the last short distance and dusting himself off. He walked over to the squire, stopping awkwardly a few strides away. The boy was even younger than he had looked at first glance. Still a few years from the start of a beard, or what passed for one among the Tallfolk. He continued to stare out where the rising mist was lost now to darkness, bright eyes pale with fear.

"Sorry," Hjorn said after a few moments, but the squire was silent. "You bound to the black-haired guy?"

The boy nodded.

"He your kin?"

The boy shook his head.

"Friend?"

No.

"You're not working for him anymore. You got someplace to go?"

Another shake of the head.

"Any family?"

Hjorn saw tears welling. He tugged at his beard, perplexed for a moment.

"Do you like stories?"

Slowly, the boy looked up. He held Hjorn's gaze for a long while.

Hjorn felt a point of bright pride welling up inside him. He stood tall.

"I have a guest room," he said.

In the ruins of the attackers' camps, Hjorn found a brace of grouse fresh killed, cleaned, and left behind. He washed them with clear water from the oversized pack of the squire's, then slung that pack on his belt. He lifted the boy to his shoulders, felt him cling tightly as he climbed.

He got the fire going with the last of the wood and a couple of bundles of broken arrows for kindling. He had been stuck on the porch for too long, would walk down to the pine grove tomorrow. Also, he had stairs to fix.

Hjorn cooked grouse for dinner and he told the story of the trickster-warrior Roinara. She had walked alone into the Fane of Last Light, bargaining with the dead heroes who dwelt there for the mortal life of Prince Glinus the Forgotten.

The boy clapped and clapped when Hjorn was done.

As he went to sleep that night, the young squire comfortable in the guest room, Hjorn realized for the first time that he was wrong before when he talked to the axe. When it offered him its dark pact the first time and all the times thereafter. Now, Hjorn thought. Only now, he had everything he needed.

Memento

THE TIMES HE JOURNEYED to the Free City, he stayed in a series of rented rooms in a dozen different wards as a matter of longstanding habit, because there were people who sought his counsel from time to time, and he was determined that it should not be so easy to find it. There had been messages this trip, left in the Smooth Swan and the Wild Godling and the Wyvern's Eye where he was known, but these were from a month or more ago, it having been three months before that and High Spring the last time he passed through the Thirty-League Gate.

Spells of warding and watching that he had placed on the single door and the dark stairs to the Urorfidith-ward loft confirmed no one passing by that he would have recognized by face or name, just as the landlord confirmed no visitors asking after him. No one skulking about with vaguely transparent inquiries regarding the dark-haired mage under any of the names he traveled by. So it was that he was pulled surprised from the haze of a dark sleep by the distant sound of the spell-locked outside door split from shattered hinges in the dead of night, and pounding footsteps along the dark hall that cleared his head in a heartbeat of all his unremembered dreams.

He slipped naked from the bed, felt the chill where the fire had died as he pressed back to the wall and was ready, the incantation on his lips by instinct, sent across the chamber with a snarling twist of both hands and hitting the intruders hard where they smashed through the dark oak of the foyer. He counted a half-dozen at a quick glance, armed and all in uniforms of dun and rust-red, save for the leader in a cloak of sable that hid his face and form as he toppled and fell.

It was an old spell and common enough, one of the first he ever mastered, but made more potent since then with special flourishes all his own. It dropped them now without a sound. Then a seventh appeared, last in from the shadows. Blade drawn as he avoided the worst of the spell's effect, faltering but not fallen. The mage made a twisted flick of callused fingers, a pulse of unseen force unleashed that cracked the figure's head back against the wall like a warrior's backhand blow.

The guard collapsed alongside all the rest. With a word, the mage threw light to the air, let it spread to scour the shadows and mark the bodies cast down in the eldritch slumber whose dreams they would try in vain to forget.

In the pale gleam of that light, he saw the spill of golden hair from the woman who had been first in, the black hood thrown back to let it fall free.

She hadn't been leading them. The shouting in the dark-paneled corridor. They were chasing her, he realized numbly, because his thought was seized in the iron grip of a recognition and a memory he tried vainly to shunt away to the shadow where it had lain for so long.

He listened now, forced himself to focus away and out from the circle of light where he stood. He had first chosen the loft in the upper reaches of the university quarter for the raucous isolation he tried to ignore now, the halls and taverns and campuses below and around him an unsleeping city within a city. Within the silence that was the alternative, he had never been able to sleep. Voices and music rang out from beyond the ruined door now, echoed from the unseen terrace behind him, the same as every night. But no sound of pursuit from either side.

The rooms were part of a high terrace that clung to the upper tiers of the old Ilvani quarter, reached by stair and bridge from across and above a broad courtyard of sculpted white stone and restless trees. It was two storeys up along the closest approach, and the fact that he heard only the mundane sounds of the street below told him that the guards and the woman who was their quarry had all made that climb unobserved, quiet under cover of night.

The same badge marked all their shoulders. He saw it, gaze focused there to force his eyes from her face. A red hammer entwined with fulvous ivy, a noble's standard, but even unrecognized as it was, he would have known this was a noble's guard detail by the cut and crispness of their cloth. A long way from home, but no dirt from the road on them. No stain of damp from the rain that had been falling for most of the past week where the winds of autumn pushed in from the distant eastern seas.

He gently lifted her with one bare foot under the shoulder, turning her. He saw her face emerge full from shadow, saw the narrow line of the mouth he had kissed for the first time when he was twelve years old.

He stared for a long moment, then turned away. He occupied himself at the bookshelves, finding what he looked for despite his state of distraction. He pulled on tunic and leggings, a high-collared jacket. Slowly. He needed to not look at her for long enough that when he turned back finally, he saw her face again as it was, not as it had been. The elegant line of cheek and jaw possessed a regal edge that it had not worn ten years before.

No, he thought darkly. Eleven years now.

A weariness to the set of the face. Lines of worry there that hid the memory of the easy smile of youth, even slackened by magical slumber. The half-open eyes were unchanged, the perfect sky blue of a thrush's egg that he had almost managed to forget.

He put his foot to her shoulder again, hard because only that would wake her from the dark sleep of his enchantment. She cried out in pain as she flinched, arms flailing for the moment it took for the magic to fade. She looked frantically around her as she half-rose, saw where the guards lay unmoving. She looked up, saw him standing above her.

He held out his hand.

Her gaze slipped down again, the guards' breathing shallow but steady, and he had no idea whether it was relief or fear he saw in her as she extricated herself from the tangle of bodies, one desperate hand still clutching tight to her cloak.

"How long will they..." Her whisper trailed off as she gestured to the six, seemingly afraid she might wake them. She spoke the Gracian tongue that once held all the promise of his youth, and which he used as little as possible now as a result.

"Get clear," he said as he unfurled the scroll he had sought and found among the books, its writing flaring as he spoke words that could not be heard and twisted one hand in the tight knot of the spellsign. Even as she scrambled away to the wall, the six bodies were suddenly wrapped in a scouring pulse of shadow that turned their flesh grey for a moment. Then they were gone.

She stared in shock. He took a moment's comfort from that before he spoke.

"I expect I don't need to ask if your father knows you were coming here tonight."

He paced away from her, judged the time by the chill of deep night in the air and the subtle change in the din from the street below. Only halfway to dawn, the songs fading to quieter voices through the dark transition of night to day, as he heard her frantically pace the now-empty floor behind him.

"You didn't..." she began. He smiled, his back to her. "You can't..."

"A full accounting of the things I can do would leave you amazed beyond any expectation. Who were they, and are there more behind them?"

"What did you do to them?" she shouted. Her voice was ice behind him, but it was her movement that set him on edge, two steps toward him and the hiss of her cloak along the wall as she swept past. He turned in time to see the sword in her hand, tip already marked across a space of two paces, dead on his heart. He could see the scabbard beneath her cloak now, set low against her leg. Slow to draw, easy to hide.

The incantation was already in his mind, set to strike her down with little more thought than it would have taken to swat a wasp. A reflex reaction built up over a lifetime of having swords drawn against him. More often than not, by people from whom he hadn't expected it.

He came to the Free City for the first time at the turning of autumn his fourteenth year, winding through the endless leagues of farm road and clustered villages that blossomed green and bright around the great walls under what had seemed an endless rain. Through all that long journey from her father's house, through all the years since, he told himself he hated her.

Until this night, this moment, he hadn't realized how wrong he was.

He felt the words of power die on his lips, fading in the same instant in his mind. His hands were shaking, forced to his side and balled to fists. As he often did, he reminded himself that it was a fine line between controlling the power that lived in him and being controlled by it. He still needed to work on that.

"I see you still recall your mood when last we saw each other," he said.

"What did you do...?"

"Sent them safely to finish out their slumber on the lawn of Ladryck Green. The last of the tavern traffic from the waterfront wards will have their cloaks and weapons pawned before they awake, but the mother of all headaches aside, they'll be fine."

He saw that she believed him, but it didn't quell the anger in her. He smiled as he stepped forward, raised his hand to push aside the blade and take the full embrace of that cold gaze. And as if he struck her, she stumbled back suddenly, screaming with a fear that he had never heard in her before.

"Stay away!" Her voice carried an edge sharp as the sword looked, but the fear fought her movements as she whipped it away from him, left herself open as she held it tip to the ground, eyes down suddenly. "You can't... You don't understand."

The blade she bore was gleaming silver, a rapier forged in a style he had never seen before, and imbued with a power he felt as a faint surge on the air, the incantation of detection second nature to him, made without thinking. Dweomer lived in that steel, had flared with her movement. A powerful magic. Old. He couldn't name the place in him where the knowledge and certainty came from, but he knew enough to trust it. A byproduct of a lifetime's study of arcane craft.

"Why are you here?" he asked at last, and he felt the fear in her again as her eyes found his.

"I need your aid."

The perfect silver of the blade seemed to ripple where it caught the light. Her hand was shaking, and his gaze slipped past the sword to note her now with rather more interest. With the cloak thrown back, she lost none of the grace of the girl she had been when he last saw her. She was tall and she was pale, in the manner of one who had grown up in good health and plenitude but been kept for too many of those young years from the world outside. But he saw the tight knots of muscle thread her arms still, marking her also as one who made up for all that cloistered time in the company of the weapon masters of her father's house.

"What help would you need that your father could not buy?" he said at last. "And of all the people you might seek it from, why me?"

"Because no coin will buy the trust I need, and my father cannot know. I need your guidance. Like all the times before."

He held her gaze for a long while. Searching for something there, but when realized he didn't know what, he turned away without a word. Near what was left of the door, he checked that the foyer remained empty as he slipped on boots and a well-worn belt of scaled hide, a dagger hanging from it. He found the black cloak that hung by the bed, slipped it on as he waited for her to realize that it was up to her to speak.

"You are not the easiest person to find," she said.

"That depends on how badly one wants to find me. If you need magic, there are easier places to seek it."

He turned back, saw her staring at the rapier where she raised it.

"I need answers," she said. "This blade. You must examine it, but you cannot touch it. I fear some curse in it, and I need to know the truth of what it is."

He felt the pulse of power again, felt it sing with a voice that was hers and not hers. A chill that he tried to ignore threaded his spine. "If you wish me to assess an artifact, you should probably be prepared for me to actually look at it," he said.

"Are you trained to the blade?"

"I can clean a trout or a would-be cutpurse with equal dexterity if pressed to it," he said. He adjusted the set of the dagger's scabbard at his hip. "But as to a real sword, my familiarity extends to knowing which end to hold. What of it?"

She motioned him forward. She held the blade near but not close, letting it catch the light again. The mage squinted. Stared. Running along the length of that steel, he saw the faint gleam of liquid. Not moisture on the metal, but of the metal. A dull sheen that anyone with a passing acquaintance of the alchemist's art would recognize.

"Quicksilver," he said.

She nodded, but a flicker of uncertainty crossed her face suddenly. "That is its name. Or at least what its master calls it. You know this blade?"

"Apt, but not particularly creative." He ignored the question as he peered closer, saw the molten flow along the delicate lines of the crossguard and down the metal mesh that wrapped the haft. At the edge of her fingers where they wrapped it tight, liquid metal pulsed like something alive.

His expression must have betrayed a sudden alarm, for she spoke. "It is safe enough, for me at least. It is a warrior's blade, or so it seems. Those who cannot properly wield it cannot touch it. Not without..." Her voice trailed off.

"Dying." He finished the thought for her. He had seen quicksilver poisoning once or twice, old-school alchemists with little aptitude and less sense driven to a madness that even the animysts' magic had trouble curing.

"But you," he said. "You hold it with a warrior's hand. Sergeant of your father's house guard by now, I should think."

"Lieutenant," she said, but he heard the hesitation in her voice.

"But no higher," he mused. "Your father making it known he had other plans for you. The diplomatic service. A marriage of allegiance, perhaps."

He felt the measured weight of the words but took no comfort as he saw the blue eyes flash cold. And in his weary mind, he weighed all the uncertainty that the sudden shock of this night had wrought. Realizing suddenly that all that mattered to him was to not have to think on what it truly meant that she was here, that she had found him, that she was even seeking him in the first place.

But he found himself wondering in the moment, despite his best intentions. How long had she searched? And in the eleven years since they last saw each other, for all the reasons he told himself she should have had to seek him, how many times had she tried and failed?

"How did you know to find me in the city?" he said at last.

"I asked," she said simply. "Your comings and goings have become easier to follow of late. You've made a name for yourself."

That much was true, he thought. "Notoriety is the best coin for certain research. I use it sparingly."

"Still seeking your secrets," she said. "Like when you were young. Staring into the shadow, eyes wide to capture the faint light." He heard a bitterness in her voice, no effort made to hide it.

Her name was one that had never needed making. Her father's daughter, sung of by the local troubadours from the day she was born. And he found himself turning now from a question he knew he wouldn't answer, had ignored through all the decade and more since they last saw each other. All that time when he had known where she was. He had always known where she was.

Why, then, had he never looked for her in all those empty years?

"The secrets I pursue now are a great deal more important that those I pursued when we last met."

"No doubt."

He felt an old antagonism rising, a subtle anger that flared suddenly at his breast like a bruise. In the time since he dwelled in the great castle on the southern coast, he thought he had set aside the heat of his youth and all the passions carried with it. Set aside anger, set aside the contempt he felt now when he thought of her father, trying to imagine him as old as he must have become. Decrepit with age, he hoped, though he knew the power of the healing that a duke's coin would buy.

"Where does it come from? The blade?"

The sword wavered in her hand. He tried to focus past the distraction of her. Felt for the power again and used it to focus a quick incantation, measuring the sword's power with a more accurate eye. Focusing on the job at hand. Research. Investigation.

He felt her hesitate, heard the moment's silence that gave him the answer even as she was thinking of a way to avoid saying it. "Your husband."

It had been that way between them, once. As youth, their thoughts intertwined to such a degree that there could be no secrets.

"No," she said at last. "Not yet."

He had been her tutor at first, only two years older than her but bluffing his way into being hired on as her father's master of languages and lore. A stolen suit of scholar's robes and forged credentials from the academies at Hypriot.

"Congratulations or condolences as appropriate," he said, and he saw the sudden flush of anger at her cheek.

"Do not pretend this is news," she said. "You must know."

"I don't, and I mustn't, and why should I?"

"Because my father remains as strong as ever, and word of his affairs spreads far."

"My disinterest in your father's affairs remains slightly stronger."

He turned for the sideboard that was the room's only furnishing besides the well-made bed and the tall shelves stacked high with scrolls and books, dust and shadows. The books were old, all of them. Collected from various forays across the Elder Kingdoms, and once or twice beyond it. He had repaired and rebound most of them at least once, a skill of his youth that had never been lost.

At the sideboard, he found the scattered pages he had been translating that night before finally allowing sleep to take him. Before she and six warriors burst through his door. He slipped them to his pocket, saw brandywine standing before him in a half-bottle that had been a full bottle that morning. He owned a single goblet that he filled and drained with his back turned, watching the distant flare of streetlight through the mottled glass of half-open terrace doors. The sound of the city rose from beyond again, soothing him.

He heard her boots pace the floor behind, louder still. Part of him hoped they would strike for the door, fade to silence, but he saw her shade in the glass of the doors move for the bed instead, sitting. Watching him.

Her father had used the magecraft of others, as did all those in power, but he had feared it more than most. As her teacher, he never tried to seek out the power in her, had never wanted to put her at risk that way, but he showed her. The mysteries of light and shadow, the glamers of image and sound. Rudimentary in their own way, young as he was then, but they were magic all the same.

"I've stolen the sword."

He filled the goblet again. Contemplated it for a moment before he took his second draught straight from the bottle. He crossed to the bed, booted footsteps heavy on the cold floor. She took the goblet when he held it out to her, still waiting, it seemed, for a reaction, but he only shrugged in response to her gaze.

"I've stolen the sword," she said again. "From his chambers. He keeps it within reach always. Carries it as his greatest treasure."

"Your husband who isn't yet." He watched as she drank, too quickly.

"If I am found out, it will disrupt the marriage. Or worse."

He nodded, thoughtful suddenly. "You're in the city together. For the wedding," he said. "When?"

"Two days time."

He felt the shadow twist through him, felt it threaten to summon up a dozen different spells that might hold her there, might bind her to him, might twist her thought and mind in a score of subtle ways. Might let him seek within her own thought for the truth of all he was to her all those years ago. The deep truth that hid behind her lifetime spent in service to a father's dreams.

Instead, he only shook his head. He let the dark hair shade his face as his gaze slipped from hers.

"Go," he said.

"I came to you with purpose…"

"Your purpose. Your affair, not mine. Take the blade and go back to him."

"I will pay you anything…"

"You no longer have anything I need."

More than he meant to say. The uncertainty in her silence told him she knew it.

The hard pulse of profit was an ebb tide that he caught and rode for his own reasons, caring not for coin and having altogether too much of it in his purse most days. But he craved knowledge. He craved the secrets that the Free City and its thousand-thousand folk held, and the deeper secrets that even the masters of lore had forgotten, trapped in ancient tomes and weathered parchments whose hiding places had become a second home to him.

He turned from her, tried to hide the hunger he felt for the power, for the secret that the rapier's magic made.

"The blade is evil," she whispered, and the fear was in her again, playing faintly alongside that other song.

"No magic is evil in and of itself," he said quietly. "Magic simply speaks to a kind of ambition that takes root more easily in amoral soil."

"I need you to destroy it."

"Again, not my affair."

"I've tried. With all the power and coin at my disposal, I've tried. Breaking, burning. Acid. Spell-fire in a flask that cost a month's expenditures of my father's treasury. Nothing so much as scratches it. The blade's strength is unnatural. It is forged in some dark legend, and it will take the power of legend to break it. You are a great mage of war. Take it. Destroy it."

He laughed out loud, saw the anger cloud the blue eyes again until she realized he was laughing at himself, not her. "I've never been within a hundred leagues of real war, and should that ever change, you'd find me moving away from the front lines at a speed that would astound you."

"I know the things you've done…"

"In the circles you travel in, you wouldn't have heard anything of what I've done. Which means you've been asking. Why?"

"Because you are the war-dragon," she whispered. "Because I need you again."

From below, the revels of closing time were spilling from the taverns into the streets. There was no night in Yewnyr, the locals said. Dark came sure enough, but that meant nothing to the constant flow and hustle of commerce and coin that was the city's lifeblood.

"My father's father wore that name and the power it represented," he said. "A name is all it is for me." He didn't have to catch her eye to know she was looking to the dragon stitched in gold at the collar of the jacket. It was a sigil he wore for the attention it received, but her attention was a thing he didn't want. Not like this.

"In all the places I have asked, all the loremasters through whom I seek a name of one with the knowledge to help me, the name I hear is yours. As if some fate has placed our paths in alignment. My need. Your power."

"If it's a curse you're worried about, any competent sage or less competent adept can set your mind at ease."

"This is no hedge-wizard's hex. I see the power that is in this blade. His moods, his manner, all of it changes when the sword is in his hand. It's been three months since it came into his possession. Three months since I last saw the man I thought I knew."

"The man you love," he said. The bottle was empty in his hand. He looked down at it with genuine curiosity, couldn't remember having finished it. "You need to go."

"It speaks to him…"

He watched the bottle slip from his hand short of the sideboard where he meant to set it down. It spun slowly, his mind holding the progression of its flight as a blur of motion, so that he saw the point of impact where the glass struck the stone tile of the floor.

"Do you believe in fate?" she had asked him the last time they spoke.

Glass was chaos controlled, the alchemists said. Solid matter possessed of no shape within, yearning to flow but trapped in its brittle state. Like life itself, caught in one aspect as the frozen moment of a single point in time. He saw the fragile potential of the bottle's construction shiver and reshape itself as it struck the floor, and with the force of that reshaping, the moment was unmade to shards that spread with a crash that made her jump.

She stared. "You know this blade?" she asked again. Her voice was a bare whisper, but he said nothing in return. Only stared at the rapier, watching light flow like liquid along the strong of the blade. He felt for its power again, felt the familiarity in the song that power made, harsh in his ears now. So that he almost missed the faint creak from the foyer behind him.

There, someone was shifting, trying to still the movement of a stubbed boot. The sound of shattering glass when the bottle fell had startled whoever was in the process of slipping through the broken outside door, unheard. Her eyes as she turned to follow his thoughtful gaze were wide with sudden fear, telling him she had no knowledge that she was followed not once but twice. Told him she knew who it was.

"He'll kill you," she whispered. She had the sword in its scabbard, vanished beneath her cloak again. "Go. Please."

"Of course," he said as he took her hand.

A shout from outside sounded like *Take them both!* Whoever's voice it was knew that any secrecy to their approach was gone now. Whoever's voice it was, he saw in her eyes the pain it carried, sharp as her stolen blade.

Footsteps erupted, loud. A dozen of them by the sound of it, waiting for the cover of the last dark to get close. He was already moving, though, pulling her through the opposite doorway before she could react, then past the tall shelves whose shadows cloaked them as they slipped across to the terrace.

He felt her weight but not the strength that he knew was in her if she wanted it. Too afraid to fight him, he thought. Already caught up in the betrayal and the scandal that this night would bring to her, to her father, to this faceless betrothed that she loved enough to steal the sword that was destroying him.

He kicked through the half-open doors, heard the cry of voices at the foyer, but it was already too late.

Around a porch of dark marble set with low railings, the city was a blaze of flickering lantern light and the eternal golden glow of even-lamps, shimmering beneath the haze of smoke-fires as an inverse sun-rise below a dark sea. She was breathing hard as she skidded in his wake, trying to stop herself. He seized her hands in response, pulled her close to him as he threw her arms across his shoulders, his own arms tight around her waist. He expected her to pull away, but she was unyielding against him, her body pressed close to his, fitted tight as though it had been carved to match him.

Without realizing he was going to do it, he kissed her. Her lips were warm beneath his, parted as her breathing slowed.

"Hold on," he said.

He saw the first figures smash through the glass doors behind them as they took to the air. They wore the same uniform as the others, the hammer and ivy badge in tawny red. He felt her hands lock behind his neck as she stiffened in fear, the sudden twist of momentum taking them as he willed the power woven into the black cloak to hurl them up and over the edge of darkness, the chill night air sharp, washing across them like the surge from the back of a fast horse as they flew.

He turned back once to see the armored figure at the terrace's edge. He was tall, red-haired and close-bearded in the manner of so much Vanyr nobility. He wore the armor of a knight of those western prov-inces in black and ice-blue, a wine-dark cloak wrapped tight across broad shoulders, legs set wide, eyes impassive as his guards stood in silence behind him, all watching.

Where the mage's arms held her tight, he slipped a hand to her belt. He unhooked it with a quick flick of his fingers. By the time she recog-nized the movement, tried in vain to stop him, the scabbard had slipped from her and was gone, spinning like a falling leaf in black and silver as it dropped to the terrace below. The guards shouted out alarm, leaping back. The tall noble stepped up to the railing, caught the falling blade with one hand.

He smiled as they soared. He judged the angle between them and the eyes below them, willed the spellpower of the cloak that spread like wings around him now to carry them higher.

The Free City unfurled below as a storm of light and shadow. The bright blazing core, edged by the spiderweb curve of its great walls. The dark lines of the great streets, cutting a patchwork swath through color and noise that was a song sung in harmony with the cry of the wind. The black serpent-form of the river, twisting in from west to east and festooned with the glimmering lights of uncounted ships carrying trade and dreams from across five kingdoms. The vast shadow of the great greens. Villages beyond the walls, dark lines of farm road edged in flickering firelight.

He held himself there, her body tight against his where she turned to stare in wonder, suspended dark against the bright crescent of the Clearmoon for an endless moment before the high haze took them away.

After a time, they descended to the darkness of the Rose Heath, a well of green shadow spreading out in the storm of light. The wide paths and endless lawn of the great park were never empty even beneath the pale fingers of dawn, but he made sure that no eyes marked them as they descended to the shifting shadows of an alder copse that marked the confluence of two great paths. Broad shapes of marble rose around them, private mausoleums like the countless others that spread as white waves across the green. The breeze was warm where it touched the grass, but the sudden stillness that followed their fast flight sent a chill through him.

Their feet touched ground together. They stood a while, arms around each other, her hands still tight at his neck. He felt them trembling, looked down upon her pale face. Afraid. But behind the fear was something else. As quickly as he tried to dismiss the thought, it clung to him. She was warm against him. In her eyes was a look he had all but forgotten, driven from him with the memory of the pain her father made.

He thought of all the things he might say, all the things he had failed to say in the years before the silence.

He asked her instead, "What does it say to him? This blade?"

"Does it matter now?" He heard her fight to find the sudden contempt in the words. A choice made, the moment broken like her fingers broke from him, pulled free as she stepped away.

He only shrugged. "Where was it found?"

"I don't know," she said. She paced away, stalked through the half-light toward the brighter shadow of a marble monument a dozen strides away. Silent and cold. The sight of it slowed her.

"A tomb," she said. She gazed up at the edifice of white stone that rose before her, first in a long line of tombs set together in a block that curved away across the shadow of the green. "Somewhere in the north country. He had the troubadours paid to claim he slew the undead that carried it, but I heard it was easier than that…"

Her voice trailed off, but as he glanced up, he realized it was his own look that stopped her cold. He saw her shock, felt the darkness that suddenly flared in him reflected in her own eyes.

"You do know this blade," she said bitterly. "You know it and you sent it back to him."

He was silent a moment. "I know one like it. Or did. A friend carried it. It was lost, or so I heard."

"What happened to this friend who carried it?"

"Madness," he said. "Or so I heard."

She struck him, the back of her hand hitting as hard as any blow he had ever taken. He felt the pain spike in his jaw as he stumbled back, watched her turn on her heel, race off with light steps toward the distant light that marked the road and the city beyond.

He thought about letting her go. Another tapestry-piece of memory to fold in with that first kiss, the last night he saw her, the beating at her father's hand that nearly killed him. He had managed to free himself from bonds and gag that day, then summoned up the spellpower that saw rage and lightning coiled in his hands where they found her father's throat. The duke still bore the imprint of the young mage's fingers across his neck, or so he had heard. A mark of arcane power that no life-magic would heal.

"You came to me for aid and guidance," he called out to her retreating back. "I'll give you both. All things are destroyed in the end, but only fate decides when that end comes."

She stopped. Turned back slowly. Her shadowed look said she wouldn't walk to him, so he went to her instead. Slowly.

"A blade of worth, of power, has a destiny," he said as he stopped, close enough to see the blue eyes gleam daylight bright in the darkness. "I don't know if it's your lord's destiny to wield this blade, nor do you, just as neither of us can know whether his doing so will taint his mind to evil. All you can do is judge whether your fate is part of that."

"You know this because you did the same for your friend?" He heard the edge in her voice, fighting tears.

"I know it because I didn't. Because I made the same choice then that you had made already tonight, to leave him to the fate he chose. You only came to me for the strength to carry it through."

She was silent a long while. When she finally spoke, he heard the strength return.

"It decides its own course," she said. "As will he."

A wind had risen from the north, carrying with it the hint of rose hedges and the last mown grass of the season from the distant gates. And in that shroud of scent, he was back in the summer gardens of her father's house, watching her dance beneath the ancient stone arch strung with grape and white creeper and the weathered Ilvani runes he taught her to read.

"Like fate," he said.

"Like love."

He felt light-headed suddenly, felt the wind shift and strengthen as if it might be seeking him. Then as with all his dreams, it was suddenly done.

"I don't know what to do," she said quietly, and there was a dread expectation in the words that he could hear.

"You do," he said. "Choose your course. Walk away."

"And where shall I walk to?"

An unwritten ending lay hidden in the question, twisting through the twilight space between the words like a serpent threading wind-whipped grass. She had come to him that night, had sought him out for fate-only-knew how long. Had pursued him through the distance of the dream they once shared, and he felt the sudden sting of that dream as he always did. Felt the protective shroud of shadow break against the pellucid frames of memory that would let all the pain back in.

"Your path is yours," he said. "I could never choose it for you."

She turned away then. Wouldn't meet his gaze. She made as if to speak but he was quicker.

"Goodbye," was all he said.

He soared up and beyond her, quickly lost to the shroud of darkness in the west that drank the last of the night sky beyond the edge of the green. From the far side of that darkness, he watched as she ran to the gate at the broad stroke of the Iresand Road, saw her flag down one of the plentiful coach cabs returning from their last runs to the nobles' houses in the wards of the mountainside ridge.

He followed her for a short while from the air, soaring in shadow as she and her cab made their way toward the twisting switchback avenues leading up into that bright night, a brilliant crown upon the city's towering head that was the herald of the rising sun. Then he turned his eyes to the darker sky and swept away.

For three days, he brooded, waiting. He took new rooms in Chrian Heath above a grudge-worn apothecary who he favored for her ability to not ask questions. He estimated what the red knight would have paid the landlord in Urorfidith to report any word of seeing him return, then offered up triple that for his silence, delivered by a rickshaw driver he used for that sort of business. When the burly runner returned with the personal effects and the books the mage needed from those he left behind, he brought news as well.

The red knight, her bethrothed, was dead.

The mage sought out confirmation, found it quickly enough by way of a private club called the Chalice, where the guard captains drank and his connections and coin could buy the ear of the serving girls. Across the Free City, the tale was spreading quickly, along with the related but less memorable gossip of how the engagement between this Vanyr knight and the daughter of a Gracian duke had been suddenly broken off by the lady herself only that day. The morning the mage left her.

Her Vanyr lord did not take it well. When the lady and her entourage made to abandon the city ahead of word of the scandal, he followed with a force of house guards in dun and rust-red. It was said that ten died that night, but details from the survivors were strangely inconsistent in describing those moments of madness.

The lady was said to be in hiding, and in mourning. He confirmed that twice more, held the knowledge in his heart for a long while.

He spent more of the coin he didn't need on information, seeking it out among those who had been there, guards and drivers and other witnesses. At the end of two more days, he found himself drinking with a young guard of the watch whose very first patrol in uniform had taken him into the thick of the fray that night, and who had nearly paid the price.

The quicksilver blade was gone, he heard. This shaken guard had seen it, sure enough. He named it without prompting, cursing the sword as he recounted the red knight dropping two men with the barest of blood-scratches from its gleaming bite. But those two were the only ones who died at the knight's hand, the young guard swore. Two more were killed by the knight's captain at arms, who seized the blade when his master finally fell, and who had seemingly been claimed by an even darker madness, laying into the city guards and his own fellows with the same murderous rage.

The young guard had seen the red knight cut down by the lady herself, defending others from his frenzied attack. A warrior's form to her movement but tears in her eyes, he said.

The knight's man fell to archers. The young guard had known the Yewnyr captain who shakingly snatched the blade up then, but could only watch in horror as a raw recruit who fought alongside him put a dirk in the captain's back and seized the rapier anew. That guard had fallen in turn, dropped by one of a gang of street bravos drawn by screams and steel to the fray. The bravos fled, just as the young guard was put down by an errant blade from one of the red knight's remaining warriors, no longer sure who they were fighting for. Two more were dead before it was done, but what happened to the blade in the end, none could say.

The mage returned to his rooms near dawn, but did not sleep. From his pocket where he had placed it, where he had avoided thinking on it ever since, he pulled the pages he had been translating the night she burst through his door. He saw the quicksilver blade sketched there in lines of faded ink whose age he couldn't guess at, a timeless facsimile that matched his memory now. The words that spoke of its dark legends were in one of the ancient Ilvani tongues slow to even his mind, but he could read them well enough.

Salinomelar, the Ilvani had called it. 'Quicksilver' was the closest approximation he was able to make, carefully extracting the name's full meaning from the ancient parchments where they spoke of the unmatched speed of the blade and the poison of its bite and the madness it inflicted on those who chose to wield it.

She would have been in her father's house by now. With the connections the mage had, with the reputation he had forged over the long years since the night he fled with the clothes on his back and a death warrant in his name, he knew a dozen, a hundred different ways he could have gotten a message to her.

"Do you believe in fate?" she had asked him the last time they spoke, and he told her yes. Even then, though, he hadn't believed it. The words simply part of the compact forged by the ardor and innocence of youth.

If she had been there to ask him now, he wasn't sure what he might say.

GHOSTSONG

HE WAS DEEP IN THE DARK of forgotten dreams when the song called him back. Raubynar blinked as the darkness shifted into focus, the fire dying across from him. He judged the time by the movement of the Clearmoon, alone in the sky. A quarter of the night, perhaps, since he closed his eyes. The fading wind was from the west, the familiar scent of the still-distant Yewnwood faint and complex where it pulled at his memory. The black branches of the budding cypress above were faint scar lines against a star-streaked sky.

He stood and stretched, feeling the song fade to nothing as dreams will do. He felt an unfamiliar slowness to his thoughts, an exhaustion threading through him that he couldn't explain. He thought he had heard the faint echo of a lyre, notes spilling through the shadows that pulled at his unwaking mind. There was a voice as well. Words that melted away the more he tried to remember them.

Across from him, Cassatra was sleeping, curled tight within the black pool of her cloak. Raub had assumed she would take a watch while he slipped into the half-sleep of the Ilvani, but it was clear she thought there was nothing on this back road worth watching for.

As he paced the clearing's edge, gathering deadfall to toss to the embers, Raub reflected that she was most likely right. Wolves and wild cats prowled the woods in early spring, seeking to fill the long hunger of winter, but the fire would warn them off. Brigands were rare but not unheard of this far off the trade roads, though Raub pitied anyone who tried to wake Cass from a sound sleep at the end of a blade.

From the most distant darkness, he heard the music again.

As far as they were from any settlement, he knew the unnatural essence of that sound even before a faint shiver up his spine warned him to be wary. Closer to the wagon camps to the east, some traveler making late-night song to ward off the spirits of the shadows would have been fitting. Here, in the isolated shelter of the cypress wood, not even insects sang at night. The Ilvani of the Yewnwood seldom roamed this far afield, the stunted groves of the scrublands shunned by them. The wall of the great forest was the edge of their world, its great roof of green and gold the only sky most of them had ever known.

It was the same faint song that had woken him, drifting nearer where the wind twisted through the shimmering grove. A woman's voice sounded out faintly, the lyre shifting within it as silver light through green leaves. But within that light, he sensed a shadow. He felt the voice seek his ear with words he didn't understand, sharp-edged like the notes that carried from steel strings.

Raub was drifting through the woods suddenly, couldn't remember stepping away from the fire. He was in leather still, a well-scarred jerkin and leggings caked with the dust of the road. Through the screen of cypress and witchwillow saplings growing low, he padded barefoot, not sure what unknown summons he was following until he slowed to gauge the shifting of the wind through the leaves. From ahead came a gleam of light. The music was louder. Closer.

He circled the bright clearing three times, made sure he was alone before he stepped out from the shadows. The Clearmoon rode at zenith, its near-full light catching the silver spread of wolf-foil and white-grass above an uneven mat of lifeless carpet vine. Gnarled branches threw a haze of shadows across day-bright ground. But brighter even than the gleaming leaves was the pool that spread in the hollow beneath a rotting cypress stump. No more than a stride across, its surface was smooth silver, unnaturally calm beneath the trace of breeze that twisted past him.

Only when his hands strayed absently to his waist did Raub realize that his weapons were back at the camp. The emerald-hilted longsword and the Ilvani dirk were still sitting where he had slung them off at the fireside. He still carried a third blade at his belt, as he always did. A leaf-edged shortsword, its distinctive shape marking it as the Ilvani style where it hung from a leather thong. But as always, scabbard and hilt alike were shrouded in black cloth and road dust. No way to draw it even if he wanted to.

Raub felt a pinprick chill twist up his spine. Afraid not of what might lie beyond the forest wall, but wary of whatever power in the song could have inspired him to follow it weaponless, seeking blindly in the dark.

In his mind, the voice he didn't understand unfurled in a gentle arpeggio, stepped tones as vivid as the colors of a loom, impossibly perfect. It was a lament, slow and ethereal. The lyre slowed to an intermittent echo of single-string chimes, lifting the voice to greater heights of sorrow.

Raub was on his knees at the pool's edge, couldn't remember stumbling the half-dozen steps across the silver glade. The scent of rot was heavy, filling his lungs so that he had to fight to breathe. Around him, the glade was shifting, the Clearmoon's light spreading now like ripples on water. The cypress stump was a dark altar, shot through by the movement of finger-long black borer beetles that had reduced the wood to a shell. Silver leaves hissed past on the wind that somehow still raised no ripple on the pool itself. He felt himself pulled forward, tried to fight a desire he couldn't explain.

Despite every urge to look away, he stared deep into that silver water and saw the faces of the friends he had killed...

"Couldn't sleep?"

As if his head had suddenly torn free of some smothering gauze, Raub felt cool air fill his lungs. The light was bright around him as he rose slowly from the pool's edge, not bothering to turn toward the familiar voice. He felt his mind clear, felt the breeze trace across his back, his tunic soaked in sweat.

The music was gone, no hint that it had ever been there. Just the faint echo of despair still twisting in his memory. At his feet, the black water of the pool was streaked with scum and a chaotic cloud of ripples spreading at the touch of the wind.

"Thought I heard something," Raub said at last.

He turned back to see Cassatra in the shadows, her crossbow nocked with a black quarrel, three more slung below the barrel and ready to be set. She had left her cloak at the camp, crouching barelegged in a knee-length shift of dark homespun that swallowed the moon's-light. Her look of calm contemplation told Raub she was worried. On her belt, she carried the handaxe the loremasters of Myrnan had called the Reaper, swinging gently within its sheath.

"You're half a league from the camp," she said. "What could you hear at that range? And if you could hear something at that range, why wouldn't you be moving away from it?"

"A voice," Raubynar said quietly. He shook his head. "Just the wind." Cass stood slowly, turned to take in the clearing, the tree line beyond. "I couldn't sleep. Don't worry about it."

From behind him came a hiss. A stand of witchwillow shifted, a dark shape rising to the air. Raub heard Cass's crossbow sing as he wheeled, fast enough to see her shoot twice. The first shot was gone into shadow. The second took the brush grouse cleanly, shrieking as it fell clumsily from the air and back to the bracken below.

Cass had a third bolt fitted and nocked as she turned to appraise the silence. Raub only shrugged.

"Breakfast is served," he said. Cass gave him a withering look.

He found the grouse easily, was carefully pulling Cass's bolt free when she called him. He heard a familiar hardness in her voice, approached to find her kneeling. He saw the flattened spread of white-grass beneath a thicket of scrub that marked the bird's roosting place. Cass was kneeling two strides away, however, the grass there bent and broken in a telltale pattern.

"Something flushed the bird," she said quietly.

Raub stepped closer, carefully ran his fingers across the spread of flattened grass. Footprints, perhaps. Cass's first shot hadn't been aimed at the bird at all.

"You thought you heard something?" she said.

At the edge of his vision, he caught a sudden glimpse of white flame and bright steel. His father's longblade. He had seen it.

In a brief flicker of memory, from the instant before Cass's voice called him away from it, Raub remembered the faces in the silver pool. He watched them shift to smoke, burn away to nothing in his mind.

He felt his hand stray to the black-wrapped shortsword at his hip.

"Raubynar?"

He blinked. The sky was lighter now, dawn coming.

"Just the wind," he said.

⁎ ⁎ ⁎

The rebuilt fire was banked to coals by the time Raub cleaned and dressed the bird. He watched in silence as it cooked, Cass pointedly ignoring him as she ate nuts and dried fruit from a drawstring bag. The sun had risen, clouds copper-stained to the east.

"You still haven't told me where we're going," she said at one point.

Raub pulled the grouse from its makeshift wooden spit, broke the charred body carefully, and began to eat. "We were moving south, last time I checked. The large yellow thing that hangs in the sky by day is the sun. You can tell direction by it, or so they say."

Cass smiled as she flicked an almond at him, sending it past his ear with a force he could feel. Though they sparred only rarely, the two of them were of a pair when it came to strength and speed. Raub was taller than Cass by only a hand's breadth, his darkness matching hers. They had been taken as kin more than once by folk who failed to note the Ilvani set of his ears beneath the rough-cut hair, the pale gleam like starlight in his eyes.

"We've been traveling south since we left the Free City," Cass said, "down a succession of cart tracks and hunter's trails that keep getting fewer and farther between. Yet somehow you manage to pick out a route from them like you know where they all lead."

She had the close, dark curls and the olive complexion common on the Gracian coast, but where she came from was something Cass had never spoken of. Barely two years since she and Raub met, that reserve was still the trait they most strongly shared. A kind of silent familiarity between them that made their time together seem longer.

"Don't confuse the ability to not get lost with having a destination," he said.

"All travel has a destination."

"All journeys have a destination. More aptly, a destination turns travel into a journey."

"And what's this, then?"

When they had first arrived back on the mainland from the Sorcerers' Isle of Myrnan, Cass and Raub spent almost a month in the Highport. First, down on the docks that were the city's lifeblood. Then moving higher from the water toward the white-terraced hills. In bars and brothels spanning the widest range of class and culture, Highport cost Raub what would once have been the fortune of a lifetime. Through an endless dance of drink and baser pleasures, he watched indifferently as it all slipped away.

Cassatra had followed him at first. But though her tastes were more subtly refined, it was the more immediate loss of her patience that saw her abandon Raub in pursuit of her own business. On their initial journey to Myrnan, in each Gracian city and town they passed through, that business was the same. Quiet meetings with loremasters in the nobles' districts. Quieter meetings with scouts and bounty hunters in roadhouses and dark taverns. Cass was searching for something she had never spoken of, and so Raub had never asked.

She came back to find him in the end, dragging him out of the drunken haze of a month's debauchery to a monastery perched among the green vineyards north of the city. These hills were still called Hypriot, the city's original name in Gracian long before "Highport" had been culled off by the rougher Imperial tongue.

The next morning, awaking with his senses more or less functioning, Raub found that the fortune he had lost made barely a dent in the fortune that plagued him still. The cold weight of platinum coin struck and minted a thousand years before. The glint of Dwarf-cut gems that were the legacy of that month the two of them spent beneath distant Myrnan.

The ruins of that dread Sorcerers' Isle left those who survived them wealthy.

Raub and Cass had survived.

"Where are we going?" she asked again as they walked. She wore leggings now beneath the shift but still walked barefoot, a kind of quiet ease in her pace. Beneath that ease, however, Raub heard the edge in her voice that told him she wasn't going to ask again.

He had worked his way slowly through the fragile bones of the grouse, cracking the last of them now to suck the marrow before he tossed them to the grass. The day was golden, sun climbing bright across the open scrubland that spread between the cypress groves and the mountains beyond. The trail he took them on met a wider cart road not far beyond their camp, heading straight for the great forest and with tracks along it fresh the day before in both directions.

"There's an Ilvani settlement," he said finally. "A frontier forest-home inside the Yewnwood, south of Nesadale." They had passed that smaller Human city two days ago now, the Free City of Yewnyr four days beyond that. All that time, he and Cass shadowed the trade road along the twisting side tracks that wound their way through rolling farm country. Always ahead of them, south and west beneath the high sun, the vast expanse of the Yewnwood spread along the horizon as a green-black shroud.

They had taken a similar road from Highport to Yewnyr when they finally left the great coastal city. The trade routes made it a little more than a month's journey for those in a hurry, but the memories of Myrnan needed a slower road to clear them. Once in Yewnyr, Cass had been prepared for another lengthy stay, and so she was surprised when Raub told her after a week that he was heading south.

"We make time today," he said, "we'll be there by nightfall."

"Something there you're due to see? Or someone?" Cass gave him a sidelong glance.

"I was born there," Raub said evenly. "A place called Anthila."

Cass was thoughtful as she adjusted her pack, half the size of Raub's and a quarter its weight. Her blanket and bedroll were the cloak she wore, a change of clothes and her weapons the only real gear she ever carried.

"You talked about it once," she said. "Anthila."

Raub felt a sudden chill against the heat of the sun, near mid-high now. The bird was done and he washed its grease from his fingers with moss and a quick spurt from his waterskin, avoiding a response. A familiar unease traced through his mind, not so much in reaction to what Cass said but to the context. If she was speaking the truth, it was a conversation he didn't remember.

Like she could sense that unease, Cass answered the question Raub couldn't ask. "You said you couldn't go back. I tried to ask you why, but you weren't overly amenable to questions that night."

In the carefully pitched tone of her voice, in the echo against the steady pace of their footsteps and the song of unseen birds in the tall grass, Raub felt the lie. Not in what Cass repeated about him not going back, but in her saying that he kept his silence afterward. Whatever he said to her then, she must have felt the hurt it carried, which told him with cold certainty that he had told her the truth.

Part of the truth, at least.

"My father," he said quietly. Repeating what he was sure she already knew. "He's the reason I didn't go back."

"Old arguments?"

"I heard word in the Free City. He's dead."

Though she hadn't been formally asked, Cass was ready to leave the day Raub set out, falling in beside him without a word as they passed through Yewnyr's Thirty-League Gate. When he told her his plans, she sensed a change in him but didn't know what it meant. As she always did, she weighed her options with an overly critical mind, every decision given an attention beyond what most of them deserved. But as she often did, she found that attention diverted by a need for company that she seldom admitted, even to herself.

She didn't know how old she was. But already in a relatively short life, Cassatra had walked enough roads alone.

"I'm sorry," she said finally. Raub said nothing, eyes on the road ahead.

Two years ago now, and a month before he met Cass for the first time, Raub had come into his first serious coin riding as a mercenary guard on the caravan routes through the inhospitable Munychion

Plains to the east. In Nesadale, he spent that coin almost immediately, purchasing the confidence of a Yewnwood trader who worked the Il-vani settlements of the eastern forest and the adjacent Human frontier. Irasol was a scruff-bearded half-Ilvani who passed through Anthila four times a year to appraise and buy the fleet grey horses of the forest clans. For the equivalent of a year's salary for any city worker, he kept his eyes and ears open on Raub's behalf.

It had been three seasons since Raub passed through Yewnyr. The last time was with Cass, bound for Highport and Myrnan beyond. Ira-sol was the one who introduced them to the broad-shouldered north-erner named Connal, who had first whispered to them of the eastern road, and of the treasures and dangers lurking beneath the blasted hills at the heart of the Sorcerers' Isle.

While they were away on that journey, the news came that Raub had waited six years to hear.

Like Raub, like Cass, like the others who had made up their com-pany when they arrived at the isle, Connal came through the madness of Myrnan's ancient ruins unscathed. The dark barbarian hadn't spoken in the aftermath, though. He simply took his share of the wealth they pulled out of that darkness, then fled for the docks at Claygate Keep and back to the Gracian mainland. He had bested the dungeons of El-tolitinus, the dark foundations of Myrnan's ancient island-castle, as had all of them who survived. But as with so many of those so lucky, Raub saw in the warrior's cold eyes the shadow of having left something be-hind in that darkness.

"So why are you going back?" Cass's voice pulled him from his dis-traction. The western wind of the night before was gone, a colder breeze from the north carrying gathering clouds.

"My father is dead," Raub said, as if she might not have heard him the first time.

"If you only just got word in the city, he's been dead for weeks. Longer, maybe. If you wouldn't go back while was he alive, why do it now?"

Raub had seen that same shadow in the others who emerged with him into sunlight at the end of their ordeal. Full-blown in the sullen Vanyr warlord who had appointed himself leader of their expedition. More guarded in the dragon-marked mage who walked at that warrior's side. He saw it in the grey eyes of the Gracian sellsword he knew only as Dilaon, a companion of Connal's who carried himself with a nobility that spoke to a story Raub never heard. He saw it in the mercenary boss who was the only one of them to have previously taken the great staircase down into the dark depths.

Eleven of them altogether walked out alive in the end. In Claygate and Highport and a half-dozen cities beyond, Raub had drunk himself to the point where he couldn't remember the faces of the dead anymore.

"Old business," he said at last.

He had done the same when he left Anthila the winter of his sixteenth year, losing himself in the taverns and roadhouses of the towns and smaller cities of the north. Drinking to forget the faces that came back to him the previous night for the first time in six years, ghostly in that silver pool. Bright like the sun and hazy as a waking dream.

* * *

As the sun rode past zenith, a wall of trees loomed before them, marking the sudden and eternal boundary of the Yewnwood. From the moment they hit the trade road, the forest beckoned them. The everpresent green of the horizon rose slowly, cresting like a great wave ready to wash across the open plain. However, not even that gradual sighting could prepare one for the experience of stepping beneath that wave, Cass realized as they approached.

The yewn was a thick tree of twisted trunk and straight branches, its broad leaves ever growing throughout all seasons. Green at birth, they faded gold as they were caught on the wind and cast away. Its only natural home was the great forest, running one hundred and twenty leagues east to west and twice as far between north and south where it split the Elder Kingdoms like a wedge. As they approached, Cass tried to judge the height of the closest trees, each estimation upgraded as they drew ever closer.

Where the wide track plunged into that green sea, the golden trunks of two great yewn rose and twisted past each other to form an arch five times her height. Beyond them, even greater trees loomed, as tall as any keep or tower she had ever seen. The wind shimmered their sweeping branches as she and Raub walked beneath them, passing suddenly from the open skies of the sunlit world into the dusk of the forest road.

The yewn for which the endless wood was named stood as gnarled shadow-shapes to all sides. Their smooth trunks were the color of goldenrod, bare where thin bark peeled off and sloughed away of its own accord to cover the forest floor. Though she felt the weight of the dark at first beneath the gently rustling canopy of leaves, it didn't take long for Cass to grow used to the wind-twisted shadows. All around them was green and gold and silence. A feeling of closeness, of shelter that she found more peaceful than she ever would have expected.

They met wagons a dozen times as they walked, Ilvani and Human traders greeting them with a wary nod as they and their horses clopped past. Even before they heard the first approach, Raub had pulled the hood of his cloak up to shroud his face, Cass noting it but not bothering to ask why.

She tried to imagine this moment for him, a half-decade's homecoming to a dead father, but she couldn't. This was a blind spot in her. A place of darkness in her memory that made her more than happy to share his silence.

The road wound its way over long leagues, crossing the flanks of narrow streams where they tumbled down from distant hills. But though Cass was wary of walking through the darkness that would swallow the trees once the sun was down, the gloom of real dusk had barely fallen when they saw the first lights of Anthila ahead.

There was no sense of entrance into the settlement. No wall to mark a defensive perimeter, no outlying farmlands to announce the slow transition to tightly packed shops and houses. Only a sudden flare of gold that filled the green twilight with the glow of first dawn.

Cass's first time in the Free City, she sought out the enclaves of the Ilvani rangers who patrolled the Yewnwood frontier, asking them the questions she always asked. As she walked the city, she had gazed in wonder at the Ilvani wards of the great island-university of Allias, and at the gardens of Gwaleldan and Lomandra Wood along the southern wall. The terraces of those wards rose as waves of white stone, supported on the smooth arches of thousand-year-old yewn. Those great trees had marked the edge of the forest long ago, when rough huts along the great river were the first signs of the city to come.

The Ilvani of the Yewnwood called their largest settlements *muirilna*. The forest-homes, great cities set within the trees. In the forest-home of Anthila, the boles of the broadest yewn stood as wide as any city block. Around those gently twisting trunks, great wooden terraces rose. Like the slopes of a sunlit hillside, they climbed on both sides of the road and into a bright haze of sculpted globes hung from low-sweeping branches. The golden light of magical evenlamps blazed here, as it lit the streets of the Free City and the houses of its richest residents. The terraces were connected by wide bridges, and by intricate wooden catwalks and ladderways hanging suspended from webs of delicate white rope, ivy-twined. A loom of light and shadow climbed up into the trees through which Anthila spread.

"It's beautiful." It was all Cass could think to say. She saw a darkness in Raub's shadowed eyes where he glanced over to her.

"Wait," he said.

As they walked beneath the supports of the great terraces, Cass could see that these were living limbs, curving out from the trunks with the precise arc of a wheel's rim. Screens of tightly woven branches were their ceilings, and from every platform and ladder came a buzz of motion and voices. Along the ground, the forest was all but silent. Stables were the only buildings she could see, but these were plentiful. Between the trunks of the ancient yewns, smaller sapling groves were clustered and coppiced to create wide-ranging corrals. Here and there, glowing ladders reached down to brush the ground, and where the road opened up to a circle of grey paving stones, two wide stairways of white-trimmed wood rose through the screen of leaves, circling past each other as they climbed.

Raub led her up the stairs without a word, and as they climbed, Cass looked down to see the sleek horses the Ilvani rangers of the wood rode. Grey and graceful as a morning mist even as they grazed thick grass and milkweed. She heard laughter and voices from within the stables, merchant ponies tethered there, and the carts they drew lined up alongside the fence. These were watched over by a pair of Ilvani boys who danced around each other with long switches of yewn. These were swords in their hands, the two striking, parrying, striking again in a focused skirmish that seemed more dance than combat.

At the head of the stairs, the haze of light and sound became a storm of activity, and they found themselves at the center of a vast market court, what would have been the central square of any Human city of the Gracian plain. The floor they walked on was smooth-worn wooden tile, dusted with golden leaves and set over a frame of woven branches. This was visible through intermittent gaps that Cass guessed were meant to sluice away rain. The throng was thick even against the rising of the night, and the voices of merchants and shoppers alike rang out like song beneath the sweeping canopy of the leaf-ceiling and the rising ranks of higher tiers overhead.

To all sides, market stalls and peddlers selling from packs and handcarts created a maze of narrow paths between them. The vendors were Ilvani, and locals by their look. Their customers were a mix of the forest folk and travelers on the long road that ran between the eastern forest and the great Ilvani cities at the Yewnwood's heart. A good number of rangers walked easy among them, armed with bow and blade. The soldiers of the Ilvani realms, aloof and deadly.

Cass caught the nods of greeting as they passed, the careful respect of a trade-city's folk, accustomed to strangers. She returned each pleasantry, saw Raub ignore them. From across the market, voices called out the virtues of silks and leatherwork, stonework and jewelry, harvest fruit and fresh nut-bread. The scent of this filled the air around them, and reminded Cass that it was a week since she had eaten anything but dried rations on the road. Successive flights of narrow stairs led to higher platforms and terraces above them, their balconies spilling over with laughter and song, and the scent of honey mead and roast meat. Beyond those were shaded terraces with what looked to be walls of wicker and woven bark. Apartments, Cass guessed, rising high into the cool Yewnwood night.

She shifted closer to Raub as they walked, spoke low to his ear. "I never took you as being one from such a place."

Raub didn't look over. "What did you take me for?"

"One of the city Ilvani," she said. "You seemed at home in Yewnyr. You must have been there a while."

He said nothing in response, changing course through the crowd. Rising ahead, wrapped tight around the bole of a massive yewn split and regrown as two intertwining trunks, a wide staircase of grey wood was their destination.

But all at once, he slowed. Cass was beside him, catching as he had a sudden ripple of anticipation spreading through the crowd, not sure where it started. All around them, conversation suddenly flagged. Cass saw Raub's hands drift to the hilt of sword and dirk beneath his cloak, but she couldn't mark the threat he felt. Couldn't catch his eye.

Down the grey staircase, a white-cloaked figure was descending. A woman, older, Cass judged at first by the slowness of her step. But as the figure stepped out of shadow, she saw a young Ilvani face, silver hair hanging to frame eyes that blazed gold and violet in the light.

The woman was limping, a white-and-silver walking stick in her hand as she made her way carefully across the market court. Like a wave, the crowd pushed back from her. The Ilvani vendors nodded with familiarity, an almost universal reverence in their gaze. The local buyers did the same, the other folk of the market looking on with interest. Sensing a significance to the woman's appearance as they fell back to watch.

A wooden bench appeared from somewhere, set down carefully where the silver-haired woman stopped near a wide cistern, spellcraft animating the bubbling flow of its water this high above the ground. She nodded thanks as she sat.

There was a voice at Cass's ear suddenly, a hand tugging at the shoulder of her cloak. The girl who had slipped up from behind as they walked was young, slender as the Ilvani tended to be where she slipped close between them to match their pace. Cass always found it hard to judge the age of the graceful forest folk. She guessed at eight years in the girl's height, though the pale face seemed younger, set within a heart-shaped frame of golden hair.

Cass had to grab the sleeve of Raub's cloak to stop him, watching his dark gaze beneath the hood as the girl raised a well-laden wicker basket. On the air came the sudden scent of spring berries and sweet spices Cass couldn't name. The buttery aroma of still-warm pies drifted up in faint traces of steam caressed by the golden light. The girl peeled back the clean white cloth that covered them.

"Cakes and pastry," she called in a clear voice, overly loud as the crowd stilled. "Fresh baked, my lady and sir. The best in Anthila." A jangle of coins came from her apron pocket as she bowed low, waiting for a nod from them both before she rose again. The mark of one brought up in servitude, Cass noted, most likely to the baker whose wares she carried now. But from all around, she could feel the sense of anticipation.

Across from her, the silver-haired woman unslung a lyre from beneath her cloak. Its strings gleamed in the golden light, its wood varnished black and set with filigree in white.

The girl dipped deftly into the basket with one hand, which she brought up holding a trio of stuffed pastries no larger than her thumb. Distracted, Cass accepted one. She took a bite and felt a sudden rush of summer. She tasted the sweet nectar of honey and wildflowers, felt a warmth thread through her that pushed away the advancing chill of the night.

The silver-haired troubadour bowed low, grimacing subtly as she shifted her injured leg. She began without speaking, made no introduction to a crowd that obviously knew her. Her fingers plucked out a gentle melody on the strings, a silver echo that rippled slowly through the silence.

"Try these," Cass whispered to Raub as she took another pastry. But her words were cut off by an expression on his face that chilled her. He was staring at the bard, seemingly caught up in the song with a degree of rapt attention that echoed that of the vendors and travelers around them. She realized that his hands were shaking.

"The pastry is my master's own creation, my lady." The girl spoke now in a bright whisper, glancing to the bard but ignoring the music. "From the ancient forest lore of our folk, a recipe known to none but the Ilvani."

Cass only nodded, watching Raub as he stepped erratically away from her. He stared around him as if he was searching for something.

The girl seemed not to notice the warrior's mood. She looked to Cass expectantly, silver brows arched above eyes the green of rain-washed spring leaves. A nod signaled the girl to scoop up another dozen of the delicacies, which were quickly wrapped in smooth white paper and slipped into Cass's hands.

"One silver, if it please you, lady."

As if the girl's voice had broken some spell that held him rapt, Raub suddenly tore himself from the view before him. He met Cass's gaze for a moment, but in response to the question there, he turned quickly away, tossing the girl a coin as he went. But he saw Cass stretch her hand out, catch it in midair. She passed the girl a silver from her other hand, and it wasn't until she tossed Raub back his payment that he noticed its weight as he should have the first time.

If the back-and-forth confused the girl, she didn't show it, nodding thanks to both of them as she slipped away into the crowd. The coin Raub had pulled absently from his purse wasn't silver, but the cold platinum whose worth gave it no value anywhere outside the largest Human cities. But even as he turned away from the girl, he stopped short, staring wide-eyed. The coin slipped from his hand.

The shimmer of the Clearmoon's light flared in a rush of wind that scoured the trees overhead, sent a sudden gust of golden leaves to the air.

Raub saw the ghost.

His gaze flitted past the troubadour again, heart tripping heavy in his chest. In her face, shining through for just a moment, he saw a flash of the one who was gone. The silver hair, the gold and violet eyes were common enough among his people. But where he watched those eyes, he saw in them the gaze of a friend dead for six years. A shaking reflection, blurred as if caught by poorly polished steel.

The name came unbidden to his mind, forced itself out through all the will that kept it hidden. *Tajomynar.*

Raub stared in disbelief. If the ghost had a sister, the bard might have been her. However, Tajomynar was the older of two sons, both of whom followed Raub that night long ago. Pride of father and family, one of the oldest lines of Anthila and the northeast wood.

It was a mistake coming back, he thought, and a sudden fear rooted deep inside him that he couldn't name. Nothing for him here. A useless errand clouded by the anger of six years and his need for revenge against a dead man. Revenge in the name of all the other dead. The faces in the silver water.

Revenge on the dead, for the dead. A fool's game.

"Are you all right?" Cass asked at his shoulder, and Raub felt himself pulled back. He met her gaze for a moment, turned quickly away, pacing toward the grey stairs and trusting her to follow.

Cass scooped the platinum from the ground where it had fallen. She tossed it to the cart of a bookseller who seemed not to notice her as she passed, listening like all the rest. Behind them, the silver tones of the lyre fell away to silence as they climbed.

Cass had turned her back on the wealth of platinum in the dark aftermath of their escape from Eltolitinus. But even then, she found herself in possession of more riches than she had ever imagined. It was a thing she would never get used to. A thing she never wanted. Watching Raub drink himself into an ever-deeper state of darkness over the past months, she came to understand that she wasn't alone in that.

With the other survivors, they spent a week in Mooncastle, Myrnan's central keep, whose ruling mages were the custodians of the hidden entrance that was the ruins' Black Stair. They had healed, and they had given their thanks to fate or their gods, and they had divided the spoils of those four weeks beneath the earth. Cass took two handfuls each of gold and silver, then packed up the rest of her one-eleventh share of coin and gems whose luster was a haze of blood to her weary eyes.

She had to strain to lift the bag when she was done, but she handed it over to the mercenary boss who called himself Lárow. He knew most of those who died, or so it seemed by the darkness in his manner each time they interred what remained of them. Cairns of cold stone marked where they fell, deep in those ancient catacombs that no blessing of sunlight would ever touch.

Quietly, Cass asked him if he could arrange for the families of the dead to share out what she didn't need. Lárow had simply nodded, adding Cass's bag to a laden leather pack. Before she and Raub left that night, she saw him pass the pack on to a trio of boys, fourteen summers on the oldest. One of them was crying, but in his eyes, she thought she sensed the grim determination of the sword fighter cut down by an arcane nightmare none of them had seen, a flurry of spectral blades hacking him to ribbons as he screamed.

Jeray was the fallen fighter's name, or so she thought. She hadn't had time to remember it. But it was then that she realized the mercenary boss had already given up his own share of the ruins' blood money for the same purpose. He looked up then to see her watching, but Cass didn't speak to him, didn't ask his reasons. She didn't give him a chance to ask her own.

She was reminded of that in Hypriot, when that first week of taverns told her that Raub had no idea why he kept his full share of the spoils. That realization cast a dark shadow in her, as it forced her to dwell unwilling for a time within her own mind. Forced her to think on her own reasons for taking the road to Myrnan, for following Raub and the barbarian from the Free City as she had.

At the time, she told herself that if anyone ever asked, she would simply echo Raub's reasons for the month-long trek east and across the water and beneath the dark earth. But in the aftermath, as she watched him collapse in on himself from an ever-increasing distance, Cass had come to understand that Raub's reasons for venturing into the shadow beneath the Sorcerers' Isle were something she might never know.

She took only one trophy from the ruins. The handaxe she now carried, which had turned the Myrnan loremasters pale when they inspected it. As with all such forays into the ruins named for the mage whose hubris and power had built the island-castle, then reduced it to rubble and ash, their group's exploration of the dungeons of Eltolitinus was sanctioned by the Myrlins, the master arcanists of Mooncastle. Some of the relics of those lost depths were claimed even before they were found, she knew. More than a few would-be fortune-seekers were distressed to see their most valuable finds stripped away in the end. Declared too dangerous to be set loose in the wider world.

Raub had lost a ring to the Myrlins, a band of linked platinum facets with a blue-red gem inset with strange symbols. It seemed no more than an arcane trifle, some dweomer of protection within it, but the masters had seized it at a glance. They wrapped it with thick layers of wool and lead foil, none of them touching it. They handed him a purse of platinum coin in exchange, Raub adding it to the fortune that was his now.

Whatever power was in the axe they called the Reaper, it had scared the loremasters, even as their unknown code gave them no claim on it. Walking past the silent warning of their eyes, Cassatra followed Raub out of Mooncastle and south for Claygate. That day was bright, she remembered, the fields to the south shining green. In Raub, she thought she felt a sense that the experience of passing through peril and winning its riches should change things.

In her own heart, she felt a conviction that nothing ever could change.

She thought about her own reasons, the real reasons she wouldn't speak of. A thing she had never shared with Raub, never shared with anyone. The reason that was the absence of any reason in the end.

When a person has little enough to live for, she thought darkly, the decisions become easy.

♦ ♦ ♦

The terraces of the forest-home showed no sign of ending. As they climbed the grey stairs, Cass began to make out ever more distant lights. Faint where they flashed through sudden breaks in the tree-canopy, then gone again. She ate as they walked, guessing by the sureness of his step that Raub knew where he was going. However, it took a serious effort to commit to memory the twisting route of terrace paths and smaller stairways that saw the noise and light of the market fall away behind them. All around, the Ilvani of Anthila were making their way along the same stairs and terraced paths, drifting slowly, voices quiet where they paid no mind to the visitors in their midst.

Between the terraces, rope bridges radiated out like the anchoring arms of a spider's web. These were little more than lattices of thin cord, set with wooden tiles and flanked by braided stays that served as railing and guy-line to either side. Raub crossed each bridge with practiced ease, Cass a little more cautious as she followed. In the empty space between terraces, she saw the wood spread above and below them. Not just the branches of the great trees rising from the forest floor below, but trees grafted to those branches as living pillars.

By their look, the lower tiers they passed through were laborers' domiciles, possessed of the Ilvani grace in their architecture but consistent in their simplicity. The dwellings of the Ilvani had an almost ephemeral quality, with walls of tightly woven wicker set on frames of loomed branches and bark. Behind those wicker screens, lights glowed to cast ghostly shadows through the haze of leaves, the bright green of new buds showing through darker green and shed gold. A yellow-shadowed carpet crunched beneath their feet as they passed through the high branches, sudden flurries of leaves falling like slow rain whenever the wind picked up.

They passed from the working wards onto wide paths flanking better-appointed apartments, and as they made their way ever higher, Cass felt Raub's silence grow more oppressive. A nagging uncertainty was growing in her, and she glanced back over her shoulder more than once. She saw no eyes on them, though, and as they continued to climb, the number of people they passed slowly waned. In the end, they were alone along the wood-tiled paths of a multileveled bower, staggered white walls rising in the distance to either side.

They had traveled more distance horizontally than vertically, but even so, Cass found herself having to guess how high they were. Beneath them, the tiers and terraces of the forest home were a widening web, crossing and recrossing each other, so that one would have been challenged to find a place to fall straight through to the ground. The night air was cooler now, the light of the lower tiers dimmed to a golden shadow that limned each terrace's edge. But in its place came the light of the Clearmoon, filtered through the screen of leaves, and telling Cass that they drew near to the very tops of the trees.

The apartments in the upper tiers were gated in a way unseen in the wards below. Beyond barriers of vine-woven branches, thickly latticed, their wicker walls were set with windows of colored glass that shimmered with the light of evenlamps and flickering fires. More than once, Cass saw the figures of guards standing at attention before gates of ironwood, delicately sculpted and firmly barred.

No one was in sight at the narrow gate before which Raub finally stopped. The barrier wall into which it was set was too thickly latticed to see through, heavy with vines and gently curved to follow the path that twisted between similar gates, other residences, on its opposite sides. Beyond the wall, higher tiers were anchored with rope stays to the topmost branches of the great tree they stood upon. Its apex was hung with a single lamp, blazing like a star in a winter sky.

"We need to climb," Raub said, and before Cass could respond, he was at the wall, easily scaling the rough ladder its branches made. She scanned the wide path to both sides, but they were alone. Shifting carefully through the shadows, she followed Raub up, watched him swing across and over to the other side.

Then she saw the sign at the gate. Faint at first, then suddenly bright beneath moon's-light that flared as leaves shimmered with the rising wind. A single-edged longblade in the Ilvani style, wreathed in flame. Gleaming for a moment, then gone again.

Beyond the wall stood a garden on three levels. Wide stairs wound around massive branch-pillars, their bark rubbed smooth and gleaming gold. The great terraces stood open to the air, their walls of wicker and rope furled to show the house they once made, standing empty and dark now. Raub stood in the middle of that first shadowed space, the flora there overgrown and unkempt.

Here and there, self-supporting walls of latticed branches hedged in overgrown paths. A dozen strides away, a huge elm stood dead within a low rise of earth. Thick branches rose to almost touch the screen of leaves sweeping down from the great trees above, its twisted roots digging deep into the floor of the terrace like black claws. Cloistered beds of flowers in a dozen varieties Cass had never seen before hissed as their spent seed heads twisted in the wind.

"Welcome home," she said at last, and there was a measure of sadness in her voice that she hadn't intended. If Raub heard it, he gave no sign.

He pushed the hood back for the first time since their arrival. From within his cloak, he pulled a flask Cass recognized. Ice wine from the winter vineyards north of Hypriot, subtly potent and most often sold by the vial. She watched Raub drink deep, shook her head when he offered the flask to her.

"It's beautiful here," Cass said, because there was nothing else to say. Raub turned from her, pacing toward the shadow of the dead elm. Beneath the tree, a faint trickle of water sounded from a neglected fountain. Its wide pool of delicately carved wood was overflowing with rotting leaves, sending a narrow stream to the ground below. "So why did you leave?"

"It doesn't matter." At his belt, Raub's hand had slipped to the black-shrouded shortsword. His knuckles were white, Cass saw.

"Then why come back?"

"That matters less."

"A destination turns travel into a journey, you said." In her mind, she felt for something else to add, found only silence.

"Why did you come?"

Once, on that long road to the Sorcerers' Isle, she asked him about the black blade. She had seen it, of course. Always carried, never drawn.

"It was my father's," he told her then, and Cass had taken it for an heirloom. A thing to be worn but not used. That changed when she saw him with it that night on the ship that carried them back to the mainland.

Alone in the cabin they shared, he must have thought her asleep, carefully unsheathing the bare blade in the faint light of the Clearmoon slanting through the porthole window. Even from the corner of her eye, she saw the edge the shortsword carried. Judging by the well-stained leather of the haft, it had seen much use. Except for the Ilvani glyphs along its length, the sword bore no adornment, but in the manner of the oldest dweomer, its glassy steel glowed a sickly blue in the shadows.

In the garden, Cass felt a chill. Old ghosts, she thought, flitting through the shadows of the windblown leaves. But even as she made to speak, Raub wheeled on her with a start. Both hands went to her cloak as he pulled her back toward the fountain, dragged her down with him as he dropped to his knees.

"Do you hear it?" he hissed, and in a heartbeat, Cass saw a change come over him, the dark eyes burning in the haze of moon's-light. With a chill, she registered the look on his face as the same she had seen in the market tier before. The same uncertainty rooting deep and sudden in him, creating a confusion she could feel.

"Hear what?"

And even as she spoke, Cass caught the faint echo of singing coming soft on the night air. A woman's voice, the language unknown. It drifted through the stillness for a moment, quickly swallowed by the wind.

In that brief echo, Raub heard the same music that had woken him in the night, a ghostly cry from forgotten dreams. Each way he moved, he heard it louder, felt it twisting in his pounding heart like a knife. His hands were at Cass's cloak again, both of them still kneeling. And as she set her own hands on top of his, she felt a great darkness, felt all the bitter spite of wine and anger focused as tightly on her as a hunter's arrow.

"This shame is my burden," Raub said with sudden anger.

There was an edge in his voice that Cass had only rarely heard. She responded, cautious. "If it was a burden you could carry on your own, you wouldn't have brought me along."

"I did not ask you…"

"Yes, you did. You might not know it, but you did. You can hide behind your silence, behind your secrecy, whatever it is that keeps Anthila something you never talked about by day, yet can't wait to confess in drink and darkness. But you didn't want to take this road alone, and so here I am."

Raub released his hold on her, pushing back in his anger as he lurched to his feet. He paced a wide circle through the dead grass. Calmly, Cass rose to follow.

"We carry our own pasts easily enough." She checked the uncertainty in her own voice, forced herself to speak evenly. "But none of us are made to carry the lives of others. Your father," she said, but even as she did, she heard the words choked off. She felt light-headed suddenly. The weight of her own secrets pressed down with a too-familiar pressure, breaking through the veneer of quiet resolve.

She heard the song again. Steel strings this time, and the voice ringing out pure and high, quavering in a gentle play of sound that slowly formed itself into words in no language Cass had ever heard. She looked for some sign of recognition in Raub, but he seemed beyond listening where he stumbled, turning back to her suddenly.

"The Ilvani live by codes. Honor and principle, strength and speed, bow and blade. Ways of life passed down to each new generation. The Ilvani know their histories back five hundred lifetimes. This knowledge is beyond you."

"I didn't mean…" Cass began, but Raub was pressing her now, his voice harsh.

"The Ilvani invented sorcery, but that greatest art was muddied and tamed by Human hands. For the thousand years that Empire bound and bent the Elder Kingdoms beneath its banner, the Yewnwood Ilvani never capitulated, never took up the Human flag. But in matters of magic, we held to Imperial rule by the threat of war. Thirty millennia is the record of our culture. Ten thousand generations of power that capitulated to upstart Human dominion in the end."

Cass felt despair suddenly, her strength breaking as she tried to fight it. Raub's eyes were a dull fire, burning black. A father gone, a lifetime lost. Something twisted in her gut, knife-sharp.

"My sixteenth year," Raub whispered, "I called four friends to my side." Cass heard the dangerous tone of his voice, felt a deepening anguish there. "And with stealth and sword and the bravado of youth, we challenged a tyrant in full view of the people, with the thought that our example would inspire them to rise against his darkness. You cannot understand."

The song was louder now, the wind carrying it from the tier below or adjacent, Cass couldn't tell anymore. "Then help me understand," she said. "As a friend."

In the time since they met, she and the brooding warrior had developed an easy familiarity between them. In following Raub from Yewnyr both times, Cass understood with a sudden and unexplained clarity that she had followed a deeper urge to push past what they were and into territory unfamiliar. But as she saw that truth, she further understood that she didn't yet know the name of that urge, or why it had spoken to her that first time two years before. She didn't know why it spoke to her a week before today, when she awoke before dawn and met him at the Free City's Thirty-League Gate.

"My friends are dead," Raub whispered. "I killed them all..."

The pain in those words hung in the empty space between them. The wind was blowing hard now, a shroud of golden leaves shimmering dead in the moon's-light. The terrace rocked gently like the deck of a great ship, its foundation limbs shifting beneath their feet.

Cass searched for words, but none came. Raub was silent for a long while. When he finally spoke, his voice carried a weariness beyond any darkness they had walked through. Greater than the self-destruction by which he once hoped to burn that darkness away.

"Our road together is done, I think."

He turned from her without a word, the hood pulled up as he tossed a bag to her feet. She knew it was coin by its sound as it hit. "For whatever debts I owe you," he said, and the insult struck with a force stronger than any blow.

He didn't look back, Cassatra staring in stark disbelief. She felt an anger close her voice off, felt a wordless challenge rising in the shadow of that anger. But before she could move, a voice rang out from the darkness behind her.

"You killed them!"

The words were Ilvani, dark and raw as the face they issued from. The gate they had climbed over was open now, an aging matron there. Her hair was the white of new snow, her features shadowed by the light of soft-flaring evenlamps in the hands of the figures behind her.

Cass hadn't heard them approach. She hadn't heard the gate open beyond the screen of green walls, but she slipped behind one of those walls now. It was impossible to get a full count of the bodies that swarmed in that light, but it was a number she didn't like. They were surging forward now, silent as death except for the hiss of their footsteps through the leaf-littered terrace floor. All their focus was on Raub, Cass watching for any sign that she'd been spotted as they pushed past her shadowed shelter. As she crouched low, her hand made its way instinctively to the Reaper at her belt.

With the words, Raub stumbled back as if he'd been struck, a fear in him that Cass had never seen before. He wrapped the cloak tight around himself, fumbling to keep his weapons and the black-shrouded shortsword from sight as the crowd circled, the aged woman stepping close.

"You, boy!" she hissed through cold tears. "You think these lost years can make difference enough to hide you from the kin of those whose blood you spilled?" With a speed that belied her age, she shot her hand forth, tore the hood from Raub's head. "Talrab, you called yourself, but you were Thrasus Talmaraub and your father's son!"

Cass shifted back quietly, still unseen. But though she waited for Raub to speak, he tried simply to slip past the old woman, only to find his way blocked by the crowd suddenly pushing forward. Surrounding him as if in response to some unseen signal.

In his eyes, Cass saw a sorrow that cut her as sharp as any knife.

"Your sire lies in shadow now and you despoil his honor by returning as a thief in the night! His line broken by your betrayal! No son to sing *thilanatir*!"

Cass's understanding of Ilvani was good, but the last was a word she didn't know. *Ghost's song,* she translated it as, but she didn't know its meaning.

"You cannot touch him now!" The woman's voice was a sibilant hiss, a lifetime's rage twisted through it. "You cannot claim their memories as you claimed their lives in the name of dark ambition!"

With sudden force, Raub pushed his way past the wall of figures closest to him, knocking three to the ground as he leaped to the fountain. There was a frenzy of movement as the crowd surged inward, the flash of more than one blade seen in the chaos. Raub went over them, hit a low branch of the dead elm, and was climbing before they could reach him. The Clearmoon's light caught him, slanting through the faint screen of higher branches above.

Cass was on her feet, shifting carefully to keep him in view as she melted back into the deep shadows. From the topmost branch of the elm, Raub jumped for empty air, snagged the lowest of the greater overhanging branches, and was climbing fast. His cloak billowed around him like the wings of a hawk in flight.

She saw him stop. She saw him seek her out beyond the edge of the chaos, the crowd raging below. The woman's voice was joined by a dozen others, screaming the same name, unfamiliar to Cass.

"Talmaraub! You killed them! They followed you and your vain dream and found only death in the end!"

From his high perch, Raub met Cass's gaze for just a moment, then he was gone into the trees. He vanished to the shadows ahead of a knife flashing harmlessly past, a half-dozen figures attempting to follow his ascent. They would never catch him, Cass knew. She had seen Raub climb before, a sureness to his movement above ground that she didn't share.

In the midst of the chaos, against the wailing of the woman's voice for six years' grieving and a son lost, Cass realized that the distant music was gone.

As suddenly as it began, it was done. The white-haired woman was on her knees, her wailing voice reaching Cass with a knife-edge sting that told her its pain was all too real. But in the movements of those who comforted the woman, those who had moved against Raub, she saw a strange slowness.

All the rage of a moment before had been drained from them suddenly, as if a tap was turned off. Cass saw anger flicker to uncertainty, then to indifferent sorrow as the members of the erstwhile mob stared at each other, uncertain as to what they should do, where they should go.

Their words were real enough, Cass piecing together a half-dozen conversations within earshot. A half-dozen versions of the story of what had happened six years before.

The bravos who thought to climb after Raub were already returning, one of them dropping to the ground a dozen strides from where she stood. Without hesitation, Cass stepped out from the shadows, walked calmly toward him. He was a smith to judge by the black of his hands and the tight ropes of muscle wrapping his arms. The hunting blade in his hand was one of the long knives of the forest Ilvani, weighted for throwing and as deadly as a wyvern's sting.

He looked up, gazed at Cass with blank eyes. She nodded in greeting, stepped past him and walked for the gate in plain sight of a dozen others.

No one tried to stop her as she went.

◆　◆　◆

The descent back down to the market was quicker by far than the long walk up, but Cass lingered at the edge of that first terrace for a while. She found a seat at an open tavern, drank a half-goblet of bittersweet berry wine slowly as her gaze traced across the crowd. Not for the figure she was intent on speaking to, who she had spotted almost as soon as she sat down. Instead, she watched the sellers, the local patrons, the drinkers laughing where they lined a half-dozen carved trestle tables.

In all those faces now, she saw the same shadow. A thing she would never have noticed before the events in the high garden, but which she looked for now and recognized with disturbing ease. Not in the travelers, though. No sign of that darkness in the scouts and merchants and wanderers who would be part of life in Anthila for a day, or a week. But as with the smith-turned-warrior, all the locals carried a kind of distance in their gaze. A weight threaded every conversation, every market transaction, every gale of laughter. A shadow passing across every set of eyes in the forest-home.

Every set, that is, save one.

Cass saw the golden hair through the crowd, dropping a handful of copper to the table as she slipped easily toward the girl and her basket and the sweet scent of butter and spice. She saw a smile of recognition as she approached.

"I trust you enjoyed your pastries, my lady." The young baker's apprentice beamed.

"They were beyond compare, child."

"Then take more for your journey. My master's recipes keep well for the road."

"Why do you presume I travel?"

"By your garb and accent only, my lady, and no offense to you." The girl cast her face down as if in apology. But Cass saw now that the green eyes were upturned, the clear gaze never leaving her. She hadn't noticed before.

"Do you have a name?"

"I am Pheánei, my lady."

Cass looked away for a moment, turning her face from the girl as if she was scanning the crowd. "Then I will have a dozen more of your pastries, if you please, Pheánei." She spoke carefully, voice clear.

When she turned back, the girl was still smiling, oblivious to what had been said out of her sight.

"Will you have more, lady?"

Cass mouthed the words without speaking aloud. *You cannot hear, can you?*

A flicker of shame passed through the girl's gaze like storm clouds across the sun. Cass saw the fear in the green eyes as Pheánei stumbled back, but she stopped her with a hand to the shoulder. As she had forced herself to so often in her youth, she smiled.

"In the place were I grew up, there were many like you. Born without the senses of other children, and no gold for the healers who value coin more than the life they claim to protect. This is no cause for shame. On the contrary, you are very brave."

The girl nodded, uncertain. The green eyes were impossibly bright against the pale skin, making her look even younger than Cass might have originally taken her for. She knew enough of Pheánei's culture to know the kind of hardship under which she lived. Physical perfection was an ideal the Ilvani lived by more so than most folk.

"I was not born this way," the girl said dutifully. "But when I was small, we lived in a village away from the forest-home. A fever came of some dark magic. It stole away sound and song from me. My parents died. My brother, too."

Cass felt something twist in her gut.

"My family, too, was lost to me." The words tumbled out without warning, past the stark silence within which they were normally held. Cass saw Pheánei's expression change, a glimmer of sudden light in the green eyes.

"I miss them very much," the girl said. "But even more, I miss the song of the wind and the birds. My mother sang with the wind and birds, and I dream sometimes that if I could but hear them again, I would hear her voice once more."

The green gaze was fixed on some vision far beyond the golden light and the shifting crowd. Cass's hand was shaking. She squeezed it to stillness as she nodded, thoughtful.

"I do not remember my mother sing. I do not remember her face, but I dream of her all the same."

The girl shrugged, the weight of a sudden sadness settling in her. "It is only a dream," she said. "It is not the world. A dream cannot fix what is broken in me."

"We carry more than one world inside us, Pheánei. And we are all broken in our own way, and the only healing that counts is that which we make for ourselves." The words sounded strange in Cass's ears. Words she had often thought but never said, she realized. Things she knew but was afraid to hear.

The girl nodded. And then she let the moment pass as if she was conscious suddenly of the unheard market around her. Remembering the task that was set for her by whatever merchant had taken her in, most likely for the debts her parents left her. She proffered the basket again. "Will you have more, lady?"

"I will, child. And what is more, I will gladly pay extra for the answers to certain questions." She patted the purse at her belt, the comfortable jingle of coin there.

Cass could read in Pheánei's expression that she didn't understand, but the girl nodded with the eagerness of one for whom every extra copper made a difference.

"On the high stair," Cassatra said, "there is a fine terrace house that stands dark tonight, and for many nights past by the look of it. Its gate is marked with a burning sword. Who lived there?"

"That is Garania Hall, my lady." Pheánei's voice carried a sudden echo of sadness. "It was the place of our forest-home master Thrasus Talmaraub Garania. He was master of Anthila for many years, until he died a half-year past."

"I am sorry to hear that. I have another question, though you might well be too young to know. Did this Master Thrasus have a son?"

The wind picked up again, a cloud of golden leaves sweeping past them, cold. "I am young, lady, but all the forest-home knows the story of our late master Thrasus, seneschal of Anthila. His was a life of hardship, from which he drew the wisdom by which he ruled our realm justly and fairly from long before I was born."

The girl turned full somber suddenly. She spoke with the easy familiarity of one repeating a story often told. "Our late Seneschal Thrasus had but one son who was his only family when his wife passed. He was named Talmaraub for his father. But this son was the dark shadow of his father in every way, unjust and scornful. The Hooded Hawk, he called himself. A masked outlaw in his youth and a stain on the name of his family. A rogue and knave, he brought near-ruin on Anthila when he tried to seize his father's power by force. Those who followed him were killed, and the son was driven into exile and never seen again."

The girl's eyes were dark, an anger there suddenly. A thing born not of her own heart, Cass knew, but of this story she retold that would have been instilled in her since she was old enough to understand it. The Ilvani fascination with lore, turning the legends of clan and race-kin into the fire of the heart and a passion strong as steel.

"When the traitor-son fled, he carried with him not only the mark of his own crimes and his family's shame, but the past of the Anthiliar. We who range and shepherd these great woods from the bright lights of our forest-home. The blade Valaendar is the Kin-Sword in the high tongue of the Ilvani. A weapon of ancient craft and older magic, predating the arrival of the Empire in the east and carried from hand to hand along the line of the rulers of these woods. From his father's own hand, the Hooded Hawk stole away the blade that was the symbol of the Anthiliar, and it is lost to us still."

"A black shortsword," Cass said. "Leaf-edged and marked with ancient glyphs of power. Ever-sharp and glowing with a pale light."

The girl nodded, surprised. "You know the story, lady?"

On Myrnan, not long before they took the Black Stair down into shadow and madness, the Gracian warrior Dilaon asked Raub in a quiet moment why he had never regaled them with tales of his own family. All the clan legends that every other Ilvani the mercenary had ever met seemed to carry with them like necessary baggage.

"Not all stories are worth telling," Raub had said then.

Not long after, in a night built on fear and the strength of dark ale, he had told Cass alone the only story she ever heard from him. The story that stuck with her still.

"Another question," Cass said to the girl. "Did you learn that story from the bard who plays in the market? The woman with silver hair?" She spoke with a degree of casualness that she realized she didn't need, the girl reading only the impassive inflection of her lips.

"She is no mere bard, my lady," the girl said brightly. "She is Halessi, our new seneschal of Anthila. She is our lord and protector, and she is very beautiful."

"Indeed she is, and her songs as well."

The girl was suddenly wistful. "I read our lady's speech when she sings," she said, "so that I know the stories though I cannot know the song. For many years, she played for the pleasure of our late seneschal Thrasus, and when she plays, she holds all the crowd rapt, as you saw. We get many bards in Anthila, traveling the forest road, but my lady Halessi's songs are special."

"Indeed they are. I would tell her so myself, would that I knew where to find her."

"I can show you, lady," the girl said happily, caught up so much in the feeling of her own importance to Cass's questions that she had seemingly forgotten the market, forgotten her life for just a moment. But as she turned to lead, Cass stopped her with a hand to the shoulder.

"Only directions, if you please. It is best if Halessi and I speak alone."

Despite her not hearing them, the girl seemed to feel the dangerous undertone in the words this time. She nodded, uncertain, but she told Cass what she needed to know.

When it was done, Cass went not for her purse but for the leather bag Raub had dropped, slung now from her belt. She slipped it into the girl's hands, watched her react to its unexpected weight.

"Find a healer, Pheánei," she said. "Hear your mother sing." Then she kissed the golden brow and slipped away.

The girl watched her go, curiosity overcoming confusion quickly enough as she tugged at the drawstrings of the pouch. Within was the gleam of cold platinum coin of a lost age, catching and reflecting the golden light of the market in green and wide-open eyes.

◆　◆　◆

The necropolis was bright in the moon's-light, the ancient vines that marked its edges each as thick around as Raub's waist. The wood of the open cemetery's half-dozen wide terraces was worn smooth with age, bleached to silver-grey by long years of rain and sun. The main gate was a rare ghost yewn, rising on a split trunk. A great white arch of living wood, its appearance suggested that it had somehow been grown from the sky down where Raub slipped beneath it.

Beyond the hedge of yewn into which the gate was set, a garden spread. The path that led into it was overgrown with muskflower and sun creeper, whose tight-clustered pods shimmered like fireflies in the night. Within the maze of overhanging branches that swallowed the Clearmoon's glow, evenlamps shone pale green through the screen of broad leaves around them.

Before, from his high vantage point above Garania Hall, Raub had watched and waited what seemed a long while to see Cass exit through the open gate of his father's house, his childhood home. The frenzied altercation there was the last thing he expected, and he felt all its uncertainty rooting deep in his mind as he slipped easily through the great canopy of branches crossing above the high ward. He fought to clear his head, feeling a kind of shame at his unexplained anger and the dark sorrow that had driven it.

Even before he climbed, he had seen Cass reach for the axe beneath her cloak as she backed away from him. An instinct against the unexpected agitation of the crowd. Sudden assault, a selectively brutal response, and a fast exit was a tactical scenario he and she were well-versed in, making use of it in more taverns and roadhouses over the previous two years than he cared to remember.

In the end, she hadn't been forced to fight her way out of the discord he left for her. But even as he waited for her to come close enough that he might call out, Cass turned west along the path that wound between the high houses of Anthila's nobles. Heading back the way the two of them had first come, he realized. And even as he did, he understood that it was better that way.

As he slipped through the shadows, Raub held the black-wrapped shortsword before him. It felt strange removed from his belt. Its weight and shape against his hip for the span of all those seasons were things he had long grown accustomed to.

Carefully, he unspooled the black gauze that wrapped it, catching the scent of road dust and well-oiled leather. He tossed the cloth to the tall grass, and the blade that emerged from the rough scabbard beneath it flashed silver in the moon's-light, then flared even brighter with the blue light born in the heart of its glassy steel. It was a shortsword of the Ilvani, its edge marked with delicate glyphs that he couldn't read. One of the ancient tongues, out of the south. His father would have known it, but had never shared its meaning.

Talmaraub was the name he had been born with. His father's name, and a thing that no one outside Anthila knew. A thing he never told Cass.

As a child, he shortened it to Talrab, which in the forest speech of the northern Ilvani was the black-hooded hawk. This was a fist-sized raptor that flew in flocks through the shadowed trees, as Raub and his friends had once run. They were as fearless then as the talrab, which would attack in swarms of a dozen to take down hare and ground squirrels six times its size, harrying with beak and claw and sheer perseverance.

Raub felt his blood beating fast at his neck, in his chest. He cursed himself for his weakness, not for the first time.

He felt the weight of the blade in his hand. He remembered the first night he held it.

He remembered the pledge he made then, to leave that blade in his father's dead heart.

With a care born of the fear that had dogged him for long years, he used the sword's light to make his way along winding paths. Dark arches of branch and moon's-shadow twisted overhead, and where the sun creeper shone, it showed the spirit markers woven of living branches into the shapes of ancient Ilvani glyphs. He saw the open biers of bleached bone, whose flesh with each passing day had been consumed and rendered back to the world that spawned it.

When he turned his back on Cass, Raub had kept climbing. Up beyond the highest tier of noble's houses that had once been his world, to ascend to the last tiers whose black-stained staircases wound up to the silent porches of the dead. Bone and ash were the paths he walked on now. Bone and dust were the dirt and loam from which the flowers of the necropolis bloomed in vivid hues through all seasons, drawing warmth and nourishment from the lives laid to rest here.

This custom was the reason the Ilvani kept their traditions of death a closely guarded secret. Not for the forest folk were the ways of burial or burning, sending the dead to the dark or the fire. The Ilvani way was the sense of connection to the life of the wood. The Ilvani way was the eternal transition of seasons, and the ceremonies that marked the point at which life ended by setting down the future's roots.

At each wrong turn and wild-grown dead end, Raub used the shortsword to hack away at screens of creeper and saplings, its touch barely felt as it sliced wood and vine as though cutting through water. Beyond the last of those screens, pale in the moon's-light, he found the spirit markers he sought.

The Ilvani way was thilanatir. The ghostsong. A ritual of binding that connected all the truths of a person's life, and by which the spirits of the dead would be joined to the memories of the living in a magic older than the fallen Empire of the Lothelecan, older than all Ilvani lore. A magic older than time.

To make the ghostsong, friends and family, fathers and daughters, mothers and sons would sing of the deeds done in life by the dead, drawing forth the spirit of those who had passed on. Memory, the Ilvani said, was the manifestation of the spirit in flesh. And so by the singing of the ghostsong, those left behind would seal away a fragment of the fallen within themselves.

Even before he fled his people and his life, Raub hadn't believed it. Not exactly. Still, he understood the greater truth of the timeless ritual, which was that the spirit possessed its own force, its own presence beyond the body by which it was confined. And so it was that for six years, he had vowed that this ghostsong would be his final gift to the father he had tried and failed to kill.

His mother's spirit marker was all but gone now, but he saw his father's set beside it in a copse whose walls were a shower of blood-red heart-vine. He was a child the first time he stood here, when his mother's woven bier had held her body for ten cycles of the Clearmoon's rites. He was an outlaw the last time he saw that bier, vines and creepers long ago grown over to consume the mortal shell that had borne his mother's grace and beauty, and to return that shell to the spirit-vault of earth and sky.

The night he fled, he named himself Raubynar, which meant the wandering hawk. Part of the name he had worn in childhood. Part of the name of a friend from that childhood who was dead now, and whose life Raub felt burning deeper into his memory each time he heard that new name spoken aloud.

Tonight, he would sing the ghostsong. He would add his voice to the chorus that told the stories that were the only things remaining now of his father's life. But the story he sung would be the one his father never told. A story that no one else would tell. His voice would be raised against the silence of the bier to curse his father's memory and spirit with the truth that only the exiled son knew.

Raub felt something cold twist through him as he stepped close. His father's body was already enclosed by its cocoon of vines, glowing faintly white with the magic by which the rites progressed. He remembered his mother's rites, all the days of silent mourning that led to the procession that had placed her here. The bier had been set with her body and its burial robes, dark to match her exotic complexion. Her rings were there, and the diadem she wore that was the gold of her eyes. These things that were closest to her were part of the rite of remembrance, and would be reclaimed in the final rites as the body crumbled. Taken by family who would bid farewell to the spirit of the dead, and who would turn away from their sorrow at last.

The darkness to Raub's features that had long set him apart from his people's fairness was his mother's. She was a wanderer, who sung him childhood stories of her travels through a dozen exotic lands. She had dwelt in all the Ilvanrand, she said, breaking nobles' hearts in each of those high courts of the forest Ilvani. But then she saw the Yewnwood and felt it claim her own heart.

Raub was never closer to her than when she was dying, and she had made him understand how the most significant artifacts of each life were central to the Ilvani rites.

An artisan's tools will be laid in his lifeless hands as he passes from flesh to dust, she said. *A ranger's bow, a hunter's rope, a warrior's blade. All the essence of life is bound up in the connection between life and the world. The things we do, the things we touch, become the memories of our actions. Impressions are imprinted on the world to create the world-memory that endures, and which will be our story when we are gone.*

He felt his mother's presence around him now as a dark haze of memory. And as he had been on the last night he came to this place, fleeing one step ahead of his father's forces and the order to bring him down dead or alive, Raub was grateful that his mother and her grace had passed before she could see what his father would become.

The shroud of glowing leaves within which the bier closed itself off was sacrosanct. It was the mark and sign of all the magic of this place, and of all the history and tradition upheld by a thousand generations of the dead consumed here.

With all the potency of that tradition pounding in his heart, Raub stepped up to his father's bier. He drove the shortsword down with all the strength of the rage that was in him, the decaying skull shattering beneath its point. He recoiled and hit again, head to foot, digging in with his heels as he slashed broadly in a single blinding-fast motion. Shroud and bier and body were hacked in two before him, this last vestige of his father's life little more than dry grass before the scythe.

With savage fury, Raub dismembered his father's corpse with the sword that was the dead man's badge of office, and whose enduring history his father had tainted with a lifetime of lies.

Valaendar was the ancestral blade of the rulers of Anthila, whose realm was the forest frontier for five days' ride to north and south. Under the Human sphere's thousand-year Imperial rule of the surrounding Elder Kingdoms, the black shortsword was little more than an heirloom. A remembrance of past glory, and of Ilvani empires against which the fifteen hundred years of the Lothelecan was the short-lived rise and fall of all other Human dominions.

The magic of the Ilvani was the magic of the unseen world, and by that magic did the necropolis reclaim the spirit of life and return it to mana once more. Body and bone, flesh and jewel, steel and stone were laid atop the bier for ten full cycles of the Clearmoon. And for each facet of the lost life that belonged to the dead, those who survived them would sing the ghostsong.

In the aftermath of Empire's fall four decades past, the blade Valaendar had become more than a symbol. By the time his father was elected seneschal in the year of Raub's birth, the power of the black shortsword had been restored by careful study and spellcraft. The old magic that would have been prohibited under the Empire, or so his father railed at every opportunity.

"Destiny denied," he called it, but it would be long years before Raub understood how the black blade's true destiny had been corrupted by his father's ambition.

That night six years past, they sought to seize that power. Raub and the four who pledged their lives alongside him, then lost those lives because he hadn't realized how far his father's malignant power had spread. Extending in ways that even the kin-faithful who worshiped the history of Valaendar would never understand.

As the black sword flashed in his hand, Raub froze.

He stepped back suddenly, staring at the grim destruction before him. The wind had slackened, his breathing the only sound.

Where he had hacked through the rotting remains on the bier, he saw his father's blackened hands. He recognized the golden ring by which his mother had been betrothed and the silver band that marked her death. Yet those hands had clutched only each other, crossed and clasped across the now-sundered chest whose wrappings were already turned to dust by the magic of this place.

Other artifacts were spread there. Scrolls of office and symbols of faith and friendship that Raub cast aside now as he tore apart the last of the funeral wrappings. He looked beneath and around the bier for the gleaming longblade that should have been there. The single memory he had come in hope of redeeming.

He raised the black shortsword again. He hacked through the tatters of remaining vines in a half-dozen places before he kicked the cloven bier over with a shriek of rage that was swallowed by the night.

Since the day he fled, Raub had yearned for this moment. For long years, he dreamed of seizing the bright blade whose magic was set in silver and white fire. A warrior's backsword that was his father's, and had been his grandfather's, and that had been carried by countless generations of his family before that. This was the sword his father's treachery denied him. The blade whose nobility and destiny his father abandoned, claiming instead the rank and rule of the black shortsword as he willingly corrupted Valaendar's name and purpose.

Had Raub been there to sing the ghostsong for his father, the ancestral blade would have lain within the bier for the mourning cycles of the Clearmoon, then been claimed by him. The Ilvani reverence for death and tradition meant that it could have been taken only by one who was heir to its legacy, but Raub was last of his line. Had anyone stolen it from this place, the protective magic of the bier would have told him so.

He clawed at the ground, hoping in vain that what he sought might simply have fallen somehow, but there was no mistake. His father's sword was gone.

Faint where the wind rose, he thought he heard the song of the moon-lit clearing.

Through the shadows came the faint echo of lyre strings, and the voice that sang in its unknown tongue.

He was wrong, Raub thought suddenly. And in the space of a heartbeat, he felt himself caught and crushed by the sudden onslaught of despair that told him he had failed. Failed in his duty, failed in his revenge, because all the hunger that fed that revenge was built on lies.

His head was pounding, throat dry. He couldn't catch his breath, unable to understand how it had all changed so quickly, how the essential piece of his vengeance had been taken from him. Did his father lose the ancestral blade? Destroy it? Cast it aside as he cast aside his son, as he cast aside his family's honor in the name of the corrupt power he had wielded through the black shortsword instead?

The memory of the silver pool in the moon-lit copse caught in his mind suddenly, his eyes burning with a rush of tears. The faces he had seen in that pool twisted around him.

Through the screen of leaves that surrounded his parents' biers, he saw the ghost watching him.

Raub felt all the breath leave him as if he'd been caught by a horse's kick. He had the black shortsword and his own emerald-hilted longsword in hand. He couldn't remember drawing the second blade as he stumbled back. He saw the young face as he had last seen it, six years before. The silver hair was long and tied back in the manner of one just past the rites of second-naming. The gold-violet eyes glimmered like the stars that shone through the translucent cast of that face.

They were five who had known each other since their first-naming. They strove in secret against dark forces, and had listened as Raub told them they were heroes, all of them.

Four had died to prove how wrong he was.

"Tajomynar…" he whispered, and he heard all the fear, all the pain of years twist through that name.

A sigh like the last breeze of summer passed between those pale lips, and Raub heard the sound twist to a whisper of fear that formed words meant only for him. A flare of white light surged and spread like the sudden coming of dawn. His hand came up to shield his eyes.

Should have kept flying, Hawk…

He felt something strike him hard across the back of the head. In the sanguine haze of his sight came ruddy laughter, bright against a looming darkness. He felt a song slip through him that was the unsung dirge of everything he had lost, and then he heard no more.

✦   ✦   ✦

In the end, it was easier than it should have been, but that only made Cass all the more wary. A canny foe and a sloppy foe could surprise you just as quickly, she had learned long ago. The only difference was in their intent, but intent meant nothing once the trap was sprung.

She was nowhere near Raub's equal at moving above the ground, but she had no choice this time. She followed the directions the girl gave her easily enough, to a high hedge-wall three tiers above the market and at the center of the forest-home. There, the council terrace of Anthila occupied a tier of its own, a broad expanse of garden and sheltered hall connected by wide bridges to the adjoining terraces.

Cass's unfamiliarity with the tangled routes that traversed the forest-home's islands of floor and the spaces between them had slowed her at first. But because she moved slowly, she began to note a flow of figures moving in the same direction she was. Subtle at first, groups of two of three pacing slowly where she waited in the shadows for them to pass. But then those groups met other groups, all moving inward and upward, seemingly following the same directions the girl had given her.

The figures were all Ilvani, moving with the sure step and silence of dark purpose. Most wore cloaks against the chill night air, but on the few that didn't, she saw the silk and subtle goldsmithing of a noble's livery. She stayed well back, shadowing them with the intentionally careless gait that would let her change direction easily if they turned to her.

She got close enough more than once to catch their eyes. The same detached gaze, the blank stare of the marketplace, was in all of them as they hurried on.

By the time she reached the last bridge, she was well back of the final figures to slip out across the well-lit span of rope and shadow. Unlike in the noble's enclave, no barrier walls surrounded the great hall of the forest-home, a combination public forum, theater, and council chamber by the way the girl Pheánei described it.

In the play of the Clearmoon through the wind-twisted trees, the seat of power in Anthila was a huge expanse of garden set with paths and courtyards of white tile. The hall itself was a broad web of gently sculpted wicker, set high upon a second terrace suspended by five great ropes from the spread of primal branches above. Cool light blazed within, a flight of grey steps rising to dark portals of polished wood. These seemed more about ceremony than security, however, set as they were within their screen walls.

The four rangers who stood in pairs on opposite ends of the bridge were the hall's only visible defense. From the shadows, Cass watched them for a time. She noted the same blank stare in them as in all the rest, but knew that having to rush the bridge to get to them would erase it quickly enough.

She went around and over them instead, scaling the walls of an estate on the adjacent tier and making her way through the shadows of its overgrown garden. At the edge of that garden, she found herself on a close-cropped common fronted by a half-dozen smaller terraced apartments. Steering clear of the lights that flickered beyond their walls of woven branches and white wicker, she slipped into the trees, climbing, then clambering carefully across a natural ladder of foliage that led her through the darkness and to her destination.

She went slowly, timing her movement with the rising of the wind that would screen any sound. Beyond the bridge and out of sight of the guards there, she saw a second rank of six sentries tending a fire on the great hall grounds. Her senses were sharp, every nerve on edge. The Ilvani held a lax attitude toward security, she knew, but not without good reason. Fighting side by side with Raub, she had witnessed more than once the combat prowess that the Yewnwood taught.

She dropped before her grip on the perch of branches could grow any more tenuous. The ranger guards were on their feet before she hit, the closest of them hurling two long knives in greeting. Cass spun the Reaper in front of her to cut the missiles cleanly in two an arm's length from her face, hafts and blades ricocheting loudly where they struck the tiled ground to either side.

The axe was a weapon whose very appearance frequently guaranteed that Cass wouldn't have to use it, which suited her well enough. In the center of the blade where she held it up now in warning, a death's-head skull grinned. Its gleaming image was embossed there by dweomer, brilliant white and edged in dark lines that clung to it like living shadow. The spellcraft that created that dead face saw it shift with the viewer's movement, its dark gaze burning into the eyes of the guards as they charged.

It wasn't much of a fight as fights go. When it was done, Cass paused to check the strength of the blood at the guards' throats. Two of them were dead despite her best effort. The rest she left inert but alive. It was a risk, she knew, but she had little stomach for execution when justice wasn't involved.

She didn't know how much time she had before they awoke, but she suspected it wouldn't be enough. As she slung the axe back to her belt, she felt its wordless voice calling to her. The confrontation at

Garania Hall had made it anxious for blood, but Cass didn't share the weapon's hunger. Not yet.

Four people were alive in the shadows behind her as she climbed the stairs, because it was easy enough to leave them that way. From childhood, Cassatra had been trained to a path of bloodless combat, the way of the refuge that was the only home she had ever known. Those instincts had stayed with her despite the long years since she turned her back on that path. Long years since she set out on another path whose destination still eluded her.

The doors were unlocked, a tumult of voices beyond covering her entrance as she slipped inside the wide white hall. The great ropes that supported the tier platform ended at its edges in thick wooden bolts, the wicker above them arcing out like filled sails. At the center of the space, a flight of stairs curved up to a second platform some ten strides across, a dais slung from a lighter web of rope that met the main supports high above.

Arched wooden rails lined the ceiling, tapestries hanging there between wall-mounted evenlamps. Rich dioramas detailed the forest and the faces of Ilvani that Cass guessed were heroes of Raub's folk, or leaders, or both. The face closest to her was a more-than-life-sized rendering of an older Ilvani male, silvering hair swept back and woven in the old style. He wore dark robes that concealed his hands but showed the hilt of an Ilvani longblade at his belt. His face was fair, but in the figure's bark-brown eyes, she saw Raub's dark gaze staring back at her.

The lower tier was strewn with cushions that might have served to sit ten score people in the wide-open meeting space. Only a quarter of that number were present here now, mostly nobles, a handful of guards spaced around them. All were standing, circling close to the raised dais platform where an unfamiliar shape stood darkly framed by the light.

Cass saw what it was. She felt her fingers tighten on the Reaper's haft.

"You are welcome to Anthila, stranger."

Over the noise of the crowd, the voice called out in Ilvani from the shadows of the high platform. Its tone was light, but Cass felt a trace of fear across the back of her neck as the words twisted through her. She focused, found the strength to shake them off. The telltale tapping of the white-and-silver walking stick preceded the silver-haired bard as she limped slowly out from the shadows.

All around the chamber, the voices of the assembled Ilvani trailed to silence. Fifty sets of eyes turned on Cass as she shifted through them, the nobles she had followed staring with a look that showed no surprise. Not that they expected her, she knew. They just hadn't been told yet what to think.

Cass wrapped her cloak tight around her as she ascended the stairs, the Reaper out of sight, warm in her hand. Halessi, seneschal of Anthila, was in the same white cloak she had worn in the marketplace, but a diadem of gold was set upon the silver hair now. The mark of the seneschal's office, Cass guessed. Hanging from a belt of pale grey dwyrsilver that cinched a tan tunic inlaid with twisting vines of yellow and green, she wore the black shortsword that had been Raub's burden for so long.

"As you can see, this a private meeting of the council of the forest-home," Halessi said as she gestured to the impassive faces to all sides. "However, you are as much a witness as any of us to the events that will transpire here tonight. More so, perhaps." The thin lips pursed to a cold smile as the gold and violet eyes flicked back to the dark shape behind her.

Raub.

Cass was close enough now to see that he was alive, the fear dimming that she had felt and focused past with her first glimpse of him from the doorway. Beneath an arch of wooden beams descending from the ropes of the ceiling, he was hanging by his wrists from a set of braided leather thongs. The seamless crafting of the scaffold was clearly Ilvani, but it had an intentionally rough quality to it that spoke to its purpose.

His eyes were shut, his breathing shallow. His bow, the dirk he always carried, the emerald-hilted longsword claimed from the darkness under Myrnan were nowhere in sight.

"We have not been formally introduced," Halessi said.

"When you're short on time, ceremony is the first thing to go."

With a smile, the bard limped across the pale white floor. "The creature of impulse seeks always the superiority of the moment. Perhaps at the cost of failure in the long term."

"I expect so," Cass said thoughtfully. "Sorry about shooting you this morning." It was little more than a guess, but a correct one judging from how the smile flickered.

"I've suffered worse," the bard said. She put a little more weight on the walking stick, her leg twisting beneath her as if to underline the point. She came to a stop before Cass, appraising her thoughtfully.

"You've been watching for him," Cass said. She nodded toward Raub without looking, tried to appear more thoughtful than afraid.

"Since the moment Irasol rode north with word of the elder

Talmaraub's death." Halessi spoke with a candor that told Cass no one else in the room would remember the words once this was done.

"I met Irasol," Cass said, remembering. "A spy of yours?"

"A spy of Talmaraub's, actually. Watching his father."

"But under your control."

Halessi smiled. "When it suited me."

"As you control all the rest of them. In command, always."

"When I need to be."

"And that's why Raub scares you."

In the light of the evenlamps, the gold-violet eyes were suddenly cold.

Cassatra scanned the wide chamber as she paced, making a mental note of potential defensive points, the lack of other exits, the best places to cut through the walls to make up for that. "Because last night wasn't about killing him," she said thoughtfully. "You wouldn't have come alone. A half-dozen Yewnwood Ilvani against two of us in the dark, asleep. It doesn't get any easier than that, but you kept your distance."

As she turned back, she saw the bard's hand stray to the hilt of the black shortsword at her waist. Cass smiled. "I'm sorry," she said. "All this talk must be a distraction to you. Far be it from me to interrupt your little game."

"This is no game." Halessi's voice was raised and pitched to carry, and Cass heard the subtle weave of the charm-song that was the bard's power thread through it. From across the room came a sudden swell of anger. "We are a people whose faith is history. The deeds and words of our kin go back ten thousand generations."

"The last generation is the only one I know about," Cass said quietly. "Who was Tajomynar?"

Beneath its curtain of silver hair, the narrow face turned pale. Halessi stood silent for a long moment. "I never dreamed that would be a story he would share," she said at last. "I misjudged him."

"You didn't," Cass said truthfully. "Raub shares very little."

The bard laughed. "A child's name is what he goes by now?"

"I suspect he has a few more, like you. That one serves him well enough, though. Ale and memory speaks through him, sometimes. He talked of his father once, and of someone named Tajomynar who he betrayed."

Halessi stepped close now, and Cass felt a shiver twist through her as the lacquered nails of the bard's string hand came up to touch her cheek. Her hand tightened on the Reaper's haft as she dug deep for the will to focus.

"That treason was only one of many," Halessi whispered, and Cass felt all the power imbued within the silver-sweet voice slip through her. "Your lover has betrayed you now, as he betrayed his people his whole life. As he betrayed what and who he was."

Cass laughed then, surprising both of them. In the echo of her own voice, she felt her sight clear against the faint haze that Halessi's words carried, as a cold wind pushes cloud away. "We're not lovers."

"Friends then."

"Something else," Cass said, and she was thoughtful suddenly. More than she had at any point of the journey that brought them here, she felt the awkwardness of her presence. She felt the urge to turn away, to leave Raub to whatever dark destiny this place was for him. But against that urge came the sudden understanding that in following him this far, she had done so for a reason.

"Some bonds go deeper than that," she said quietly. "Some bonds have no easy name."

Halessi stepped back then. She hammered the walking stick to the floor, raising it high as it burst into white light that wrapped it as a sheet of flickering flame. It was a weapon in its true form, Cass saw. A single-edged longblade, the image she had seen on the gate, blazing so bright that its steel could barely be seen within the flames that wrapped it.

"*Iastora!*" the bard shouted, and Cass recognized the command. *Sing.* Halessi's voice was pitched again to carry to the crowd. "The anger that lingers in the heart of Anthila runs deep! Anger for lost sons, for lost faith!"

The backsword flared even brighter, setting the bard's face in stark shadow as the assembled nobles surged to their feet. The diatribe was for their benefit, Cass knew. Raub's summary sentence. Judgement, then execution. True to the Ilvani custom, the nobles were uniformly well armed, most with the long knives of the woodland hunters, a few with swords of their own. The blank eyes watched as Cass took it all in, the room around her wholly under the bard's direction and the song the sword made.

"You are outnumbered and surrounded," Halessi said. "Every blade in the room waits for my order to put you down. However, the lives here have value to me, and I am loath to spend them needlessly. I hope I needn't worry about you doing anything foolish."

"No worry at all."

With a fluid motion, Cass spun toward the bard, the Reaper a blur in her hand as she threw it, but Halessi was ready. She twisted away easily to watch the axe sail past, realizing only too late that missing her was exactly what Cassatra intended.

She had stalled as long as she needed to, watching carefully for the subtle shift in Raub's breathing that told her he was finally conscious. As Cass hoped, whatever injuries he suffered had left him with enough control to hide his waking. The Reaper spun through the air as a silver blur, slicing through the leather thongs a finger's-breadth above where they bound Raub's hands. Even as he fell, his eyes shot open, dark gaze fixed hard to the bard as he hit the ground.

Halessi was sprinting toward him as he kicked the Reaper back across the floor, Cass scooping it without looking. The violet of the bard's eyes was black now, burning against the gold with a seething rage. The bright blade flared white-hot as the silver-sweet voice summoned up a spell of command.

"Kneel!" Halessi shouted, and Cass saw Raub stumble with the effort of resistance. It was the moment's distraction she needed to leap the distance between her and the bard, hitting hard from behind, a solid slash to the shoulder that cut through the robe and what felt like tempered mail beneath it and the bone beneath that.

As Halessi staggered forward, Cass reached for the dwyrsilver belt. She drew the black shortsword with her free hand, the bard too slow to grab it. Halessi had taken the crippling strike in silence, but she screamed now.

The white-flaming backsword flared again as she lunged, but Cass was faster, lashing out with a kick that shattered the bard's jaw and forced the spell she was speaking to die in her throat. The Reaper followed, arcing for Halessi's neck even as a desperate thrust shot her sword up to meet it, a gout of white flame arcing off as the axe was deflected wide.

That the bard's blade could survive the Reaper's touch showed the strength of its magic. Cass stumbled back but Raub was there. As if they had practiced it, she threw the black shortsword to him, Raub catching it as he slashed down, hitting Halessi at the line of shoulder and neck with a two-handed killing stroke. A gout of blood sprayed to the air, catching him as the bard twisted and collapsed to the ground.

The flaming backsword was sprawled across the floor. The wooden tiles burned beneath it, Halessi's fingers still traced across the grip. Cass was wary, watching the crowd of nobles where they shifted in silence.

She waited for a sign that Halessi's control was broken. In the instant, she realized what not seeing it meant.

Looming over the fallen bard, Raub reached down to liberate the burning blade. Even as Cass shouted a warning, the sword came up, slashing hard at an impossible angle. It struck Raub with enough force to knock him back, his jerkin smoldering.

As Halessi lurched to her feet, she laughed. The runes on the bright blade flared ebon black within their shroud of white flame, so dark that it hurt to look at them. Raub and Cass moved at the same time, but the bard was faster, scrambling back with blade up, blazing as it blocked attacks from both sides.

Blood mottled Halessi's cloak and tunic, but the gaping wound at her neck was already healed. White flame was flowing up her arm, coursing across her body as her strength returned. The voice of sweet silver that Cass had crushed a moment before rang out with mocking laughter now.

"Your legacy," Halessi said to Raub. "This blade you dreamed of wielding some day. Yet your father knew your weaknesses so well that he would not trust you with the knowledge of its power."

Raub's eyes were locked tight to the bard's as they circled each other. And in that gaze, Cass saw a recognition she didn't fully understand.

"This blade has a name. *Palas Eryvna*, it is called. But your father never even told you that. Did he?"

"Show yourself," Raub hissed, and that dark whisper held all the anger of his exile. All the anger that had sent him to the Sorcerers' Isle and underground, and into a dark madness that Cass hadn't understood until it was almost too late.

The bard laughed as she paced past him, the silver voice bright as she discarded her ruined cloak behind her.

"Do I know you, friend?"

"Aside from myself and my father, only four others knew of that blade's power to control the minds of those around it. Because I told them of that power the night we swore to seize and throw it down."

"And you succeeded, young Talmaraub. Succeeded beyond your wildest dreams. The old order put down and a new hope for freedom in its place. You never came back to the glory you sought, though. You were the Hooded Hawk, a hero to them all. At least you were until your father and I told them differently."

And even as Cass watched, the silver hair blurred. The eyes shimmered as the body beneath the bloodied grey tunic changed. It was done in a heartbeat, and standing in Halessi's place was an Ilvani male who could have been the bard's brother. Their features were the same. The silver hair, the gold and black eyes bright in the magical glow of evenlamps all around.

For a timeless moment, all Raub could do was stare. Then he feinted, struck hard, but the flare of white fire sent the black shortsword wide as this new figure let the burning backsword bite deep at the shoulder. Raub's cloak flared and smoldered, blood suddenly welling there in a wide swath.

"The bright blade has many powers," Tajomynar said. The voice had changed, but it carried the same confidence, the same silver sheen that threaded through Cass's mind. "Your father had no need for this one, at least as far as I know. It takes some getting used to, but it makes a powerful disguise for a dead man."

The bard glanced to Cass, raising his voice to the nobles below him. "Kill the outsider! Justice for the traitor is mine!"

Raub and Tajomynar traded off a fast flurry of strikes as the Ilvani of the council swarmed toward the stairs and Cass like a living wave. She didn't wait for them to reach her. Leaping from the edge of the dais, she hit hard in the heart of the frenzied crowd as she let the instinct take her. The training that was her childhood had taught her to fight by the sheer grace of every balanced motion, by sense of touch as much as sight. As fast as they came within range of fist or foot, the Ilvani dropped around her.

In all their eyes, she saw the same emptiness she had seen in the guards outside, and as it had then, that blank stare kept the Reaper at her side. However, Cass already had her sights set on a better target for its edge.

On the dais platform above, the glow of the black shortsword was bright in Raub's hand, a dull blue cast washing across his features as he circled. Tajomynar was across from him with the backsword that was the blade of Raub's line, the two trading strikes as they tested each other.

In a moment of brief respite, Raub whispered. "It was you..."

Tajomynar laughed again, the silver voice threading through the chaos of the chamber. Below, Cass was moving. In the circuit she made earlier, she had carefully noted the lay of the guy-ropes whose thickly woven trunks suspended the floor of the hall. Now she retraced that route, twisting past the blades of a quartet of young nobles that she clubbed senseless one by one with the Reaper's haft.

"It was me," the bard said. "So wonderfully obvious that it took only six years for you to understand. All that time, blaming yourself. All that time, seeing our faces..."

"Get out of my head," Raub hissed.

Tajomynar laughed again. "Your mind is an open book, Hawk. I need no more skill than a carnival soothsayer to lay open its secrets."

As the bard struck, Cass jumped, flipping backward over two more sets of outstretched arms. Within reach of the closest rope, she slashed out at its thickly wrapped pillar of steel-strong Ilvani weave. It would have taken a dozen blows from a woodcutter's axe without so much as fraying, but she felt it part like paper at the Reaper's touch.

With a sickening lurch, the central platform of the hall collapsed. From all around came the tearing of cord and screen as the sculpted walls tore free, twisting in a sudden storm of white. The remaining four ropes were more than enough to hold the floor up, but with its balance lost, the chamber dropped and lurched. The nobles who were closing in around Cass a moment before were upended, spilled to open air and the outside terrace below.

The dais platform in its own web of ropes remained level, but the stairs were torn away above the sloping floor of the main chamber below. Still trading blows with Tajomynar, Raub swung wide, watching the bard step back from it easily. His arm was aching, the lighter weight of the shortsword unfamiliar in his hand. He was overcompensating, hitting from the shoulder, too hard.

"We are alike in all ways," the bard said, smiling. "I was angry, as you were. I sought to make things right, to reclaim the glory that was Anthila as you did. Like you, I saw the weakness in your father. Unlike you, I saw the opportunity there."

Below him, Cass was clambering up to the high side of the fallen floor, trying to close the distance to Raub. She found her footing easily enough away from the severed anchor point, pulling herself up along a makeshift ladder of shredded wicker and fallen ropes. Unfortunately, more than a few of the combat-ready nobles were doing the same.

"You betrayed us to him," Raub whispered, and he understood it now as he should have understood it long before. He cursed himself for his folly. Cursed the memory of that face framed by silver hair, and of the love held in his memory that had turned to bile in a heartbeat.

Six years before, they fled the forest-home as outlaws and had ridden unseen in the deep woods for more than three seasons. *Arnos Iranthilia*, they called themselves. Anthila's Watch.

Raub had seen Tajomynar die that night. He saw them all die, felt their blood wash over him like a red-black rain.

Over long years before his exile, the ranger garrisons of the Ilvani had slowly begun to shift out from the deep woods to the unstable

Gracian frontier. The destruction of the Imperial capital at Ulannor Mor was on the far side of the world and a lifetime away now. However, every province of the Elder Kingdoms, every forest-home in the Yewnwood had its stories of the breakdown of rule in the aftermath. Gracia and Vanyr, straddling the mighty Yewnwood like a yoke, had fought wars for the throne of their long-lost kings. In the northern freeholds of Norgyr and in Ajaeltha to the south, they were fighting still. Would-be tyrants and warlords forging new conflicts from the legendary wars of the past.

In the aftermath of the Empire's fall, Raub's father played the fear and ambition of his people like a bard bent to a dark song. Under his hand, more and more power was drawn to the center, concentrated in the nobles and the merchant lords he controlled. Anthila prospered, even as the outlying villages became little more than work camps, their people toiling in the name of tithes and fealty to the new order.

As the Arnos Iranthilia, Raub and the others made short work of the bosses and bandits that ruled in his father's name, drawing the folk of the outlying villages to their cause of freedom. The five were the strong core at the center of something larger, putting Raub on a collision course with the rule of a father whose name and corruption he had turned away from. In short time, the talk of uprising that spread throughout the deep wood made its echo felt in the forest-home. Anthila's own rangers were sent to hunt them, and with the four he had set out with a year before, Raub crafted a daring and dangerous plan.

They rode for Anthila that night, determined to bring an end to it. One swift stroke, the blade falling on the soft neck of the elder Talmaraub's corruption. They had the advantage of surprise, of strength, of youth and purpose.

None of it mattered in the end.

As they made their careful way up the forest-home in the dead of night, Raub's father was ready. He had known their every move to the great terrace of Garania Hall, it seemed, where the seneschal should have been sleeping, alone.

Raub and four others rode for Anthila that night. Only he rode out again.

On the twisted floor below him, Cass was fighting for her life. Six foes pressed in around her, half of them young gentry with long knives in hand and a speed that suggested they practiced hard with them. She had already seen the guards she left outside fighting their way toward her, caught up in the spell of the bright blade as were all the rest.

Like Raub, the Ilvani were natural climbers, slinging their way one-handed through the shredded rigging of the walls. She had to work to stay in position without slipping, the platform twisting now beneath the weight of combatants whose weapons threatened to turn it into a killing floor.

Most of these weren't warriors, she reminded herself. These were nobles and merchants years away from hard labor or the warbands, but they were Ilvani all the same. A lifetime's training to blade and bow burned in them, one grey-haired elder demonstrating that prowess with an elaborate double-feint that made it past her. He tagged her shoulder, a flare of white-hot pain rising where he cut her to the bone.

In the end, she let the Reaper sing. She felt the scene around her slow to a precise storm of movement, dropping to take out two knife-fighters with a pair of back-to-back strikes that bit deep. Their blank eyes showed no pain, no understanding as the life flickered out behind them. Cass watched their bodies slide in pieces down the slanted tiles, but if she hoped to give the others pause where they fought to close in, it seemed only to increase their rage.

Above her, Raub and Tajomynar fought in a blinding fury, but with every strike, Raub felt his strength flagging. Steel wasn't enough, he knew. Steel alone had never been enough. He needed more, needed to push against the fear he saw now reflected in the bard's black eyes.

Since the year he was born, his father had been seneschal in Anthila. His father was lord of the forest-home and the wide wood beyond it, the borders of the Ilvani dominions of the Yewnwood marked by secret sign and ancient treaty. But for as long as Raub could remember, he had seen through the facade of nobility that his father wore like armor against any threat to his increasingly dark rule.

Raub had challenged his father even before his own first-naming, possessed of that arrogance of the Ilvani that makes all things seem so possible. He challenged his father with what he had seen, accused him of controlling his people. Bending the will of the forest-home to his own ends, manipulating the nobles, the merchant lords.

His father laughed then. The voice that carried the fate of a people sounded out bright, sunlight on water.

"Minds as weak as these call out to be controlled. You will understand some day."

Tajomynar struck hard, pulling him back from the darkness of distraction. The bard was defiant, Raub's blows ineffectual even when he landed them. The bright blade that had been his father's healed away all hurt as its master fought on.

"You held the right to both these swords your whole life," Tajomynar laughed. "Son to the seneschal. Last of your line. You threw both away to play the rebel. Breaking your father's law in the name of village rabble. I had more ambitious plans."

"I do them a favor," his father said. *"I grant them direction. I shape their collective fears to contentment, twist the conflict in their hearts to peace."*

"You rode with us, Mynar." Raub had to fight to force out the words. "You believed in the greater good before you betrayed us to my father. Or have you rewritten your story so effectively that you've come to believe it yourself?"

"You were a coward," Tajomynar hissed. "You are a coward. Afraid of what you should have been."

Raub raised the shortsword, defiant. He slashed out twice to lock with Tajomynar, the black blade and the white crossed for a long moment between them.

"These weapons are what I am," he said coldly. "This blade, I brought back in the hope that Anthila might raise up a leader worthy of carrying it again. That blade you hold is coin for my father's treachery, and in my hands, it will mete out a lifetime's justice to pay that balance in full. For your betrayal, Mynar, the first blood it claims will be yours."

The white flames that wreathed the backsword flared as Tajomynar grinned. "Your father is dead, Hawk. Your line ended when he placed this blade in my hand and let its power pull me back to life that night. When he bade me sing the ghostsong over his passage to memory."

Below him, Cass felt the surge against her redoubled, but three clashing strikes set the Reaper hacking through a half-dozen blades. The closest attackers leaped back, a haze of blood telling her the axe had cut through bone and flesh as well in its cleaving arc.

"Anthila is mine!" Tajomynar shouted in triumph. "Palas Eryvna the bright blade and the name of Thrasus is mine!" He stepped back, pointed the white-flaming longblade at the black shortsword in Raub's bloodied hand. "Valaendar of the Anthiliar is mine!"

"Then take it if you can…"

Steel had never been enough.

Tajomynar lunged again, three quick strikes parried and returned as he shifted, but Raub was ready for him. He swung up and to the side, so that the burning blade slipped wide to block. It was a fool's parry, Tajomynar's left side wide open for the moment it took to make it.

Raub hit hard, drove his fingers deep into Tajomynar's eye even as he slammed forward, smashing into him shoulder to chest.

He felt the edge of the dais slip away beneath them. They fell for a timeless moment, then hit hard, Tajomynar shrieking as blood fountained from his ruined eye. Raub managed to find his feet as he swung down hard. The bard was faster, raising the bright blade to block as he rolled away and scrambled up.

They were at the top edge of the upended central platform, feet set to find a precarious balance. Cass was a half-dozen strides below them, but a sudden silence fell around her now. Where Tajomynar's scream rang out, it stilled the crowd in a way she didn't understand. The power in the voice was broken somehow, the surging horde stopped where they clung to the ruined platform or spread out across the garden tier below it, blank eyes gazing upward.

Raub had to fight to find the breath to spit, thick with blood and bile where it hit the tiles at the bard's feet.

"You're finished," he hissed. "You're a shadow that the light will wipe away. This performance you play is as false as the face you wear..."

"All life is performance, fool." The silver hair was hanging in red streaks now, Tajomynar's face a mask of blood. Already, the eye was healing itself, its torn tissue knitting, but his voice was still shrill with the pain. "You play a role now as false as the one you chose for yourself as a child. Pretending to be the outlaw, the rebel. The hero."

"Even as you play the dead man." Raub felt the leg that the bard had cut threatening to buckle, had to lock it to prevent himself from falling. "You've walked the ground these six years in another body. Hiding behind another face. Who's the pretender, Mynar?"

The eye would heal as long as Tajomynar held the blade, Raub knew. The time it would take was all the time he had.

"Tajomynar died, Hawk. I believe you were there." With a surge of speed, the bard struck twice, the black shortsword up barely in time to parry. "By your father's grace and the passing of this blade to my hand do I live and breathe," he hissed, "but your death is the only thing that wipes away the pain of that night."

Below them, Cass had the Reaper balanced in her hand, ready to throw. She had a straight line and clear sight to the bard, but Tajomynar was in command now, his strikes coming fast enough that the slightest distraction would be Raub's last.

A feint. Strike and counterstrike. Raub nearly slipped, catching his balance only by luck.

"You killed them," the bard whispered. "You killed us all."

Raub felt the words burning in his mind like sudden fever. Something dark passed across his eyes, and then he was looking down to see

Cass below him suddenly. She was caught up in a tight press of attackers even as she shouted a warning he couldn't hear.

In a blur of steel, Tajomynar cut him across the forearm even through the haze of his bloodied vision. The black blade of the Anthiliar lurched where Raub's hand spasmed, and he saw Tajomynar almost break his defensive posture to lunge for it. Through blurred red, he saw a trace of madness suddenly. The bard's hunger for the shortsword and the power it promised showed raw for an instant in the gleam of his black eyes.

"Should have kept flying, Hawk…"

Raub lunged. He threw all he had at Tajomynar, watched him easily evade the uneven thrust as he knew he would. The bard struck hard on the return, wheeling as the white-burning blade cut under and past the black shortsword.

Raub was waiting for it. He took the lunge, twisted to catch it straight on. He felt the flaming blade punch through his shoulder, a moment of numbness there flaring to a crescendo of pain like he had never known. Tajomynar was an arm's length away, but Raub twisted in and down. With the guard of the black shortsword, he caught the flaming steel of Palas Eryvna just above the hilt, twisting his body hard. His shoulder was the fulcrum on which he wrenched the bright blade from Tajomynar's hands.

With a surge of white flame, the backsword sang, punching through Raub where he stumbled back. He let Valaendar slip from his grasp, tossing it up before Tajomynar. He saw the black of the bard's eyes flash suddenly back to violet, glazed over with mad desire as he snatched his prize from midair. He had a moment to shout in triumph before he died.

Raub wrenched Palas Eryvna from his shoulder with a scream. Then the last of his strength drove an arm's length of flaming steel through the bard's heart, the blade that had been his father's shunting out through ribs and mail and a spray of blood across the white floor.

He blacked out for a moment. When his head cleared, he was on his knees. He heard the sudden silence in the wide chamber around him, broken by the pounding of his own heart. He smelled the tang of blood, tasted metal in his mouth. He saw Tajomynar lifeless in a spreading pool of red before him.

Raub's blood-soaked jerkin was still smoldering where the burning blade sundered it, but he felt no pain. There was a warmth at his ribs and in his leg where Tajomynar had cut him. The bleeding had stopped, torn flesh scarring over as the power of the bright blade restored him. He lifted it slowly, felt the unfamiliar weight in his hand. His father's sword, and everything it meant.

That night six years before, they had been caught with ridiculous ease. His father was alone as Raub knew he would be, a brazen assault within the forest-home inconceivable even to his dark paranoia. But even alone, his father's sorcery was a storm that struck them down in a hail of black fire the moment they set foot within the house.

They had been brought from Garania Hall to the council. Put on display and bound as the condemned. With his will controlling the minds of the nobles who would have decided their fate, his father didn't bother with the pretense of a trial. Just killed them all, one by one.

That night, a renegade son was his weapon.

"Raub."

He shook his head to clear it, turning to see Cass below him. A circle of combatants around her stood in stunned silence. He felt a kind of subtle panic in the Ilvani nobles, a disconnect between what they had just witnessed and their ability to react to it. Against that uncertainty, Cass displayed the same preternatural calm as always.

Raub kicked at Tajomynar's body, gave it enough momentum that it slid slowly down the sloping tiles. A wide swath of blood trailed out behind it, marking the corpse's path as it toppled off the edge beside Cass and fell in a sodden heap to the floor below.

Six years ago on this very floor, the charm-song of the bright blade in his father's hand had worked Raub's muscle and mind like a puppet, turning the blood-fury intended for the seneschal against the others. Against the friends who had followed him.

Tajomynar had been the first, too shocked to understand what was happening as Raub gutted him from navel to neck.

Having witnessed Tajomynar's fall, the others understood. Their screams and Raub's had shattered the dull silence and the pale glow of the chamber's white walls.

"Iastora," Raub whispered. He remembered Tajomynar's command as he remembered his father's from long ago. White flame danced along the blade of the backsword, an unheard music flaring in a song that spoke of new beginnings. Raub tried to find his voice, an unaccustomed fear in him as he felt the power of Palas Eryvna filter through him. He sensed a connection to those around them, felt his thought press out to touch them. He felt their minds waiting for his commands, attuned to the blade over long decades of control.

He thought of the retribution he had waited years to deliver, but the shadow that dogged him all that time still shrouded him now. Something else needed to finally clear it.

To the stupefied nobles, he spoke the last command the sword would give them.

"Know the truth," he said, and across every face that watched him blankly, there came a sudden rush of shock and fear.

A moment's silence hung before chaos erupted. Two score voices were shouting, screaming, as the elders of Anthila pressed in around the shattered remains of the seneschal who had betrayed them. Cass could pick out only fragments of the fast-spoken Ilvani, but she heard the awareness there, felt the rage in those who circled closest to their fallen former master.

In the tumult, she slipped away. She turned back once to see the black blade that was Valaendar, the symbol of the Anthiliar and the badge of their leadership, driven down into the blood-streaked wood of the crippled floor.

Though she tried to find him in the frenzied crowd, Raub was already gone.

◆　◆　◆

In the bright green of the vine walls outside the necropolis gardens, Cass waited as the sun rose, the day dawning bright and unseasonably warm. She had slept for a while as the Clearmoon set, her back to the white arch. Each time she awoke, it was to the expectation that she would see Raub sitting across from her. But as day broke, she began to make plans for the road back to the forest's edge. What might lay beyond there, she didn't know.

She had made her way down to the market in the aftermath of the events on the council terrace, moving quickly but still arriving behind the news from above. Even against the clamor she had seen earlier, the market was chaos, every shouting voice spreading the same shocked story of lies and retribution. On the forest road below, she could hear horses in motion, couriers heading out by the last light of the Clearmoon, she guessed. Taking word of the night's dark events into the forest and beyond.

She gathered up her cloak, picked two handfuls of early berries from a vine-strewn lattice, and packed them carefully for the road. Idly, she found herself wondering how long it would take for an entire clan of people, for all its settlements forest-wide, to reclaim a collective memory denied them for so long. She felt the twinge of an old sadness then, and a familiar ache that she set aside as she always did.

All memory was precious, she thought. If Raub's people hadn't realized that before, they would know it now.

"Ilvani tradition holds that the spirit lingers for a time in the mortal world."

Cass hadn't heard Raub approach, his movement silent through the trees as all Ilvani seemed able to do when they put their minds to it. He was crouched a dozen strides away at the edge of the terrace, looking not at her but at the white arch above, the great trunk twisting together as it rose into green shadow.

"The life force exists outside the body it inhabits," he said. "The spirit takes time to have its life read to it by those who know it. The final words of those who shaped our lives, imbued with all the emotion engendered by our death, are the ghostsong."

"That's why you came back? To sing the truth?"

Raub threw his hood back but didn't answer, seemingly lost in thought. Cass approached, dropped to sit three strides away. Dried blood still marked his face, hair streaked red-black. But in the light, she could see that the wounds of the deadly fight were gone.

His bow and quiver were still missing, as was the emerald-hilted longsword that had been the greatest treasure Raub carried out from the darkness under Myrnan. Instead, Palas Eryvna, the black-runed bright blade that had been his father's, hung at his belt.

"What did I tell you?" Raub said.

"I don't know what you mean," Cass said truthfully. Even with the snatches of sleep, she was exhausted, her thoughts slow. Caught up in the old sadness that she couldn't shake.

"That night that you said I spoke of my father. I don't remember it. What did I tell you?"

Cass was silent a while. The wind was warm again, coming from what felt like the west, but she had little sense of direction within the silent expanse of trees. "I was in the market this morning," she said by way of not answering. "To a person, all Anthila is talking about the Hooded Hawk."

"Let them," Raub said, and only in saying it did he realize how little it mattered to him now. "How did you find it?" he added. "This place?"

"I asked a deaf girl where your father was interred."

Raub weighed the answer, didn't bother asking the obvious questions in return. "And how did you know I'd be here?"

"I didn't."

Above them, the wind dislodged a cloud of golden leaves. And even as they fell, their slow drift was suddenly disrupted by a half-dozen dark shapes shooting out from the shadow of the trees. A phalanx of fist-sized hawks shrieked and soared on fast wings, flashing black and gold in the light for a moment, then gone.

"What did I tell you?" Cass heard the edge in his voice that told her he wasn't going to ask again.

"All of it," she said.

Raub stared out toward the edge of the tier, a screen of branches there framing blue sky beyond.

"I don't know what that means."

"It means you told me all of it. What he was, what you did. You standing against him, fighting for your people. What he made you do in the end. What you tried to do after."

"Remember this."

Those who had followed him were dead, and their blood drenched his shaking hands.

"Remember this," his father had said, and then he turned away, and Raub felt the power of the bright blade Palas Eryvna in his mind break beneath an aching rage he had never known before.

That night six years ago, he stumbled forward, seizing the short-sword where it hung at his father's belt. His father was old even then, too slow to stop him. He died quickly, the sword Valaendar that was the symbol of his rule and the corruption he had visited on his people buried deep in his back. The flaming backsword was still in his grasp as he fell, the black blade wrenched free and in Raub's hand as he fled.

In the resultant chaos, he stole a horse and rode for the Free City, far from the reach of Anthiliar law. With the sword of his people in his possession, he lived on the coin the horse brought as he waited for long days, then for weeks. He expected to hear the news of his father's death made public, word of his corruption exposed. Expected to return to Anthila with Valaendar in hand, the black shortsword ready to be presented to the new leader of the forest-home.

It was well into winter, raining cold when he heard from a group of Gracian traders that his father was alive and well. The one called the Hooded Hawk had disappeared, they said. The fools who followed the traitor had been slain by his own hand.

For six years, Raub felt his father's corruption lurking in the short-sword that had slain him. For six years, he fought and failed to shed the dark spirit that dwelled beneath that tight-wrapped black cloth.

When he left the Free City, he fled by horse across the plains of Munychion with the thought of abandoning Valaendar in the dragon deeps of the south. More than once, he almost left it behind in the depths of Eltolitinus, dreaming of the black blade lost in that place of death and madness until the end of time.

On the ship back to Highport, his spirit broken by a darkness that eclipsed even the night of his exile, Raub decided to cast the sword overboard, watch it sink deep into the blue-black depths of the sea. He unwrapped it that night for the first time since he fled, trying to find the strength to follow through. In the end, though, he felt the hold the blade of the Anthiliar had on him. A feeling finally laid to rest now.

At his belt, the black-runed backsword hung, imbued with the ghostsong of countless older generations whose presence would wash away his father's darkness in time. A deeper history, waiting for him to set aside who his father was. To become who his father might have been.

For long years, he wondered why fate had spared his father that night. Tajomynar was right. His father never told him of the sword's powers, save for the strength over other's minds that Raub had discovered on his own. His father had rejected him from the start. His legacy and the blade that was the symbol of it, both denied to Raub. He had never even known the sword's name.

"You carried that knowledge all this time and never spoke of it," he said to Cass at last. "Why?"

"Because if you'd remembered that you told me your story, I would have had to tell you mine."

They sat in silence a while longer. Then, as if they were in touch with each other's thoughts, both rose.

They slipped out of Anthila easily enough, Raub taking them down little-used paths and ladderways that descended in time to the forest floor. By side trails, they made their way to the road, and though they passed couriers riding at speed in both directions for the better part of the day, they walked unrecognized and, finally, alone.

The sun was down and the Darkmoon up when they passed beyond the forest wall, the shadowed scrub plain and the southern mountains seeming larger somehow after the close confines of the great forest. They made camp in a pine bower atop a rise whose crest was a shattered stone dyke, the last vestige of a frontier outpost tumbled and fallen in one of Gracia's endless ancient wars.

They walked the day in a silence both welcomed, neither speaking more than was necessary until they had eaten by the fireside. Cass felt the ache of the night before and the long road in every joint, even as the last of Pheánei's pies filled her with the warmth of a forgotten spring and the urge to do nothing but sleep. But as she watched Raub throw scattered deadfall to the flames, she suddenly spoke.

"I don't know who I am."

She hadn't realized she was going to say it. Hadn't felt the words slip out from the place where they had been held tight inside her for long years.

Raub looked up, dark eyes catching the firelight where Cass watched him.

"I have a past," she said, "but it's closed off to me. I have a family I don't remember. My father, my mother. A brother. I can see them sometimes. Only their faces, not even names."

In the refuge where she was raised, they were taught to look within. But in looking inside herself, Cass had only ever seen the emptiness that her memory made.

"I remember... a castle. Where I was born, I think. A man in armor, wearing a crown. I seek out the rangers, the loremasters, the bounty hunters for word of old stories. A girl, lost. To see if anyone's looking. There's been too much war, though. Too many lost..."

It was the emptiness that had forced her in the end to look outside herself. To look back on the past that was lost and leave all else behind.

"You can't blame yourself for being the one who survives," Cass said. "The one left behind." And in saying it, she realized how long she had waited to speak those words.

She laid down then, curled close to the fire. Raub watched her for a while, feeding wood to the flames as the Clearmoon rose and the distant call of wild dogs sounded out against the silence of the night.

"Where are we bound for tomorrow?" he said at last, but she was already sleeping.

A Prayer for Dead Kings

– ONE –
Rite of Fire

THE CHAR-BLACK DRIFT OF CROWS writhes like smoke above distant fields. Rising wind flows cold from the east, carrying the echo of a woman's laughter. A ringing like a clear bell, faint shimmering of silver on the air. The dawn-sweet scent of spring's thaw. The foul air of the unburned dead.

And when Gilvaleus first saw the Lady Aelathar among the ranks of the Healers, he swore his love for her upon the Sword of Kings, saying 'Thou art most fair of all the courts of Gracia, and the Forest Kingdoms of the Ilvanrand, and all the isles and far lands of these Elder Kingdoms, and when this war is done, with my love will I honor thee.'

He sees the thorp from the little-used forest road. A league distant in the light of dawn, but he recognizes at once the stillness of death that feels far closer. This place has a name, once. No more. A cluster of a dozen farmhouses, sod walls and ridgepoles. Canvas and plaster and thatch are shimmered by the gusting wind as he approaches. Broken doors are burned by a mark he does not recognize.

He walks through a score of bodies lying unmoving, blood anointing frost-kissed ground in a dark benediction. He is an old man, feet bare. Back bent as he drags each corpse in turn to lie in rows beside the mound he builds from fence posts and deadwood, lamp oil and the last hay of winter, unneeded by the horses found slaughtered in the grange.

In the smithy, he finds flint and steel with which to light the pyre. He finds three boys there, throats cut. Left to slip slowly to the darkness that comes for all the others in the end.

He hefts the bodies as if they weigh nothing. The muscles of arms and back twist like double-knotted leather beneath his tattered rags. With an old strength, he lays the fallen to their makeshift bier one by one, but the limp that carries with him speaks of wounds even older.

He burns the boys first.

"Take this offering to the mountains' winds," he whispers, only to himself. "Ash of the body, heal the spirit now set free."

And Aelathar's power was the old magic of the Druidas, so a garden Gilvaleus vowed to make for her at the King's Seat at Mitrost, to which she would call the splendor of Summer in all seasons. And they walked together in the empty ruins where that wonder would be raised, and he told her they would pledge their love beneath bowers white and green.

Blue sky flares, breaking through cloud only to be scarred by the reek of black ash. Thick columns of smoke rise and are torn away on the wind. One by one, the dead receive the rites of Danassa, goddess of the harvest who watches over them while they live. The rites of Herias, god of the long night of death where they walk now. Folk of the fields, living lives unchanged for ten centuries of Empire.

Then her laughter rang on the white stones that glimmered by the stars that were fair Aelathar's name, and whose light was in her silver hair and pale eyes. And Gilvaleus the High King kissed her for the first time beneath those stars, that watched them both with all of fate and history's unseeing eyes.

Stone walls twist across fields, rubble-strewn. Thin grass breaks the dead-brown stubble of winter, the green left gleaming where frost turns to dew, then mist.

And in the end, the Companions of Gilvaleus the High King rode to the Plain of Marthai and met the Warriors of Astyra the King's-Bastard, who had called to him swords from the Duchies of the Northlands, and uncounted blades of the Norgyr besides, who sought revenge against Gilvaleus for Thoradun the Usurper, their long-dead Lord.

•

He thinks of the boys. Tries to remember their faces through the black shroud of burning. He tries to think on how many winters it might be since they last sleep in their mothers' arms, before the gods' call and mortal steel makes men of them.

He feels a wetness at his eyes that he does not understand.

Then the skies were shrouded black with cloud and crow-wings so thick as to block the sun, and a dark rain fell that covered all the field with a clinging mist to thwart the eye of Archer and War-Mage alike. And the High King was wrathful, and fought with the strength of ten, killing the best Knights of the Northlands. And all the while in the fray was heard his voice, calling for his Son to come to him, and to embrace the dark destiny of his betrayal.

He tries to not think on these things anymore.

The day waxes, wanes as he keeps the fire burning and throws each body to it in turn. Dawn sun rising weakly, pale gold in the east, grazing clouds born of the distant sea. High sun passing warm, touching his robes that are the pilgrims' white once, long ago. Stained by countless leagues of travel but still recognizable by their shapeless cut, by the cord belt, unknotted.

A weathered scar rises chest to neck to cheek, half-hidden by a ragged growth of beard the same grey as the White Pilgrim's hair. He is shorn, but badly. A rough knife-cut that he administers only when weather and blood-mites remind him to. His knife is a slip of rusted steel, barely a blade at all. He uses it to cut the ropes that bind the three boys, keep them from struggling in the end.

And ere the battle was done, the Field of Marthai ran red and black with blood from steel and spell-fire that rained dark as night, bright as noon. And all around them were the dead that lie and the dead that walk, returned to the fight by the dark Animys of the Necromancers of Astyra's ranks, and denied the gods' blessing and the long rest of earth and sky. Then the mottled light of the Darkmoon shone down upon the plain to stain the mud of the field blood-black and glistening, like the blood that stained Ankathira the Whitethorn, Sword of Kings, that cut fearless through the ranks of the Kings'-Bastard's unholy force in Gilvaleus the High King's hands.

He lets image and memory-scent flit past his mind's eye, a constant shadow play of blood and memory. By day, he sacrifices himself at the altar of madness remembered. By night, he sleeps the sleep of no dreams.

"This is the bargain the gods have struck," he whispers, only to himself. This is who he is, is why he lives. A new lifetime of atonement for the life, for the future, that ends so long ago.

Then Gilvaleus looked about him, and saw that all the Kings'-Bastard Astyra's force was broken but circled. And with weeping eye, he beheld that of his Companions, yet lived only Nàlwyr, who had returned to his High King, and Baethala the brave, and Fossa who was his Brother, but all were near death and fighting far from the High King's side. And Gilvaleus cried out, saying 'Woe to all that this day should come, and an end to all we fought for.' And from the dark smokes around came the voice of the King's-Bastard, who cried 'Father, thou hast won the field but lost all thy cause, and thou must face me now!' So did Gilvaleus the High King spy through shadow the adamantine spear of he whose treachery so much death had sown, and drawing strength from the Whitethorn did he advance against his Son, crying 'Traitor, the death thou seekest is here!'

This life is given back to him, then given in turn to the gods whose gift life is. A new lifetime of dark dreams to pay for the old lifetime that spawned those dreams.

Then did the power of the Whitethorn cut down Astyra the traitor, but the King's-Bastard drew breath through foul Animys even after blood and spirit had left him. And with his spear, he slashed at his Father's face to scar him cheek and neck, and Gilvaleus fell back with rage in his heart and bloodied gaze. So did Astyra rise to thrust his spear through the heart and spine of the High King, who fell at last. Then with his final breath, Astyra witnessed this curse upon Gilvaleus his Father, saying 'I die at dismal peace with knowing that thy last sight will be the Son thou slayest, sired in the darkness of thy heart, and the price of all thy sins. Father, remember me...'

Dusk and sunset are blood-red across darkling sky to the west, and the burning is complete. The last of the dead are set to the cleansing flame that their fate denies them. The village is scoured two days past, to judge by the state of the bodies. Eyes gone to the birds, maggots not yet unweaving pale flesh.

The White Pilgrim sees death too many times before. He knows what these things mean.

He works with no scarf or scent to mask the rankness. For him, the air carries no stench to note because the taint of death is always with him. Carried from the Plains of Marthai a lifetime ago. Blood on his hands slick like oil, burning like spell-fire as he plunges them through the mud crust of a filthy trough to wash them by the failing light.

And as Gilvaleus the High King lay dying, he was cradled in the arms of Nàlwyr, who spoke his grief and rage to the empty field.

He tries to not think on these things anymore. The memories all but gone now. Gone for good, soon. Taken by the darkness that is all he has left.

'I ayra la mea Gilvaleus Haroya? Quèla sort es déicen a mai, ayra que vou apartes de mi, resta seol amba tos els meus nemicas a la mà?'

Benediction in the tongue of Gracia, echoing through long years.

'And now my High King Gilvaleus? What fates are left to me, now that you turn from me, left alone with all my enemies at hand?'

A man might turn away from the friend he betrays. Might walk away from the warrior's death that the gods deny.

The warrior's death is good enough for some. Not for him.

A man might walk away from a killing field. A man might turn his back on the past and disappear into history.

He tries to not think on these things anymore.

And the High King spoke, and said 'Thou must take comfort in thyself alone, and look to the hope of these days to carry thee. For I am taken into Orosan to heal the wounds that are my heart and memory. But in that time when name and heart are cleansed by the memory that takes me, then all Gracia that I saved shall embrace that memory, and I will return for all who speak this Prayer for Dead Kings.'

He is walking along the farm track that twists between the wan mud of spring fields, bare feet not feeling the cold. The pyre's last bodies spill fat-black smoke to the shrouded sky, and that sky is split suddenly by a shrieking cry and the storm of wings above him.

A howling rattle on the wind is the passage of a phalanx of hassas overhead. He counts six of the great winged horses, circling back with a speed that belies their sheer size. Soaring low enough that even through the falling dark, he sees bright eyes watching him, sees the darker masks of helmed riders tracking as they pass. Their tightly reined movement on the air, the faint glow of their dweomered bard-ing marks them as beasts of war. They circle to drop around him one by one, touching down at speed to stop in a storm of dust and shredded turf.

Light springs from hand and sword. The White Pilgrim is caught in a shimmering circle of white, against which the dusk beyond can no longer be seen. The riders are warriors by their look. Dark leather, weather-stained. A red band at the shoulder of each cloak is set with the sign of the black boar. The White Pilgrim recognizes it. Cannot remember. Bright tokens are pinned there, blades in white that mark some manner of rank.

The closest hassas rear up, cry out a challenge. They expect him to run through the spreading shadow and the mud of track and field, but no thought of running enters his mind. The great beasts shake foam from their flanks as their wings are furled. They trample dead-grey earth as they circle, upthrust stands of winter grass shading newer green beneath.

A leader rides among them, set astride a coal-black stallion whose hooves are shod with steel spikes that churn the earth as it tears at the bit. A leader set with visored helm, lacquered black steel to match the plate of his armor. He wears no armband, no white blades. The others slow as they move past and around the stallion, hemming the White Pilgrim in.

The dark figure pulls the helm off easily, sets it under his arm as his gaze meets the White Pilgrim's. Holds it fast. Lines of age and anger are etched in a handsome face. A scar at his neck. Hair hanging to shroud eyes that are black even in the haze of dweomered light.

"By whose leave do you walk this road?"

The Imperial tongue, harsh-clipped in the accent of Norgyr. The leader's voice is twisted with fatigue, but an edge of anger covers it. The White Pilgrim never hears this voice before, but he knows the tone that threads it. Anger born of no specific event or evil, but simply the way of things. The rage that is the heart of every leader of warriors who lives long enough to claim that mantle.

"I asked a question, old man. You would be wise to answer."

The warrior's cloak is steel-grey once, but the stain of too many leagues darkens it to mottled dun and black. A woman rides behind him, hair the silver of midnight frost, and from her hand flies a standard that is altogether fresher. The black boar on red. A banner the White Pilgrim sees above a dozen other warbands in days past. Weeks, perhaps. He cannot remember.

"I walk no road, lord, but the land between roads." Careful words, spoken slowly because the White Pilgrim in his penance leaves words behind. He must think now when he speaks, throat rough with days of silence. Weeks, perhaps. "I have sought leave from no lord or master save Menos, god of travelers, whose grace carries with all who walk within his sight and favor. I make my way in his name and the name of all the Orosana, and have no quarrel with you or any other."

He says the words or variations on them uncounted times before. He is used to the challenge of knight and outrider, farm lord and brigand. From the glance the leader gives to the rider next to him, he hears words like them before.

"These are dark times to be abroad, priest."

"I am no priest. Only a pilgrim in all the gods' names."

"And the dead behind us burned themselves?"

The White Pilgrim glances back to the pyre. Brighter now as darkness and cloud scour the eastern sky. "In the absence of a priest, any of the faith might perform the rites of new life and death."

"You and your fellow pilgrims will find precious little new life in Sannos, old man."

The Duchy of Sannos. Heart of Gracia. Broad hills rolling green with forage and cropland. Broad rivers cutting through sable soil to reach the sea. The White Pilgrim remembers, but he knows not why.

"I am not of these lands," he says simply. But his vision is a wash of light suddenly, and he thinks on his endless road.

"Do you have a name, pilgrim?"

"The name I once bore is lost to my sins and past, my lord…"

The Empire is gone, fifty years and more ago now. And with each year come more folk to walk the leagues-long trek of four seasons. Each year brings a dozen new fanes along the old roads that carry him between the mountains, Drachen's Teeth to Shieldcrest, north to south. Other roads draw him east and west, sea to forest and all the broad lands between. A lifetime of wandering. Seeking solace that never comes.

"I am duke, old man."

"The name I once bore is lost, my duke."

The White Pilgrim feels the light pass, swarmed by shadow. He forgets now. Content to live by the shorter cycle of light and dark, step by step, day by day.

"You are thoughtful, old man," the dark figure says. "Why?"

"The death you seek is here…"

Only as he hears his voice does the White Pilgrim realize he speaks aloud. He knows the words, cannot remember.

A subtle shift marks the dark warrior's gaze. The curiosity of a man used to being feared, who senses now that the White Pilgrim has no fear anymore.

"We kill only those who stand against us," this Black Duke says. "They will stop, in time, and so shall the killing stop with them. I am come to heal Gracia. To see it rise once more to the greatness taken from it."

"The blood of children is on your hands and mine, my duke…"

From the corner of his eye, the White Pilgrim sees the standard-bearer's hand come up. A pulse of spell-fire flares there whose power she draws forth from her blood, her voice. Five other hands hold weapons at the ready in response to the White Pilgrim's words, but he does not flinch.

He sees the Black Duke raise his own hand to stop them all. A dismissive gesture, the warriors under his command obeying without thought. The black boar charges on its crimson field, twisted by the wind.

"I am Arsanc of Thorfin," the dark warrior says evenly. "I am a freelord of Norgyr and duke of Gracia, and I will kill any man or woman who stands against my rightful claim to the throne of this land. But I do not kill children."

"These were boys. By the forge…"

"The villagers are killing their children themselves." A dark weariness to the voice speaks to the truth it tells. "Their faith in your gods of the Orosana runs strong enough that they are willing to embrace the sacrifice of life that all faith demands in the end."

The White Pilgrim feels the words twist in his mind. A thing he cannot think on.

"It is said that the Black Duke fights in the vanguard of his own forces, while the dukes of Gracia linger behind stone and spell-wall." The White Pilgrim recognizes his voice again. He remembers these things, but he knows not why. "He sweeps down from the snows of Norgyr and through the borderlands like a dark storm." Words overheard in shrine and fane. Tales told by refugees across meager fires in the night.

The Black Duke, Arsanc of Thorfin, laughs aloud. The White Pilgrim hears the edge of respect in his voice. Does not understand it.

"You are an observant one. Tell me what you see in your wanderings. Tell me what you know."

If they are razing homesteads, it means that the main brunt of the fighting is done. No one risks warriors and mounts in skirmishes against farmhands if real war yet has any chance to be fought. The forces of the black boar are moving village to village, seeking fealty to a conqueror. When it is not given quickly enough, they burn settlements razed and rebuilt in the aftermath of war a year before, and five years before that, and on and on back through three generations of war that seeks and fails to claim what little remains of Gracia's ancient soul.

"I am only a pilgrim, my duke."

He tries to not think on it. Tries to drive the sense of what this war means from his mind, but it lingers like all the rest of his lost life. Images graven into his dreams by knives of shadow.

"So you said. In all your gods' names." Arsanc laughs again.

The doors of the farmhouses are burned with a mark he recognizes. The black boar of the standard, carved by spell-fire. The White Pilgrim sees the same mark in every other village he passes through on this leg of the long journey. Eastbound this time. The light of dawn at his eyes as the endless leagues carry him closer to the days of the High Spring.

"Your dead gods will stay that way, old man." The Black Duke slips his helm back on, but the strength of his voice does not waver. "Take that message and this one to every temple and mud-shrine you see wherever your wanderings carry you. Duke Hestyoc has sued for peace, and orders his folk to accept his fealty to the black boar. The lands on both sides of the Farwash and the Vouris are under the stewardship of Arsanc, Freelord of Thorfin and Innveig, Duke of Reimari, protector of Mundra, Liana, Lamitri, and Sannos, and heir to the empty marble throne of Gracia."

No sense of hubris carries in the words. Only the dark familiarity that says they are earned and paid for.

"I am not worthy of a place in the gods' fanes," the White Pilgrim says quietly. "But I will take your message to any who might listen."

But in that time when name and heart are cleansed by the memory that takes me, then all Gracia that I saved shall embrace that memory, and I will return for all who speak this Prayer for Dead Kings.'

The Black Duke laughs. "Your impudence marks you as either wise or a fool, old man."

"Very much the fool, my duke."

And with only a flick of leather leads, the dark figure is gone. His great steed leaps to the air with an unfurling of black wings, limned by the last light of day. Shadows slash across the White Pilgrim where he stands. The other warriors follow, thrashing the air to a sudden storm of thunderous wing-beats and the cries of the hassas as they climb, racing each other to the height of the settling darkness.

The White Pilgrim watches for a long while, sees them bound for the east. Gleaming wings dwindle slowly against the black line of the sky.

He walks far by darkness. He passes where the road snakes into dark woods, so that he might escape the sight of the pyre whose glow will outlast the night. He sleeps in a copse of sweet heather and spring lilac. Perfume shrouds the deep descent of night beneath the haze of the Clearmoon, its clipped face sinking within a dark sea of cloud.

In the darkness of that sleep comes the dream.

– TWO –
PILGRIM'S DREAM

HER SKIN IS FAIR ONCE beneath the crust of grime. The dirt of a long road hides her features, her age. The cusp of womanhood, thirteen summers behind her.

Early morning, approaching a market village with a name lost to memory. Within the dream, the White Pilgrim feels a vague recollection of a day he passes there, long ago, but he sees it now with a clarity of sight beyond the softness of his aged eyes. In the distance spreads a wide copse of white cottonwood, branches gleaming leafless and fire-bright as they screen the rising sun. A tumbling creek wends its way north, the grey walls of a mill standing mist-shrouded against the forest behind.

Twisting away from the creek, the ruts of a farm track mark the progress of a wain loaded with flour sacks as it passes. Two emaciated oxen labor heavily as the cart's wheels bump along toward fields cut by low stone fences draped in a haze of hanging smoke.

A few paces behind the wain, caught in the shroud of its dawn shadow, the Golden Girl walks.

For the better part of a week, she follows the farm tracks that parallel the twisting course of the wide-flowing Farwash, four leagues to the east. Her eyes are the blue of burnished steel. Her hair is long, the gold of rain-fresh straw. Tied back and swept beneath the collar of a travel-stained and much-patched cloak. The wind catches this as she walks, revealing a shapeless pack of black leather at her back, a thin blanket tightly rolled.

A third bundle is slung between pack and blanket, more than half her height across back and shoulder. Wrapped and rewrapped in rough homespun, concealed again as she quickly wraps the cloak tight around herself.

She slips away from the cart as it rumbles on where the field fences meet the road. The rough shapes of close-clustered houses stand beyond, dull with the grime of passing winter. Two reluctant goats are dragged along by an unsmiling youth. A peddler leading a laden mule calls out his wares with little enthusiasm.

The Golden Girl ignores all of it. She walks a little more quickly than casual. Around the closest shanties and the muddy sheep track that circles them, the smoke-shrouded fane comes into view.

A thatched roof rises over walls of rough fieldstone, primitive. Shuttered windows are open to the air. The main doors, the two side doors, all of banded planks, stand closed. Above the main doors, a woven crown of white beech branches is set with three stones. She eyes it warily as she pushes inside, is hit by the haze and warmth of the fire that sends a shiver through her, seems to remind her how cold she is.

A broad rust-iron brazier sits atop three stones where a hearth once stands, long ago. A memory of when this place is the village's great hall. Incense is set along the edges of the great bowl, twice-burned charcoal blazing within it in a haze of yellow-white flame. A narrow chimney sits above at the confluence of the ceiling's great beams, venting twisted snakes of smoke to the bright sky. The beams are old but newly carved in the signs and faces of the gods of Gracia. Newly restored to the faith of village folk north and south from Staris to Kannis, west and east from the walls of the Yewnwood to the Leagin coast.

The Golden Girl opens her cloak but does not step toward the fire. A look around to make sure she stands alone, then she adjusts the belts that hold her gear in place, always shifting as she walks. She feels heat thread through her, feels the chill of the oblong bundle lashed tight to her back even through leather, armor, and cloth.

"You are welcome to the fires of the Orosana, pilgrim."

The voice precedes the shuffling steps behind her. The Golden Girl pulls her cloak tight as she fixes the set of her tunic to cover the talisman on its leather thong, cover the chain shirt that lies unseen beneath that. The talisman is the symbol of her father once, who gives it to her mother, who gives it to her. Steeped in the dweomer of protection by the essence of her mother's own life and blood before she dies.

The priest newly slipped out from the shadows wears the livery of a speaker of the Pantheon. The long-dead Orosana who dwell in the twelve mountain peaks of the north and south. His body is soft, rippling beneath the grey robes whose cleanliness shows how infrequently he leaves this dark hall. Eyes set small in a doughy face, porcine in their gaze. A ceremonial mace hangs at his belt, strong enough to deal out injury to a not overly large rat if one happened by.

The Golden Girl takes him in at a glance. She lowers her voice, lets it find the tone of the fatigue she feels. "I am no pilgrim," she says. He will not hear the well-practiced mockery in her tone.

"All travelers are pilgrims in the eyes of the Twelve, and shall carry the blessings of the Orosana if they walk with faith."

In most of the fanes she stops in, the faithful whose faces mark all the endless leagues of her young life are born of the unseeing memory of youth. The legends of Empire and the traditions of the dead faith of the twelve gods of the Orosana are both equally mythical to those who never know either. This priest is older than she expects. Might well remember the last days of Empire. Seeking solace in a dead faith because at the end of his life, he has no time left to hope for the return of the world he knows.

"I seek a pilgrim, though," the Golden Girl says quietly. "An older man, grey hair and beard. He travels alone in the gods' names, passing Miandale four days ago. He did penance at two different fanes outside the city, then left along the farm roads, they said."

"Many pass this way, child."

"He is scarred, this one. On his neck and cheek, an old wound. A limp that cannot heal."

"A soldier?"

"Once. Perhaps." A trace of uncertainty twists through her, hidden as quickly as it comes. She distracts the priest's gaze with the sudden glint of copper in her hand, pressed to his palm.

"I saw one such in the village," the priest says with carefully measured gratitude. "He did penance in the dawn rites. Two days past, I think it was. His health appeared poor, so I bade him take shelter with us, but he was gone before the morning broke."

"He did only penance? Did not stay to rest, to sleep, to warm himself?"

"No," the priest says. "Not while I was here to see, at any rate."

The Golden Girl fights to control the hope that threads her voice.

"Where had he come from?"

"I did not see him arrive..."

"What did he say? What did he speak of, what was his path?" She does not need to ask the destination.

"That he came from the north is all I know. He talked of having crossed the Farwash within sight of the Free City at the spring flood. I expressed surprise that he survived that journey with all the roads of Mundra and Liana teeming for war, but he showed no sign that it concerned him."

The Golden Girl knows that road. She walks it often enough. She turns from the priest as if he vanishes from her thought and attention, already focused on the end of her long journey.

"If the pilgrim should pass this way again, who should I say is seeking him?"

In his voice, the Golden Girl hears the twist of uncertainty. Her focus is back, and sharpened. She meets the priest's faint eyes in the shadows. Knows that it is not on his own behalf that he asks. "Only an old friend. Seeking counsel."

The pig eyes narrow in dark assessment as she turns, but the voice calls out in last hope. "Join me at the fire of Denas the all-father before you go. Join me in prayer for your safe journey in Menos of the road's name." The priest steps to within a pace of the brazier, bends to his knees in a well-practiced ritual.

The Golden Girl turns back, the cloak swirling to let slip a glimpse of the scabbard she wears. High and just behind the hip, letting it slide with her leg as she walks. Easier to conceal but slower to draw. Not that it matters.

She measures the three paces to the brazier, catches its wide edge with her spit. It hisses there, the priest stuttering as he starts to his feet. A look of horror on his face, hands up to make a supplicant's pleading motions to the empty images graven across the fane's smoke-blackened beams.

"I am no pilgrim," she says again as she turns to go.

She keeps her days long. Awake and on the march well before dawn, then adding the moons' light to the steady spring lengthening of the sun. She can only hope that her quarry does not do the same. She takes the time to eat, gnaws a crust of bread as she moves quickly along the northward track. Her pace quickens as she shadows the stone fences.

Two days. Her face shows the effort of trying to hold the calm she feels slipping from her. Six seasons of searching, and seven long years before that, and she is never this close before.

The Golden Girl feels the talisman that is the memory of her mother and father lying cold against her breast. She presses her hand to it through cloak and leather. A reminder of the things her father fought for, dying without knowing whether the lost dreams of the Empire that had been sacred to him would one day be drawn forth from the shadow.

The peddler seen earlier is on his way out of the village already, no buyers that morning but still shouting out for custom. His voice punctuates the sucking of his cart's wheels in the mud.

At her chest, the talisman still held within the flat grasp of her hand, the Golden Girl feels a sudden warmth like the summer sun.

The heat of the charm's warning spreads through the chain shirt against which it rests, pulses in time with her heart, quickening now.

The magic of her mother, long dead but still watching her. Protecting her as it does so many times before.

The Golden Girl hears the wet thud of hoofbeats on the road ahead, rising over the shrill cries of a herd of goats that scatters at their approach. She moves absently off the track, kneels in the shadow of a stone wall as if searching for something lost in the mire at her feet. From the corner of her eye, watched carefully, four armed riders appear at a slow canter. The peddler is forced to scramble, dragging mule and cart aside to clear their path as they come.

From the corner of her eye, she sees the black boar. Her pulse quickens.

She rises, keeps her eyes cast down. She feigns a limp as she hunches low in her cloak. She changes her shape, changes her height, her gait. Letting their eyes pass over her where they search.

She almost succeeds. But like the tingling that marks a foot fallen to blood-sleep, she feels the faint trace of spellcraft twist through her.

A shiver takes her despite her best efforts to quell it. No way to tell the nature of the spell, but in the instant, she pushes all thought, all understanding from her mind. In the recognition of magic, she must force herself to not recognize the magic. She concentrates on the muddy ruts at her feet, counts her steps, whispers a childhood song her mother once sung to her, a lifetime ago now.

She hears the muddy drumming of frantic hooves behind her as the riders rein up, spin around. The thought-magic. The incantation of detection.

She is running, not bothering to look back. Vaulting the low stone fence takes her away from the road, into the cluster of houses and poultry pens just passed. A voice comes from behind her, threaded with a rage she hears too many times before.

"The girl! There!"

But she is already gone.

The Golden Girl runs furiously through the village still just coming to morning life. She dodges surprised folk at walk, slips with ease through sheep bound for the spring meadows. Behind her, she hears the horses thundering along the track, then breaking hard to cross onto the muddy turf of the common in the direction where she disappears. She counts on that, cuts hard around a stone shed and back to retrace her steps.

She risks a glance behind her, sees the company slowing, searching. Their leader is tall, hair shorn in the manner of a seasoned campaigner.

She recognizes him from twice before. Three times? Her memory blurs the faces, each new set of pursuers. No telling how many of the Black Duke's forces are searching for her.

Chaos erupts behind her as the riders plow through the common without care. Villagers scramble to get out their way, a cart overturning when its startled horse bolts. She slips beneath the slats of a rude wooden fence, a handful of goats bleating sudden surprise. A shout from behind, horses spurred on as she is seen.

As she races toward the cottonwoods where they spread close to the rutted eastern road, she feels a pulse of power behind her. She drops by instinct a stride from the low stone fence, hears the crack of shattering stone as the bolt of white light meant for her bursts to tendrils of seeking flame above her. Then she is up and over, two more blasts of spell-fire lashing out behind her as she disappears into the shadow of the trees.

She hears them clear the fence but knows they cannot follow, needing to cut around the wood and pick her up on the other side. She breaks hard south, races back to follow the road where it twists to meet the creek and the mill there.

The Golden Girl is slowing, tired. She fights to adjust the bulk of the tight-wrapped burden on her back as she sprints for the millhouse door, pushes through. Rough planks slam shut behind her. No bar there and a latch a child could break, so she grabs up a battered shovel set nearby and rams it between door and frame like a wedge.

Her eyes draw detail from the shadows as she slips within. Three rough-walled storerooms frame the millworks, loud where the stone turns in steady motion. The movement of the wheel can be glimpsed where the creek flows by below the wide-gapped mouth of the floor.

She moves quickly, seeks out a second entrance and finds it off the larger of the rooms. A narrow window above grimy sacks of grain, haphazardly stacked and the perch of three bone-thin cats that eye her warily. It opens south, out to the forest and the road beyond. The cats scatter as she pulls herself up with tightly muscled arms. She holds there on the wall long enough to gauge the width of the opening against her shoulders.

Then footsteps behind her bring her back to the ground, and from beneath her cloak comes a flash of steel. The rapier is out of its scabbard in a fluid motion. Silent as a serpent, steady in her hand. Her body locks in a warrior's crouching stance. Ready.

A boy stands before her. A millhand, gone from startled to deathly afraid in the blink of an eye. He is young, not much older than her. Thirteen summers behind him.

A distant shout from outside. Faint hoofbeats along the road. She raises the tip of the blade in a smooth arc to alight at the boy's throat.

"One chance. You tell them I slipped out through there." The Golden Girl nods to the window. The millhand boy can only stare. A dull gleam in her other hand. Five copper coins that are likely a month's wages for the boy are slipped to his shaking palm.

"One chance," she says again.

Then the rapier is back in its scabbard even as she moves to the open space of the floor, the wheel flashing below in its steady thrashing movement. No hesitation as she jumps, catches the wheel's edge in a sure grip, swings off it and down. No sound of her fall over the steady hiss and thrash of dark water below.

She does not cry out as the sharp chill cuts through her. She is gone from sight where she wraps the cloak tight around herself, slips into the flow of shadows. Her gear draws her down, but she holds herself high in the water with strong kicks, arms pumping, only her face exposed to watch.

Above the line of the riverbank, she sees horses at the mill, raised voices faint over the wheel's steady din. She has time to watch the four warriors mount up again, heading south along the road and away from her. Then the creek twists round a bend and she is gone.

– THREE –
LINES OF FAITH

THE DREAMS ARE THE LAST SIGN of madness. Last coin paid to the un-seen weaver spooling out the endless thread of life, never-ending by the doom of failure, of weakness, of all mortal sins.

The White Pilgrim remembers these things. He feels the thoughts come to him as he walks, but he knows not why.

He does not recall the point when he comes upon the creek, but he follows it. Its banks are steep and spread with crocus and aconite, flanked by the ruts of intermittent wagon traffic, and by the muddy tracks of sheep and cattle that tell him folk dwell nearby. A village ahead. He remembers.

He remembers also a village behind, filled with the unburned dead. How long ago, he does not know. He remembers the dream of the Golden Girl, knows the vision comes only that morning. He counts the days by the dreams, tries to remember when last he ate but cannot.

He remembers other dreams. Of a friend he betrays, looking for him. A Golden Girl walks with the friend, close at his side. Faint imag-es, half-remembered. Sticking in memory like a bone cutting the back of the throat.

So it was that in the seventh year of his reign, Garneus the King, who had led all Gracia through the Fall of Empire, was called to Orosan in his greatness, to be Herald to the Triad and the Twelve. So did Eurymos ascend to the marble throne, and pledged to uphold his Father's justice and the strength of Gracia reborn. But those also were the days of Thoradun who would be the Usurper, who ruled as King in Sannos, and who with sorcery and secrecy tainted the minds of the Lords of the Northlands. And those Lords railed against the rule of Eurymos, and did fight among themselves and against the Southlands for long years. And in the end did the Lords of the Northlands send messages to Aldona, which said 'Eurymos is King in the South, but we of the North must choose our own path.' And Thoradun was named their King, and the Wars of Succession had begun.

As the rough track twists around the edge of an ancient alder copse, the farmland fane swings into view. Set within stony fields edged on three sides by twisting lines of younger trees, it stands bro-ken-walled and hunched like some great beast.

Farm thorps scattered to the distance are faint beneath the gleam of sun and muddy fields, low stone fences following the ebb and flow of hilly soil. No sign of burning here, save for the fane. The walls are whole when last the White Pilgrim passes by. Now he sees a slack-fallen spread of stones, splintered beams, charred thatch.

Then in the ninth year of the reign of Eurymos as King, which was the third year of the struggle of the Southlands against Thoradun the Usurper, there came the black Day of Death. And on that day in the courts at Aldona and Aynwel, Charath and Valos, Maris and Cosiand, Princes and Lords and their Overseers, their Captains and Advisors were stricken by the Fell Sorcery of Thoradun's Necromancers.

Scorched lines along the ground and around the fane run too straight to mark the heat of anything but spell-fire, burning itself out as it unleashes the full potential of its destruction. The sign of the black boar is etched across the stones of a still-standing wall.

And Eurymos the King was slain with all the rest by the Dark Magic that despoiled body and soul, and prevented the return of the soul, and among all his kin and people, there was despair.

The day is high and hot, and burning in concert with the pain in his chest to sear the dreams from the White Pilgrim's mind. He knows the road from two seasons before. Three seasons. He shakes his head, cannot remember. No matter anymore.

As he approaches the fane, he watches them work with unceasing effort beneath the heat. A dozen. No. Fourteen he counts as he limps toward them, tracking along rough islands of dry pathway twisting through the mud. They shore up what remains of the roof of the fallen building with fence rails. Woodworkers labor to plane new posts as the tumbled wall is carefully taken apart, sized and reset again, course by slow course of stone.

They see him approach. They hear him. No one looks up.

"By the grace of Denas and the Twelve, take the blessings of this wanderer upon you." The White Pilgrim speaks slowly, fights to remember the words.

They work on in their sullen silence, the weight of stone and timber made heavier by injury. The White Pilgrim notes the mark of fire and blade on the arm and shoulder of the broad-nosed farmer who is the only one who speaks. "A blessing on you, old man, and best you move on."

"Keep your tongue civil in Denas's house, Olan. And mind your manners."

The new voice comes from the one who directs the efforts of the carpenters. A priest by the grey of his tunic, its color not noticed beneath the grime of his labor until he turns.

"Denas's house has no roof, and won't if every beggar passing by interrupts the work." The man Olan sends a dark look toward the White Pilgrim, who sets his eyes down before the priest's gaze, speaks humbly.

"I am no beggar, lord, but am willing to work for my share of whatever repast you might spare. All hands do the gods' work if the gods' plans are the work of the heart."

"We got folk enough we can't feed already without…"

The priest's raised hand cuts Olan off. A power in the gesture that speaks to the strength of the gods' laws among the folk of green fields and grassland.

"We have men enough on the wall, pilgrim," the priest says gently, "but could use more stone from the fields. Our repast is yours to share, of course, in Danassa's name."

Danassa is goddess of field and furrow, her breath the touch of spring ready to bring new life to the world. The White Pilgrim nods as he turns back, shuffles into the mud and bends to the task appointed him.

And on that day, Telos, Brother to Eurymos and Father to Gilvaleus, was with his Brother, and would have been slain by the Usurper if not for the intervention of Irthna the Silver Sorceress, who was Mother to Gilvaleus and had counseled Eurymos long years since leaving Telos her lover's side. And Telos had pledged his life to his Brother and King through long years of fealty, and wept at Eurymos's side now, and said to Irthna 'Why did thou not leavest me to save him, our King and best hope for our land?' And Irthna swore that for the love she granted Telos and always had, she saved him, and that their love that had saved him was the sign of fate and the choice of the Gods that Telos be King and avenge his Brother for the sake of all Gracia.

The White Pilgrim blinks. The sun moves, sloping toward the line of sky westward, burning gold against twisting cloud. Around him, stones are set in three piles by his labor, equidistant. The sign of the Triad of Brothers. Denas, the storm lord. Rhilos, the hammer and shield. Phion, the earth and sea.

He stands silent a while to quell the pain at his heart and in his leg. His back and neck are set with the full ache of the afternoon's stooped labor. He watches to see where the others work with focused determination, one ruined wall of the fane rising near to full height once more. So it is that he is the first to see the dark figures advancing along the field walls.

His eyes are watering, blinking back dust. The figures come from the east along the dusky line of the sky, so that it takes time to recognize that these are more farm folk, advancing with fork and staff in hand. Their voices follow them, angry words caught and lost on the rising wind. The White Pilgrim sees the reaction in the priest and the others, their work forgotten as they spread out before the fane's fallen doors.

"Caris!" The one leading the group stands one-eyed and hulking where he shouts. Bare-chested and clad in leather below the waist. The labor of countless seasons twists along his arms like knotted ropes, beard flecked with grey and a staff in his hand. "You and all the rest, get back to your families. Your work here's done!"

The priest answers to the name called. "Hold there, Gadro."

"I'll hold not while you and your faith-snakes call down the wrath of the black boar again! You played the fool for dead gods once and paid the price. You won't make me and mine pay it a second time."

A surge of anger spills out between both groups as the advancing farm folk slow. They face friends and neighbors along a rough line marked by fear. Subtle movements, eyes shifting side to side. Tools are held tight to become weapons in work-worn hands.

"The Black Duke is usurper and tyrant…" the priest begins, but he is quickly cut off.

"Arsanc's peerage is no concern of mine!" the one called Gadro shouts. "Nor do I care who sits on Mitrost's broken throne. I'm Sannos-born and bred, and paid tithe all my life to a duke that's never set foot on my lands. Paying tithe to Arsanc instead is no care to me, so long as me and mine are left to our lives in peace, and you and your gods stand in the way of that!"

"These are the Orosana's lands." The priest Caris speaks in a voice of booming authority, meant as much for the farmers at his back as for these newcomers, the White Pilgrim knows. Fear pushes all folks' minds too quickly to the edge of changing. "The dukes of Gracia once governed by the Twelve's laws, and will again, gods willing. Arsanc and his heathen law…"

"If it's no gods at all that Arsanc will bow to, then I'm heathen with him. Ten generations, my folk have farmed these lands, and never once saw the hand of your gods in any harvest, good or bad. Nature is as nature does, and mortal magic makes its difference when it needs to."

"Our magic is the gift of the gods…"

"I call down the weal of the druidas as well as any in my line ever did, priest, and I never asked no god for the gift."

The priest spits. Unexpected anger in him. "Your Empire's faith of self is a shell of deceit. You raise your hopes and dreams on fragile ground, and they will fall."

"Weren't my Empire anymore than Arsanc is my lord, but I leave well enough alone so I can go my way. Farm my lands, heal my folk…"

"The beasts of the field know not that Denas the high father bestows the sanctity of life and speeds the blood in their veins. By the same ignorance, you ignore that it is the gods' healing power that flows in you…"

"You want to believe it, that's your right and welcome to it. But Arsanc has no patience for your gods, and Arsanc's band made clear when they smote your gods' hall. You raise those walls again, they burn our farms!"

Druid and priest press close, and a sudden surge of power sends followers on both sides scattering. Caris clenches one hand to his chest, the other raised to a fist that pulses suddenly with white light, squeezed out from tight-locked fingers. Gadro raises the staff and whispers a fragment of incantation, the old magic, black oak at his hands suddenly studded with a surge of thorns that gleam in the golden light of setting sun.

"Peace be with you both…"

With a start, priest and druid turn in equal surprise. Each is so focused on the other, on the dark uncertainty twisting between both groups that the White Pilgrim hobbles forward without being seen. He stares darkly as his words hang. Hesitates as if uncertain whether the voice that speaks them is his.

"The way of folk is to choose sides," the White Pilgrim says. He feels a weakness in him suddenly, the pain in his chest flaring. He shuffles a step forward that he does not mean to take, the closest in both groups shifting back, cautious. "The way of gods is too often to divide faith from faith, but it need not be this way."

The priest appraises him with a dark curiosity. The druid merely laughs. "One priest intent on burning in the name of faith is enough for us, old man."

"I am no priest. Only a pilgrim in all the gods'…"

A twisting of gnarled hands, and the thorn staff is a blur of black as it swings for the White Pilgrim's flank. But the White Pilgrim is gone, two steps to the side suddenly as a blow that would lay him out lashes only empty air.

The druid Gadro stumbles back. He is off balance, nearly falls before he rights himself. All the anger in him is redirected from the priest in an instant.

"Spry for your age, father," he says darkly. "The gods' grace be with you?"

Another swing, too fast to see. The White Pilgrim shifts with it, feels the staff slip past him by a finger's width. From behind the druid, two figures move, rough cudgels of firewood raised. A dangerous energy threads the air suddenly. Anger and fear twist through friends facing neighbors, seeking opportune release against this stranger.

Then even as Telos swore his hate of Thoradun the Usurper and took up his Brother's crown to quell the fear of the Lords of the Southlands, he bade Irthna take Gilvaleus their Son, now the Young Prince, and keep him safe from the Usurper's shadow lest it strike again at him and those closest to him. So was Gilvaleus, with fifteen Summers behind him and ready to take his place in the ranks of his Father's Knights, taken from his Father by Irthna his Mother, and then were great Spells of Enchantment placed upon him that hid away his name and memory, to a secret place that only Irthna's choice or death could unlock.

He blinks.

Something is changed. The fight is done.

The druid Gadro, the priest Caris both lie in the mud to either side of him. Gadro is motionless, choking breath through the haze of blood from a shattered nose. Caris is moving, scrambling back with one arm hanging, the bone broken to judge by the pallor at his face and the pain that turns his breath to a rasping hiss.

Three others are down, crawling away. All the White Pilgrim can think on is that he cannot remember which side they stood for.

Then was Gilvaleus sent to Kalista Keep in Magandis in the North, where King Astran was a most fair man, but in the conflict between King Telos and the Usurper did acknowledge Thoradun, who had promised to leave the lands of Magandis free as long as its folk paid fealty and fought at Thoradun's behest. Thus did Irthna know that her Son would be safer in that city than in any of the courts of the Southlands where Thoradun might think to seek him, and no suspicion cast on him there.

The White Pilgrim looks to see blood on his hands. A torn swatch of someone's tunic is clutched in shaking fingers.

"I will not fall..." he whispers, but he knows not why. The cloth slips from his grasp, twists like a sanguine leaf as it falls to the ground.

So was Gilvaleus named as Guderna, and was called a Squire's cousin's son as he was sent into service in the armories with name and memory not his own. But there was he quickly made a source of scorn, whereby the sons of Squires and Knights called him farmhand, and Gilvaleus-who-was-Guderna soon grew the repute of a hard fighter, who would not turn from taunt or jest. And all such affronts were met instead with all the strength of the Young Prince's heart that not even the mighty magics of Irthna his Mother could undo, which told him that against taunt or threat or the beatings of those that were his masters now, he would not fall.

"Trust to the gods," he stammers. "Trust to their judgement, but do not…"

Then one day was the Young Prince assigned to a Knight's train as handler of arms to walk alongside the pack horses, and in this train were two Squires on horse who were two that had taunted the boy they called Guderna, and who laughed now to see him under their own orders. And in the train was a Fair Girl, in the livery of a noble house but cloaked and hooded, who was to be escorted from Kalista to the City of Lysar.

"Others will not understand. Others will claim to see the truth of one thing… of other things. Do not make yourselves… Do not make your faith the target of others' wrath."

"Begone, heathen!"

But on that road at sunset of the third day was the Knight's train attacked by the White Giants of the Northlands, that pressed down for their dark hunt from the icy shoulder of the Drachen's Teeth. Brave fought the Knight but was thrown down, and his Squires did flee to save their own lives. Then the Young Prince did take up fallen sword and stand alone against the horde, and shouted that the Fair Girl should flee, and on his life he would stand and fall in her defense.

The priest is on his feet now. Folk who stood facing each other just moments before stand together now behind him.

"Leave your fane as rubble for the Black Duke's eyes," the White Pilgrim says, "as you take your faith to hearth and field and make all your places holy…"

"Begone! Take away your false words and the blood on your hands!"

But the Fair Girl did not flee, and standing back to back with the Young Prince, she threw off cloak and hood and he was sore amazed to see the Daughter of the King Astran, fair Cymaris, who carried the power of the Sorcery that was her blood birthright from her Mother. Then fighting side by side did the two vanquish the howling threat of the Giants, and Cymaris slew their master, though the Young Prince Gilvaleus who she knew as Guderna was sore wounded and near death.

Nothing more to say. Nothing more he can do. The White Pilgrim stumbles as he turns. He feels a new ache in his shoulder, the knuckles raw on his bloody hand. Through the mud of the field and toward the track, his eyes are watering as he limps toward the setting sun.

And with magic draughts that were her Father's gift, Cymaris brought the bloodied Young Prince to health. And she said 'Thou wilt come with me and be safe, for I see the strength in thee and would not squander it for service to those less than thee.' And seeing her, the young Gilvaleus who knew not that name knew her fairness, and felt a longing unaccustomed as she held him and they took horse and rode away.

Ahead, the alder copse is beaten copper, black branches clawing at the molten sky. Raised voices echo from behind him, but the White Pilgrim does not hear. He blinks away the pain of the light, casts all thought aside. Tries to begin the process of forgetting what happens here.

From the edge of the tree line, a figure watches him.

A smooth silhouette stands against the flame-roiled sky, holding in the lee of a twisting trunk. Diffuse light etches rough-skinned bark, arm-branches raised overhead as in warning. Through the blur of his sight, the White Pilgrim sees the shadowed face, the straw-gold hair. The girl's blue eyes are bright. Watching with a look that tells him she watches for some time.

And then she is gone, slipping back into shadow with skirled cloak and the faintest trace of footsteps across the forest floor. The White Pilgrim stumbles, slows even as the sound of distant hoofbeats rises and falls. Riders are passing on the well-traveled wain road to the west. A haunted cry comes sharp in his hearing as a sunset-hunting falcon is flushed from the distant trees.

Then all is quiet again. A breath of wind rises, seeming to whisper in words. It takes the White Pilgrim a moment to realize that the words are his.

And in the court of King Astran did Guderna who was Gilvaleus find himself presented to Cymaris's Father, and on her word, the King made him one of his Daughter's protectors, and claimed for him rank and pay besides. So did the Young Prince's hand once more hold the sword that he had been trained to, the best blade in his Father's court at twelve Summers. Then soon was he training Cymaris to the blade, so that her skill was awe and wonder to her Father and the court, and the Young Prince claimed the captaincy of her Father's guard, and Cymaris with her Sorcery was her Father's advisor and heir. And the Young Prince loved her, and sought his life at her side for all time.

He feels an emptiness twist through him, but he knows not why.

The White Pilgrim is cold suddenly. He feels the call of the track he follows, the track that leads him here, that will lead him past the copse where the Golden Girl stands a moment before. The track he knows he must follow, though he knows not why. He pushes through a screen of black saplings and copper shadows and is gone.

– FOUR –
FOUND AND LOST

DARKNESS IS CLOSE, the sky cut by claws of shadow. His pace is hobbled by the pain at his heart, and by the new ache he carries as a reminder of the fight he leaves behind. He stoops once to wet his hands with the rank milk of black toadstools, scouring the blood from them with clods of dead leaves.

He listens, not sure what he fears to hear. In the shadow that fills his mind suddenly, he sees the Golden Girl's face. A vision that he quickly forgets, letting the image slip away as he gazes beyond it.

Only a dream, he tells himself. He does not understand.

Ahead, the trail rises gently to be lost in a clearing. A broad well of stony turf and leaf mold spreads within the sloping tree line, grey in the last light of dusk as he approaches. Something presses on the White Pilgrim now. He is wary, but he knows not why.

Ahead, a ring of giants are hunched in the shadows, lurking in wait. He falters. His hand strays to his waist by forgotten instinct, grasping only empty air.

He shakes his head to clear his sight, vanquishing the trick of the eye that transforms a cluster of ruined huts. The clearing is a hunting thorp long abandoned, wind blowing faintly through bare trees. From behind him, a nighthawk calls.

And in that time, the greatest Knight of Marthai and Veneranda was Nàlwyr, of the Ilvani of the Danawood, who had learned his skill at arms at the hands of his Father, who was a bandit and rogue and bard of great legend of that forest. But Nàlwyr had broken with his Father when but a youth of fourteen Summers, and made his way to Hypriot and sought service in the Prince's Company but was rebuffed for lack of noble blood.

"You fight well for a greybeard."

He hears the voice as laughter, ringing like a clear bell. Six paces away, a wedge of stone thrusts up from grey grass. The Golden Girl sits there, nearly invisible in the falling dark. Waiting for him. Watching with eyes the blue of burnished steel.

Then the young Nàlwyr made challenge to the Captains of the company, and the Captains scoffed, saying 'We fight Warriors, not children full of pride and hubris, so go now boy, back to thy family and thy fate.' And Nàlwyr's eyes of steel blue flashed as brightly as his blade as he issued challenge again to Sergeants and Knights and Squires in turn, who scoffed and turned away, except for one.

The White Pilgrim sees those steel-blue eyes following as he twists his gait, sweeps around the Golden Girl as if she might be puddle or sinkhole, a rock or bole blocking his path. Her hair is long, the gold of rain-fresh straw. Tied back and swept beneath the collar of a travel-stained and much-patched cloak.

He sees silver at her ears, a bright gleam even in the failing light. Four rings at the left, two at the right. The twist-thickened silverwork of the forest Ilvani, the style of all the folk of the Great Woods. The White Pilgrim does not notice before. The Golden Girl's face not seen so closely in his dreams.

He stumbles where his foot is clutched by a gnarled stump of root, thrust up from the ground, unseen in shadow. He remembers a dream. Riders in a village, hunting a girl whose name he does not know.

And that one was the Prince Sestian himself, who trained with his troop in their armor and in the livery of a Captain, and was accorded no sign or symbol of rank in battle, for he had pledged to fight always as the companion of all those who served him, and to fall at their side if fate so decreed. And Sestian said to Nàlwyr 'In this time of war, any who offer to lay their blade and life for Land and People shall be accorded the respect of a Knight, even though they lack the skill and heart.'

The White Pilgrim walks on into shadow. He hears the Golden Girl's soft footsteps fall into place on the path behind him.

He tries to not think on these things anymore.

"You've traveled far by your look," she calls. "Pilgrim, are you?"

The huts vanish into darkness behind as he falters at the edge of the clearing. He seeks for a moment to find another trail twisting into the trees, barely visible. Black branches grasp like witch's fingers as he pushes through.

"You must have a name, wanderer," the Golden Girl says, voice close at his ear. His mind judges her size as he sees it, gauges the sound of her step and finds it harder than it should be, even for a long road. A weapon at her hip. Armor to make the weight he hears. And something else.

"Call me Justain. My father named me for the justice and the peace that is the legacy of the true high king."

"You prattle, child."

The White Pilgrim hears the anger in his words as if from a distance. Someone else speaking with his voice. Something is wrong. Something is changed, but he does not understand.

"I mean no offense, sir, even as I note the fall of night. Two travelers on the same road by chance would be wise to camp together, this far from the villages. I have food that I am happy to share. A tale, perhaps."

"I walk alone."

"I have walked alone. For too long. I grow tired of walking alone."

Then the Prince Sestian faced the boy Nàlwyr, whose blade sang the song that his Father had taught, and who disarmed his Prince and master never knowing his name. And Sestian's Captains and Knights were enraged and came to their Prince's aid, but Sestian bade them hold, and ordered each of his Knights in turn to face the boy.

"You do not walk," he says. "You run. At the sound of horse by sunset. Hunted by the Black Duke's riders."

And when each Knight had fallen to Nàlwyr's arm and the bright singing of his blade, then did Sestian order his Sergeants to the field, and then his Captains. And in the end, all laid down their arms and begged quarter of the boy, and the Prince Sestian called Nàlwyr to him and made known his name, and Nàlwyr bent to his knee and was ashamed for the hubris he had unwittingly shown his Prince and Liege. But Sestian named him Knight, and said 'Thy days of shame are done, and legends will be made of thee.'

The White Pilgrim does not look back, but he feels the fear that threads the Golden Girl's silence. "You've seen them?" she says at last. "The riders?"

"No."

"Then you know nothing, old man."

"I know that no forces save the Black Duke's ride in Sannos now. Duke Hestyoc has sued for peace. Arsanc controls lands on both sides of the Farwash and the Vouris."

"Arsanc's ambition is as empty as his deeds. This land belongs to the people, and a true king worthy of them."

"This land belongs to the Orosana and those who hold the faith of the Twelve who forged Gracia from rock and iron."

Her pace quickens then. She slips through the trees alongside him, will not lose him, a pale blur in the shadow. "Arsanc is a pretender to greatness. He claims the legacy of a past that does not belong to him, as he claims a nation he has no right to rule."

"I care not who rules Gracia, any more than I care why a wayward girl holds the Black Duke's interest."

The twisting trail breaks suddenly to a wide dell, a dark slash across its heart marking the east-west road that they are circled around to meet. First starlight streaks the trail and the trees, and the haze above that marks where the waning Clearmoon hides out the day in the darkening sky. The White Pilgrim stays his course toward the road, intent on pushing past the Golden Girl where she walks facing him, her light step avoiding obstacles she cannot see.

But then from the corner of his eye, he sees her falter. Hand to her breast, she clutches at something beneath her tunic.

The hoofbeats come a moment later, faint in the distance. Fear in the Golden Girl's face, in her voice as she spins to scan the black track behind them. "We must get off the road." She holds a rapier in hand, drawn too quickly for the White Pilgrim to see it. Its fine blade is a line of silver starlight in the gloom.

"I walk alone," he says.

Torchlight through the trees now. They come from the west, cantering fast. The steady thud of their approach is a deadly drumbeat, muffled by the trees.

"Please..." she says.

"Please yourself and get back to the woods."

"I can't."

He hears the pain in those words. He does not understand, but his anger wavers. "I will tell them I saw you near the fane. You headed south across the fields. Menos keep and watch you."

"I won't leave you. I've searched too long for you..."

That stops him. The White Pilgrim turns, stares through starlight and shadow.

"Gilvaleus..." she whispers, but he only shrugs his aching shoulder. Not a name he knows.

They are standing that way, face to face, the Golden Girl's blade still drawn as the horses thunder in. They pull up short with shouts and a haze of dust. Four riders in tight formation, all with torches blazing and cloaks wrapped tight against encroaching night. The leader is tall, hair shorn in the manner of a seasoned campaigner. He barks an order in the rough tongue of Norgyr as the riders spread out, surrounding the White Pilgrim and the Golden Girl as she turns to go back to back against him.

A circle of shifting horses and weapons surrounds them. Two crossbows. Two of the short sideswords that the Norgyr favor from horseback, blades triple-tempered blue-black and razor honed. The four warriors are road weary, eyes dark. Keeping close, but wary of the Golden Girl's blade hanging steady in her hand.

The leader raises a torch. He meets her defiant gaze with a cold smile, but it is the White Pilgrim he speaks to.

"Your name, old man?"

"The name I once bore is lost to my sins and past, my lord. I am only a pilgrim in all the gods' names."

The warrior laughs. He is younger than the gaze of his dark eyes, face seamed with the faint scarring that healing magic leaves behind. Like so many of the Norgyr, his skin is burned by wind and sun even in the nascent spring. His pale hair hangs long, beard short, both knife-cut roughly. He wears leather like the others, a shirt of ring mail hanging loose over it. Like the others, he wears the black boar on the red band at his shoulder. His is set with two blades in white that mark his rank.

"I am Gareyth, sergeant to my Duke Arsanc," the warrior says. "What business have you with this girl?"

"None, my lord. She met me on the trail and ignores my pleas to leave me be."

Behind him, he hears her breathing quicken. She is afraid now, which makes him realize she has no fear before. Not caring about the Black Duke's forces, but cut by the White Pilgrim's words.

"Let me help you then." The sergeant lowers his sword, swinging it behind him to mark the White Pilgrim's path out of the circle and into the empty night beyond.

"Denas walk with you," the White Pilgrim says to the Golden Girl as he goes. He looks back to her, sees her eyes wet as he limps carefully between the horses, head bowed.

The sergeant, Gareyth, speaks to the Golden Girl. The White Pilgrim is already forgotten as he slips into the darkness.

"Days to the king's conclave, and half the armies of Thorfin and Reimari are scouring Gracia for you, bastard brat. The pains you've put me and my troop through, you should be thankful that my Duke Arsanc has ordered you brought to him undamaged."

The White Pilgrim hears but does not understand. He is a dozen paces past the Golden Girl, past the riders. The empty altercation is already on its way to being forgotten.

But he slows. A compulsion he does not understand twists through him as he turns back.

The Golden Girl's response to the sergeant's threat is a blur of grey steel that arcs out as she moves. The closest rider fires a crossbow, aiming low for the leg. The Golden Girl counts on that, leaping as the bolt strikes dirt behind her, then using the force of her movement to drive the rapier through the soft back of the warrior's leg and into the flank of his horse beneath.

The beast screams in pain, bucking backward even as she ducks below it. The warriors with crossbows find their line of fire broken. They draw swords instead, joining the sergeant as he fights to keep his horse in position, block the Golden Girl's escape.

She makes no move to flee, though. The White Pilgrim watches her weave between two of the northern knights, defying the advantage of elevation as she parries both their blades, drives the rapier through the hand of one and sends him tipping from the saddle. His torch tumbles to the ground, his uninjured hand groping for his fallen sword, but the Golden Girl sends the blade outside the circle of combat with a furious kick.

The torch is snatched up in her off hand, the Golden Girl spinning to lock it to the rapier as she cross-blocks the sergeant, slashing at her shoulder. She hurls the flaming brand at his horse in turn, the beast rearing as it dumps him unceremoniously to his back.

The last rider vaults from the saddle, not trusting his horse in the sudden chaos. The Golden Girl meets him, darting in fast and low as the incantation he utters marks him as the battle-caster of the group. His hands are twisting through the precise pattern of his magic even as the Golden Girl drives the rapier through one of those hands. The mage's spell dies in a cry of pain as he staggers back. He raises his good hand by instinct as if to ward her off, so that the Golden Girl's blade takes him through that hand just as cleanly, crippling his spellcasting in twin jets of blood as she screams.

"En nom du haroya!"

An oath in the tongue of Gracia, echoing through long years.

In the name of the High King…

She tries to reach the sergeant before he rises, but the Norgyr warrior twists serpent-fast. He rolls to his feet to parry her initial thrust, pushes forward with three fast strikes. One tags her cloak, slashed out in a feint as she slips past him. The second two crash off the guard of her blade. A second feint to slip back, but another of Arsanc's knights is there suddenly. Then the third, leg bleeding as he screams in rage.

Caught between them, the Golden Girl turns one to the other, dropping to a defensive posture. They fight in deadly rhythm by response, timing their strikes as she turns.

Not even her speed saves her this time.

The sergeant cuts hard at her shoulder, but his blade shrieks as it rakes steel, the armor she wears revealed as her tunic is slashed through. Tightly woven chain gleams the pale grey of dwyrsilver, but though the strength of that armor protects her, the force of the sergeant's attack twists her off balance. He shifts behind her to strike low, cutting deep into her leg.

The Golden Girl does not cry out as she falls.

The sergeant pins her rapier hand beneath his boot, his mouth a wolf's grin as she struggles in vain to escape. But then he spins on his heel suddenly, a hand at his shoulder. A look of surprise as the pommel of a Norgyr sword shatters his nose.

The White Pilgrim is there, torch in one hand, the blade that the Golden Girl kicked free of the fray in the other. A moment of shock on the faces of the Black Duke's troops as their sergeant staggers back, collapses to his knees even as they leap to the attack. Not fast enough.

Torch and sword move in tight arcs, locked together to block and parry, then swung free, striking hard. Blades flash to left and right of him, but the White Pilgrim twists away like wind-blown smoke, driving one guard back with fire as he disarms the other with three furious strikes. The Norgyr's blade is sent to the shadows behind him, his sword hand cut to the bone.

The sergeant tries to rise, face a mask of dust and blood. His shaking legs go out from under him as the Golden Girl drives her knee to his stomach. She drops on him, his back cracking as she raises the rapier, gripped tight in both hands.

The red-limned tip of the blade touches his neck. The White Pilgrim sees. Stops. He limps back from the one guard still standing, who dares not move.

The Golden Girl fights to slow her breathing. The wound at her leg is a blossom of red-black. Shaking hands let the rapier slip, trace a razor-line of jagged red along the sergeant's skin. His eyes are tight on hers, bruise-dark pits against the flickering firelight of the White Pilgrim's torch.

"Why do you follow me?" she says. Pain threads her voice, teeth set as a grim line against it.

"My Duke Arsanc's orders."

The White Pilgrim watches the sergeant spit blood as he speaks. Gareyth, the young warrior's name is. He does not remember why he knows it. Uncertain suddenly as to why he stands there.

"Three years since my father and I first saw the black boar, in Charath. Roaming Gracia in secret a full two years before your duke was even thinking on moving against Reimari. Why?"

"My Duke Arsanc's orders…"

The sergeant closes his eyes, will say nothing more. He waits to die.

The Golden Girl stares for a long moment. Then she stands slowly, keeps the blade at Gareyth's throat until she steps quickly away, out of any reach. He is on his feet in an instant, stumbling back. The White Pilgrim is there, sword up in warning.

"Leave your weapons," the Golden Girl says. "Ride."

In the sergeant's pack as he helps the wounded to their horses, the Golden Girl finds glass vials packed in sheepskin. They gleam with a pale blue light, the telltale sign of a healing draught. She takes two, leaves the other two for the sergeant and his warriors to sort among themselves. The White Pilgrim watches as she drinks, sees the blood at her leg staunched, the set of her wounded shoulder slowly straighten itself.

The Norgyr move out at the slower speed of the wounded horse, hoofbeats vanishing quickly into the utter dark that their single torch leaves behind. The sergeant Gareyth is in the lead. He does not look back.

The Golden Girl hurls three shortswords to the forest, cracks the stock of each crossbow with well-placed kicks. The White Pilgrim looks wonderingly to the borrowed blade in his own hand, thinks to throw it after the others. The fight is already fading in his mind. He slips the sword to his belt instead.

The Golden Girl stands listening to the silence of the night, ensuring that the Black Duke's soldiers are truly gone. And only then, the White Pilgrim sees her resolve crumble.

Her bravado breaks for the moment it takes to reveal the child she is. She fights back tears, the weeping that wracks her slight frame, eyes squeezed shut. The dirt of a long road hides her fear. Thirteen summers behind her.

Then the moment is past and the steel-blue eyes are dry. She passes the healing draught to the White Pilgrim, but he shakes his head. She slips it within her cloak. Stands in silence, watching him.

"You fight well for a bastard brat," he says finally. Dismissive. The Golden Girl's blue eyes are cold as the White Pilgrim turns, heads off with torch held high. She follows a half-dozen steps behind.

– FIVE –
DEAD LEGENDS

THE WHITE PILGRIM WALKS until the torch begins to sputter, breaking only then from the track of the road for the darker wood beyond. The Golden Girl follows, stays close to see the faint trail he finds and walks along. She glances behind her, as she does all the time since they set out. As she has before, she sees only darkness there.

He moves with a slow certainty. Realizes that he passes this way before, long ago. The trees shift to gnarled scrub pine, tight-set bough to bough, a wall of shadow. And just as the torch threatens to gutter out, he leads the Golden Girl to slip past that wall and into the sheltered grove beyond.

The White Pilgrim stoops where he remembers the shallow firepit scraped out from ancient soil. He finds charcoal fragments spread there, covered now with a skin of winter-dry leaves. He sets them burning with the last flickering of the torch, lets that kindling flame consume its stump. He shuffles in the shadows, finds branches that he adds slowly. Faint tongues of fire feed hungrily as they rise to a bright blaze.

In the light of that blaze, the Golden Girl stares to the wall of forest where it marks the boundary of a great-stone circle that rises around them in the darkness. Slabs of white granite, rough-struck and planed. They taper faintly along their length as they rise to twice her height, set in a perfect ring within which the ground is clear. The old magic of druidas. The tree-priests marking the consecration of this place.

The White Pilgrim feels the power lurking within the whispering pines, kneeling to face the tallest stone as he murmurs thanks to Menos, god of travelers, for his grace and protection. When he turns back, the Golden Girl is sitting close by the fire, holding deadfall with which to feed it. Her cloak is a shroud of shadow where she crouches within it, stares to the darkness.

Justain, her name is. He remembers.

Her waterskin and pack are set out across from her, bread and salt pork waiting to be eaten.

"Save the bread," the White Pilgrim says as he paces. The strength of the battle just fought is still in his limbs, pushing the pain away for a time. The Golden Girl says nothing, flicks her gaze to meet his.

He feels something familiar in those eyes, so he turns away.

He sits finally, remembers that he still wears the Norgyr warrior's shortsword when its narrow guard catches him hard in the ribs. He pulls it naked from his belt, stares at its edge against the firelight for a moment before he sets it aside.

Justain eats a piece of the pork, chews slowly to soften it. Thoughtful. "Bread ill-feeds the exertion of battle," she says finally. "Wounds need the nourishment of meat to heal. A warrior would know that."

He answers by tearing a piece of bread, peeling mold from the crust before he eats.

"You were a soldier once?" Her voice is flat, emotionless in a way that draws his attention to it. Hiding something. "A general? Something more?"

She calls him a name, before the fight. He tries to remember it but cannot.

"I saw that limp you have," she says. "I thought you might have been a soldier."

"Think what you like."

"I think you know who I am. So why do you pretend?"

With a twisted length of pine branch, the White Pilgrim banks the fire, sending sparks to spiral up past the standing stones. Dark shapes against the star-streaked sky. His hand shakes, a hint of anger in his gaze. She sees it.

"People have too many things to remember," she says. "Too many regrets. Do you have regret?"

"A man who dies with no regrets dies without having lived." His voice tells him he is angry. He knows not why.

On the closest stone, the White Pilgrim sees weathered runes in a script he cannot read. Not Gracian but older. Their meaning hidden now, lost over the endless years of Empire that shaped language and thought to one unbreakable whole. Likely no one left in any land who can still read all the stories that only the past now speaks.

Then at the High Winter did Prince Sestian of Marthai and Veneranda declare for Telos, and so did war press finally to the borders of Magandis. And King Astran did send forth Guderna who was Gilvaleus, in lead of two hundred Knights of his realm, and in those battles he did acquit himself in great heroic form.

"My father died a year ago. Before he did, he told me he had only one regret," the Golden Girl says.

And standing singly against full scores of Sestian's best swords, the young Captain Guderna took no wound, and showed his foes great quarter and did turn countless of them against their Lords and to King Astran's side. And Telos fighting in the South heard word of this new Captain but had no knowledge then that his Son had been bound to the Daughter of his enemy's ally, and neither could know the other across the gulf of war in the North.

The White Pilgrim waves his head to show his disinterest, drinks from her waterskin. He realizes how parched he is only when he hears himself speak, throat tight, voice raw with the fear he cannot place.

"And what was that?"

"That he never saw his high king again…"

With the words comes a weight of loss and apprehension. She looks up to the sharp light of the stars, then back. The White Pilgrim does not meet her gaze.

"You are Gilvaleus," she says.

"No…"

A single name. So small a word in response, but he fights to force it out. He feels a pain that stabs at his chest like a rusted blade plunged in, then again, again.

"He followed you from the field at Marthai. When you turned away from him. He followed you like he'd followed his whole life."

"No."

Then it happened that Nàlwyr heard of this brash young Captain of Magandis who had defeated all his Prince's best, but who tempered victory with mercy and had claimed full hundreds of Marthai and Veneranda's force to the armies of Magandis. And he marveled 'This is a Knight of great heart, and woe to the times that make us enemies, and the fates that will force me to face him.'

"But he lost you when he fell sick outside Odradale," the Golden Girl says. "It was winter."

"You don't…"

And at the High Spring, they did face each other at the head of two great forces along the banks of the River Konides that flowed with the full rage of Winter, and could not be crossed save at three narrow fords whose claim and hold would be paid in blood.

He feels the anger like a black flame suddenly, burning at his heart and in his hands where fists squeeze blunted nails into his palms. Pain there like the pain at his throat, where the words he means to say are caught tight.

The Golden Girl stands slowly, cloak wrapped around herself. Small in the shadows. Justain.

"My father. Nàlwyr."

From within her tunic, she brings forth the thong of leather at her neck. The talisman hangs there, an oval of pale gold to catch the light.

At its center, a dragon rampant in blood-red, claws of black. Eyes of silver gleam where it coils its tail around itself, ready to strike.

The White Pilgrim is on his feet, does not remember standing. The fire is before him but he circles, the Golden Girl across from him, risen to pace away from him, angry. Justain.

"They all say you died. That Astyra the king's-bastard had slain you before he fell. Priests and fools announcing that your body was carried on a chariot of fire up to Orosan, taken to the lap of the gods, but you walked away!"

"You do not know!" he shouts at last. He tastes blood at his tongue where he must have bitten it. He does not remember. "No one knows these things! Memories and lies! All of it, lies!"

"This is no lie. This is what my father said to me before he died. Captain to the high king, first of the companions of Mitrost..."

"You do not know!"

The White Pilgrim turns from her, cannot bear to look at her anymore. The bottomless blue of her eyes, her face blurred with tears to match his own. Footsteps around him mark where she follows as he tries to rub his eyes, feels the burning of the blood still clinging to his fingers from the fight.

He tries to get away. He must get away. He tries to not think of these things anymore, the memories almost gone.

"He came to you at Marthai!" Her words are a blade, cutting open the oldest scars. "He came back for you, out of exile, out of the wilderness for you. He fought by your side, offered you his life. He watched you crawl out from a field of shattered bodies, and he followed you, he begged you!"

'And now my High King Gilvaleus? What fates are left to me, now that you turn from me, left alone with all my enemies at hand?'

He hears her father's words in the Golden Girl's voice, sharp with the edge that betrayal makes. Hears the rage there handed down to him like a dark judgement for all his deceit, all his weakness.

"He begged you and you walked away. He told me..."

He twists from her grasp as he strikes her arm away with a shaking hand. The darkness of his look stuns her to sudden silence where she stands.

No. Not the look. The shortsword in his hand that he cannot remember picking up. It thrusts out to touch the paleness of her throat, so fast that she has no time to avoid it. A point of blood rises there, spreading black in the firelight.

"And how good are you?" the White Pilgrim whispers.

The Golden Girl stares. Does not understand.

Her hand strays to her belt, the scabbard hanging there. Slowly, slowly in the hope that he does not see. A stripling's trick, where a veteran would draw at speed to distract the foe.

"Bastard brat. You steal a man's memory. Try to steal his name. You don't know…"

And with blinding speed, the White Pilgrim thrusts through the pale throat, all the force of leg and shoulder punching through flesh and bone, blood and spine. The blackened steel of the Norgyr sword is a deadly shadow in the blaze of firelight.

Except the Golden Girl is gone.

There and not there, forcing herself back as she falls beneath the killing stroke. She rolls two paces away, dropping her cloak as she rises again. The White Pilgrim is on her, going low for the right side, opposite her scabbard. A savage strike, no way to block it, but his blade hits steel. A flash as her rapier comes up, slashes out and down, too fast to even see.

"How good would you have to be?" he screams, a dark rage in his voice that is stilled for long years. "How good to prove that Nàlwyr's blood flows in your veins?"

Her silence answers as she wheels, tears the torn sleeve of her tunic free to take no chance on it hindering her movement. The tight-woven links of the chain shirt twist like silvered snakeskin as she lurches back from the White Pilgrim but he presses, relentless. Slashes down and across with a series of killing strokes, speed driven by the lightness of the Norgyr blade.

The Golden Girl retreats again, gets no quarter as she parries, no room to take advantage of the longer rapier as she sends strike after strike wide by a hand's width. She parries his next blow with the same cross-hand movement as the last three. The White Pilgrim feels himself set for the follow-on. Then he watches her blade suddenly flash down and across, slipping beneath his. The repetition of her defense lulling him into a pattern of counterattack he cannot see.

She takes the advantage, lunges in with a thrust that catches his tunic but misses his arm as he twists wide. The White Pilgrim drops his sword to deflect her next attack, a low thrust from the opposite side, impossibly fast. And then she has the offensive, the razor tip of the rapier weaving a bright pattern in the firelight as she strikes, strikes again, swords meeting in a clash of steel that rings out against the silence of the stones and the night beyond.

He finds a respite when she stumbles in a patch of thistle, winter-grey and invisible in the dark. He unleashes a savage windmill strike, fast as an uncoiling thicket-serpent, but she slides past it as if he was standing still.

The best blade in his Father's court at twelve summers. Memories and lies.

The White Pilgrim fights like a man half his age, strength and speed a reminder of the skill he once has. The Golden Girl fights like a veteran twice hers. Her prowess is a reminder of something else.

He is as fast as he ever is. As fast as he can be, but she is faster. Her blade weaves a mandala in the firelight as she strikes, furious now.

The darkness in her gaze is a thing the White Pilgrim recognizes. A thing he cannot face.

She forces him left, left again, pushing him back as she tags his sword arm twice. The fire is behind him now, blocking further retreat. A fool's error. She comes in low, a blurred stain of red and black, fire and shadow, and through it the flash of steel as the rapier bites deep at his shoulder.

Then Nàlwyr, seeing this Captain Guderna in the foreguard, called to him and said 'Our companies are even matched and the river's flood a third foe that all face at our peril.' Then both approached under sign of Herald, and Guderna who was Gilvaleus saw that this captain of the best armed and armored Knights wore only a shirt of chain set of dwyrsilver links, and that his blade was the slender silver of a serpent's tongue that looked like any blow might shatter it.

The White Pilgrim feels the bright shard of pain. He feels a numbness that wraps him like the embrace of a lost friend.

He sees himself reflected in her eyes as he stumbles back. Sees a fear in that reflection that he does not feel for so long now.

And Nàlwyr spoke and said 'In the even fierceness of our force, this fight shall be decided by my blade and thine, so let us spare the blood that should not stain the hands of any Knight so noble as thee and me, and make a pact of single combat that shall decide the day.'

The Golden Girl's movements are a deadly song, are a dirge of blood and iron that will best him in the end if it continues. But it is a deeper blow that drives him back, sets his feet to falter.

The blade in her hand. The rapier, recognized in a heartbeat.

And Captain Guderna agreed, who had never lost a bout, and so faced Nàlwyr who had never been bested at arms, and both fought within a narrow bend of stream that fed the torrent of Konides down a bright falls, and where their forces were lined, and watched amazed. And through a long day the two did clash, sword to shield and sword to sword, and in the end did the speed and sharp bite of Nàlwyr's blade draw blood from Guderna whose true name none knew, and did send him down.

He feels all the space of memory filled in. Black water seeping to fill the cracks of the soul. He knows the speed of her movement, the singular grace that is the form of the greatest warrior who ever lives, long ago. The greatest friend.

He tries to not think on these things.

The Golden Girl drives past his defenses, slashes an arc of red across his sword hand. The strong of her blade catches at his hilt, snapping the shortsword free of his hand to twist and fall six strides away.

The White Pilgrim freezes before her, weaponless. The rapier touches his own throat now, a look of fury in the Golden Girl's gaze. Justain, her name is. He remembers.

She sees the recognition in his eyes. Falters. She looks past him, around him like she realizes only belatedly where she stands, what is happening. Who she fights.

"Gilvaleus..." she whispers.

And the White Pilgrim falls to his knees. Justain stands over him, still poised to strike. Not letting her guard down, always expectant. The old lessons learned well, the rapier held stone-steady in her hand.

And all the force of Magandis was wroth and prepared to attack against their Captain's fall, but Guderna the War-Captain felt the nobility of Gilvaleus whose name he did not know, as he spoke and called 'Hold, for this Nàlwyr is a noble Knight whose grace and skill hath saved ten score lives today.' And as Captain Guderna, he ceded the river to Nàlwyr and to his Prince Sestian, though he knew what wrath his own King Astran would extend against him, and retreated to Kalista with his host. And Gilvaleus marveled well at the skill that had bested him, and thought for the first time of the goodness of those he fought against, and wondered at the part he played in war that threatened all Gracia now with steel and fire.

At the last, the White Pilgrim sees the father in the Golden Girl's eyes.

"Nàlwyr..."

A moment's memory is let free of the darkness that is the past. The White Pilgrim sinks fully to the ground, Justain watching, unable to speak. Stepping away at last. Stumbling back in tears to the fireside.

The night passes. The half-full Clearmoon drifts to darkness in the west. The fire is dying, so the Golden Girl gathers wood again, feeds it to a bright blaze once more. The White Pilgrim stares into the twisting weave of flame, shivers despite its heat.

The Golden Girl is watching him. She is Justain, he remembers. Named for the justice and the peace that is the legacy of the true high king.

She waits for him to speak, but he is mute in the shadow of his memory. In the end, she speaks instead. "My mother was a healer. In the house where my father was brought after Marthai."

And with weeping eye, he beheld that of his Companions, yet lived only Nàlwyr, who had returned to his High King...

"He tried to follow you but was too badly injured," she says. "She nursed him there. Cared for him. I was born there."

And Gilvaleus cried out, saying 'Woe to all that this day should come, and an end to all we fought for.'

"You should be with her," the White Pilgrim says. Barely a whisper.

"She's dead," Justain says. "Four years past. When my father took me with him for the first time on the long road."

And as Gilvaleus the High King lay dying, he was cradled in the arms of Nàlwyr, who spoke his grief and rage to the empty field.

"I am sorry," the White Pilgrim says.

"Thirteen years, he searched for you. He picked up your trail again as soon as he was able. The plains folk spoke of wounded soldiers passing west and south in the aftermath of the battle. And one that more than a few remembered. A pilgrim in white, sick with fever. Crying to the old gods for forgiveness for the death of his son."

'Father, remember me...'

"He thought he'd found you once. He missed you by days, he said. Down south in Aldona where he said you were born. For a time, he thought you'd gone over the mountains. He feared that you knew he was following you."

The White Pilgrim sits in silence a long while. "You don't know," is all he can say in the end.

"I know you are Gilvaleus. You are the high king, lost at the Plains of Marthai in the battle against Astyra, the king's-bastard of Mirdza."

"There is no name..."

"Do not forsake who you were, my king. Who you are."

"There is no name!" The White Pilgrim circles around and away from the fire. The Golden Girl is shifting past him, careful. Afraid that he will run, he realizes. He does not remember rising.

"Legend supplants the truth of what a man is," he says. A weakness threads his voice that he cannot fight. "The sins of the father, too quickly forgotten."

"Gilvaleus is legend now," she says. "Legends cannot die..."

"The blood of children on my hands…"

He hears the words hanging, not sure whether he speaks aloud until he sees the Golden Girl's questioning look. She waits for him to say more, but he will not. Cannot.

"When my father pursued you, he had one goal."

"In the morning," he says. He shakes his head. Watches her with clouded eyes, the tracks of tears fallen and dried along the grime of his cheeks. "We must talk of this in the morning."

"My father wanted you…"

"In the morning, child. Justain. Please."

He is on the ground again, cannot remember sitting. He closes his eyes, the lines of age on his face etched by the light of the fire. Seams of black and red like a patina of blood across the skin.

She watches him for a long while as he lies down on moss and gravel, cloak drawn tight around him. When he closes his eyes, he can see himself through her gaze. A weary old man. Something broken in him where the weight of the world presses down.

Time passes. She keeps the fire burning hot and low, harder to see it from the woods. The White Pilgrim knows this spot, though. He knows that their isolation will keep them safe from the sight of anyone passing by night, even along the nearest trails.

When he closes his eyes, he can sense what the Golden Girl feels as the talisman lies cool against her skin, tells her they are safe for the night at least. She trusts its power to warn her of enemies close by, as it does since the cold day at High Winter when her mother slips it to her neck and breathes her last.

Time passes. The White Pilgrim curls up in exhaustion, not stirring when the Golden Girl pulls his cloak tighter about him. She watches curiously as his eyes flicker beneath heavy lids, cracked lips twitching with unheard words.

Time passes. She sits with her back against the standing stone closest to his, trusting its cold touch to help her stay awake. Shivering with the descent of the deep night, she closes her eyes for just a moment, the rapier across her legs and clutched tight in her hand.

The haze of light is bright in her eyes as the Golden Girl shocks herself awake, groping blindly for the talisman by force of habit. She is cold as the shroud of mist that rises with the dawn, sends fingers of light twisting through the screen of trees.

Across from her, the fire is burned down. The White Pilgrim,

Gilvaleus, High King of Gracia who her father serves and loses and seeks and dies never finding, is gone.

– SIX –
GODS AND MEN

A VILLAGE SITS AS A BRIGHT CROWN atop a cluster of green hills, familiar to the White Pilgrim from one of the endless seasons that bring him here before. A wide road is set with grass-graded flagstones, speaking at once to some importance in the past, and how that importance is forgotten now.

This place has a name, but he cannot remember. He does penance at the fane there, long ago. Bright walls, whitewashed. Twelve mosaics newly cut for the twelve gods, set deep in alcoves of stone. Twelve carved columns line the portico, for the twelve mountains from which the gods watch over these lands of Gracia, whose every tree and blade of grass they first sowed in the dark before time began.

He glances back at intervals, looking for something. Someone behind him. He tries to recall who it is, but his gaze is blank. Images like sifting sand in his mind. Gone.

He walks the day away. Red cloud seethes in the west as he passes through twisting stands of apple and pear, their first green shaking off the dark of winter's sleep. He sights the farms as twilight presses down, heightening the light of bonfires scattered across spring fields. Wreaths of wicker and woven straw are lashed to masts, set alight beneath the shroud of darkening sky.

The White Pilgrim judges the feel of the air. He judges the warmth of the season, the length of the day. This is the celebration of life and new growth. The rites of High Spring. Danassa is the god of field and fertile sowing, who wears the flaming wreaths that are the sacrifice of spring, and whose bonfire smoke seeds the spring rains that are the goddess's soft breath.

He hears bright voices on the dark air, singing in Gracian and in the common trade tongue that is the Imperial tongue of Lothela before that. He sees the fires grow closer together where fields turn to farmsteads, as farmsteads turn to the low walls marking the edge of the meadows that are the village's start and end. Tight points of red and gold are strung against the darkness of cloud and night. A circlet ring of firelight, above which the half-globe of the Clearmoon is a silver blur.

The crowds are thickest where the road reaches the wall. The village is small to judge by its scattered houses. Ten score souls dwell here, perhaps, but ten times that number are here this night, flocking from all the nearby farms and thorps. Ready to eat and laugh and drink and love through these seven days and nights beneath the goddess's bright blessing.

Copper kettles blaze brightly, steaming with the scent of fruited stews and spiced wine. Slow-roasting mutton glistens and turns on a dozen scorching spits, and the White Pilgrim is drawn toward the feast even before he becomes aware of the tight knot of hunger twisting in his gut.

From the corner of his eye, a shadow crosses the Clearmoon's pale haze. A twisting ripple of great wings, carried fast on the wind. Then gone within the shroud of cloud and night. Too quick to see had he not been looking.

It reminds the White Pilgrim of something. Gone now.

He slips through the crowd, feeling the course of laughter and song push past and around him like a warm wave. But in the voices, he hears the undercurrent of fear that laughter and song hides.

In his mind, he sees a ruined village. A cluster of a dozen farmhouses, sod walls and ridgepoles, canvas and plaster and thatch shimmered by the gusting wind.

In his mind, he sees folk divided from and against themselves, a surge of anger spilling out between friends and neighbors along a rough line marked by fear.

He shakes his head, feels the memories fade. Gone now.

The mutton is thick sliced, dripping blood and grease to his fingers. Its taste is autumn grass and winter grain and sweet roots, and he knows to eat slowly, sparingly. Pacing himself, he chases the meat with bread and water to prevent the iron pangs of an empty belly suddenly overfull. A soldier's instincts, drawn from long campaigns fought on the barest rations.

"We share the warmth of firelight, welcoming the bounty of spring with the sharing of the last of winter's stores. By the green spirit of Danassa, life is restored to the land and its people, whose faith weathers the dark season and its storms."

The voice is deep, ringing out like the tolling of a great bell to still the sea of closest voices. The White Pilgrim feels a shadow thread his thought.

"The Triad of Brothers protects our rite with thunder and hammer, blesses us with skies swept clear by the wind of the sea. Beneath those skies, we give our thanks to Danassa the sister-daughter. Sharing our joy that the Twelve might hear us. Sharing our laughter and song that the Twelve might know our love, and that they might hear our contrition for the breaking of our faith under the yoke of heathen Empire, and our prayers for the heroes of faith who have thrown our conquerors down and will do so again."

A broad rise of white stone stands within the triangle of the three gods' fires that burn brightest of all at the center of the celebrations. The fires are the sign of the Triad, the white slab the spring stone of Danassa, and the stage where the speaking figure stands.

"These are dark days for the faithful. War crosses our borders. But we remember other days and other wars, and those whose allegiance to Gracia made the difference in those wars."

Safe in the leeward shadow of a woodpile close to the fires, the White Pilgrim sits alone, unseen by those closer by. Over their heads, he spies the speaker's bearded face. His arms are spread wide, grey robes unfurled. A priest of the Orosana, an oaken staff in hand.

"We remember that when word came that Ulannor Mor had fallen, with it came the joy and hope that all the Lothelecan was fallen with it. But even so, the Lotherasien who were the Imperial Guard, the blood and steel that bound the Empire, did endure to threaten that the rule of Empire would not pass, and that as its power was once, so it would be."

The White Pilgrim holds a mug of wine. He cannot remember who thrusts it into his hand, some one of the dozen laughing maids that skip up to embrace him as he eats. He holds it for warmth, avoids the temptation of its sweet scent for the sake of the sleep already rooting deep in belly and mind.

"But in those dark days that were the First Wars of Succession in Gracia, even as Telos the King dwelt in exile in Vanyr and sought to build the army that might challenge the unjust rule of Thoradun the Usurper, there came word of the dispersal of the Lotherasien. And it was said that the Knights of the Imperial Guard had vanished from the face of Isheridar."

Farther from the circle of listeners pressing in around the priest, dancers robed and unrobed circle within the gleaming light in a frenzy of song. In the even farther dark where the White Pilgrim watches, forms shiver and twist and come together in the passion of the rites of spring. Caressing and coupling, oblivious to inhibition and the chill of the clear night.

"But in Gracia's darkest time did one such knight of the Empire turn from that heathen path, and she claimed a place among the gods and her people by denying her past. And this was Irthna the Silver Sorceress of Aynwel, and lover to Telos the king and mother to the young prince Gilvaleus who dwelt in Magandis, broken from his past and the name that was his. And neither Telos nor his princeling knew of Irthna's place among the Lotherasien, nor had the fallen Eurymos, nor Garneus the Great who was father to Eurymos and Telos, and last regent of Imperial Gracia and first king of this reborn land. So with her vow to the Lothelecan broken for the greater good of the land she loved, the Silver Sorceress to her lover came, and she spoke, saying 'By my word and oath have I kept secret these long years a power that might save all for which you and your line have fought.' "

The White Pilgrim feels the chill of night suddenly, cutting the warmth of fire and wine that spreads through him.

"And saying so, the Silver Sorceress took Telos to a secret cove of the Bronae Ashtal, which is the Whitewater of Maris. And at that ashen lakeshore, she summoned for him Ankathira, called by legend the Whitethorn, sword of kings, that for those thousand years of Empire had been lost to Gracia."

The priest's voice carries, the faces at the more distant fires now turning. Laughter and song are dimming, the warmth of light and laughter twisted through by shadow now in the White Pilgrim's sight.

"And bestowing the blade upon Telos, Irthna said 'By the ancient legend of the sword of kings, you shall command the fealty of the lords of the south, who will be the army that rises up against the Usurper as must be. But by the ancient power of the sword of kings, you will gain access to the greatest secret of the Lothelecan, and shall strike into the heart of Thoradun's force like the most furtive blade, and the Usurper's blood shall water the grey plains of war where the greatness of Gracia will grow once more.' "

The White Pilgrim hears the voice as a harsh echo in his mind. He tries to breath but cannot. He tries to turn away but cannot. Something is changed.

"And in the days of the Lothelecan, it was spoken of how the armies of Empire could cross from any point to any point within the Elder Kingdoms in an eye-blink of time, and of how the forces of Empire would move in a day's march from Ulannor Mor in the farthest westernmost reaches of all lands to Daegraleth beyond the Leagin in the east. So to Telos, Irthna showed these secret ways, and showed him how the arcane power of the Whitethorn could fuel the portals of the Lotherasien, and so would sweep the forces of Telos past the bulwark of the Usurper's defenses, then into Sannos in the north that was the heart of Thoradun's rule."

The White Pilgrim is on hands and knees. He vomits up the last of what is eaten, swills the dregs of wine from his spilled cup to clear the acrid taste from his mouth. The priest's voice is a hammer in his head, a searing blade of pain behind his eyes. His vision blurs wet as he tries to stand.

"And so with a force of knights and war-mages that had sworn their lives to the sword of kings, Telos did return to Aldona that was his home and the seat of his line, and announced his return to the Usurper, who laughed in his northern hold. So did Thoradun send his forces to the narrowest breadth of Veneranda and Lamitri, there to forge a wall of steel and spellcraft against which the king's forces would break. But unknown to even the Usurper's most powerful seers, Telos and his force took the secret paths of the Lotherasien, and struck from Aldona straight through to Sannos and the great fortress that Thoradun had raised at Beresan."

The White Pilgrim blinks to see the priest's face change, the voice shifting. A shimmering panoply of other faces, other voices, comes quickly then is gone again. Then only the familiar echo remains of the words he hears before, hears endlessly through uncounted springs, uncounted summer celebrations, uncounted tales at fires shared to keep off the chill of a winter night.

"But even as the gates of the Lotherasien were opened by Irthna channeling the power of the Whitethorn in Telos's hand, the Silver Sorceress had held a dark secret from her lover and king, which was that to reopen the gates of the Lotherasien would cost her life. And so she sacrificed herself, and as she died, the Silver Sorceress cried aloud a word of final prophecy that was a vision she would leave to king and son alike, whispering the name of 'Astyra' that Telos knew not."

"Mother…" The White Pilgrim is whispering, weeping, but he knows not why. "Remember me…"

"Then Telos's pain became the rage that fueled the battle cry of all those who followed him, even as in far Kalista, the young prince Gilvaleus felt that pain that was his father's heart. For on this day, when he had passed twenty summers into manhood, finally were the sorcerous wards that held his name and memory prisoner roughly shattered with his mother's death. Then knowing his mind and past for the first time, he shook off the pain as he tore the badge of his once-King Astran from his shoulder, and vowed that he would ride to his father's side. But Gilvaleus, too, heard the name of Astyra as his mother's voice echoed in his own mind, and wondered at its dark foreboding..."

The priest's voice breaks off suddenly. From the darkness above comes the shriek of hassas and a storm of beating wings.

They sweep the fire line like soaring ghosts, low enough that the wake of their passage sends spiral pillars of spark and flame twisting skyward. Cinders tear at the assembled revelers like a blood-fly swarm.

The White Pilgrim hears shouts of fear, cries of attack and treachery in the night, but he does not move. He only watches as the dozen winged horses circle back, carving wide loops around the gods' fires. In their wake, they forge a frenzy of movement as folk flee for the shadows, are pushed back into a wall of fear that holds fast.

Then the hassas and their riders are down to hedge the circle, dropping to shred the ground as they slow the great speed of their flight. Countless smaller fires flare to sparks amid clouds of wet-clodded earth, torn up by gouging hooves. Their light is shrouded in the steam that rises from the wings and flanks of those great steeds in the chill air.

Aside from the White Pilgrim kneeling alone in the shadow of his woodpile, only the priest holds fast, anchored to his stone dais by the anger that turns his hands to fists. The largest of the hassas drops directly before the grey-robed figure, a great black stallion that rears in seeming rage at having been reined down to still ground from the endless air. The spike-armored hooves tear turf and earth to strike sparks off the stones below.

All is silence as the hassa's rider removes his visored helm. The Black Duke's gaze is cold as he lets it wander the huddled crowds, hemmed in by firelight and the steady circling of his riders in the distance. "A clown in grey," he calls to the priest and the crowd at once. "Telling tales of mirth to please the common folk, no doubt."

"Show respect for the gods and their servants." The priest's voice is rage, but it carries an edge of dark fear that says he knows who it is he speaks to.

The Black Duke swings from the saddle to the ground. As he strides forward, he is taller than he seems against the great bulk of his mount, which paces back now to paw the ground.

"I mean no offense, priest. Continue with your fables. You have a rapt crowd. Tell us of your gods. Your dead kings."

And Gilvaleus fled Magandis that had been his home for five years and all his memory, and which had shaped his allegiance to the dominion of Thoradun, who he knew now as enemy to him and his line, who had killed his Uncle as King, and many lesser Kings and Princes and Knights besides, and for whom Gilvaleus swore now vengeance in the name of all those dead and his Mother lost.

No sound but the hiss of the fires and the hassa's steaming breath. A challenge roots in the Black Duke's eyes, the priest's gaze defiant in return.

"I can tell you tales," the Black Duke calls, and all who stand within sight hear the words. "I can tell you of the kings of Gracia. A hundred generations of history reduced to an endless slavery of faith."

And before he left his once-homeland, the Young Prince sent word by trusted messenger to Cymaris whom he loved and who was in her Father's house. And this message said 'I must leave and thou must follow, for my doom is told as the Son of Telos and heir to all Gracia, and the love I have borne thee these years of youth will be a danger to thee when my true name is known.'

"Blasphemy…" Behind Arsanc, the priest finds his voice. "I was a child at the court of the High King Gilvaleus at Mitrost. I have stood at the white table, whose stones were cut from the twelve peaks of Orosan, and were the holy sign connecting the rule of the high king to the rule of the ancient lines of kings…"

"A sign connecting to the corruption of that line." The Black Duke paces, sets his hand on the hilt of his sword as if in warning. "A hundred generations of mud-streaked priest-lords who fought and died for their gods and sired sons to kill each other in the name of other gods in turn."

Then even into Kalista came word by Seer that with fell magic had Telos brought his armies to face the Usurper at Beresan, which was burning and all its forces in the South scattered. But as the host of King Astran gathered to ride racing to Thoradun's defense, its captain was nowhere to be found, as Gilvaleus rode out alone, weeping for those who had once followed him, and cursing the war that would yet divide them all.

"The white table stands sundered now," the priest says, "as the sign of the sacrifice that Gilvaleus made, and of the gods' favor of that sacrifice that will see those stones made whole when a high king worthy of Gilvaleus rules this land once more."

"The white table was cracked by the magic of mortals," Arsanc shouts, laughing. "And it will be rebuilt by mortal magic before the Clearmoon rises full again. The king's conclave meets when the rites of High Spring are done, and there will be a high king at Mitrost before that conclave ends."

And when after sixteen days and nights by dark road, Gilvaleus sighted the Usurper's hold at Beresan, he saw how the armies of his Father were routed by the return of Thoradun's forces from the South, and all were broken, and the banners of the Dragon, red on gold, were surrounded and would soon fall. Then did the Young Prince feel the answer to the call of his mind and memory, and fought his way through the press of defenders, blade and spell, and he slew as he cried aloud 'I am Gilvaleus, come to my Father's side!'

"I will tell you a story of your Gilvaleus," the Black Duke cries with a sudden dark rage. "Hear the story of the high king and his lords of Mitrost. Hear the tale of brave Nàlwyr, betrayer of his king, lover of his queen. Butcher of children."

And many fell before Gilvaleus, and more fled from his wrath that was a burning fire in his heart, let free and unleashed of all the full passion that his Mother's magic had long denied in him. Then did many of his Father's side that were surrounded and threatened with surrender and death throw off their chains of fear and fall in beside him, lending their voices to his as they cried 'We follow Gilvaleus returned, Son and Best Blade of the King!'

Where he huddles still in the shadow of the woodpile, the White Pilgrim convulses. An unnamed fear wraps around him like a tightening noose, his eyes closed, opening again so that the dark dreams might pass once more. But even against the bright light of fires and the Clearmoon, the shadow twists across his sight.

Then coming finally to the ruined court where Telos his Father fought beneath the Great Dragon that was the banner of his company, Gilvaleus and his newfound troop shattered the press of Thoradun's force to free the King's position and the guard who fought around Telos and had sworn their lives to the last. But then did the Young Prince weep to see his Father already fallen, and there was a darkness in his flesh as of black Necromancy, so that the magic of his loyal Animysts could not heal or bring him back from the threshold of life that he had passed. And in the bloodied ground before him was thrust the Whitethorn, Sword of Kings, which Telos's dead hands still clutched and which none of his retinue dared to claim.

The memories almost gone now.

Then did Gilvaleus seize the Sword of Kings and draw it forth, and he held it aloft to feel the power of the line of Kings that had claimed the Whitethorn before him, and to understand his destiny in that power as he cried 'Warriors of Free Gracia, rally to me and to the Sword of Kings!' Then with all the survivors of Telos's sortie did Gilvaleus fall back from Beresan, with his Father's body and the Sword of Kings, whose power was bound to the Unseen Pathways that the Lotherasien once walked.

He tries to not think on these things.

"Liar and blasphemer and heathen in the sight of Denas!" The priest shouts to match the timbre of the Black Duke's voice, but he cannot equal its rage. "The gods curse you and all your heathen line!"

"And there is the voice of your dead gods." The Black Duke laughs darkly again. "A fool in grey shouting whispers of vengeance in the night. The Empire's only failing was not burning the old gods clear from history and the hearts of the weak as well as they did from the mind and memory of the world."

So were the Unseen Pathways of the Imperial Guard made known to Gilvaleus, that were the gates whose sites and secrets were held now within the Whitethorn, and he was sore amazed to seem them all in his mind's eye. Then did Gilvaleus lead the surviving forces of his Father's assault, and many in those ranks were sore wounded, and all were weary, and even in their amazement as they followed Gilvaleus, they despaired to return across endless leagues of enemies to their homes in the Southlands from which they had followed Telos.

"Heathen masters for a heathen age." Even standing as tall as he can, the priest is still stooped beneath the gaze of the black-armored figure before him. "Lost to a millennium's decadence and the consort of fiends that rained down death and black fire on Ulannor Mor and all its host of darkness!"

But within Gilvaleus now was all the knowledge of all the Pathways of the Lotherasien that crossed the Elder Kingdoms, and in the Whitethorn was the power that Irthna his Mother channeled with her life to open those ancient gates. And even as Thoradun's forces pursued them, Gilvaleus and his army passed onto those Unseen Pathways and vanished as if taken by the air.

"Fifteen hundred years of glory," the Black Duke shouts. "A hundred centuries of peace in the Elder Kingdoms, until a king of deceit abandoned the faith of self and let the land suffer the fate of all those who embrace the faith of lies that dead gods make. Whole generations lost to war under Eurymos, Telos, and Gilvaleus. Uncle, father, and the son who imposed his will with the magic of Empire but turned from its example. Letting the treachery of his own soul infect a land that still bleeds for his sins."

So did Gilvaleus cry to his company to follow him, and through dark archways of shadow did they come at once to the Vale of Cotanas in Aldona, which were the lands of his birth upon which he had not gazed in long years. And he brought his troop hence even before the sun had set on the battle at Beresan, twenty days and more of road to the north and west.

"Gilvaleus betrayed the power he stole." The Black Duke presses closer to the priest, circling the white stone now. "He and his faithful succumbed to the base temptations that are the gods' promises of power. The lust for blood and the weaknesses of the flesh. Not worthy of the faith of self. Not worthy of the crown he wore."

And Gilvaleus did not rest, saying to all 'Bring the worst wounded to where they might heal, and those wounded who can, ride in search of healing and return, and those who cannot, build a bier for my Father where he might lie. But those who can yet fight, for the glory of Gracia and the Gods, follow me!'

The Black Duke draws his sword in a smooth motion, swings to strike the spring stone. But even as he does, a pulse of black fire explodes from the ground before him, rising as a roiling wall from which he steps back.

A shout comes from somewhere. Four of the Black Duke's warriors are moving where their hassas circle, two with bows drawn, two with spell-fire at hand even as the Black Duke waves them to a halt. The priest is drawn up to full height where he clenches his staff tight, controlling the black fire that pulses with the power of animys, channeled by his spirit and flesh.

"Show respect for the gods and their servants," he says, cold. "Leave this place."

The Black Duke only laughs.

"Fifteen hundred years of Empire showed that the gods are nothing more than a child's fear." Arsanc turns his back to the priest, a dangerous show of defiance as he calls to the shadowed eyes still watching. "This priest claims to channel the power of your dead gods and holds sway over you in that power's name. But any of you can command that same power, shaped and honed by animysts of Empire for a thousand years after the last gods were only memories. No prayers shape the magic of life. No begging power from unseen masters, for the Empire taught us that we are our own power. Humankind and all its kin."

"You will kneel before the altar of Denas!" The priest's voice is a knife's edge of purest contempt, but the White Pilgrim hears the fear there. That voice and the Black Duke's spill over into the voice of mind and memory that he tries to force away. "You will beg mercy to north and south and all twelve mountains of the Orosana for your insolence! You will worship the truth of their power!"

A crack like shattering stone splits the air as the priest screams an incantation born of blood and thunder. "Denas! Rhilos! Phion!" He swings the staff around and down in another pulse of black fire that lashes the ground, burns earth and rock to ash in a bright circle around the white shelf of stone.

The burning flare of shadow threatens to blind the White Pilgrim. But he forces his gaze back, eyes open when he hears the Black Duke laugh.

Dark fire surrounds Arsanc, the full force of the priest's spell caught and held by the Black Duke. Twisting like pale smoke on an unseen storm wind. "You will worship none but the high king of Gracia," Arsanc shouts. "And you will recognize me when I sit on the marble throne at Mitrost and my power has made the white table whole."

The Black Duke directs the power of the magic he steals, shaping and reshaping it as lines of molten fire that spin around him, wrapping him like armor. "You will worship me!"

And with fingers twisting tight to fists, he pulls both hands downward with a shout of rage. In a sudden screaming storm of light and brimstone, a column of white fire descends from the clear sky, the priest wide-eyed in his fear as he disappears within it.

"Call the power of your storm god!" The Black Duke screams it, the conflagration shaped by the power he controls flaring brighter with his anger. "Call the shield of Rhilos, call the rains of sea and sky to quench you!" But no calling comes. No spell or prayer to protect the priest where his figure is a skeletal outline of white and black now. Just the guttural voice of a dying man, abandoned by the gods whose names are lost in the endless scream that is his last benediction.

In the space of heartbeat, it is done. The fire fades, boiling down to the ground and seemingly swallowed by it where a mound of ash and bone smolders atop the charred white stone. In the crowd that watches, the panic spreads with the horrific speed of the fire itself. Folk scatter, shrieking. Falling back to the darkness of wall and field, meadow and orchard.

The White Pilgrim is moving with them, does not remember standing. He limps shadow to shadow, pushing for the scattering edge of the crowd where it breaks around Arsanc's riders and their winged mounts. And even then, the Black Duke motions with a tight circle of a mailed fist for his warriors to unleash the fear for which the banner of the black boar is known.

The hassas shriek as they charge. Spell-fire flares to all sides, reflected in the clash of blades. The White Pilgrim does not look, seeking only the space to move, but his way is blocked by white wings unfurled suddenly before him and a dozen others. A wind-beating wall lashes him, one of the Black Duke's beasts vaulting skyward to drop into the midst of the seething crowd.

The White Pilgrim stops short. He stares at the hassa's rider beneath his black helm. The face is burned by wind and sun, pale hair long, beard short, both knife-cut roughly. Seamed with the faint scarring that healing magic leaves behind. The scar at his nose, broken and healed, is freshest of all.

The sergeant stares wide-eyed. Gareyth, the White Pilgrim remembers, though he knows not why.

"My duke!"

The shout rises over the cries of the fleeing, reaches the ears of Arsanc as he wheels. The sergeant Gareyth lurches his hassa back with a great beating of wings, his sword drawn. The White Pilgrim holds where he stands, movement to all sides as other riders break away from where they drive into fleeing villagers with spell and blade, wing and hoof.

At their center, the Black Duke strides forward, still on foot, his night-black steed following two paces behind. He takes in the White Pilgrim at a glance. A flicker of memory in the depths of dark eyes. A look to Gareyth, who speaks. "He travels with the girl."

"No, lord." In the White Pilgrim's voice, in his eyes, is an honest confusion that drives the young warrior to a state of rage.

"Perhaps your memory needs refreshing, old man…"

A quick spur drives the hassa forward, a pulse of wing-beaten air nearly knocking the White Pilgrim off his feet. He casts his head down, does not understand. More hassas rear around him even as the Black Duke stays his sergeant with the barest movement of his hand.

So did Gilvaleus take a host of twenty Knights once more along the Unseen Pathways, and using the sight of the Whitethorn did he sense a gate close by to the Keep of Kalista. Then riding forth from that gate by cover of dark, the company made for the Keep and made their way within by secret ways known to Gilvaleus, who spoke not of what he sought, which was the King Astran and his Daughter Cymaris. For none knew that the Young Prince had dwelled in these lands, understanding only that they followed their liege.

"When she escaped, along the farm roads south of the Vouris," Gareyth hisses. "He was there."

"Then search the road and the field tracks from here to the forest," the Black Duke says, and the bright wings of the hassas are a thundering storm as they take to the air. Their wake batters the White Pilgrim where he stands, stirring all the nearest fires to a corona of sparks and white-hot ash before the silence descends once more.

"Well met," the Black Duke says. "Again." The light plays across the dark eyes, the etched face as he sheaths his sword. Thoughtful.

And when Gilvaleus found King Astran, he was met with fury, for the King had read the message the Young Prince left in secret for his Daughter, and in it, he saw the confessions of a traitor and intelligencer. So was he sore amazed to see his late captain, for word of Gilvaleus's flight from Beresan had only just reached the Seers of Kalista, and fearing Sorcery, the King attacked with no warning. And

Gilvaleus, though the love he had borne for his King was strong, was blanched in heart by the death of Mother and Father both, and swore 'So be it,' and set upon his once-liege with a fury, and by the Sword of Kings was Astran slain.

The White Pilgrim feels the shadow of memory press down, the pain a burning brand behind his eyes. "You send your riders to search the road," he says, because he must say something to try to force the vision from his mind. "For the girl. Why do you not search the houses?"

The Black Duke laughs. "For you to ask the question confirms you do not know her. She is the butcher-knight's daughter, possessed of all the arrogance, all the hubris of her father and the king he killed for. Whatever else the fault of her blood, this girl does not hide."

Then did Gilvaleus see that Cymaris whom he loved was hidden close and had watched her Father die. But even as she came to him, he felt his vision clear as from the shadow of a fever, and saw in her the betrayal of his love, and said to her 'Thou hast forsaken me who once loved thee, and who might have turned thy Father's heart against the Usurper and to the cause of right, and dead he lies for thy dark betrayal.'

"I do not know her…" The White Pilgrim tries to hide his uncertainty, feels the Black Duke's dark gaze on him.

"But you met her."

"She came to me," he says slowly. Remembering. "On the road. She spoke to me."

"Spoke to you of what?"

"She spoke… words, but I cannot…" The White Pilgrim tries to summon up her voice to mind, but all that comes is the memory of the blue eyes, burning bright with accusation. A name slipping down into shadow.

And Cymaris denied her deceit, saying that the messenger it was who was betrayer, whose trust Gilvaleus had claimed. For with devious thought had the words of the fleeing Young Prince been brought to Astran his King, whose wrath was great. Then did Cymaris tell how she had been brought before her Father, who accused her of complicity in Gilvaleus's plots, and though she swore her innocence, she was kept under guard and lost favor in her Father's sight.

No. Something is wrong. He feels it.

Cymaris does love him. He feels the pain of her lost touch, knows that the messenger betrays them both. He remembers, but he knows not why.

And Gilvaleus was sore enraged, and with the power of the Sword of Kings, he saw through the fair Cymaris's deceits, and thought of all the times of their love turned to ash in memory now, and so he made their love one last time at the place where her Father lay. And when it was done, she had paid for her unfaithfulness, and Gilvaleus raised the Whitethorn in triumph over her and in warning, and spoke, saying 'This blade of my Father and of the Kings of Old is the scale of my justice, on which all my betrayers shall be judged.'

"I have forgotten many things, lord..."

He loves Cymaris with all the passion of his youth, but the memory is cut through by seeping shadow. Twisting within the grain of his mind like the rot that sets into aging wood.

"Including forgetting to name me duke, old man. That can be dangerous."

"I am sorry, my duke." The White Pilgrim feels a shame he cannot explain. He will not meet Arsanc's gaze.

"For the girl's interest in you, I might have taken you for one of the companions. The butcher-knight's fellows of the white table. All the blades of Gilvaleus and of Mitrost who stood by and watched their king debase and abandon the throne they won for him. But the companions are dead. I've made sure of that."

Arsanc paces to circle the nearest of the gods' fires. He wraps his cloak around himself, thoughtful. A weariness fills him suddenly that the White Pilgrim senses more than sees. A thing that the Black Duke will not show.

"High Spring is done in three days, and my company and I must be in Mitrost then," he says. "I have captains there already, who curse me quietly for my absence, but the girl is near and I have searched for too long. Do you know Mitrost, old man?"

Then when Gilvaleus and his Twenty fled the Keep of Kalista, they returned not to Aldona where his host rested and spread the tale of the new King. But instead, Gilvaleus sought in the Unseen Pathways of the Lotherasien a route to the Ruin of Mitrost, which once had been the seat of the Kings of Old but was now fallen and forgotten. And Gilvaleus saw the Domed Hall where stood the Marble Throne, impervious to time and age by the ancient Sorcery that pervaded its stone. And he saw the floor where the White Table once stood, whose twelve panes of stone were cut from the Twelve Peaks of Orosan, and which was a sign of that gift of the Gods that was the rule of Gracia, united as it once had been.

"Aye, my duke..." The White Pilgrim feels the touch of a chill he cannot name.

"The king's conclave convenes there when the High Spring passes. When the conclave is done, it will have named me Gracia's high king, and I will be the easiest man in the nation to find."

And before all his company, Gilvaleus named Mitrost the seat of a High King, and vowed that though his home was the Southlands, this place would be the center of his rule. And he said 'So shall these ancient stones form the foundations of a great city that shall be capital over all Gracia, as the greatness of our past shall form the foundations of the future!' And the Twenty of his company became Heralds and the first of the King's Companions, riding forth from Mitrost even before dawn to send the word forth in Marthai and Veneranda that Gilvaleus was High King, the first that Gracia ever knew and a King to rule all other Kings and Princes of the realm, and that the Usurper's time was done.

The White Pilgrim starts as something flashes before him. Two coins that the Black Duke tosses to him, fumbled and caught with unexpected dexterity. Not just coins, he sees. It is the Black Duke's face struck there in profile, his name beneath. The pale gleam of gold is bright against the grime of the White Pilgrim's hands.

"I know wealth means nothing to a man of principal like yourself," the Black Duke says. "So I will ask your favor instead. Do you know the story of Nàlwyr?"

A heavy silence. The crack of pitch flares white-hot in a dying fire at the White Pilgrim's back. "I have forgotten many things, my duke…"

Where it stands stock still behind him, the Black Duke's hassa watches the White Pilgrim with a too-thoughtful gaze. Its bright eyes catch the fire, pulsing blood-red.

"You might have forgotten the legends. Not many ever knew the truth behind them."

In the sky above, a flare of white wings eclipses the Clearmoon's light. The hassa riders are returning, no sign of their quarry. The Black Duke looks up, staring to the darkness. "I seek the butcher Nàlwyr's daughter," he says at last.

The White Pilgrim simply nods. He knows that the Black Duke carries more that might be said, but he does not ask. He cannot ask.

"There is unfinished business between my house and hers. For the blood of a brother."

Through the shadow of his sight, the White Pilgrim sees the Golden Girl's face through firelight for a moment. Then gone. "I understand, my duke."

"Understand this. One of the coins is for you, and spend it well. Save the other. Use it as a token. If the girl seeks you again, whatever her reasons, stay with her and send coin and word to Mitrost by any soldier of the black boar you find. Keep her close until we get to you. Deliver her to me and your reward will be yours to name."

The great shrieking crashes down on them as the hassas alight. The sergeant catches the White Pilgrim's eye, staring darkly. The Black Duke turns to where his own steed stands behind him, vaulting to the saddle with a single swift leap.

As he seizes the reins, he looks down to the White Pilgrim. Considers. "For most of a man's life, he has the luxury of killing only when he needs to. For honor. Against the threat of being killed."

"Yes, my duke."

"I live a life wherein people die at my word only because killing them is easier than finding a reason to let them live. You are alive because you amused me once, pilgrim. You are alive again because I have use for you. If we meet a third time, I might need more."

The night passes with no memory. The White Pilgrim is walking, recalls having slept but not where.

The sun is barely risen, mist hanging between him and the dawn that tells him he makes his way east. A muddy pathway follows the edge of orchard and field, the village familiar to him from one of the endless seasons that bring him here before. Passing out of mind again as it disappears into the long shadows, a bright crown atop the green hills behind him.

He glances back at intervals, looking for something. Someone behind him. Images like sifting sand in his mind.

He sees movement against a distant stone fence. A dark figure walks a white horse turned to gold where the dawn touches it. The image blurring from the wet of the White Pilgrim's eyes as he strains to see.

He looks back again, sees the horse and the figure gone. A great white bird soars above where they stood just a moment before.

The image is fled from his mind by the time he no longer turns back from the light of the eastern sky.

– SEVEN –
REGRET AND MEMORY

THE SUN IS LONG BEHIND HIM when he finally stops, a hard day's walking firing the pain in his chest, in his leg to the touch of a white-hot blade. He does not slow, does not stop save to drink at a stream reached at midmorning, whose banks he follows in the time since with a hazy familiarity. A winding ribbon of muddy water twists west, joining other streams, other rivers in a chaotic course to the sea. A path starts, disappears, starts again before it finally becomes a rutted track that makes him quicken his painful pace.

Now in Hypriot, the Prince Sestian had long held Marthai and Veneranda from the conquest of Thoradun, as the Usurper directed the iron and fire of his armies against Telos in the South. And from his Seers at dusk of one day, Sestian heard of the fall of Telos who was his friend and King, and the Prince despaired, having pledged his sword and his realm to Telos who was fallen, and he wondered at what fate and the gods might hold for Free Gracia now. But then came the name of Gilvaleus who had returned and who carried the Sword of Kings, by Herald at the rise of sun. And the call was sent forth through the Northlands by spellcraft and messenger that the new High King was come, who would revenge himself upon the Usurper for his Father and his Mother and for all Gracia.

He cannot recall how long the visions walk with him. He knows where he is, cannot remember it against the storm of shadow that scours his mind. The waking, walking dream.

But Sestian asked how it were possible for the Son of Telos to appear at his Father's side and claim the Sword of Kings, it being known that the Young Gilvaleus had been hidden away far from Thoradun's dark magic long ago. And Nàlwyr, captain to Sestian, came to the Herald as he rested with his Prince and awaited fresh horse, and he heard the tale of Guderna who had been Captain in Magandis and was Gilvaleus, Son of Telos in secret hiding for long years. And Nàlwyr remembered the ceding of the River Konides and the honor of this Captain, and said 'My Prince, I know this High King, and as I will follow any King with a heart as noble as he hath shown me, so must you.'

Isolated stands of black oak shimmer leaf-bare branches, a rising wind driving shoals of cloud before it, wet from the east. Beyond the trees, broken walls of vine-cloaked grey mark the edge of a once-great estate, lost to the upheaval of the half-century since the Empire falls. A manor house beyond it slumbers now as shards of marble swallowed by grass, scavenged to the bare bones of rubble too large to carry away.

Then Nàlwyr assembled a host in Hypriot and rode for Mitrost before six days had passed, by which time all the North knew the name of Gilvaleus the High King. But the Usurper Thoradun, laughing dark in his citadel in Beresan, called his allies and armies of the Northlands to him through Mundra and Liana, and bade his forces of the South turn toward Veneranda and Marthai. For there, Prince Sestian declared openly his allegiance to Gilvaleus at Mitrost, whose ruin was a camp now, where all the forces of Sestian were gathering to the High King's side. And Thoradun's challenge was to cage the upstart High King, and press him on the field with forces to all sides, and destroy this Gilvaleus as his Father was destroyed.

In the fading light beyond the ruined house, he sees the shrine that is raised where once stood an outbuilding of the main. Weathered fieldstone is packed with sod, growing green on three sides. Blackened by mold along the northern wall, out of sight of the sun.

A bathhouse, the White Pilgrim thinks. He knows it, cannot remember. A hot springs that are once a noble's private retreat, benched with white marble and gold leaf. Turned to a shrine of the Twelve and Crecinu the healer now. A quadrangle of four long wings flanks a central open court unseen at the center, hidden behind roofs of cracked and weathered slate. Tall windows bound with white shutters. The sign of snake and staff above the rough-hewn planks of the door.

And many Knights were wary, for Gilvaleus tarried to build his force, but knew that even all the host of Marthai and Veneranda would not stand long against Thoradun's unified strength. But Gilvaleus told them 'Fear not, for the power of the Lotherasien is ours to command, and as the Empire held peace through the Unseen Pathways, we shall now wage war, and the strength of Thoradun's host will not avail him.' And saying so, he chose just one hundred of the best Knights who swore to serve him, saying to the Prince Sestian that all the forces pledged to the High King would be his to command, and would defend the lands and folk of Marthai and Veneranda from the Usurper's spells and steel.

A half-dozen acolytes break the ground of spring fields, digging in the winter-rotted vines of pumpkin and snowroot as he approaches. They pay him no mind, recognizing him as one of their own. The last sun passes cold, touching his robes that are the pilgrim's white once, long ago.

He stops at the well for water, finds two coins in his pocket. The pale gleam of gold is bright against the grime of his hands. He sees them before. Cannot remember as he places them in the stone bowl before the well. A scattering of copper is set there. Polished stones, tokens and totems of wood and bone for those who carry no coin but give the thanks of travelers to Menos all the same.

But though Nàlwyr had shaped the will of his Prince and led Sestian's host, and was accounted First Captain of Marthai and Veneranda, he turned away from Gilvaleus when called to the High King's company. And Gilvaleus was sore amazed, and asked him why, to which Nàlwyr said 'In the host of the new High King come many from Magandis, and the most of those speak only of their love for the Captain Guderna who was Gilvaleus. But from Magandis also comes word of the High King's killing of the King Astran, who was a noble man, and of the High King's defilement of Cymaris, his Daughter.'

The shadow is sharp behind his eyes as he collapses before an ancient ash. Its black branches are limned with green and gold in the first days of spring, the last light of the sun. Its twisting trunk is the span of his outstretched arms, for so he kneels before it.

He cannot remember how he comes to be here. He stares to see the shrine before him. The acolytes finish in the fields, the faint echo of a day's-end song heard above the call of crows that rises with the dusk. He turns behind him, looking for something. He tries to recall what it is, but his gaze is blank.

And Nàlwyr would not take the King's Commission, which was the Dragon of the High King's house in red on gold, and he spoke to Gilvaleus, saying 'These acts of thine were not the acts of a King, nor of the Captain I fought with honor. And if that honor I saw is not the true heart of thee, then I cannot follow thee.' And Gilvaleus was chastened, and said 'Then stay by my side, my friend, to help remind me of what I have done in anger, that such anger might not be part of me again. For thou must be sent to me by the grace of the gods, thou whose heart will not quail beneath any darkness, and who will help guide my own heart when the haze of loss and anger obscures my sight.'

The White Pilgrim gazes upon the ash as he does long ago. The ground is loam and gravel where he kneels. It is spring now, but in his memory, he kneels in the spring before, and the spring before that. At the base of the great tree, he sees the stone whose carefully carved letters are flecked with mold, worn smooth with the passing of years and the weeping of the sky.

A single name is graven there. He reads it. Remembers.

Then in Cosiand and Valos, the forces of Thoradun held all folk and Knights in a dark grip of ruin, but there were many who broke and fled north, and so did even more Warriors and War-Mages and Healers and Seers come to Mitrost and pledge themselves to Gilvaleus for the freedom of all Gracia. And in the ranks of those Healers was the Daughter of two noble Gracian lines of Human folk and

Ilvani, but her Father and Mother had been executed for fighting against the Usurper's rule, and her name was Aelathar.

"Nàlwyr is dead," he says. He recognizes his voice as he speaks, but the words take longer.

The name of Aelathar atop the stone echoes in his mind, half-remembered at first. Held for a moment, gone again. And then it is there and a part of him, and all the pain of all the lost years twists through him like a blade.

From the shadow comes the light. He remembers where he is. Touches the stone with a shaking hand. "It is good," he says, "to see you again."

And when Gilvaleus first saw the Lady Aelathar among the ranks of the Healers, he swore his love for her upon the Sword of Kings, saying 'Thou art most fair of all the courts of Gracia, and the Forest Kingdoms of the Ilvanrand, and all the isles and far lands of these Elder Kingdoms, and when this war is done, with my love will I honor thee.'

"I should have wept before," he says. "There should have been tears for you then. For all the grief I caused you, and for all the thousand hurts I inflicted upon you for the love you granted me."

And Aelathar's power was the old magic of the Druidas, so a garden Gilvaleus vowed to make for her at the King's Seat at Mitrost, to which she would call the splendor of Summer in all seasons. And they walked together in the empty ruins where that wonder would be raised, and he told her they would pledge their love beneath bowers white and green.

"I curse this fate," the White Pilgrim says. "I curse this life that denies me death and the chance to be in your arms once more. And so I am glad," he says, "that Nàlwyr is with you again. Watching over you as once was his charge. Kept for too long from the side of those who loved him…"

Then her laughter rang on the white stones that glimmered by the stars that were fair Aelathar's name, and whose light was in her silver hair and pale eyes. And Gilvaleus the High King kissed her for the first time beneath those stars, that watched them both with all of fate and history's unseeing eyes.

"And when you see him, tell him that folk still remember the good we did. Tell him the virtue and greatness of Empire lived in him. Tell him he was the best of us all, and bound to the goodness that lived in him as in no other."

His eyes are wet, voice breaking. The wind is rising from the east, stealing the last warmth of the day. His sight blurs through shadow and tears, the visions faded but the gloom of sunset wrapping him now.

"Tell him I am broken for what I have done, and that the sins of his king are washed from him by the penance and pilgrimage I make. And by the grace of the Twelve that keeps me alive to pay the endless price for the blood on my hands. And when you see Astyra, tell him his father weeps for his birth and life, and pays now for ending that life before its time. And when you see Cymaris, tell her I loved her, and that I beg forgiveness of her and will always, and that I am spared the death that should be mine to spend a hundred lifetimes in pilgrimage that might pay for my sins."

He hears footsteps behind him. A faint whisper of boot leather and gravel caught by the wind. He turns slowly, feels the ache of the road in his chest, his back, his legs.

The Golden Girl stands there. Watching him.

He remembers the road. Remembers her blade bright in the fire-light.

He turns back to the stone, squeezes one hand to a shaking fist that is touched to his dried lips and kissed. Pressed down to the cold of the graven name for a heartbeat that is a life of lost time. "I bring the greeting of spring," he whispers, as he whispers every year on this day for long years. "Fare you well, my love. I pay the price that must be paid for wronging you."

Familiar words. The memory twists through him for a moment. Gone again.

He rises stiffly, shaking as he limps toward the lantern light glowing warm now at the shuttered windows of the shrine. He hears a whisper of leather and gravel behind him, remembers that the Golden Girl is there. Following him. He does not look back.

Incense mingles with a haze of smoke to shroud pillars of blackened pine, marching in ranks down the length of the main hall of the shrine. The White Pilgrim slips in the open doors, the Golden Girl behind him, still silent. Rough stone walls are smooth with whitewash, ash-flecked from the fire that smolders in a great brazier. Set on three stones to mark the triad, venting smoke to a rough hole in the rafters above. The healing altar stone of Crecinu stands beyond it. The shuttered windows are touched by rising wind that twists the light of torches along the walls.

"The Black Duke searched for you," the White Pilgrim says. "At a village…" He remembers suddenly. He holds the image in his mind's eye, feels it fade.

"Let him search, so long as he does it from winged horseback so that even the blind could see him coming."

"I did not tell him where you were."

"Tell him what you like," the Golden Girl says, and he hears no fear there. "Run where you like. I'll find you again."

Doors of oak stand beyond the altar, dark with walnut oil and framed by torches where they mark the approach to the central court. Canvas covers the entrances to the two adjacent wings of the shrine. Dormitories, kitchens. The White Pilgrim remembers.

A handful of acolytes work where a smaller fire burns at a blackened hearth in the far corner, snowroot bread tended to in the coals. They look up to acknowledge the White Pilgrim with a nod, his face familiar to them. The lay of the shrine, its shadowed light and sweet scent are familiar to him. A thing he knows without knowing.

"We almost found you here. A year ago. The High Spring."

The Golden Girl stands across from the White Pilgrim as he bows his head at the brazier, the benediction of thanks for safe journeys. He does not remember kneeling.

"My father came back to us when my mother took sick. He told me the story of how he followed his high king. How he lost you, then followed you again. He told of watching you walk away from the field at Marthai that day, stripping your armor as you went. Disappearing naked and bleeding into the night. He said it as if it would make me understand why I couldn't remember who he was."

Her hair is a faint streak of shadowed gold against the dark of the cloak wrapped tight around her. Her standing at the fire of the Orosana is in violation of custom, the darkness in her gaze showing how little she cares. She spits to the coals, a hiss of steam marking her careful contempt.

"I'd seen five summers when my mother died, but I don't remember them anymore. Only the road. Across Gracia for eight years. The length and breadth of the land, beyond the Free City to the borders of Mundra. Almost into Vanyr. Down through the south, into Aldona. He worried countless times that you had fled and he had lost you. Across to the Kelist Isles, over the Shieldcrest to Ajaeltha. The dark of the Yewnwood. But always, you turned back. Wandering toward the heartland again. My father knew you must be circling back to somewhere, but he was never close enough to catch you here."

"They call it Angarid," the White Pilgrim says. The name is clear in his mind. "Shrine of Crecinu."

The Golden Girl appraises him, cannot hide the fading hope of her gaze. "These things I say to you. Who you are. Do you understand?"

"The queen came here." The White Pilgrim speaks as though he does not hear. "After the tryst with your father that drove her from the king's side. The love between them that the king's madness made. Gilvaleus seeking to hate Nàlwyr for what he was, so I sought to unmake him. Break him to my obedience. Force him to..."

The words choke off, hanging in a silence marked only by the White Pilgrim's suddenly labored breathing, the hiss of the brazier as its charcoal burns. "He sought to unmake him," he says, the barest whisper. "In a dark madness, the high king was..."

He falters as he feels the Golden Girl's arm at his shoulder. She kneels beside him, turns her blue gaze to his. Speaking carefully.

"You are Gilvaleus. You are high king of all Gracia and master of the marble throne of Mitrost. You rose up against the usurper Thoradun who slew your father, and putting him down, you forged peace. Do you remember?"

"Justain," the White Pilgrim says. Thoughtful. "Your name."

"Yes."

"You are Nàlwyr's daughter. You bear his blade and mail. His sword arm. No one else could have trained you to that."

Her hand is shaking in the manner of one who hopes for something, then sees that longing turn to the fear of never finding it. "Do you remember?"

"Aelathar was her name. A queen among pilgrims." His voice falters as he feels a light flare at the point where the name hangs. Breaking the shadow in which the visions hide. "She fled Mitrost and left all she was behind. Made a life here. Became once more the healer she was born to be, but not even Crecinu's grace could heal the hurts of the heart that I made for her..."

The shadow rises again, the light draining from the White Pilgrim's gaze like a sudden fall of night. He feels the blur of memory and history, watches it slip away.

"A pilgrim comes to her gravesite that spring," he says. "He returns every spring after..."

"You are the pilgrim," the Golden Girl whispers, and now it is the light of her voice that cuts the shadow. "You are Gilvaleus. You must remember. You must!"

The words ring out loud against the silence of the shrine. The acolytes at their fire look up, uncertain gazes focused on the White Pilgrim. He glances up, makes his apology for the outburst with a nod.

"We show our faith by silence in the gods' houses," he says.

"Your gods can do without my silence, and darkness take them all."

But the anger that threads the Golden Girl's voice carries an edge of pleading now. "You are Gilvaleus."

He stands quickly, no time for the pain in his leg and his chest to stop him. The Golden Girl falls back where the force of his movement shrugs her off, but she is on her feet before he takes his first step away from her, toward the darkened doors ahead.

"My father's only god was his faith in the greatness of the folk he served and died for," she shouts. "For the high king he served and died for." Her voice is knife-sharp, echoing from the blackened rafters.

The acolytes stare darkly. One rises as if expecting confrontation, but he shrinks back from the chill of the Golden Girl's gaze.

"My father told me you carried the faith of self in your heart. He spoke of you with the reverence you show for your dead gods. He spoke of hope that the peace and greatness of Empire could be restored in a Gracia fallen to plague and war and the ambitions of petty kings."

Then with the host pledged to him as High King, which held Knights of Marthai and Veneranda, and of Cosiand, and of Valos, and of Magandis and all the free lands of the South, Gilvaleus set forth his challenge to Thoradun, sent by arcane craft and voiced to all who stood at the Usurper's side.

"What changed you, then? What made you embrace a mythology dead and buried a thousand years? What made you afraid?"

The White Pilgrim stops before the doors as her footsteps approach from behind. He does not look back, cannot see through the storm of shadow that breaks like a thundering wave within his mind.

And the voice of Gilvaleus rang out there, saying 'The time of the Usurper hath ended, and in the name of the gods of the Orosana who have returned the Sword of Kings in this darkest time, the High King of Gracia will make amends.' Then did Thoradun's forces forge a wall of iron and spell-fire around Beresan, and waited for the host of Gilvaleus to break upon that wall as a single storm wave upon the unyielding stone of endless cliffs. But Gilvaleus had learned from his Father's death in the siege of Beresan, and was content with dark purpose to let the Usurper await his assault.

"My father knew he was dying and he wept for you," the Golden Girl says. "He wept for Aelathar. But he never gave up the faith of heart and mind. He never once gave up the dedication to life that is the first thing sacrificed on the braziers of your Orosana. The dead gods buy the faith of folk with promises that this life means nothing, and so can be thrown away because the next life promises so much more."

For when the forces of Gilvaleus set forth, with Nàlwyr in the van and the greatest hundred Knights of all the Free Lands and Peoples, Gilvaleus took them to a great stone arch atop the cliffs a league from Mitrost. And those who had ridden with him from Beresan knew this entrance to the Unseen Pathways of the Lotherasien, but Nàlwyr and others were left to amazement when Gilvaleus cried 'Behold!' and drew forth the Sword of Kings, whose power set the archway stones alight, and set open the Secret Gate through which all Gracia lay waiting.

"Life is its own end and purpose. This was the faith you embraced as a son of Empire. The faith that drove you to save Gracia…"

"I broke my faith," the White Pilgrim says. Voice low, wracked with a pain that is a part of him through every step of a pilgrimage toward a death that will never come. "I failed. In everything I tried to do."

"Then fix that now. Fix what has been done. Change what will be done."

Then with the war cry that was the Triad and his Nation's name and the name of the Sword of Kings, Gilvaleus led his host through the Gate and along the Pathways of the Lotherasien to the city of Aradorg, a two day's ride from Beresan and head of the great supply convoys that fed the Usurper's fortress. And in the gloom of dusk, the forces of Gilvaleus fell upon the city and its defenders, and all were surprised, and most were lost, so that Gilvaleus and his army slipped back to the Unseen Pathways and returned to Mitrost before the moons had risen in that night sky.

"The past is the past," he whispers. "There is no future except that which pays for the past. You live in dreams, girl."

"My father had a dream," she says.

The White Pilgrim hears the dark determination that threads her voice to replace the fear, the pain. A thing she waits to say. A thing she tries to tell him at night before a fire beneath the watch of the standing stones.

Something is changed, but he does not understand.

She steps past him where he stares at the shadows of the doors ahead. He remembers that he was walking there, but he knows not why.

"My father searched for you because he carried something of yours, my high king. Found on the field at Marthai. He knew you were alive, even as the lies and legends grew like weeds in the aftermath of that battle. Gilvaleus claimed by the gods and waiting to return in Gracia's time of need. But he did believe that you would return before the end. His dream was to make that happen, but seeing you now, I give thanks he died when he did, for to look upon what you've become would have killed his spirit as surely as fate took his body in the end."

So began the breaking of Thoradun, whose forces soon were enraged with the fear of the High King Gilvaleus and the Knights he named his Companions. And for bloody month after bloody month, Gilvaleus led his Companions along the Unseen Pathways, and passed through and across every part of Gracia in the course that the High King's strategy made. Then one by one, the Usurper's strongholds were assaulted, and many were broken, and those that were not broken were left scarred with the fear of a foe who traveled seemingly along the air itself, and descended like the most sudden storm.

"You do not know…" the White Pilgrim says, but the pain in his heart has spread roots to his throat. He is pacing, does not remember walking.

"I know there is war to all sides of us," the Golden Girl says, dogging the White Pilgrim's steps as he circles between the brazier and the altar's shadowed slab. "Or had you not noticed? Arsanc the Black Duke forges a hold over the northern duchies with Norgyr steel. He is the usurper reborn, and he will claim the marble throne because the only one who can claim it from him is you."

"Arsanc can have his throne. Him or any other. No difference…" The White Pilgrim fights to breathe. He forces the words in a rush of anger that builds, kindles itself with the heat of all his pain. "The dream died when the Empire died. A world at peace. A hundred nations, a thousand peoples spread across five thousand leagues of Isheridar. Have you ever seen a map of the world-land? Seen the scope, seen the impossible vision of a world's worth of life held together as one?"

He is shouting, voice breaking with a strength he does not hear for so long. The acolytes at their fire rise as one suddenly, slipping through the canvas-curtained doorway at a run. His mind is clear. He does not understand.

Then battle after battle, Gilvaleus and his Companions cut away at the cords of steel and stone and spell that held the Usurper's Kingdom strong, striking without warning in the Far South of Charath, then appearing days later in the Spring snows of the Mundra Mountains. And folk called the host of Gilvaleus the Ghost Dragons, whose red-and-gold banners blazed in the light of dawn as his force rode down garrison and patrol, then vanished again to elude the pursuit of the anguished captains of the Usurper's scouts.

"Fifteen hundred years, the Empire held a world," the White Pilgrim says. "Created a golden age by the wisdom of its masters and the knights of the Lotherasien who were its virtue. A thousand years of peace in the Elder Kingdoms, and I sought only to remake that glory in this smallest part of the world, then destroyed all I worked for in a single lifetime of hubris and deceit."

And though Thoradun in his rage did threaten and pledge that a hundred years would be only the beginning of his dark reign over Gracia, it took but a single year through which Gilvaleus did harry and assault the forces and citadels of the Usurper, and day by slow day did his Companions win back the hearts of Gracia and break the will of those who were yet bent to the Usurper's rule.

"No nation can rise above the weakness of those who lead it," The White Pilgrim says, quieter now. "Weakness is a scourge that plagues us all."

Then in the bright Spring of that next year, the realms of Charath and Staris were reclaimed, and the lands of Andrezou and Aynwel by Summer, and then Valos and Cosiand, and Eudorin, and the Southlands were united once more, as the Kingdom that Eurymos held before the Usurper's black treachery on the Day of Death. Then was Maris routed by the armies of Prince Sestian and claimed by his line, and the Usurper's forces driven back across the River Vouris for the first time in nine long years.

"The dream still lives in your name," the Golden Girl says. "The legend lives, and you are the legend. You can bring back the glory that the folk of Gracia yearn for. Your story does not end yet. Your right to the marble throne…"

And the White Pilgrim laughs, the sound ringing out darkly in the empty shrine. "And tell me, girl, how a dead king proves himself? Fourteen years have I walked to pay the penance of my sins." The White Pilgrim knows that number perfectly now. His mind is clear, all the past laid out before him suddenly. "Tell me how I walk into the king's conclave and claim a legacy lost to mind and memory?"

The Golden Girl undoes the clasp of her cloak then. She lets it fall to one side as she shifts the bundle that she wears lashed beneath it. More than half her height across back and shoulder. Wrapped and re-wrapped in rough homespun that she tears free with shaking hands, revealing a gleam of white and gold beneath. A scabbard of ivory and gilt leaf, no trace of dust clinging to it despite the grime of a fourteen-year road that sheds from its wrappings in a dark cloud.

The Golden Girl is on her knees. The White Pilgrim does not remember her moving.

He stares as she lifts the sword to him, clutches it through the mask of rags, hands shaking. Without knowing how, he understands that neither hilt nor scabbard is ever touched by her bare hands. The Blade a thing she holds for so long, keeps only for him.

Then the horns of war sang in the South, and Thoradun's forces of the Norgyr broke and fell even as the Gracian folk of the Northlands took up arms against them, and so was the rule of the Usurper undone at last. But the traitor would not yield, and called Gilvaleus to him at Beresan, and stood waiting at the ruined court where the High King's Father had fallen.

The hilt where it meets the scabbard is ivory and grey leather, and he reaches for it by forgotten instinct. Feels a surge of warmth thread through him as he grasps it. Feels the pain of his heart gone suddenly, the shadow that clings to sight and mind cast aside as he draws forth a longsword with a whisper-silent hiss.

The cross-guard and fuller are in steeled gold. Ancient glyphs of prophecy and power are scribed there in white, pulsing with a faint glow. An edge and ridge of dwyrsilver steel shed the shadows like water spilling from oilskin.

And when Gilvaleus came to him, the Usurper laughed with dark malice, saying 'Thou art a boy who seeks power he is not fit to hold, and my lasting curse on this land is to bequeath it to thy weakness.' But Gilvaleus said 'I am the chosen of the Sword of Kings, and carry the age and anger of all its masters before, and thy power is as a child's against mine.'

Ankathira. The Whitethorn is held in his shaking hands. He remembers.

And with Dark Sorcery did Thoradun attack, but the power of the Sword of Kings protected Gilvaleus as he struck. Then long did both battle within the circle of Companions, and in the end, the Usurper fell. Then with the King's Sword the Whitethorn, Gilvaleus ended the dark reign of Thoradun in blood, and called the name of his Father and his Mother as he did.

"My father carried it from the field," the Golden Girl says. "He kept it for the dream of seeing it in your hand once more."

The White Pilgrim fights to find the words, wracked with a fear and a longing that he knows once before.

"I saw you…" he says. Not sure who he speaks to. Memory of a dream, early morning at a market village with a name lost to memory. A vague recollection of the day he passes there, long ago.

He remembers those visions he sees through the Blade when he holds it, long ago. The sight it grants him when the Whitethorn is the sign of his reign, the ancient sword of kings. Resting for the thousand years of peace that is the Lothelecan, then rising again in a time of war. Seeking the hand that can wield it to rule this land.

Then the fighting was done, and Gilvaleus in triumph returned to Mitrost with Nàlwyr at his side. And Aelathar was there, and walked with Gilvaleus as he called for the Keep to be remade, and for the city he had named as his capital to be built around it. And in that peace of Autumn and the Winter that followed, Gilvaleus sealed away the Unseen Pathways that led him to victory, for they were opened by the power of the Whitethorn, and the power of the Sword of Kings was to be shaped to peace.

And he understands now. He feels it clearly as the sight returns to him, the sword of kings in his hand. All the pain of seeing the Blade. Of understanding how long it is separated from his touch.

Then the Kings and Princes who had shown their loyalty to Gilvaleus were crowned and named the Dukes of the new Gracia, and those who had too long held fealty to the Usurper were set aside, and new Dukes named in those lands and in Magandis and in Mundra and in Liana whose Princes and Kings had fallen in the last of the Usurper's War. And the High King swore his love again to the Lady Aelathar, and with all the Dukes of Gracia in attendance and Nàlwyr at his hand, they were bound in marriage at the High Autumn that marked the days of Gracia reborn.

"No," the White Pilgrim says.

He feels that pain like a white fire at his breast as he forces the Blade back to its scabbard. Feels the hiss of steel and velvet shiver cold through his hand like a viper's kiss. The Golden Girl stares in shock as he returns it bundled to her hand. She makes to speak but is interrupted by footsteps behind them.

The White Pilgrim turns, sees the priest whose shrine this is slipping through the canvas with two acolytes at his heels. An older figure, bent and hairless save for the wisp of a beard tucked into the grey robes. A look of recognition dulls the anger in his gaze.

"There is nothing to fear," the White Pilgrim calls to him. The Golden Girl is on her feet, the Blade behind her suddenly, wrapped within her cloak. "We will take the healing waters." The White Pilgrim bows thanks before the priest can respond, forcing the wizened figure to simply nod as he retreats back through his curtain.

The White Pilgrim limps once more for the dark oak doors, hands shaking as he pushes through. The Golden Girl stands alone for a long moment before she follows.

– EIGHT –
BLOOD OF CHILDREN

GREY STONE IS SHROUDED by darkness and the shimmer of steam that curls along the walls of a broad courtyard. A latticed roof of black wicker cuts a cloudy twilight sky to grey haze, brighter beneath where evenlamps hang from posts along all four walls. The magical light of nobles and lords, a last testament to the status and wealth of whatever family line ends here in the aftermath of war.

Then the scarred land was cleansed by the healing power of Druidas and Animys, and Aelathar herself traveled throughout all Gracia to lead the Druids in the reclamation of earth and soil, glade and stream burned through by the arcane force that Thoradun's War-Mages had unleashed.

The baths of Angarid sit in open air within the center of the four-armed quadrangle of the shrine. The White Pilgrim stands bent along the edge of the dark pool, sulfurous waters clinging as a crust of yellow to grimed marble.

And for the love he granted her, Gilvaleus sent Nàlwyr as the captain of Aelathar's company, and Nàlwyr swore to his King that no hurt should come to her while he breathed, and that in the union of Noble King and Fair Queen was found the beauty that would be the reflection of a land made whole again.

Carefully, he pulls off the robes that are the pilgrim's white, long ago. He feels pain flare in his chest and shoulders as he carefully folds them. He is weary as he catches sight of the faintest of reflections in black water. A weathered scar rises chest to neck to cheek, half-hidden by ragged growth of beard the same grey as his hair. He is shorn, but badly, a rough knife-cut that he administers only when weather and blood-mites remind him to. The face of an old man.

The Golden Girl carefully closes the doors behind her. A rippling and a splash ahead heralds the bent and pale figure slipping naked to the water. The White Pilgrim's expression is dark as she paces around him, looking to all four shadowed corners of the open court as by reflex. Making sure they are truly alone.

Her shock is gone, and the expression of the betrayed that he will always recognize. The anger threads her voice again. "Why did you walk away from Marthai? From who you were?"

The White Pilgrim hears her voice as through shadow, must turn to see her before her words can be heard. He remembers her. Justain.

But in the dark of that Winter of the Peace of Gilvaleus, there came word from the North of the death of Cymaris, who had been set aside after her Father's death, and who fled Magandis for Mirdza and a life held in secret from her kin and the life she had known.

"You must be weary from your journey," he says. "You should take to the waters. One of the customs of the Empire you are so fond of."

The Golden Girl only sits at the black pool's edge, lets her fingers curiously touch its steaming surface. The silence is broken by the dark-stone echo of faint dripping. The wind is rising, rattling the lattice of the open roof. The White Pilgrim's back is to her as he speaks.

"The sins of Gilvaleus cost him his throne." He fights to find his voice, hears the weakness in it that he sees in his reflection. "They pre-clude him ever taking it again. Sins of avarice and madness and murder that cannot be forgiven."

And Gilvaleus heard at night the voice of Cymaris that he knew, which spoke to him as cold bitterness and said 'Thou hast a Son, my king, who is born and raised in secret, and will be the legacy of the love and hate thou grantest me...'

"You are king," the Golden Girl says, and in her tone, he hears that she does not understand. "Kings will kill for the sake of what is right."

"You do not know..."

And Gilvaleus awoke in a fever, not knowing whether it was Sorcery or Dream that filled him so with dread, but even as he rose came word from Mirdza that Cymaris was dead by her own hand. So it was learned that in the time before, she had given birth to a boy whose Father she had not named, and which she had sent away with trusted servants before her end, and whose place and whereabouts where known by none now. And the name of the babe was told to Gilvaleus, who fell to dark thoughts when he heard it as 'Astyra,' that name of prophecy that had been his Mother's last word to him.

"A king must slay those who stand against him," the Golden Girl says.

The White Pilgrim shivers even in the heat of the ancient spring. Alone in the darkness. A frail old man.

"The blood of children on my hands..."

Then Gilvaleus drew upon the sight of the Sword of Kings that had shown him the treason in Cymaris's heart, and he saw her dead and on her bier, and the child gone as the messenger had spoken it. And he felt again the moment of his Mother's own death in his mind, and heard the fear in her voice as she spoke the name of 'Astyra.' Then accepting the sight of the Whitethorn, he knew that his Mother's final word was a warning to him, and that all he had built was threatened by the babe that was the fruit of Cymaris's betrayal, and that the peace of his new King-dom was in peril unless that threat was faced.

"Do you know why Arsanc's forces pursue you, child?"

"He hates my father as he hates all the companions," she says, too easily. "His lackeys brag of it. They say he killed Fossa himself, two years past. He drove Baethala into exile and death beyond the Shield-crest. He found where Gauracta and Ilfamor and Lutain were burned and interred after Marthai, then he scattered their bones for the dogs."

The shadow twists through the White Pilgrim, squeezes tight his heart. They are old names, the memories of them burning like cinders in his eyes.

"My father was the last," the Golden Girl says, "and his burial place is what Arsanc seeks, but he will not find it through me."

"No, child."

And through endless long days, Gilvaleus sent forth the sight of the Whitethorn to seek the babe that Cymaris sent away, but the power of her own sorcery had bred with the subtle treason of her heart and mind, and the boy Astyra was hidden from even the sight of the Sword of Kings. Then came the turn of the third year of the Peace of Gilvaleus, and the return of Aelathar and all her Healers, and Nàlwyr her servant leading them.

He rises slowly, feels where the heat turns the pain at his leg to a duller ache. The pain at his heart still burns, no balm that can cure it. He pulls himself to the slick stone steps and ascends carefully, claiming his robes where he left them.

"Against you, it is a darker revenge that Arsanc seeks," the White Pilgrim says. And though he tries to push the shadow of memory away, he feels it weave around him as dark mist and chill light, drawing forth the dreams like venom from a wound.

And that High Spring was the most joyous celebration of peace across all Gracia, but the mood of Gilvaleus at Mitrost was dark, for in both Aelathar and Nàlwyr upon their return, he felt a change in the love they granted to their High King. And using the sight of the Whitethorn, the High King saw for himself the secret ardor that had developed between his Captain and his Queen, and the darkness of Cymaris's betrayal paled beneath the pain of this new deceit. And the vision of the Whitethorn counseled patience, for Gilvaleus knew that more years would pass before Cymaris's betrayal could be met, and he knew what must be done.

He tries to not think on these things anymore.

"The Black Duke calls your father the butcher of children," the White Pilgrim says. "I do not know yet why it tasks him, but in the fifth year of Gilvaleus's reign, your father went in secret to a Reimari refuge on a mission of murder. The high king believed that the proph-ecy that Irthna had made held the kingdom, held the future of Gracia in its grasp. Only by the death of the king's-bastard Astyra before he came of age might the doom of Gilvaleus be undone. For the sake of the kingdom, Nàlwyr went to ensure that the child king's-bastard would be slain."

"You lie…"

The new anger in the Golden Girl's voice has the edge of splintered stone. She is away from the black water, bootsteps ringing out loud as she paces to the White Pilgrim, the steel-blue gaze holding him fast. "My father was no murderer. My father was the soul of the honor of your court. Nothing could have made him take such a path."

The White Pilgrim does not remember the Golden Girl standing, does not remember having dressed again. The shadow roots deep in his mind, feeds the dreams in the name of the pain he cannot fight.

But in the end, the sight of the Whitethorn found the boy Astyra whose name was as a wound in the High King's mind for long years now, and saw him dwelling in a refuge that was called Stondreva, where the Sons and Daughters of nobles were schooled. Then Gilvaleus called Nàlwyr to his side and found the words that had burned in him for just as long, and speaking, said 'Thou art my Captain and my friend, and I know the love thou bearest me. But also I know of the deceit thou weavest with thy love for my Queen, and by my name and the power of the Whitethorn by which I rule, I call on thee to pay the price for thy betrayal.'

"An order from his king would have."

The Golden Girl's eyes are bright in magical lamplight, blue and gold like the summer sunrise. An age in those eyes beyond the paltry years of her childhood.

"An order from his king did," the White Pilgrim says.

And when Gilvaleus gave his order, Nàlwyr fell to his knees and despaired, and pleaded innocence in the matter of the love that Gilvaleus had seen pass from him to the Queen and back again. But the Whitethorn saw through the deceit of his friend, whose lies cut as deep as any blade, and Gilvaleus ordered Nàlwyr to stand before him as a Knight, and his Captain wept, and pleaded 'What dark counselor hath directed thee so?' But Gilvaleus only turned away, and Nàlwyr was broken by the will of the Whitethorn and the weight of his betrayal, and determined that Gilvaleus's will be done.

"Gilvaleus believed that your father loved Aelathar the queen, and he was consumed by madness as he watched the love grow between them. Knowing that he loved both too much to send either from his side."

And that night, Nàlwyr went to the Queen Aelathar, and the darkness that was in him shocked her to grief, and she begged him 'What hath been done to my Captain that looks to have broken all the goodness in thee and sown this darkness in its place?'

"Gilvaleus in his madness, in the fever of dark dreams, believed that ordering Nàlwyr to break his own code of morals would force him to fealty. Shatter his love for the queen. And instead, it pushed the great knight to the place where having lost his honor, he had nothing left to lose by that love."

And Nàlwyr wept, and would say only 'Not what I have done but what I will do, in my High King's name.' And Gilvaleus was watching with the sight of the Sword of Kings as Nàlwyr and the Queen held each other, and he watched as Nàlwyr rode out alone at next dawn.

"An order was given on a dark night of rage." The White Pilgrim cannot meet the Golden Girl's gaze. Cannot fight the tremor at his hands, the racing of his heart. "To break the will of the strongest of the king's companions, an order to kill all children in the refuge, and thereby ensure that the king's-bastard would be among them..."

"You lie!"

The Golden Girl's scream hangs in the darkened silence, is swallowed by mist and lamplight. The White Pilgrim seeks to lose himself in that silence, feels it fight the shadow of memory. But in the end, the words are stronger than he is.

"The madness of the high king scarred those closest to him. Aelathar, betrayed by despair and come to Angarid to forget. Nàlwyr, broken by conscience. Fleeing the court at Mitrost, not to be seen by Gilvaleus again until he came from the mists that morning at Marthai. To stand by his king's side one last time, and to watch Gilvaleus slay his son in a last act of madness and accept the retribution of the gods for all his sins."

The Golden Girl wipes away her tears, consumed by anger and by the terrible uncertainty and fear of a life betrayed. Memories and lies. But through her tears, the White Pilgrim feels the strength renewed in her voice, fighting to keep from breaking as she speaks the words again that are the legacy of the father she knows.

"You are Gilvaleus."

"No..."

"You are Gilvaleus," she says. "Nothing else matters."

Then to the refuge of Stondreva came Nàlwyr, who in the madness of his High King's order slew the guards and masters of that place, shouting aloud the name of Gilvaleus his High King, and told himself he did them mercy, that they would not live to see the children slain. But as he advanced upon the dormitories, there stood one child against him with blade in hand, and all the other children standing fearful behind him.

"That name is broken. That name is lost."

And Nàlwyr said only 'Thou diest for the High King Gilvaleus, boy, so close thy eyes that thou might not fear the end.' But to him the Boy spoke, and said 'I do not fear thee or any High King who would murder babes in the night, for I know honor, and with honor I will stand against thee.' And with speed and mercy did Nàlwyr slay the Boy, but even as the children of Stondreva wailed their fear, Nàlwyr saw the blood of the Boy on his blade and hand, and then did he flee in grief and pain, and did not return.

The White Pilgrim stalks away, limping again. He is shivering, he realizes, wet air touching him now with chill fingers. "By the grace of the gods who made us," he says, "we pay for our sins in death, but death will not have me. Spared from the end at Marthai, because the peace of death would have allowed me to forget what I had done. What I had become. And so I pay with my life. Walking the land I betrayed in the name of my own weakness, and watching its fall into ruin and war. That is the penance I do for the past, until the gods are done with me."

Then in passing days did a message come to Gilvaleus by courier of horse, which was in Nàlwyr's hand and said only 'The blood of children is on thy hands and mine, my Lord, and so I walk the paths of penance to which my King hath sent me.'

He feels the Golden Girl's hand at his shoulder. She is tall, he realizes suddenly. Possessing the wide innocence of her father's eyes, the steadiness of her father's hand as she grasps his, holds it tight.

And Gilvaleus was pleased, and in his pleasure, the sight of the Whitethorn did not sense the boy Astyra and all the rest scattered to their folk as the refuge at Stondreva was emptied, and the spells of warding that Astyra's mother had placed upon him sealed him away from the sight of the Sword of Kings.

"Only the good has been remembered," she whispers, weeping. "The people need their king, who vanquished the usurper and restored to Gracia its honor and peace. The darkness will be forgotten. Your legend has undone all sins."

And even as he reveled in the peace he had long sought, word came from servants and from the sight of the Whitethorn in response that Aelathar had fled. And the voice of the Whitethorn told him that Nàlwyr was broken, and that Aelathar was scoured by her guilt, and all would know of their betrayal, and Gilvaleus turned his sight from them and was content.

"I have heard the legends…"

From outside, through the wickered darkness where it meets the shadowed sky, the shriek of hassas splits the night.

He remembers suddenly. Shadow unravels like fading storm clouds, scattered by cold wind. He sees movement against a distant stone fence, a dark figure walking. A white horse turns to gold, turns to a great bird soaring. That very morning, they watch him. They follow him. He is a fool.

Shouts rise outside the shrine and within, a challenge raised, but the words are too faint to hear. The Golden Girl draws her father's blade, a blur of silver shadow. The other hand is behind her, slinging free the scabbard belt that holds the wrapped bundle at her shoulder.

She holds it out to the White Pilgrim.

He hears the voice of the Blade call him with its ancient hunger.

His hands stay at his side. He fights to slow his breathing, lets the voice wash over and through him, and he is stronger than it.

"You must go," is all he says.

"I will not leave you. My father searched for you, to return the sword of kings to you. You must…"

"Go!" he shouts, and his voice is the voice of the king he spends long years forgetting. The memories slip down into shadow, wrapped tight and slowly smothered, and he is gone from the pool court before the Golden Girl can speak again.

Bursting through the doors of dark oak, he runs for the main entry of the shrine by instinct, slowed by the pain at his chest. He sees the Golden Girl from the corner of his eye slip in from the courtyard, ducking down behind the great brazier to wait. He sees the priest and two acolytes at the door, frantic as they struggle to fit the battered wooden beam that will bar it.

He tries to warn them, but the White Pilgrim's shout dies on his lips as the door disappears in a blast of force and a scouring shroud of flame.

The dying scream of the priest is cut short by the mercy of death as the acolytes flee. Out through the canvas doors, shouting prayers to Crecinu for salvation. The White Pilgrim stumbles forward, feels the heat of spell-fire even as it fades and an unfurling darkness follows it.

A hulking form of armor and shadow steps in from the night as Arsanc and his steed are the first through the doors. The hassa's wings furl to raise a cloud of dust and ash as the charred body of the priest is broken beneath the great beast's hooves. The Black Duke leaps down from the saddle, stepping forward as his mount rears behind him.

The Golden Girl is there suddenly, cloak off and rapier drawn. The White Pilgrim pushes forward, keeps himself between her and Arsanc's force where they push in on foot. More appear to both sides, coming in from the dormitories, from the kitchens. No blood on their blades tells the White Pilgrim that the acolytes are safely fled, and he holds the sudden hope that he understands and can shape the single purpose that brings Arsanc here. A quest of the Black Duke's that the White Pilgrim can end.

He feels the Golden Girl go to his back, pushing close within a rough wall of blades and black armor. It is the sergeant, Gareyth, who steps in to grab the White Pilgrim by the arm, drag him from the side of Arsanc's prize.

The instinct of old battles threads through the White Pilgrim suddenly. He drives arm and shoulder with a strength that belies his age, so that the young sergeant is caught off guard. Too sure of himself as always, the same bravado that sees him bested on the dark road. A fist finds the open space of armor at his waist, and the White Pilgrim sees the telltale lurch of pain that grants him the instant to swing one foot up, strike at the sword arm.

He has Gareyth's blade in hand before the sergeant can even react. Another kick sends the young warrior sprawling even as Arsanc shouts an order. The White Pilgrim cannot hear it over his own battle cry as he strikes.

Back to back, they fight. The Golden Girl stands single-handedly against four of Arsanc's company as the White Pilgrim disarms two warriors who step in where Gareyth stumbles back. They let the fight come to them, keep a screen of bodies around them for cover against spellcraft as they move. No word between them, but their tactics are matched perfectly. Two down, then three where the White Pilgrim drops a warrior with a fast strike to the leg. Low and dirty, slashing muscle and tendon at the armor's weak spot behind the knee.

Fighting in such close quarters, two of Arsanc's company stumble. One falls back, exposed for just a moment, a killing stroke left open. But the White Pilgrim lets it go, watches the warrior slip back into a defensive posture. Enough blood already on his hands.

The Golden Girl fights to make up for him. Two more down on her side who will never rise again, her blade flashing lightning-fast. Then comes a sudden break in the circling press of weapons and bodies, and the White Pilgrim shouts for her to run.

She stands fast as he knows she will, because he knows the mind of her father. And so she leaves herself exposed where a bolt of spell-force from outside the circle catches her cleanly.

The White Pilgrim feels her scream. He hears the bones of her sword arm shatter beneath the force of the blow. He sees the silver-haired mage, the standard-bearer from the ruined village. He remembers, images like a flood in his mind as he pushes past Justain, swings down on the mage, and is suddenly lifted off his feet.

Arsanc's spell is a song of pain and sorrow that courses over him like an acrid rain. His body is thrown against the wall, slamming to the ground as the Black Duke laughs.

The White Pilgrim feels ribs broken as he rights himself. He fights through pain and the blood-red shadow of his sight with a fury that sends the closest warriors scrambling back. The blade he stole from Gareyth is gone, so he snatches up Justain's rapier where it falls. He strikes hard to take the silver-haired mage through the flank, away from the fast blood but dropping her. Two lurching steps take him back in front of the Golden Girl where she writhes in pain.

"Kneel!" the Black Duke shouts, and the White Pilgrim feels the power of spellcraft anchored within the word as it drives him to the ground.

His will is split and splintered. Silence in the shrine except for the bark of steel on stone where Arsanc's hassa paws its spiked hooves. The Black Duke pulls off gloves and armguards, passes them to the closest of his warriors. A grim smile.

But beneath it, the White Pilgrim sees the sadness of mourning in the black eyes. He feels a pain there that he cannot understand. Something is changed.

"I owe you my thanks," the Black Duke says, as a nod to the limping Gareyth sees the Golden Girl picked up from the floor with a stifled scream. As the sergeant and two others carry her to the altar stone, the White Pilgrim can only watch.

Arsanc motions another of his warriors in, who kneels at the White Pilgrim's side with a whispered incantation, and the burning pain is calmed suddenly by the cool shudder of the healer's touch.

He feels his breathing slow, a preternatural calm twisting through him. With it comes the shadow, twisting to cloud his sight. Memories like splintering glass, reflecting smaller and smaller fragments of the light.

"My duke..." The White Pilgrim's throat is tight, words choked by the fear he feels. "My duke, the girl has no hand in your quarrel with her father. Please..."

The Black Duke laughs. "The girl will pay for the sins of the father," he says. "You as a pilgrim should appreciate that. Your kind believe in the payment of life-debt in the old gods' names. You believe that the Empire fell for its transgressions. Men seeking the power of the gods and paying the price. Is that not what the stories say?"

"Nàlwyr's crime was not his making. He followed the orders of his high king's own madness. You seek to break the scabbard that held the executioner's blade, but the blade itself is laid now before you."

"This is blood feud, old man, and no matter of yours. I told you that should we meet again, I might need a reason to let you live. You've given me that reason and more. Be on your way."

Two of Arsanc's warriors lift the White Pilgrim to his feet. A pouch is thrust to his hand, heavy with coin. The open space of the destroyed doors stands behind him. He feels the cool of the night, feels the shadow drawing him on. Telling him to turn from this, to close his eyes to the Golden Girl, writhing where she is pinned to the altar now. Surrounded, hands and feet seized tight, mouth covered by gloved hands.

Her blue eyes find his, the fear in them revealing the child she is. Thirteen summers behind her.

The White Pilgrim shouts as he hurls the pouch to land at Arsanc's feet. "For the girl's life, I beg your mercy, my duke!"

He tries to find the voice that he knows is his. The voice that once commanded the armies that turned back a tide of blood from the north and restored the legacy of his father and grandfather in a land of peace. But the Black Duke turns on the White Pilgrim with a sudden fury.

"I will show her the mercy Nàlwyr showed when his blade took my brother through the throat!"

The echo of that voice silences even the great black steed in its restlessness. A trace of shock shows in the Black Duke's own expression. This is an anger he does not mean to show.

But in that anger, in the pain that threads the voice, the White Pilgrim understands. He knows the horror that lingers behind the dark eyes, the lined face as it steps close.

"Folk forget the legends." Arsanc's voice is the ice of the northlands that are his home. "Not many know ever knew the truth behind them. Would you know that truth, pilgrim?"

"My duke... you do not understand..."

"I will tell you of Nàlwyr. Lover of queen and whore," the Black Duke whispers. "Right hand and sword of the high king Gilvaleus, and I carry the memory of my brother's throat slit by that sword. Havar was his name. A fox cub killed by a hound knight, torn to pieces by that butcher's blade."

The bitterness, the emptiness that rings out in the Black Duke's voice is a thing that the White Pilgrim recognizes. A madness built on loss and on empty years.

"My brother had twelve summers on him." The distant gaze of memory fills the black eyes. "And he stood alone with a stolen blade in hand and a dozen terrified children behind him and no one else to stand with him against the butcher."

"You are Arsanc of Thorfin, Innveig, and Reimari," the White Pilgrim whispers. "You do not kill children." He clutches at the words from distant memory, a faint shard of hope held there.

"For long years, no explanation, no knowledge of who attacked that night, then fled. A lifetime of waiting while he hid behind his fear. Nàlwyr the brave. Nàlwyr, killer of children. My brother stood against Nàlwyr and he died to save the others…"

The White Pilgrim turns from the Black Duke. Cannot meet he dark shadow of those eyes, blurred with tears to match his own.

"For my brother's life, the life of Nàlwyr's daughter. A fair exchange. Would that the butcher had only lived to see it."

"My duke, her death cannot bring back life lost…"

And the Black Duke laughs loudly, voice wrapped tight by a lifetime's pain. "Her death is not your concern, old man. I have waited half my life for revenge. I will take the rest of my life to carry it out if I can."

Arsanc turns away then. He walks to Gareyth, whose hands hold down the Golden Girl's broken arm. The Black Duke nods.

A knife in the sergeant's hand is pressed to Justain's throat as a convulsion of fear takes her. The blade draws blood as it cuts through the leather thong of the talisman, down the line of her breast as it slashes her tunic to reveal the armor beneath. Laughter around her as she screams while the chain shirt is pulled roughly off. A girl who pretends to be a warrior. Shirt and leggings are torn away by armored hands.

"I am Gilvaleus…"

He whispers it to the silence. The Black Duke is at the altar, a figure of steel and shadow that shrouds the pale shape beneath him. The Golden Girl no longer moves, no longer fights through the tears and the terror of what will come.

"I am Gilvaleus!"

The White Pilgrim shouts it now, and all eyes turn to him. His voice carries all the weight of that confession, the shadow drawing down on him. Denying the truth to his own mind even as he fights to hold it clear. Fights to remember the truth of who he is. Of what he has done.

"I am the source of all your pain, Black Duke. I am the madness that ordered Nàlwyr to murder. I am the hand that wielded the sword anointed with your brother's blood, and I offer my life to you as debt for blood, here and now."

He feels the confusion from the scarred sergeant, from the silver-haired mage, from all the rest. Only Arsanc meets his gaze.

"My blood for your brother's," the White Pilgrim calls. "My life for hers. Let the girl go and my fate is in your hands."

And Gilvaleus on the Marble Throne of the Kings of Gracia sat alone, and his Court and Companions were of one voice in their allegiance to him, for all knew that no treachery could stand against the sight of the Whitethorn that was their High King's power, and the sign of the strength of his reign. And Gracia endured the Peace of Gilvaleus for long years, and sang of the glories of his rule and the Sword of Kings.

The Black Duke lifts a hand to the White Pilgrim with the effort that might swat an errant wasp. And in the movement of that hand, he is a puppet. Lifted and twisted and smashed to the ground in a searing pulse of pain that is the longing for death that he carries with him for endless years. The pain of living, which only the release of death can end.

"Fool of a pilgrim. You could have saved yourself."

He is dying, cannot move where the magic of the Black Duke throws him a dozen strides across the chamber, breaks him at the foot of the brazier. He feels his back shatter as he hits, but the sudden numbness is a relief from the pain of Arsanc's spell that can only scour his mind now.

He is dying, cannot move, cannot close his eyes, so that he stares at the altar stone, sees the Golden Girl fighting again as Arsanc strips away his armor, piece by piece. He sees one of the assembled circle break from their witness position, Arsanc's force holding to watch as their master's dark revenge is made.

It is the sergeant, Gareyth. The White Pilgrim remembers his face. Remembers all the anger in the young eyes, remembers how he stole the warrior's blade. Humiliated him, enraged him. And all that is gone now. Only pity in his gaze for an old man dying slowly, in agony. A blade in his hand flashes bright as he moves closer, but Arsanc's voice carries, halts the sergeant with an echo of endless contempt.

"Leave him to his gods…"

'And now my High King Gilvaleus? What fates are left to me, now that you turn from me, left alone with all my enemies at hand?'

•

He is dying, cannot move as feels the shadow slip across his sight. Blinding him to match the numbness, so that the voice of the Golden Girl fills all the remaining spaces of his mind, her screams echoing endlessly from cold stone.

– NINE –
WHAT MUST BE DONE

HE IS DYING, CANNOT MOVE. Cannot close his eyes, so that he stares at the empty altar stone, sees it gleam with the bright lines of dawn squeezed through shuttered windows.

His back is broken. Limbs numb to all feeling, the freezing cold of stone against his cheek. He slips into blackness, slips out again.

He is dying, cannot move, feels the pain that is the mailed fist of the Black Duke's power fading after endless torment. An endless night. A trembling in his fingertips, the pinprick pain of frostbite threading his legs.

He tries to think on how long he lies here. Tries to remember where he comes from. Who he is.

And then Gilvaleus arose in light from the Field of Marthai, and looked to North and South to the twelve peaks, and East and West to the Great Yewnwood and the Raging Sea of Leagin that were the bounds of his Kingdom. And a host of the Twelve descended on chariots of storm and fire to stand around the High King, and their leader was Denas the High Father, who spoke and said 'You bleed for the land, High King, and by your blood the land will one day be healed. And so come and let your hurts be healed in the halls of Orosan.'

No. Something is wrong. He feels it.

He is alive. Does not understand. A spike of anguish twists through his gut like hot iron as he lurches, splays across the floor with the endless scream of having been reborn. All the memory rushes through him of all the suffering he ever bears or inflicts in a long life of pain.

"Denas who is my father the storm lord," he whispers. "Triad-brothers who are shield and sea, the Orosana who are the grace and life of us all, why?" But he hears no answer come.

The last time he holds the Whitethorn, he kneels on the bloody ground of Marthai and watches as the hilt of ivory and grey leather twists and falls from his shaking hand.

He hears the voice of Blade in his mind like the shriek of steel on stone. He feels its pain as it calls to him. Feels its power as it tries to hold him, denies the death of the mortal wound that Astyra's spear makes. Punching through armor and ribs, heart and spine, armor again even as he raises the Whitethorn and carves his son from neck to navel with a cry of vengeance that is the end of all his dreams.

He sees the destruction that his greatness wreaks. Something moves before him, and he wipes gore from his brow to see Nàlwyr watching. He sees him speak, his friend, his captain, grown so old in the long empty years since he fled. But no voice can be heard through the haze of blood and the scream of the forsaken sword of kings.

A man might turn away from the friend he betrays. Might walk away from the warrior's death that the gods deny.

He knows nothing except that he should die. He knows that he is spared, feels the sins of his reign hanging about him like unseen chains.

He limps from the battlefield. He feels the shards of pain that claw his chest, his leg with each step.

He does not look back.

The White Pilgrim lies there for time beyond the reckoning of his senses. He feels a warmth thread through him. Feels it centered in his left arm, twisted under him where the Black Duke's magic cast him down.

He struggles to move, fights to breathe as he reaches outward, fingers clutching spastic against cold stone. His voice is the faintest whisper, hanging in bright silence.

"Why will this life not end, and why do others still suffer by this hand, by this madness, by this weakness?"

Then his fingers touch rough homespun, burning with a heat that no earthly fire ever made.

"What is your plan for me...?"

And in answer, the White Pilgrim hears the voice that calls to him for the last time on the field at Marthai fourteen years before.

Beneath the brazier, tucked in and out of sight where the Golden Girl hid it, a bundle wrapped in torn and dusty cloth seethes with a pulse of white light. The White Pilgrim strains to reach it, feels the power of that light already threading through him. Keeping him alive even across the distance between them, long after the Black Duke's wrath should claim him. Taking all the pain from him as the Blade touches his hand.

He tears through old cloth with a vigor he does not feel in fourteen years. He grasps the hilt of ivory and grey leather as he stands, drawing forth the longsword whose edge and ridge are dwyrsilver steel, crossguard and fuller in steeled gold, burning white where ancient glyphs of prophecy and power speak the name of the sword of kings and send its strength coursing through him like a dark wave.

Ankathira the Whitethorn. Claiming him. Accepting him.

He remembers.

He kneels at the side of the fallen priest and speaks the rites of Danassa and Herias, but he has no time to burn the body in his haste. He walks to the altar stone but will not look upon it in his rage. He sees instead the broken leather thong cast to the floor, the talisman that once hung at the Golden Girl's neck. Justain. The blood-red dragon set in pale gold. Her travel-stained cloak lies beside it, a dark pool on the floor.

He understands the dreams now. He remembers the sight that the Blade gives him, long ago. Visions of light and darkness. His mother's fear as she dies. His father's lament for the nation he tries and fails to save. The dream of the king's-bastard Astyra sent into hiding by a mother he loves, a women he breaks in body and mind. The love of his best friend. The love of the queen he spurns. The sight of them together, a fire in his mind that burns for long years.

He will not turn away from these things anymore.

He sees the Golden Girl in his dreams. He sees her for long months, walking the endless road of hamlets and farmsteads as she follows him. He sees her father in dreams, long ago. Following that same road. He remembers now.

When he carries it before, the Blade gives him sight beyond that of other men. Beyond even the vision of his mother Irthna and the sorcery that is her gift. The Blade in his hand as high king gives him the power that lets him strike against the usurper Thoradun, lets him channel the magic of Empire to reclaim the Empire's glory.

He loses that sight when he loses the Blade, letting it fall from his blood-soaked hand on the field where his son lies dead before him. And so separated from him over long years, held tight to the will of Nàlwyr and Justain as they seek him over endless leagues, five thousand days of hope and pain, the Blade's vision watches him instead.

These past seasons, the dreams he has. As the Blade comes ever closer to him, he sees it because it is the Blade that seeks him. Not the Golden Girl. Not Nàlwyr, now gone. The two of them are only agents for the hunger of the Blade that is a sign of his connection to it, manifesting as the hunger he feels now at the sight of it, the touch of it.

All this time, the Whitethorn, sword of kings, has been seeking its master. Showing in dreams the way that leads back to its power in the end.

•

The White Pilgrim steps from the shattered doors of the shrine into bright morning. He kneels at the torn turf where the hassas descend, sees it dry and guesses that two nights have passed.

He paces quickly to the great ash. The pain at his chest, in his heart, his mind is gone. The ache at his leg, the ache of age is gone. He embraces the rage that replaces it. Kneels in prayer at Aelathar's stone one last time.

He takes the talisman that is the Golden Girl's. The sign of her father's faith, her mother's love. He lays it on Aelathar's name.

"Until you see her," he whispers, "keep this safe."

He rises with the strength granted him by the Blade he wears now. Its scabbard belt is slung below the cord of his robes, unknotted in the manner of a pilgrim.

"Tell Nàlwyr I am broken for what has been done," he says.

He goes to the well, to the stone bowl where he retrieves one of the token-coins Arsanc gave him. The profile face of the Black Duke shivers the shadow in his mind, whips it to the seething darkness that he welcomes like an old friend.

"Forgive me," he says, "for what must be done."

With the Whitethorn in hand, the White Pilgrim summons up the sight once more, and in that sight, he sees the Black Duke's course through a sky bleeding golden dawn along the line of white sea. A view he knows, rooting deep in heart and memory.

He looks to glimpse the Golden Girl, just for a moment. He sees her bound and tied behind the sergeant, Gareyth, where he rides. Her eyes are closed in merciful sleep.

The blood of children on his hands.

He sets the cloak the Golden Girl wore to his shoulders, concealing the Blade as he walks off into the dawn.

The voice of the Whitethorn is in his mind now, and he remembers it all.

The Empire of the Lothelecan falls the year he is born, and Gilvaleus is the Empire's child. Grandson of Garneus who is the last regent of Gracia-under-Empire, then first king of the new Gracia that shares the year of Gilvaleus's birth. That new Gracia fractures into petty kingdoms and bloody war the day his grandfather dies.

Gilvaleus is only a boy, seven summers behind him. Nephew of Eurymos, who claims the crown from Garneus his father, and who fights and fails to hold the nascent kingdom together. Son of Telos, who claims the crown in turn when his brother is murdered by the usurper Thoradun.

The usurper is Lord of Sannos, where stands the shrine of Angarid and Aelathar's resting place. Sannos where Arsanc speaks to him outside an empty village. White Pilgrim and Black Duke, the burning of the dead. Sannos where Justain comes to him, tells him who he is, where he fails her. Blood on his hands.

He remembers now. The power of the Blade reshapes his mind as it mends his body.

He remembers it all.

He is the Empire's child, is trained to its standards and tactics, to its ideals and nobility. He has passed twenty summers when his mother gives her life to channel the power of the sword of kings. When his father falls in battle against Thoradun. When Gilvaleus rides to his side, too late. Seizing the sword of kings from dead hands. Vowing revenge.

He is the Empire's child, and grows up with the faith of self that denies the old gods their power for a thousand years. The belief that neither gods nor any other mystical force controls the fate of the world and its countless peoples. The belief that the destiny of the mortal races is theirs to decide, safe from the slavery that worship and pantheon make. The faith of self sees all folk free to seize the powers of mind and magic that previous generations claim as a boon of the gods, to be bestowed only on the faithful.

He is the Empire's child, and he seeks to rebuild its greatness in Gracia. Seeks to forge a lasting peace, a rule of law. A freedom from fear and tyranny to last another thousand years.

On the Plains of Marthai, it all ends.

The distance to Mitrost is thirty leagues along the straight line of the sky. Two day's journey for Arsanc and his company, the hassas flying at speed. High Spring is done at tonight's sunset, and the Black Duke must be in Mitrost then. The seat of the high king that Gracia is denied for fourteen years of strife and war.

To walk that distance will be ten days or more along the twisting tracks that lead to roads that shadow the great River Vouris. Seven days, perhaps, if the White Pilgrim walks the grassland border of the river valley, cutting overland on a straight course south and east for the sea. All of it too long, the king's conclave starting with Arsanc's arrival. No time left to him.

He carries the Whitethorn, sword of kings. He knows another road.

A strength he does not know in long years drives the White Pilgrim as he runs. He passes by the farmsteads and hamlets of these fertile lands at a distance. He sees the same scars of war that have haunted him on this spring's journey. Fields burned, fanes leveled by spellcraft and the force of blood and steel.

These are old lands. He knows it. Remembers it. The confluence of cultures that defines the heartland. Gracia that is the war-torn present. The Aigorani that are the fathers of Gracia, the Aclicians from across the broad Leagin who settle here even before the first Aigorani city-states are raised. The Empire of Eria that is built on the bones of Aigoris, and which first binds these lands as a nation with animys and iron.

These are old lands, and in them are the old ruins in which the unseen pathways of the Lotherasien are hidden away.

He knows those hidden roads. They are a part of him now where the Blade feeds him that knowledge. The memories that are his mother's, long ago.

The sun is setting pale as he finds the archway he seeks. Standing isolated in a lonely stretch of beech forest whose ground betrays no sign of any traveler but him. Far from the road, far from the farm tracks. Grey stone tumbles as if part of a wall once, only a wide archway still standing along a roughly flattened yard of flagstones slumbering beneath moss and long grass.

He feels the pulse of power in the Blade as he approaches. He remembers it. The lifeblood of kings flows through the dweomer of its steel, through him.

Thou must take comfort in thyself alone, and look to the hope of these days to carry thee. For I am taken into Orosan to heal the wounds that are my heart and memory.

He should die on the Plains of Marthai that day. It is why he casts the Blade aside, lets it fall to the blood-mire of that killing field. He feels the mortal wound that Astyra deals out, lets it take him down into shadow.

But as long as he is bound to Ankathira the Whitethorn, he cannot die. This is his fate, he knows now. This is his curse.

Long ago, the faithful of the old gods whisper that the Empire falls because it seizes and suppresses the gods' own power. The magic of mind and mana, life and sun harnessed by mortal hands. The magic that destroyed the Imperial capital of Ulannor Mor in a cataclysm whose aftershocks set the structure of Imperial power crumbling.

The practice of the priests states that emperors and kings can only ever be the supplicating shadows of the gods who give them life.

Forced to bend their reign beneath the same yoke of subservience, of faith, worn by all mortals. So it is that the Empire's greed for power pushes its leaders to hunger for and seize the power of the gods. Until the true gods, grown impatient in their might and majesty, strike them down.

He awakes alive in Marthai as he awakes alive in the shrine, feeling the dark power, the hunger that is Whitethorn's coursing through him. Claiming him. Accepting him. Healing the wounds of the body but leaving mind and spirit shattered at the sight of a son's lifeless form. The memory of a young girl's scream.

He draws the sword of kings. He feels the flood of power flow from Whitethorn to the ancient stones and the portal the Lotherasien built there. The arch and courtyard are set out by careful hands to take the appearance of ancient ruin, keystones glowing now with the symbol of the Imperial Guard. Three blades and three moons are set touching, overlapping, held to each other in a tight embrace.

Within the archway, a grey light flares and burns away as dark mist, and all the hundred hundred destinations that connect within the portal network of the Lotherasien fill his mind.

This is the Empire's power, which wins him the kingdom of his father, his uncle, his grandfather with only twenty summers behind him. This is the Empire's power, with which he attempts to reforge a nation. And in doing so, he follows that Empire's own doomed example.

He remembers the place he goes to. His thought and spirit are clear now, the shadow gone that plagues his sight through long years of exile and wandering. The curse he bears. The penance he pays for the sins of the king he is, long ago.

Over long years of wandering, he hides from the question, hidden from the essence of what he is, long ago.

Asking himself how he can be punished by gods in which he never believed.

He moves through the archway, through the burning mist, stepping through to a changed light. The sun still hangs low but the sky is shrouded, bright but cold above the sea. It is a different ruin whose far side he steps through. A great stone arch atop the cliffs a league from Mitrost, spread beneath a sky of dusk and dark cloud that shreds away on the wind. The portal's power twists through him as the sign of the Lotherasien on its keystones fades away.

From the edge of a long grove of green-budded cypress, he looks out upon the last of a great valley, thick with farm thorps. These crowd together and push toward the feet of a great stone city set astride the twisting blue-black of the Vouris as it rolls to the sea. Mitrost is bright against the dark slopes of that endless water. From long ago, remnants of the glory that is the legacy of Gilvaleus seep into its shadowed stones, white banners twisting in the wind.

The last sun casts knives of blood-red light down through the clouds. The White Pilgrim kneels in shadow, feels the chill of dusk but ignores it with the warmth of the Blade flooding through him.

He rests with clear mind, no thought, no fear. He sees the light of fire and evenlamp begin to flare in the surrounding farmsteads and the city below. He waits for the fall of full darkness that will mark the beginning of the end.

– TEN –
White City

AS NIGHT DESCENDS ON MITROST, a shadowed figure walks down from the goat trails of the hills. A pilgrim by his look. He gains the farm tracks, no notice given him from the lighted windows of sod houses and weathered huts.

He slips unnoticed onto the main road, which despite the time of night still runs heavy with wains, merchants, laborers, other pilgrims, all moving for the city. No one caring that history is made here as sunset marks the ending of the High Spring. Only seeking the commerce and the blessings that come with that.

The keep that rises at the center of the city atop its great hill is all that can be seen over serpentine stone walls. Long years ago, Mitrost is the White City. Now, those long years cast even longer shadows, the deep scars of fires arcane and mundane marked as a dark stain upon the stones. Signs of the battles that erupt in the aftermath of Marthai and bring the reign of Gilvaleus to its end.

Four decades before that end, his grandfather is Imperial regent. Elected from among the ranks of the nobility of Gracia the Great, the heart and most powerful province of the eastern Empire. It is under Empire that these lands are named the Elder Kingdoms. A legend bestowed with careful thought, designed to quell the last of the ancient hostilities between Gracia, Norgyr, Vanyr, Ajelast, Kelistae. A name that speaks to the ancient power of these nations, but whose official rendering in the common tongue of Lothela makes clear that none of these five cultures will ever again challenge the Empire for power.

Fifteen centuries ago, the Empire claims the mantle of Empire of all Isheridar. However, the five endlessly warring nations abutting the western Leagin Sea make that grandiose title a lie as they laugh off the overtures of the Lothelecan.

Those greatest powers of the east ignore the will of Empire for two hundred years, their independence a dark stain on a banner of Imperial unity. They fight that unity for three centuries thereafter. The War Kings of the Kelist, declaring that their sons and daughters will build a wall of their own flesh, blood, and bone around the green isles before the Imperial banner flies there. The Norgyr and Vanyr, never conquered and never at peace, and as happy to turn their berserker blood-lust against the Lotherasien as each other.

In the end, the corruption of ancient Ajelast is the weakness that lets the strength of Empire spread. In those desert lands that are Ajael-tha now, the khanan-emperors fall to the manipulation of the Imperial Guard. As Ajelast deals in secret with the west for Imperial magic and lore, those riches are the key that unlocks the gates of Isheridar's last free lands. However, it is the lords of Gracia who ultimately make the case for Empire, seeking the peace with Norgyr and with Vanyr that is long denied them. Peace with which they quickly rise to dominance in the unified east, spreading their culture, their language to the Imperial realms on both sides of the sea.

When Gilvaleus names Mitrost the seat of the high king, it is a ru-ined last legacy of Gracia's greatness. A remnant of Eria, whose empire is the center of civilization in the east for five hundred years, and on whose bones Gracia is built. A crumbling maze of stone walls, and the legendary citadel of the Gracian kings of old. Before the long wars of history. Before the peace of the Empire that rewrote history.

The White Pilgrim follows the road through wagon camps and farmsteads, pays as little mind to shepherds and mercenaries as they do to him. The farmlands around Mitrost are fallen into disuse, the city less than half the size it is when Gilvaleus rebuilds the white table.

He sees this and thinks on all that he does, long ago. All that is un-done in the aftermath of Marthai. All he throws away.

The road swells to its widest where it swallows the last of the farm-stead tracks, passing in through the main gates of the city that are as heavily guarded tonight as they are at the height of Gilvaleus's rule. He sees the armor and livery of a dozen different forces, sees the barely concealed hostility with which those forces work toward common de-fense. Banners fly that he does not recognize. Three score armed and armored figures line the approach, watching the steady flow of wain and foot traffic.

The black boar of Arsanc is not among the guards of the road, the White Pilgrim sees. A subtle statement of power from the Black Duke. Already setting himself above the rank of those he means to rule.

He watches fully a third of those who approach turned away at the gates, left to drift back to the hamlets and tents that surround the city walls. Beggars and pilgrims. The desperate, the too well-armed. The White Pilgrim slows his own pace so that he falls back, walking alone. He approaches the great bridge whose solid stone deck and columns sweep up in a continuous line, shaped by the power of animys.

The White Pilgrim feels the eyes of the guards on him. He sees spears lowered in a gesture of casual threat.

He has the Black Duke's coin in hand, held out only for their eyes. He slows. Does not stop. "The Duke Arsanc expects me." No longer the pilgrim's voice. No longer the weakness of age, the shadow that clouds his sight.

Only a moment's hesitation before the spears are set aside. He passes between them, passes between the sullen faces that mark his steady pace through the cavernous gate house. The evenlamps that once burned here are long gone. Torches replace them, sending flickering fingers of light along weathered stone. He feels the cobbles beneath bare feet, hears a familiar echo lost to the shadows and the noise of the city as he passes through the wall.

Long years ago, when this place is the seat of Gilvaleus the High King, the tightly set streets of the wall wards are tenements and houses, shops and market squares, academies and guild halls. When this place is the seat of Gilvaleus the High King, the ancient ruin of the keep is rebuilt in the white stone of the Marthai quarries. Surrounded by a royal court of merchant stalls and sages' workrooms, of stables and alehouses, courtyards and apartments. All that space is open to blue sky, and lit at night with a magical glow imbued into the white stones of the keep itself.

The courtyards are long gone now. The White Pilgrim sees the streets darkened as he passes through, keeping a bearing for the high hill where the keep stands. The light of its walls seeps from beneath the grime of long years, shedding shadows that are the silver-gold of first dawn. A pale gleam that makes the glow of torches and watchfires along its walls seem brighter.

Set on the empty coast of Marthai and Veneranda when they are one land under Prince Sestian, the city is abandoned when Gilvaleus claims it. Forgotten. The ancient castle is shrouded in legend and rumors of dark magic, both the legacy of the kings who do not survive their final conflicts with the Lothelecan. Lords of old Gracia whose memories are quietly swept away.

The White City is built at Gilvaleus's direction and from his own design. A citadel whose strength is its isolation, declared as a free capital separate from the lands that surround it. It is the high king's wisdom to set himself above the conflicts that endlessly splinter and cripple this ancient realm. To show those who will need to follow him that there exists another way. A shared history that all in Gracia must embrace. A common purpose and culture.

Only closest to the keep does the city cling to new life now. Pavilions and tents dot wide fields of dead grass and rubble that are the grounds and stables where the king's companions of the white table train, long ago. Couriers and servants, skalds and whores throng here this night, a shifting storm of figures drifting from flag to flag. Following the unseen courses where Fossa and Lutain, Ilfamor and Gauracta and so many more once faced each other in tests of strength and loyalty to their high king.

The White Pilgrim knows that the king's conclave brings all nineteen companies of the duchies of Gracia to assemble here. Ten thousand troops at a guess, and he recognizes the banners and standards of fewer than half of them. Flags change over time. The dukes of old are long dead, or break with the past. The dukes of a new day come together at this site of ancient power to seek a king and an end to fourteen years of war.

Hostility rages here this night between the nineteen factions. Knife-sharp and seething like the mist that settles within the walls to turn the firelight to yellow-orange islands in the dark. The Second Wars of Succession they call these days. The tales told by refugees across campfires in the night.

In the fourteen years since the fall of Gilvaleus, the eighteen dukes of Gracia govern and fight and push constantly to the crumbling brink of civil war. For fourteen years, folk call for a new high king to rule the dukes. Four conclaves are set and summoned in those years that all end in dark oaths, pledges of war. Assassination, more than once.

At this conclave, the nineteenth and newest duke of Gracia will see it done. Things the White Pilgrim hears on the roads, in the shrines.

Garneus it is, Gilvaleus's great-uncle, who calls the first conclave so many lost years ago. In the aftermath of the fall of Empire, Gracia is a void within which seethes a storm of fear that will sweep ten centuries of peace away. Garneus is Imperial regent, respected for the quickness of his mind, the slowness of his temper. To his castle in Aldona, he calls the lords of Imperial Gracia, speaks to them of a vision for the future. A Gracia united under common law, common will, with Garneus as the first king to rule this land in a thousand years.

For too many centuries, the only tools known to the princes and petty kings of Gracia are strength and spellcraft, starvation and steel. Tools whose edge is too easily broken. Telos is Gilvaleus's uncle, and heir to the nation that Garneus built in the aftermath of the Empire's fall. But Telos has not his father Garneus's heart for diplomacy and easy reason, and attempting to rule from strength, he sees his power crumble. Each declaration of a new kingdom outside his rule, each new border marked and claimed comes at the cost of Gracian blood.

In those years, the land turns against itself, ready for the strength of Thoradun of Sannos to claim. Thoradun the Usurper, who knows only how to break the will of those he rules, and who wields the strength of ten thousand Norgyr who are the heart of the mercenary force on which he builds his power.

Around the keep of Mitrost, the factions of Gracia have carefully staked out positions according to allegiance and strength. The flags of what the White Pilgrim guesses are the northlands are clustered tight away from the castle, the white bear of Kannis the only banner he knows. Isolated and distant from the larger pavilions of Marthai, Veneranda, what he thinks he recognizes as Lamitri in the west.

And at the center of all, the banners of the black boar twist in the mist-white wind. The abandoned ruin of the once-great temple of Mitrost rises behind them, spectral in the firelight. Its twelve pillars are pulled down, the twelve faces of the Orosana little more than remnants of colored glass. Arsanc chooses the site of his troops' encampment for its symbolism. A calculated display.

The Black Duke's camp is alive with firelight and revelry, music and drunken shouting, the hiss and crackle of pine fires. The fat-sweet scent of venison rises, roasting whole on the spit. In the shadows at the periphery, the White Pilgrim slips close along the edge of the stores tents, servants racing to and from the fires with torch and lantern, cask and crate. Tents and pavilions are marked with the sign of the black boar, long tables set with cloths and laid in with heaped trenchers and overflowing mugs. All the trappings of a royal banquet, the image adding to the strength the Black Duke's force presents here this night.

The hassas rest nearby, the great beasts herded within a wide patch of muddy field nearly as large as that claimed by Arsanc's tents. They are penned in by stakes of black oak whose heads pulse with the violet glow of protective spellcraft. The White Pilgrim sticks to the shadows there, ignored by the winged horses in their slumber. He avoids the bright fires and the brighter laughter that spreads beyond as he circles, appraises the tumult before him.

He sees officers, soldiers of the forces of the Black Duke that sweep their way south from Reimari in six short weeks of devastating war. The tales told by refugees across campfires in the night. But the warriors are not what the White Pilgrim seeks, cannot give him what he needs. Not without the battle he does not want to make. Not yet.

At a secondary barracks, haphazardly raised beyond the crisp lines of the soldiers' tents, he slips in through the crack of canvas. He sees rough bedrolls spread direct to the ground. Six children within. Pages and drudges, stable hands and couriers look up in surprise as the White Pilgrim pulls the tent closed behind him.

Two stand within reach, their legs kicked out with a lightning-fast strike, dropped to the ground with muffled cries of fear. Three eat at the small brazier that is the only light at the tent's main pole, upending their trenchers as they scramble back. He catches the scent of scorched meat and bitter smoke.

The sixth turns to face him, throws up an arm against the imminent threat. The White Pilgrim is taken for a sergeant or servant-master, and he is on the boy in an instant, hurling him to the ground, the same fear in his eyes as in all the rest. They see too late the ragged robes, no insignia or sign of rank. Not understanding for the brief moment in which he will take what he needs.

He drops to kneel astride the boy, judges him at fifteen summers. Older than the others. Hair the color of dead leaves, a twisting scar touching his face from eye to cheek. Taller, an edge of arrogance in his manner that speaks to a position of authority that makes him perfect for the White Pilgrim's needs.

He has the Blade in hand. He cannot remember drawing it. Its razor tip is pressed to the boy's throat, and the White Pilgrim must focus to force it to stillness. The boy cannot blink, cannot breathe.

He whispers in a voice whose rage he does not recognize. Speaks to all at once, the leader who is only a boy and the children who follow him. "Any sound, any movement, this is the first of you to die."

With the sight of Whitethorn, he sees the Golden Girl curled tight in shadow. She is not moving, the White Pilgrim hoping that she dwells still in the painless deep sleep of the mind. Darkness around her, the air close and stale, her hands and feet bound. No clue as to where her cell is, but he will learn that now.

"Your Black Duke travels with a girl. He arrived here with her as prisoner. I would know which tent of the Duke's company is hers."

A stammering voice rises across from him. One of the others, a black-haired girl cringing in fear. "The Duke Arsanc's forces have brought many with them, lord…"

The White Pilgrim drops the child with a backhand blow that is unleashed before he can stop it. It takes all his strength to hold the Blade back from the throat of the boy beneath him, weeping now. He sees blood there, pearling as three perfect drops where the tip of the Blade scribes a trembling line in the flesh below.

"No. Not this girl. She is Arsanc's alone. A prisoner." The White Pilgrim's voice chokes off, words lost in the desire to strike. A desire to kill this stripling as a warning to the others, to see if blood will loosen their wretched tongues.

"The Black Duke holds court within the keep," the boy leader whispers, voice twisted through with the certainty of death that he feels. Speaking not in any hope of mercy, but from the obedience that all grant to death in the end.

"The Golden Girl…"

"He holds a prisoner there, in his tents. I heard the soldiers say it. I have not seen…"

"Where?"

"There is a garden, lord. Duke Arsanc holds court in the domed hall, but the knights who serve him in the conclave have tents in the garden."

The White Pilgrim sees it in his mind's eye. He feels the sight the Blade grants him trigger a resonant rush of memory. He sees the scarred boy at the altar, holding Justain down while Arsanc strips away cloak and armor, laughing. He will have his vengeance for her pain, will have the blood that pain demands.

No.

He shakes his head, tries to clear it.

Something is wrong, but he has no time. He feels the shadow thread through him, fights it with a will he barely remembers.

"Hold…" he whispers, and he does not know who he speaks to. He fights to stay the killing stroke, both hands locked to the Blade now, shaking.

"One man must die tonight," he says to himself, to the weeping faces cast down before him, to no one. "Along with any others who stand in the way of that deed."

And even as he says it, he feels the hunger in the Blade that is the shadow scouring his sight. The hunger that is the voice that seizes his mind, tells him who he is now, who he is long ago, who he is again before the end.

"Do not be in that number," he says.

The power and the hunger. The desire for greatness. Feeding him as it always does.

The White Pilgrim feels a chill twist through him. He feels pain at his arms that are locked to the Blade in a grip of iron.

He remembers now.

He fights to recall where he is, who he speaks to. He kneels in a darkened tent, six children on the ground before him. All waiting to die.

"Stay here," he whispers, hoarse. "Say nothing. Do not bargain your lives for the sins of…"

He loses his thought, cannot focus, cannot think. The haze of shadow grows stronger on the fear that shifts and washes around him. It flickers in his mind like the guttering of the brazier's light as he goes.

– ELEVEN –
DARK GARDEN

HE FINDS HIMSELF ALONG the edge of the encampment, cannot remember having moved there. In his hands, a dark bundle of clothing. He cannot remembering seizing it.

The White Pilgrim sees the bright patches of firelight surrounding the tables where Arsanc's followers celebrate the events they expect this night will bring. He cannot be seen in turn where he shifts from shadow to shadow, sees faces he recognizes. He feels them laid out before him in the quickening sight of memory. The farmhouse pyre, the night on the road with the Golden Girl, the song of rage that threads through him that is the memory of the altar at Angarid.

He sees the young sergeant. Gareyth. Dark eyes bright with laughter at the head of his table. The two blades of his rank gleam beneath the sign of the black boar at his arm.

The White Pilgrim watches in silence. He waits, unconscious of the passage of time, of the muscles of his legs locked to hold him crouched low. Unconscious of the weariness he should feel after the open road and the passage along the unseen road. All the things that bring him to this place once more.

All he feels is the heat of the Blade in its scabbard, his hand wrapped tight around the grip. A pulsing force that courses through him like a draught of slow-smoldering fire.

All he sees is Gareyth moving, finally. Staggering to his feet as he shouts with the easy voice of one whose battles are all done. He walks the length of the tables, slaps a dozen hands, returns with vigor the salutes he receives.

The White Pilgrim rises. He drifts through the darkness to shadow Gareyth as he makes his way to the edge of the firelight. An empty space of grey grass and rubble spreads between the Black Duke's camp and the tents of the dukes he means to rule before this night is done. The young sergeant drifts with faltering steps toward a twisted stand of scrub oak, gaunt branches scraping the night sky. He fumbles with shirt and leggings, whistling as he pisses.

The sergeant's back is to the darkness, from which he hears a whisper of footsteps across dead ground. He turns back as he finishes.

A moment to scan the darkness, to shake off the torpor of wine that shows in the dullness of his eyes.

In those eyes, the White Pilgrim reads the suddenness of the young sergeant's fear. A stranger behind him. A moment of distraction that no soldier ever allows himself in the field, but the Black Duke's pavilion is already marked as a site of victory this night. This place is the end and endgame of the lightning-fast invasion of the northern duchies, from which one man will remake a kingdom in his own name.

Then comes a moment of recognition, and the fear fades. Gareyth smiles darkly, appraises the grey face, its gaze as blank as the mist-night that swells around them. No light to betray the Blade held motionless in the White Pilgrim's hand.

"You are a determined fool..." the sergeant begins, and then he dies.

The darkness swells where the Blade comes up, lances out with all the strength of a lifetime's rage held quiescent. A rage confined to the shadow of memory for long years. The speed behind its force belies the White Pilgrim's age, defies the exhaustion that should wrack the hunched figure in the name of all the leagues of his endless road.

Three strikes. The first is through the throat to silence him, but a man might die slow, noisily that way. Not enough. Again, through the spine to drop him, paralyze the pain of nerve and the thrashing madness of the moment of death, by which a man might alert others to his passing even as he falls. And again, through the heart because the Blade's power demands it. Ankathira the Whitethorn drinking deep of the blood of the unfaithful. Traitors to the cause of the high king.

He hears dead grass whisper in the rising wind. The travel-stained cloak that is the Golden Girl's is dropped to the body at his feet. The White Pilgrim wears the cloak that Gareyth wore, does not remember donning it. He sees the red band and its black boar, sees the dark stain that mars the steel of the Blade.

Ankathira that is the Whitethorn pulses in his hand with the steady frantic rhythm of the heart that it stills this night. The first blood the Blade draws since Marthai.

The White Pilgrim remembers the madness in his son Astyra's eyes that is a mirror to the madness in his own. He remembers the mud of the field, blood-black and glistening. The bodies scattered across it swallowed as if by a drowning pool.

He remembers the young sergeant's face as he turns from the altar at Angarid, moves toward the White Pilgrim lying broken in the shrine. Pity for an old man dying slowly, in agony.

He tries not think on these things.

He bends to adjust the cloak to cover the body. A darker stain in the fog-shrouded shadows, invisible from the pools of light and laughter beyond. As he does, he sees the scabbard at Gareyth's hip.

He recognizes the hilt. The Golden Girl's blade that is her father's. The young sergeant dies with no chance to even reach for it.

The White Pilgrim takes the rapier that is Nàlwyr's, lashes the scabbard to his waist below the rope belt that now carries the Blade in its scabbard of ivory and gilt leaf. He takes the young sergeant's purse, covers himself with the dark cloak that is the sign of Arsanc's guard. He draws the hood up as he slips away.

Toward the main gate of the keep, the White Pilgrim walks with a purpose and detachment that carries him through the shadows between the watchfires of a dozen different camps. He returns salutes where members of Arsanc's contingent pass him, not acknowledging any face directly. He ignores the dark stares that come from beneath other banners, other badges of loyalty at shoulder and sleeve.

No challenges are made. No one even in Arsanc's own force looks past the sign of the black boar, the rank marked there. Soldiers' instincts softened by drink and the more potent elixir of assured victory.

Their master is the most powerful freelord of Norgyr. The newest duke of Gracia. Arsanc will be high king of Gracia by the time the king's conclave ends. Tonight, perhaps. If not, tomorrow, or the tomorrow after that. Nothing left that might stand in the Black Duke's way.

Torches and braziers burn bright against the fog at the perimeter of the keep's curtain wall, its towers rising to their crumbling height of shadow above. It is quiet here. No traffic save for those on the business of the conclave. Knights and lords, foot-couriers under close scrutiny.

The White Pilgrim watches from the ruins of an abandoned stable, scorched stone and timbers cracked and open to the sky like an empty tomb. Two score guards are stationed at temporary shelters where the crumbling gatehouse once stood. Wood and canvas and steel form a bright wall, the old guard posts broken like the stables. All the rubble that is a monument to that day when Mitrost falls.

The gates are closed, the guards stepping forward at their first sight of him, swords drawn. A routine antipathy marks their movements, focusing on the lateness of the night, the dark importance of the business unfolding within the keep's walls. The same knife-edge of open antagonism in them as that seen between the factions outside the city wall. The warriors of lesser dukes, staking out their claim to Arsanc's service while they can.

"Speak your business at the king's seat at Mitrost," the closest guard says in Gracian, "and swear your fealty and liege to Gracia."

The old oath, or an approximation of it. He hears it uttered countless times, long ago.

"Arsanc," the White Pilgrim says simply. He hunkers down in his stolen cloak, lets his gaze drift face to face. He feels an anger thread through him. The voice of Whitethorn unspools shadow as it whispers, sends his gaze across the closest guards. His hand strays to the hilt of the Blade beneath his cloak.

He fights to clear his vision, forces his hand away from the scabbard and into the sleeve of his unseen robes. When he brings it out, it holds the token of the Black Duke, pale gold gleaming in the swirl of mist and torchlight from high along the walls.

"Arsanc," he says again. He sees eyes slip from the token to the sign of the black boar at his shoulder.

Grudgingly, the guards step back, swords lowered as a knock is hammered out at the gates. The scraping of bar and bolt, a flare of firelight and evenlamp. The brighter light of magic slips into the fog like white fingers, the gates swinging wide. Another six guards stand within, their dark looks joining with the looks of those outside as the White Pilgrim passes them.

He walks down a wide hall, floor set with flagstones that were white once, long ago. They spread splintered now, ground grey with dirt and ash. He hears the gate crash shut behind him. Hears the murmur of voices fall and fade as he passes by empty alcoves, walls lined with the cracked shadows of shattered mosaic and relief.

Within a great circular courtyard, four staircases climb. Pillars circle around him like advancing giants wrapped in white. The open air above shows a wash of stars, the sky pale in the west where the Clearmoon wanes. A blood-red haze to the east shows where the Darkmoon climbs.

He feels the last fragments of the scales of time fall from his eyes. He gazes out upon the ruin that is his legacy.

Long years ago, Mitrost is the White City and the keep is its gold and silver heart. A castle-town within a city. Home to five thousand of the high king's closest companions and servants, mages and scholars who are the backbone of a reign built on visions of greatness. Now, those long years leave barren shadows in their wake. Apartments and markets, emporiums and barracks are long gone. Only carcass stones remain, as fragile in appearance as the wall of wind-shivered bark that lingers when the great oak is eaten away by rot from within.

These crumbling foundations are still strong enough to support the battlements and halls that are the heart and height of the keep. Firelight burns bright there this night, in the domed hall where the white table stands shattered. The king's conclave is there. Deciding the fate of all that Gracia lost in the tale Gilvaleus tried and failed to write.

The White Pilgrim hears voices in the distance from two directions. Heavy steel footsteps. Guards on patrol, at least as many as those that watch at the gate by his guess. He tarries too long.

Cursing memory and vanity, he slips past the closest pillars and into the shadow of a passageway. This twists within the north quarter of the keep, largest of the four wings set off from the circular courtyard. He watches the guards pass, sees not the mix of uniforms and sigils of the gate but a singular slash of red on all the dark cloaks. Arsanc's troops, patrolling out from where their master holds court in the domed hall above.

He feels the routes he must take there, locked into a memory untouched now by age or shadow. He knows the way he must walk before this ends.

He knows it is time.

He moves by instinct, taking back staircases and forgotten passageways rank with mold and shadow. He listens for footsteps ahead and behind, shifts all but silent around them. An unseen shade in his cloak of black. Bare feet a whisper across the rubble that dusts the ancient marble of empty corridors, the crumbling stairs he climbs.

From the darkness ahead, he catches the sweet scent of rot and age, and he is there.

When Aelathar comes to him, her power is the old magic of the druidas, and so a garden he promises to make for her at Mitrost. With walls of glass and shimmer-glowing gold, it opens up beyond the domed hall and the king's seat, and from that throne of state, he watches her distant figure walk paths of white gravel in the company of doves and summer moths.

He clambers over a wall of white stone that glimmers silver in the starlight. He pushes through a shroud of grey boughs and bearded moss. The low walls of the garden are crumbling in the embrace of ivy and decay. The regular ranks of smooth-barked peach and apricot and plum that once marched here spindle to intermittent stands now, splaying moss-crusted fingers to the air.

He watches two guards walking the near edge of the darkness, easily times his movement between them. He knows that more lurk within the light that seethes in the distance, the glow of fires and evenlamps bright beyond a twisting wall of mist and shadow. He knows that they do not matter to him yet.

The trees are ranked like dark sentinels, but he holds the allegiance of the night as he slips through them, bare feet silent across loam and leaf fall. The haze of light swells, and through mist and distance gleams a weaver's loom of glittering shards that he knows marks the shattered windows that are the garden's edge. The lost entrance to the domed hall where the future is made.

He feels Arsanc there without needing the power of the Blade to see. The eighteen other dukes of Gracia are with him. The best warriors of two nations and nineteen armies, but they do not matter to him yet.

Through the mist, he sees a lone pavilion set amid the trees. The banner of the black boar hangs unmoving in the chill air.

Two more guards pace out slow movement that he reads with ease. He draws on the power of the Blade, acknowledges its hunger as its sight shows him the unseen spaces within the mist-shrouded tents. Shows him the empty shadows he walks through as he finds the single tent he seeks. Shows him the spot away from the light where the darkness hides him, lets him cut his way through and into the deeper darkness beyond.

They keep her in darkness for the terror that the darkness brings. The pain she suffers scars her thought, so that the mind left alone feeds on itself. Creating terrors more potent than anything that can be visited by the world outside the mind.

The scent of filth and fear. A faint line of grey light at the main spar of the tent marks an evenlamp shrouded with black cloth. The White Pilgrim frees one edge of the glowing crystal sphere, just enough to set the interior of the pavilion as a silver haze. Enough to show him a rough table and stools, a brazier burned low, blankets piled haphazardly.

He hears the catch of her breathing in the dark. He follows the fear to the corner where the Golden Girl lies.

She is opposite the sealed flaps of the doors. He crouches so that he can listen, can watch for any sign of approach even as he knows that no one will enter. She is Arsanc's prize, and none among the Black Duke's forces will dare to sully his vengeance. A thing that their duke seeks since before the Golden Girl is even born. The girl he destroys, will destroy, in the name of that vengeance.

She is bound hand and foot, eyes shut tight where she curls in the corner. A blanket of rough homespun is slipped off her, covers only her legs. The chain shirt of dwyrsilver that is her father's is worn against her bare flesh. No doublet or shirt beneath it. He sees where it rubs her raw, her broken body anointed with the armor that is the sign of her conviction and purpose. Returned to her as some kind of mocking trophy.

He sees the bruises that color her face, her arms and back. Sees dried blood streaking her cheek, her shoulder, her belly.

The White Pilgrim shifts closer in the red haze of his sight. He fights to keep his hands from trembling as he reaches for her. Closer, and he sees that her eyes are open, faint slits of shadowed steel-blue that gauge his movement. Close enough that she can spit through cracked lips to catch the black boar at his shoulder, can swing her legs around, driving them for his stomach like a ram.

He stops her, gently. Pulls the hood of the cloak back so that she can see his face.

The sight of the Blade courses through him. It fills him with her pain in a searing instant of understanding, and in that sight, he realizes how young she truly is. Understands how much of her strength is the mask of her father that she wears. He sees the world through the blue eyes that cleave all life, all things, cleanly into light and dark, right and wrong.

The Blade lets him see himself through her eyes, only for a moment, so that he can see the horror in himself. The pain and remorse that is the sight of her. The coldness in his gaze that is the hunger for vengeance that is all he knows now.

No words pass between them. He grasps her hands to quell their shaking as he unties the cords that bind her. She wraps herself in the blanket, shifts close to the brazier for the last of its heat. From within his cloak, the White Pilgrim retrieves the bundle he took from the children's tent. Clothing, boots, a jacket. Sized for the boy leader, all too large for her, but it will do.

She dresses in silence, hands shaking as she slips the chain shirt back on over a dirt-streaked tunic. She covers it with the jacket, sets her mouth with the pain of each movement. The sleeves of the jacket, she leaves long. Covering the red welts of ropes at her wrists.

From beneath his cloak, the White Pilgrim retrieves the sword that is the weapon of the Golden Girl's father. He hands it to her with head bowed but she barely looks to it.

"The king's sword," she whispers, voice cracked like old stone. "Where is the king's sword?"

"It is safe," the White Pilgrim says. "You must go to Angarid." He opens the purse that is the sergeant Gareyth's. Copper, silver, and gold gleam faint within as he slips it to her hands. "Take the farm tracks. Pay your way with copper, keep the rest hidden. The healers will have returned to the shrine by the time you make your way there. Let them care for your hurts. Let them keep you safe."

"Where is the sword of kings?" she cries, and the pain in that voice threads through the deep sight he feels to bring back the old ache of his heart. Cutting him with all her fear, and all the longing of her quest. "I left it for you. You must…"

"A king's subject does as she is ordered," he says. He finds the old voice, sees the force of it reckoned in her weeping eyes. "A king's companion does her liege's will with honor," he says, more gently, but the grief as she looks away cuts deep through the Blade's sight.

In the end, he cannot bear that pain. Cannot stop his hand as it flips his cloak aside, reveals the ivory scabbard slung there. The White Pilgrim sees a light return to the blue eyes. He sees a hope there that he does not recognize anymore.

He takes her hands in his. Draws her to the dark back of the tent and the entrance he makes there. The sight of the Blade shows him the silence beyond, lets them slip safely out and through.

The Golden Girl's hand is in his as he draws her quickly through shadow and shrouding branches, leads her to the wall of white stone. He senses the movements of the distracted guards in the darkness around him, pacing his approach to their silence.

"Keep this in hand," he says as he presses the golden token of the Black Duke to her palm. "It will get you past both gates, but do not let Arsanc's guards find you before you get there. They walk so that the whole world hears them, so listen, wait, move in the silence. Follow the shadows. When they ask at the keep wall, you are sent from the Black Duke himself with a message for the captains of his pavilion in the city. Do not be afraid."

The White Pilgrim pushes her hair back, wipes dried blood from her cheek. He stares into the blue eyes that he understands have never known the thought of abandoning her father's quest. He tries to help her scale the wall, but she is up without the aid of his hand. A strength in her that is Nàlwyr's, the old determination in her as she holds herself there.

"My father's dream," she whispers, as if she knows the White Pilgrim's mind. "You remember."

Not a question this time. He feels her gaze on him, knows that she senses the strength of mind, of body that floods through him now.

"I remember," the White Pilgrim says.

Her father dreams of this night, long ago. Gilvaleus with the sword of kings in hand, stepping forth to the witness of all the dukes of Gracia. He sees it in his mind. He feels the hunger of the Blade embrace the power in that image.

"Do not cross over to the side of revenge," he says. He hears the tremor in his voice, tries to fight it. "To the embrace of hate. For once hate holds you, there is nothing left."

She hears it also. An uncertainty threading his words that should not be there. "My king, you must show yourself. Tell them your name. You are the legend, and the legend is all that men remember now…"

"When the past is reckoned, the future will be made," he says. "Do not lose what you have. Your life, your faith. Your goodness that is your father's."

"My king…"

"Go," the White Pilgrim says, and he is gone from her. Disappearing quickly into the darkness of the sleeping trees.

– TWELVE –
A Prayer for Dead Kings

WITHIN A SPACE OF SHADOW, he once more approaches the light. Walls of shattered glass are flanked by white stone at the orchard's edge, marking the gabled exterior of the domed hall beyond. The center of the keep is its highest point, broken like all the rest of its crumbling edifice. Little more than a shadow of the past.

Crystal shards cling to twisted spindles of rusted steel, the gold leaf that long ago catches the glistening dawn stripped away. Walls of canvas hang here now, spiked to the stones above. Clipped together against the open air, the chill of night.

He stands at the canvas, can reach out to touch it. No way to see within, but the sight of the Blade takes him there.

The domed hall. The king's seat. The throne room of Mitrost that is his, long ago. The great council chamber where the future and fate of a kingdom is decided. Will be decided again.

A charred haze paints the walls, frozen fast. Signs of the fires that burn here when the keep is lost. White stone mold-streaked to grey rises to curved buttresses overhead, etched with mosaic scars that are the only remnants of the images of legend that adorn these ceilings, long ago.

Once, the trials of immortal Pheretas are rendered here, who labors across the breadth of the mortal world to return the six lost scrolls of good and evil, life and death, memory and madness to Denas his father. The visions of Acasyma, whose prophecies of the future bring destruction or fortune to all who hear them. Creusa the mariner, who travels the seven Ports of the Dragon Kings around the Leagin and returns with their ancient secrets. The reign of Cassatra who is the dragon queen of Eria, and who all the kings of Gracia that arise thereafter claim for their bloodline until that bloodline ends at the Empire's word.

The stories he grows up hearing. The tales of the past that live on as song and shadow play, lesson and memory. A hundred years from now, a thousand years from now, his life should join the lives of those who come before him. Memory turned to legend turned to myth by the passage of time. But he is not worthy of that fate. Not anymore.

The White Pilgrim hears the words spoken in the domed hall, then hears beyond them. He feels the senses of the Blade slip into mind and heart, reading the fear and rage that threads the room and the small circle of men and women gathered there.

The nineteen dukes of Gracia stand alone in conclave. No captains or guards at their sides, no entourages of heirs or petty nobles. They meet alone by ancient tradition, face to face so that no shows of false support, no gainsaying of fervent followers can distract them.

The dukes of Gracia are secure in the power of spellcraft that each brings with them. Ancient incantation, the dweomer of armor and cloak, charms and wards. The strongest magic in the nation, perhaps. Granting each ruler the power of a demigod, even as it reduces each to equals. Nothing to mark the conflict of this night except sheer force of will and the strength of the followers that each holds beyond the walls of the keep, the city around it.

But that strength is broken tonight, and Gracia will never be the same.

Through the sight of the Blade, the White Pilgrim sees nineteen thrones of stone that circle the sundered white table. All that remains of the court that once stood here. The thrones are the chairs of the king's companions, long ago. The table's great panes are split and shattered, broken down the middle and cracked to two crumbling sections across the floor.

For this endless day, the dukes of Gracia are on their feet. They speak to show their rank and strength without break or surcease. They fight with word and threat since before the sun fades. Sparring and shouting endlessly all the earlier day, even though by tradition and agreement, the conclave begins only at the mark of night that is the High Spring's end.

This is the king's conclave. The summit started by his grandfather, who is Garneus the Great and Imperial Regent. In the aftermath of word from the distant west that Ulannor Mor has fallen, it is Garneus alone who can bind together the lords of Gracia to acknowledge the need for one leader. One voice who speaks for all. One king whose rule reclaims the greatness that is and is always.

That first king's conclave is in Orlach in Aldona, long ago. The great city of gardens where Gilvaleus is born in the year of the Empire's fall.

The second conclave is in Mitrost, the seat of power that Gilvaleus forges to mark the rise of a new age that he vows will equal the old. He is the High King, who slays the usurper Thoradun and drives his forces back to the ice lands of Norgyr once more.

Within the circle in which the dukes stand, the White Pilgrim sees in his mind's eye the great slab of stone as it shatters and is thrown down by the sorcery of Astyra, the night he challenges his father for the throne. An assault of sorcery breaks even the magical defenses of the keep, the high king cast down as the white table is sundered by the king's-bastard's unbreakable adamantine spear.

Long ago, the white table is the seat of the high king's companions and the symbol of the justice of his reign. An artifact of the city of kings, lost to time but rebuilt at Gilvaleus's direction by sorcery and engineering when the walls of Mitrost are raised.

Its circular face comprises twelve interlocking panes of stone, recut from the twelve holy peaks of the Drachen's Teeth and the Shieldcrest. Assembled by spellcraft and ground to a clear mirror-brightness.

Along its edge stand a score of kings and princes, who by threat of war or love for Gilvaleus name themselves dukes and accept the reign of the high king that will make Gracia whole once more. A sign to connect his rule to the rule of the ancient lines.

Astyra's assault is put down that night. And in the end, the companions of Gilvaleus the High King ride to the Plain of Marthai to meet the warriors of the king's-bastard. The swords he calls to him from the duchies of the Northlands. Uncounted blades of the Norgyr, who seek revenge against Gilvaleus for Thoradun the Usurper, their long-dead lord.

At the head of the white table, a single figure from among the nineteen commands the attention of all. Armor of black lacquered plate. Lines of age and anger etched in a handsome face. A scar at his neck, hair hanging to shroud eyes that are black even in the light.

"Consider the choice before you." The Imperial tongue, harsh-clipped in the accent of Norgyr.

Arsanc stands before a high seat of white stone, pitted and cracked with endless age but standing tall by virtue of its ancient dweomer. The throne carved of a single block of Magandis marble, it is said. An artifact of an age before history, beyond even the Empire's power to destroy, so they simply erase that history. Leave the marble throne empty so as to be forgotten.

The sight that is the Blade's lays out the endless threat and debate that leads to this point. It focuses the White Pilgrim's mind and senses to the final ultimatum that the Black Duke lays this night at the feet of those he means to rule.

Arsanc is a freelord of Norgyr, one of the dozen war-clan chiefs and tribal kings who rule a disparate collection of nation-states that collapses to blood and chaos when the Empire is lost. He is young when his father dies and leaves him the lands of Thorfin in the far north. A hardscrabble spread of steppe and forest that is perfectly set to the Black Duke's ambition. An isolation there that reminds him he is alone. A starkness that cannot warm the cold of heart that comes with a brother's death years before.

Then long ago, word from the south changes all that.

From a skald sent into Gracia in exile, a tale returns to Arsanc's court, bargained against clemency for the various crimes that see the bard exiled in the first place. The story he offers is the truth of what happened to Arsanc's brother Havar that night in Stondreva, gleaned from the drunken rantings of squires and fallen knights. Proven in the confession of a blue-eyed warrior who wanders the fallen lands of Gracia in constant search of a thing he will not name. A broken knight who confesses to the murder of children. Whispers of the dark rot of the spirit that eats away the heart of Gilvaleus's reign.

His whole life, the Black Duke lives with the sadness that lingers now in the space where the love for his brother is once held. Now, that sadness is replaced by a dark hatred and a thirst for vengeance against a king long dead. A vengeance that will be taken against all Gracia in the end.

War is a constant in Norgyr, though the Black Duke spends his life avoiding its costs. He builds his forces claiming the need to defend his lands, holding a peace that means nothing to him anymore, as striking from Thorfin, his forces take Innveig Freehold to the south. Then into Reimari where his brother dies, long ago, and down to the borderlands of the Duchy of Mundra that is the wall of Gracia to the south.

The fields and steppes of Reimari have long been disputed territory. A realm of rich grasslands that are the frontier between Vanyr and Norgyr, Norgyr and Gracia. Then so does Arsanc who is freelord of Reimari in Norgyr declare himself duke of Reimari in Gracia. And only then is the Black Duke's ambition revealed.

With the strength of three freeholds behind him, Arsanc is the most powerful lord of Norgyr. He leads an army of the north that perches above Gracia, waiting like a tide to be unleashed. Even before the invasion of Mundra begins, the threat of invasion is enough to cripple the northern duchies and their leaders, weakened by the years of deadly struggle between themselves that the fall of Gilvaleus wreaks.

"The newest duke of Gracia will lead you," the Black Duke shouts.

"Or the war that begins today will shatter the shadow that is all that remains of this land."

The White Pilgrim feels an ache twist through him as shouted voices erupt throughout the domed hall. Capitulation and defiance, the dukes of Gracia jockeying for power in the midst of the unthinkable change this night will bring. He feels the Blade echoing the hunger of the Black Duke's words. He remembers Marthai. Remembers his son's blood on his hands as he forces the hunger away.

"Hold…" he whispers, and he does not know who he speaks to.

Arsanc's forces push across the border, engaging in isolated strikes. Mercenary tactics, hit and run assaults on merchant trains and farm towns shatter the resolve of Mundra's people, just as the tactics of the usurper Thoradun do four decades earlier. Truces are forged quickly in fire between the Black Duke and those who cannot stand against him. Treaties open the roads into Lamitri and Liana, the green fields and mountain mines of northern Gracia that are the anvil on which the hammer of destruction will strike.

Around the broken white table, the three dukes of Mundra, Lamitri, and Liana stand closest to the Black Duke. Marshalling support for an ultimatum.

Arsanc's forces wage a lightning war in Sannos and in Mirdza. Mirdza will yield up Marthai when it falls, and fair Hypriot at Marthai's heart. With Hypriot comes control of the Sea of Galvas and its great cities and its hundred smaller ports, from which comes control of Cosiand and Valos and Aynwel in the green south. The trade of Galvas and the south pushes north through the Free City of Yewnyr, whose wealth and power stand in Mundra, and so back to the north, where the Black Duke's forces form a wedge set to thrust down and into the heart of Gracia like a bloody spear.

"This is the doom before you," Arsanc says in triumph. His voice threads the White Pilgrim's mind as the Blade feeds the words, the haze of emotion into him. "This is the weakness of your race, your kings, your gods. Gracia was the jewel of the east, and will be again. But you are children, and your games of rule and conquest and petty wars are over."

The Gracian dukes have only one option, all knowing it even before Arsanc speaks. Arsanc is to be made high king, elevated from the ranks of the fractious dukes that have fought over Gracia for fourteen years and could do little more than watch while it crumbled away. All have heard their doom that day in ultimatum and private audience, and in the days before that in the whispers of advisors and courtiers.

"The king's conclave is the assembly of dukes, who will choose from among their own ranks a high king to rule all Gracia, and in whose name the dukes will uphold the peace and law of Mitrost."

The White Pilgrim hears the power in the Black Duke's voice, hears the echo of history in his words. The same words Gilvaleus speaks in the domed hall when the usurper falls.

"You will know greatness again by my hand," the Black Duke shouts. "You will know peace, or your people will know death. Your choice stands before you."

The White Pilgrim feels the shadow press down upon his sight. He hears a voice thread that shadow to tell him that there stands a third place between peace and death.

Death is the ending of things. Death is a part of the natural order, the settling of accounts, the passage from what is before to what is now and what is tomorrow. Peace is the beginning of things, the time before the breaking that comes when all the natural forces of life and nature are unleashed.

The place between is his life. All the peace from long ago, burned into memory like a book of scars that he must read and read again. All the pain that is tomorrow's, driven into his flesh like iron nails as punishment for what he is.

"My lord?"

The voice rings out loud in the stillness of his mind. He feels the echo that differentiates it from the voice of the Blade, repeating the signs and shadows of the conclave in dark whispers.

The White Pilgrim wheels, finds himself face to face with four guards. The armor and cloak of the Black Duke. Faces he does not recognize. Two have swords already in hand, the other two drawing as they see him. No warning of their approach, his mind and senses focused inward, into the domed hall and what unfolds there.

He feels the hunger twist through him like something alive. Through the Blade's sight, he sees himself through these strangers' eyes. An old man, bent. The black boar at his shoulder makes them approach carefully, taking him for one of them until he turns to show the road-grimed robes beneath the cloak. A belt of frayed rope is loose above a scabbard, from which the White Pilgrim draws a longsword whose weight is seemingly too much for him. It hangs in his hand, trembling with the effort of clutching it.

Their looks are something between humor and pity. The warrior with the two blades of a sergeant at his shoulder detaches himself from the others.

"Yield," the White Pilgrim says. He hears laughter from all four as the sergeant strides forward. "One man must die tonight," the White Pilgrim says. His voice has an edge they too easily ignore. "Along with any others who stand in the way of that deed."

The guard sergeant raises his blade, a slow arcing strike. In a flash of silver, his sword is gone from his hand. A second flash and the hand is gone.

He stares in shock as the White Pilgrim grabs him, spins him, anchors all his weight and strength by deadly instinct to send the sergeant hurtling through the remains of the garden's wall of glass with a scream.

All the shouting, all the blustering and bravado of the domed hall is shattered in an instant. The canvas that blocked the night and the open air of the garden comes down as the sergeant flies through it, hitting hard and sprawling in a nest of blackened shards.

More figures follow a heartbeat behind. Three in the uniform of the Black Duke swarm the fourth at their center, a blur of grey and white, silver and red. The White Pilgrim fends off attacks from three directions, the Blade singing in his hand.

Chaos erupts in the hall, a dozen blades drawn at once. Skirmishes flare between the leaders of Gracia, who are reduced to brawling fear in the instant. Accusations shouted of ambush and betrayal, the incantation of spellcraft, animyst and arcane power filling the air.

The White Pilgrim threads through it like a deadly shadow. He discards the cloak of the black boar where it limits his movements, spins at the center of a web of blood and steel. The three guards who pursue him are fought to a standstill, screaming for aid as they fall back beneath a staggering series of fast strikes.

He attacks relentlessly. He feels the hunger of Whitethorn even as he fights it, forcing his strikes to sword and armor rather than the soft flesh of arm and neck. He parries without counterstrike as he feels his way through the movement around him, feels the sight that is the Blade's mark out the field of combat. Feels it flood him with the fury that will drink deep of the blood of betrayers this night if he will only let it.

"Hold now! Hold now!"

The voice booms out over the chaos of screams and steel. The Black Duke's warriors respond first to their master's call, falling back where they press the White Pilgrim, who turns. There at the edge of the broken table that divides the hall, Arsanc holds his sword in one hand, his other clenched within a globe of light that flares to every corner of the chamber.

As the dukes of Gracia shield their eyes against the brightness, the great doors of the domed hall are cracked wide with the echoing boom of stone on stone. From the corridors and side chambers beyond, the captains and war-mages and guards of nineteen dukes spill through from where they have held their own court, awaiting word of the business of their masters.

Some dozens make it to the sides of their lieges before Arsanc himself snarls an incantation. A shimmering black fog rises, congealing even as warriors and mages fall back to either side. In its wake, the doorway is sealed in a shroud of dark stone that echoes with the anger of voice that created it.

"Hold now!" the Black Duke shouts again. "Spell and sword, all stand down!"

A sudden silence twists through the throne room. The dukes of Gracia, the knights and war-mages who defend them, all fix wary eyes on each other, on the Black Duke, on the White Pilgrim. They cluster around the chairs of the king's companions, a force of magic and military strength as formidable as any ever assembled in the Elder Kingdoms.

It would take very little provocation for all the leadership of Gracia to perish here, the White Pilgrim realizes. He senses the power held in dangerous check, the rage and fear that threads the chamber. The Black Duke's ultimatum.

One man must die tonight.

The White Pilgrim steps toward Arsanc. One of the Black Duke's defenders slips in from behind with axe in hand, ignores his duke's orders in favor of a perfect unseen strike. The White Pilgrim swings back without looking, takes the attacker cleanly at the wrist, cutting to the bone. Then around from the other side, cutting deep at the shoulder as the axe spins away. His gaze never leaves Arsanc across from him.

"Hold!" the Black Duke shouts again. No one moves, save for the White Pilgrim as he continues toward the broken cleft of the white table, collapsed inward to a crevasse of rubble and dust.

He fights the call of the sword to strike again, strike hard. Drink deep of blood and the power it provides. The dead Gareyth, the Black Duke's men in the orchard all laugh to see him.

Arsanc is not laughing.

"I told you I was the source of all your pain," the White Pilgrim says. "I told her they would not listen."

Arsanc does not ask how this ancient man, this wreck of a man could possibly have made his way here, left for dead two days and thirty leagues away. He does not ask how the White Pilgrim still lives. His shadowed eyes betray the darkness of his understanding.

"Those who would actively seek the crown of kings betray an ambition that makes them wholly unsuitable for rule," the White Pilgrim says. He hears the tone of command in his own voice, sees the reaction in the assembled dukes as they look from him to Arsanc. They fall back to leave space around the white table where he paces, bare footfalls steady in the silence.

"You cannot…" Arsanc whispers. "You cannot be."

His own blade pulses blue-white in his hands. One of the great blunt-ended broadswords of the Norgyr. Runes of magic flare along the length of its steel, Arsanc channeling its arcane power.

The power in the sword of kings that is Ankathira that is the Whitethorn shivers through the White Pilgrim, who hears the voice of the Blade as a dark laughter in his mind.

A hatred flares in the black eyes of the Black Duke. The shadow that a lifetime's pain inflicts on others, because the target that pain should seek is dead and gone. Forever out of reach.

The White Pilgrim looks from face to face as he passes the dukes of Gracia in turn. He seeks for familiarity in those eyes, sees only shadows staring back at him. Too much time passes. Old faces that might be faces he knew, reshaped by long years. Young faces to replace the old who fight at his side and kneel in this chamber and pledge their rule to the high king's law when the fighting is done.

Sons and daughters. Usurpers and new blood. Time passes for them as it does for all folk, all things. Flesh and life fading, images graven in stone and mosaic, sketched in charcoal or pigment. All worn away in time.

All things end. All things but him, and the sins he bears that hold him here.

"She was wrong," he says to himself, to the faces staring stunned around him, to no one. "The things we remember, good or bad, are no matter."

He feels the Golden Girl's hand at his shoulder. She is tall, he realizes suddenly. Possessing the wide innocence of her father's eyes, the steadiness of her father's hand as she grasps his, holds it tight.

"A king might return from the dead," he says. "Speak his name and be cast aside as a fool. An old man, senses lost. No face to be recognized because the memories have left him behind."

"Only the good has been remembered,' she whispers, weeping. Long ago. "The people need their king, who vanquished the usurper and restored to Gracia its honor and peace. The darkness will be forgotten. Your legend has undone all sins."

He tries to reach for her hand, but she is not there. Only a dream now.

He tries to reach for Nàlwyr, for Aelathar, but he is alone.

"Only by deeds," the White Pilgrim says, shouting now. "Only by what we do are we remembered. The best and worst of what we are. Our humility, our hubris, our fears, our courage. We vow our lives to those who follow us, to those we lead, and so our lives are reckoned in the end only by how we die!"

He turns back. He looks to Arsanc once more where the Black Duke stands cold, a dangerous darkness in his eyes. The White Pilgrim fights to keep his breathing slowed in the silence.

"Do you remember me now, my duke?"

Arsanc is a dozen strides away as he raises his sword for a killing stroke. But then the single step he takes toward the White Pilgrim consumes him in a flash of light that disgorges him again a single step distant. Whitethorn is up to parry, faster than thought, three furious strikes sent wide as the White Pilgrim twists away.

Arsanc stares in stark disbelief, falls back into a defensive posture as the White Pilgrim counterattacks. Whitethorn is a blur of silver where it lances out, meets steel twice before cutting beneath Arsanc's sword arm with the force of all the Blade's hunger behind it. The White Pilgrim feels the sword of kings strike but glance off, the Black Duke's armor flaring white for a moment beneath a shimmering shield of arcane force.

He staggers back, watching Arsanc as he halts. A moment's respite.

"It does not matter," the White Pilgrim says. "Who I am. All that matters is what was done. What will be done in answer."

Arsanc unclasps his cloak, casts it aside. "Here is my answer," he whispers, and from a scabbard at the back of his belt, he draws a blue-bladed dirk as he strikes in a blaze of steel. The long looping arcs of the sword set up the dagger as it lashes out like a serpent from the left arm, the Black Duke fighting effortlessly, drawing on the dweomer of the broadsword to augment his strength. The sight of the Blade senses this, the White Pilgrim hearing it in the voice that guides his hand as it parries, blocks, parries again.

The Black Duke makes a final onslaught, the broadsword howling as it strikes the side of the white table where it slopes up beside them. A chunk is hacked from its marbled edge, smoldering where it falls.

"Your day is done," the Black Duke shouts. "My blood's revenge is on you."

A quick strike from Whitethorn arcs off the broadsword cleanly, the Blade shrieking in the White Pilgrim's ears now, ravenous. "The sins of the father lost cannot be paid for by the daughter," he calls. "No more than the guilt of the father can be cleansed by the innocence of the murdered son."

"My brother's life is not bartered in platitudes! For my brother's blood, the butcher's daughter is mine, and I will bestow on her the death that should have been her father's when she begs me in the end!"

"I am the one you hate!" the White Pilgrim shouts. "I am the one whose madness cost a brother's life!"

"Then show me your children, old man, that they might feel the same pain you will feel when you fall here!"

"I gave the order that sent Nàlwyr to Stondreva and your brother to his doom!"

The White Pilgrim feels the weight of the truth slip from him. A confession left unspoken, uttered twice now for the first time in long years. And even as he speaks, he sees and understands the subtle shift in the Black Duke's gaze where the words sink in through a lifetime of pain.

"What do you remember, old man?"

Arsanc strikes hard, a newly fired rage in him flaring as he pushes the offensive. As the White Pilgrim falls back, he understands that something is changed.

Arsanc is as ready to kill as ever. But more than that, now and only now, the Black Duke is ready to die. Finally. No way out anymore from the pain he carries. Nothing else beyond this moment when everything ends.

"I remember it all," the White Pilgrim says, and he does.

The power of the Blade clears his mind, feeds him the hunger that is the lifeblood of his reign. The power of Whitethorn threads through him, replaces his strength of self as if his blood were black shadow suddenly, fed and pumped by the heart of steel in his hand.

"Havar was the brightest light," the Black Duke screams in a voice churned of raw malice. "My brother was a scholar. A poet. Something better than the bloody line that got him."

The White Pilgrim feels the Blade begin to lead him in, too close. He leaves himself open as Arsanc attacks in a relentless flurry. The dirk takes him clean through the side to slash skin and muscle, staining the robes that are white once with a stream of blood. The pain staggers him even as he feels the power of the sword of kings staunch the wound, begin to knit torn flesh whole again.

The assault gives him an opening as the Blade cuts for the throat. But the Black Duke only disappears, flashing back a half-dozen steps to let Whitethorn cleave empty air.

"I sent him into Stondreva," Arsanc shouts, "so that he might become more than what I was. The potential in him to lead, and to follow his conscience like he did the night he stood against Nàlwyr and laid down his life to protect children who were nothing to you!"

The White Pilgrim feels a sudden chill root deep in his heart. He feels the pain at his leg flare, only for the instant that the hunger of the Blade abates. Long enough for him to feel the shadow twist inside him.

Arsanc sees it. A realization shines bright in the black eyes. "What do you remember, old man?"

Whitethorn makes a brutal slashing attack against the leg, the broadsword down to deflect it. The backswing comes in high, straight for the chest, but the dirk sends it wide. The flare of white light again as the dweomer of the Black Duke's armor turns the glancing edge of the blow.

Another flurry of strikes is exchanged, Arsanc shifting backward to cross-parry. And then he slips in the loose rubble of the floor. Only a moment to regain his footing, but it is enough.

Waiting for this moment, the White Pilgrim lets himself succumb to the fury of the Blade. He feels the shadow take him, lets it call his body to service as he lunges, strikes hard. He ignores the wards of the black armor, finds the softer flesh of the Black Duke's dirk hand. He drives through and back so fast that the Blade shows blood only as it pulls away.

The dagger spins away as the White Pilgrim blocks a desperate swing from the broadsword. In a flare of light, the Black Duke is gone, drawing on the power of the sword once more to cast himself back across the chamber, to the far side of the shattered table.

The White Pilgrim is ready for him. Already moving with the warning of the sight that is the Blade's, he leaps across the table to slash down as he drops, cutting deep against the Black Duke's sword arm. The spell of shielding flares again, but the Blade tastes blood, cutting through spell and armor, flesh and bone.

The broadsword falls from the Black Duke's hand. He tries to grab for it but Whitethorn bites a third time, taking him through the shoulder as he staggers back.

An absolute silence hangs in the domed hall of Mitrost, chamber of marble throne and white table and the fate of a nation. Arsanc twists his fingers as he snarls, the distant broadsword torn from the ground with the power of spellcraft, but the White Pilgrim catches it with his bare foot, slams it down hard.

The Black Duke stands weaponless. No fear in his eyes. Quick movement comes from behind the White Pilgrim as Arsanc's own men break for him. A half-dozen are seized and held by the captains and bodyguards of the other dukes, as many breaking free to rush the frozen figures at the center of the hall.

A flick of Whitethorn brings the tip of the Blade to the Black Duke's throat. Holds it there.

Arsanc makes no move to wave his warriors back, so the White Pilgrim does it for him. The Blade trembles in his hand, tastes a trickle of blood along its razor edge. Six swords are drawn against the White Pilgrim. The Blade senses the threat of spellpower from two of those closest to him, two more in the crowd that he can see.

But farther back, around the great chamber and from the corner of his eye, the White Pilgrim sees the dukes of Gracia kneeling.

One by one, they slip to the ground. Captains and war-mages follow their lead, all staring at a sight that cannot be. A sight denied by all the history, all the legends they have ever learned.

The White Pilgrim shakes his head. Does not want to see. "One man must die tonight," he shouts to himself, to no one. "Along with any others who stand in the way of that deed."

Down the gleaming length of the sword of kings, he meets Arsanc's black gaze. "Do you remember me now?"

The Black Duke spits his answer, catching the White Pilgrim on the cheek. He wipes it away absently with his free hand. He shakes his head to clear the shadow, tightening like a noose around him now.

"My brother did not yield when your noble Nàlwyr cut him down," Arsanc says, pitching his voice for all to hear. "Do you expect different from me?" A moment's defiance before the end.

And the White Pilgrim steps back. Lowers Whitethorn to his side.

"No. The mercy denied your brother by the high king's order is yours."

The Black Duke's warriors are too startled to react, holding where they stand. Arsanc's eyes are black pits, seething with a lifetime's rage. But the White Pilgrim sees uncertainty showing in that gaze for the first time.

He feels that same rage coursing through the Blade where it and his hand are locked tight together. Something is changing. Something is changed, and the Blade knows it.

Its shrieking fury pounds through him, the memory of all the nights of darkness spent alone. The taste of the long campaign in which he raises the banner of his father and uncle before him, hunts the usurper's forces across burning fields and through gates of magic to north and south, to the coast, to the forest wall. The scent of death that threads the mist of Marthai as falling bodies churn the mud of the field to bloody foam.

Of all the things lost to him, this is the last to return. The memory of the voice that whispers to him when he first takes the sword of kings from his dead father's hand. Telling him of the things he will do, the power he will wield. The land he will unite under his banner.

Then comes the memory of that voice as it whispers of other things. Betrayal of the heart. The thirst for vengeance that drives him against Thoradun, that spikes the hunger for retribution against Cymaris. The shadow that turns his heart to ice for the sake of a lost son and the prophecy he is become.

The White Pilgrim takes a step back. He does not think on what must be done, because he knows that to think on it would betray the action to the Blade where its sight twists through his mind. He thinks instead of a woman's laughter, ringing like a clear bell, faint shimmering of silver on the air.

His thoughts are clear. Truly clear for the first time in all the long years of exile that scar body and heart and mind.

It takes all the effort of his will and the strength of both hands to let Whitethorn drop to the ground before him.

The White Pilgrim feels a peace that he never knows. He lets it settle in on him, slowly. A chill threads through him that is the cool touch of old stone, the heat of blood suddenly stilled where the Blade hits the floor with an echoing clash.

"Too much of the blood of fathers and sons, daughters and brothers has already been spilled in the name of this same madness," the White Pilgrim says. "My blood must end it. My life is yours."

He drops to his knees.

In another place, in another battle, another lifetime, he falls into the embrace of death because death is promised to him. He falls at the hands of his son, the legends say. He feels Astyra's spear like a dream of endless falling, endless agony as it shatters ribs and spine, pierces his still-beating heart.

In that moment of dying, as in this moment of dying, he realizes how long he waits for that death. Biding time for the chance to make atonement for the darkness he carries. A death at the hands of the son destined to slay him will somehow wash away the blood on his own hands. Astyra, Cymaris. Aelathar, Nàlwyr. Havar, who is a scholar and poet. So many more who die so that the marble throne might be his.

"Forgive me," he says to himself, to no one.

A step away from him, Arsanc flicks his fingers. The sword of kings is pulled from the floor on threads of unseen force, snatched up to his hand. The White Pilgrim sees the Black Duke measure the weight of the Blade, feels the shudder as its power threads through him.

Arsanc turns so that the light of the domed hall shimmers on the cross-guard and fuller in steeled gold. Ancient glyphs of prophecy and power are scribed there in white, pulsing with a faint glow. An edge and ridge of dwyrsilver steel shed the shadows as the light of the Blade draws forth the dark murmur that is risen from the kneeling dukes, their war-mages and sword captains.

"You know this blade!" Arsanc calls. The White Pilgrim feels the Black Duke seize the power of this moment never looked for, never dreamed of. A final and unexpected piece of the fate that will be made here this night. "The sword of kings decides the destiny of Gracia! Returned from the dead to exact the justice denied by the betrayal of a king!"

No one moves. The song of blood and hunger that is the voice of the Blade rises to a new crescendo. The White Pilgrim hears an answer to that song as Arsanc laughs.

He is ready. He walks beneath the dark weight of his sin for a lifetime.

The Black Duke wheels to face him, swings back the sword of kings in an executioner's arc. In that last moment, the White Pilgrim sees himself reflected in Arsanc's black gaze.

Looking down on himself, there in his own eyes, the White Pilgrim sees nothing but acceptance.

Then a silent blur of naked steel erupts in a fountain of blood from the Black Duke's throat.

A scream from somewhere. Arsanc staggers, Whitethorn still held high as he clutches at the rapier punched through his neck like a lance. Choking, spinning, he lurches away from the fallen canvas across the chamber, the wall of shattered glass from which the weapon is thrown.

The Black Duke's closest warriors are in motion, but none are as the fast as the Golden Girl. She sprints in from the black shadow of the garden, slips past the clutching hands of two, four, a half-dozen frantic figures. She vaults to Arsanc's back as he stumbles away in fear.

The White Pilgrim cannot move, cannot stand. Forced to watch as the Golden Girl grabs her father's blade, tears it from Arsanc's neck with a scream of rage and the grinding of bone. Twisting off, she parries two strikes from guards behind her, spins to run the staggered Arsanc through the hand.

She watches the fight, the White Pilgrim realizes. She sees all the Black Duke's strengths of magic, the protective power of his armor. All the weakness of his rage carefully assessed while she waits.

In a heartbeat, the domed hall is a battlefield. Arsanc's forces try to press the Golden Girl but are drawn back by attacks from the followers of the other dukes. An uproar of voices echoes from the buttressed walls, prayers and threats screamed over the clash of steel, the pulse of spell-fire erupting within the chaos.

The White Pilgrim cannot move, cannot stand. All his strength is gone, drained from him as the darkness of his blood is cleared. The memory of the sword's voice in his mind, its shadow in his heart, fading now.

Unhindered, the Golden Girl presses hard, but Arsanc brings Whitethorn up to parry despite the grievous nature of his wounds. And even as he falls back, the fountain of blood at his throat slows. The White Pilgrim feels the power of the Blade, pulsing in time with the frenzied beating of the Black Duke's heart.

The Golden Girl spins. Two fast feints, Arsanc slow as he follows, left out of position. The Blade cuts back where he tries to find an opening.

She thrusts with all the strength of her body. She drives her rapier through the unprotected wrist of the Black Duke's sword arm, drives it further to strike the black armor. The force of that armor's shielding magic flares within her blade, flowing into Arsanc's arm through a conduit of blood and steel. Then back into the armor in a blinding pulse of arcane feedback that lets the rapier punch through plate steel, chain and leather beneath, muscle and bone.

Arsanc makes no sound despite the pain as his arm is pinned to his chest. The Golden Girl drives one fist to his eyes, uses the other hand to grasp Whitethorn by the cross-guard and tear it from his blood-drenched hands.

Arsanc screams then. The sound of a soul sundered. A lifetime of vengeance sought and promised and taken away.

The Golden Girl is Justain. The White Pilgrim remembers. Daughter of Nàlwyr, the best blade of the kingdom.

She has her father's eyes, open wide in blind rage as she twists around Arsanc to punch the sword of kings through his back, shredding cloak and armor, flesh and bone.

The Black Duke staggers, clutching for the Blade with his one good hand as it is torn from him again, ribs splintering, Justain spinning. Using the momentum of her movement to hack Arsanc's head from his body in a fountain of blood that catches her as she screams.

The White Pilgrim screams with her.

The sword of kings slips from her hand. The Blade drops to the floor as the body of the Black Duke falls.

Something is changed.

The White Pilgrim kneels with the Golden Girl in his arms, feels her body wracked with sobs as she clings to him.

"There is no absolution," the White Pilgrim says to no one. "There is no ending for Gilvaleus…"

The throne room of Mitrost is in chaos, the forces of the Black Duke fighting to get to his body. Steel and spell-fire ring out loud as the forces of the other dukes of Gracia splinter off to factions, screaming betrayal, calling for justice.

"You lie to yourself. You said it before. Deeds and words are one and the same. You have earned your absolution a thousand times over."

The Golden Girl's voice at his ear. He hears the fear in it that reveals the child she is, thirteen summers behind her. He holds her but he does not know why. He tries to remember.

"The gods have denied me death," he says, "and I will never know their reasons…"

"Then make your own reason for living. Make that reason count."

He looks up then, and even in the chaos, he sees the eyes that watch him. Arsanc's body is gone, figures rushing past toward the garden, toward the main doors where the stone wall is shattered and brought down by the thunder of arcane force.

Something is changed. He is walking, cannot remember standing.

"Tell them who you were," the Golden Girl says, pleading now. "Tell them who you are." Her father's bloody rapier is clutched tight in her hands. The White Pilgrim does not remember her retrieving it from the Black Duke where he lies.

He tries to remember who he is. Tries to recall a vision of peace, of a land freed from the fear of what the future brings.

All he remembers is blood on his hands. All the violence done in the name of that dream of peace.

"If there was some good in what was done in the lifetime of Gilvaleus, take it for what it is," he says to himself, to no one.

"Make the future," he says. "Do not mourn what was."

"Tomorrow belongs to you," he says to himself, to the Golden Girl where she kneels at his feet, blue eyes bright, blood and tears streaking her face as he turns away.

The Blade is gone but its vision wells in him one last time. Showing him that the Golden Girl will flee this place, hidden safely by the chaos that flows from the death of the Black Duke who would be high king.

The connection from him to the Blade is broken in his anguish. In its anguish. It calls to him, but he will not answer.

She tries to follow him, but the White Pilgrim moves by instinct, taking back staircases and forgotten passageways rank with mold and shadow. He hears her footsteps fade after a time, hears the shouts of panicked dukes and courtiers grow ever more distant in the dark.

The gates of the keep are open, the guards scattered to respond to the madness that this night wreaks. No one notes him as he slips through the frenzied crowd.

The tents of the city are pandemonium as word spreads beyond the keep. No one stops him as he makes his way through the shadows.

The gates of the city are open. He slips out with the throngs fleeing Mitrost, fleeing the darkness of this night, the uncertainty for what the future brings.

Long ago, he does not need the road where it twists away from the city and through the dark farmsteads beyond. The shadow hides a secret way, but he cannot remember. He recalls only that he is walking the grassland border of the river valley, cutting overland on a straight course north and west from the sea.

The Black Duke is dead, and in that death, all the pain of life is done. The White Pilgrim knows that, understands it. Cannot remember how.

He lingers along the riverbank for a time, washing by the light of an abandoned campfire. He cleans blood from his hands, from his robes that are the pilgrims' white once. Long ago. He is not sure how the red-black stain sets itself there. Then he forgets even that he wonders as he limps off into the night.

– EPILOGUE –
IN THE END

IN THE END, THE AIR IS WARM and green, set with dappled shadows that twist across the flaking plaster of the walls.

A last image. A dream he has, long ago.

A memory.

He lies in a bed near the tall windows of the dormitories, a haze of shadow spreading except where the shutters are thrown wide to the sun and air of spring beyond.

He returns here, but from where he does not know. A long journey of days. Water and forest and field, leading him back to isolated stands of black oak, broken walls of vine-cloaked grey.

He knows where he is, cannot remember.

They find him beneath the ancient ash at dawn, sprawled across the stone whose carefully carved letters have worn smooth with the passing of years and the weeping of the sky.

He does not remember them moving him to the dormitory. Does not remember them feeding him, washing him. He only knows the sweet sleep. The light of dawn threading the shutters. The light of real day when the shutters are opened by the Golden Girl who is already there, first to find him. First to his side beneath the great tree, holding him as she weeps.

He sees a talisman at her neck. A dragon rampant in blood-red, claws of black. Eyes of silver gleam where it coils its tail around itself, ready to strike. It reminds him of something.

His days are gold and green, bright sun and the buds of new leaves just starting, spreading through the trees whose wind-song dance he watches from his bed. His nights are dark, and peaceful, and in that peace he finds himself hoping for the end. He does not remember why.

Not yet, he thinks. Fate not done with him. The gods, perhaps.

He does not know anymore. He is content in that, finally.

His wounds are healed by the craft of the acolytes, but his body is old. He spends his days watching sun and sky, and speaking to the Golden Girl when she sits at his side. He tells her tales that she repeats back to him so she will not forget, but he himself cannot remember the words when she is done.

He feels something calling to him. He dreams of Aelathar who is his only love. Dreams of Nàlwyr who is his greatest friend. Dreams of all the rest, the names gone but their faces with him now, shimmering as his mind drifts in the golden light.

He dreams of Cymaris and Astyra and wakes with wet eyes, begging the love and absolution of mother and son. He feels their forgiveness, feels the Golden Girl's hand in his as a voice tells him that he earns his absolution a thousand times over.

He is glad of that. He feels the faint echo of an ache that dogged him once. Gone now.

Something is changed. The leaves are full, the ash and oak shimmering green in the haze of dawn, the heat of summer. The shutters are open to the day and night now.

He lifts himself from the bed one day at dawn. He feels the ache in his leg and at his chest as he slips on robes that are the pilgrims' white.

Something is changed. He kneels beneath the ash, crouches at the stone, squeezes one hand to a shaking fist that is touched to his dried lips and kissed. Pressed down to the cold of the graven name for a heartbeat that is a life of lost time.

"It is good," he says. "To see you again."

He only realizes he is fallen when he feels the Golden Girl lift him. A last dream. Long hair tied back, the gold of rain-fresh straw. The red dragon on gold, hanging now from a chain at her neck.

A rapier at her waist, the gleam of dwyrsilver beneath her tunic. Her father's blade, the chain shirt he once wore. The only burdens she carries now.

The memories are gone. All set to rest by what the future might hold.

Then was it told how Gilvaleus the High King returned from the dead and from the court of the Orosana to stand against the Black Duke as he had stood against the Usurper in life. And with the Sword of Kings in hand, he slew Arsanc of Thorfin and Reimari as he would slay all those who would covet the glory of Gracia for their own.

In his life, he has been light and shadow, bright king and killer of children. In his life, he has claimed a kingdom but let wither the heart and soul that might have ruled it.

And when it was done, Gilvaleus walked back into shadow, but said first to those Dukes of Gracia who knelt before him 'Know, all of you, that I shall not return again, and so let my name now be lost to that memory that takes me. Then each of thee, take comfort in thyself alone and yourselves as one, and look to thy faith of self to carry thee. And let all Gracia know that the greatness of this land is in all folk and the Lords who lead them justly. So shall you say to all folk, Seize the peace that is this land's destiny in each of thy thousand-thousand hands. And speak no more prayers for Dead Kings.'

In the end, all is darkness. But from the shadow comes the light.

Then her laughter rang on the white stones that glimmered by the stars that were fair Aelathar's name, and whose light was in her silver hair and pale eyes. And Gilvaleus the High King kissed her for the first time beneath those stars, that watched them both with all of fate and history's unseeing eyes.

In the end, all is as it should have been, and he accepts in that end the darkness and the light, and is cloaked tight finally in all of eternity's welcome embrace.

FICTION BY
SCOTT FITZGERALD GRAY

WE CAN BE HEROES

A PRAYER FOR DEAD KINGS and Other Tales

CLEARWATER DAWN — Book One of "The Exile's Blade"

BLACKHEATH (with Quinn Hamilton)

THE VOICES OF THE DEAD — Dark Tales & Lost Souls

TALES OF THE ENDLANDS
The Twilight Child • Shadow to Shadow • The Moonsign Scar
Daeralf's Rune • The Game of Heart and Light • The Voice
Black Run •A Space Between • Stories

ONE SIZE FITS ALL (as Gary Scott)

Scott Fitzgerald Gray is a specially constructed biogenetic
simulacrum built around an array of experimental consciousness-
sharing techniques — a product of the finest minds of Canadian
science until the grant money ran out. Accidentally set loose during
an unauthorized midnight rave at the lab, the S.F. Gray entity is
currently at large amongst an unsuspecting populace, where his
work as an author, screenwriter, editor, RPG designer, and story
editor for feature film and fiction keeps him off the streets.

More info on Scott and his work (some of it even occasionally truthful)
can be found by reading between the lines at **insaneangel.com**.

COLOPHON

In the convoluted process by which the disparate pieces of
A Prayer for Dead Kings and Other Tales have come together,
the following people have been instrumental. This will undoubtedly
come as a surprise to many of them, but life's like that.

The Dukes of the White Table
David Otterson, Mitchell Wylie, Ron Graves, Kevin Harris, Mark East

The Clan-Singers
Colleen, Shvaugn, and Caitlin

Razeen's Library Scribes
Colleen Craig, Shvaugn Craig, Mitchell Wylie, Gerrard du Flanchard

Chief Mosaicists of Mitrost
(studio)Effigy, Alex Tooth, Ricardo Guimaraes, Jose A.S. Reyes

The Imperial Guard
Dead Can Dance, John Debney, Harlan Ellison, Lisa Gerrard,
Mike Grell, Richard Harris, Ernest Hemingway, Robert E. Howard,
Guy Gavriel Kay, Joe Konrath, Fritz Leiber, Thomas Malory,
Bear McCreary, Neal Morse, Vangelis, Hans Zimmer

A Prayer for Dead Kings
AND
OTHER TALES

Published by Insane Angel Studios
insaneangel.com

Cover, Design, and Typography
by (studio)Effigy

Cover Illustration by Alex Tooth
alextooth.com

This is a work of fiction. All names, characters, places, objects, and incidents herein are the products of the author's imagination or are used fictitiously. Any resemblance to actual things, events, locales, or persons living or dead is entirely coincidental. Except for that one bit? Where that guy does that thing? That's totally about you.

ISBN 978-1-927348-17-8

v1.1
November 2012

We try to make sure that no errors creep into our work, but publishing is a chaotic enterprise at the best of times. If you spot a typo or a formatting glitch in an Insane Angel Studios book, email insaneangel@insaneangel.com with details (including which e-book version you're reading, if applicable). If any errors you spot are ones we haven't yet caught and are in the process of fixing, you'll receive one of our e-books of your choice for free.

www.ingramcontent.com/pod-product-compliance
Lightning Source LLC
Chambersburg PA
CBHW071102250626
47159CB00002B/558